Notes on Cracker Barrel Napkins

Old Seventy Creek Press

2018

What others say about *Notes on Cracker Barrel Napkins* and Todd Moberly*:*

"These are stories from another generation, retold imaginatively here by avid listener and able writer Todd Moberly to save them from the dust bin of time and forgetfulness."
      Loyal Jones, author, humorist, Appalachian Scholar.

From a letter to the author, concerning **'Blind Jenny's Gift"** (with title revised to print in the collection as '**Fiddling to the Wolves'):**
"VERY TOUCHING...WOULD GLADLY PUBLISH IF I WAS AN EDITOR...."
      Wendell Berry, American/ Kentucky poet, essayist, farmer, novelist, philosopher, and scholar.

"This wonderfully wrought collection makes us reflect on the past, focus on the present, and find the strength to face the future. It is a captivating, compelling, and enjoyable work of fiction."
      Gwyn Hyman Rubio, author of the best selling **Icy Sparks; The Woodsman's Daughter,** and **Love & Ordinary Creatures.**

I laughed. I cried. I smiled. Reading these stories brought back memories of my own childhood home of Fordville.
Well-developed characters. Resolution of conflicts. Wisdom gained. Readers couldn't ask for much more.
      Julie Whitaker, former English teacher.

"Todd Moberly's southern storyteller's voice gently nudges the reader into the center of a dusty, peach-scented location where distinctive and picturesque characters gather to share stories that are unique and absolutely unforgettable in time and place."
      J.B. Hamilton Queen, Author of **Raincrow; Imminent Reprisal; Masters the Breed; Sweet Gums; Dagger in the Cup,** and **Sting.**

"Kentucky characters come to life in these Appalachian tales of a time gone by. I highly recommend this read!"
      Angela Correll, author of the **May Hollow Road trilogy**.

"Todd Moberly showcases the very best of Appalachia, each story like a colorful quilt that wraps round you and leads you home. Well done!"
    Laura Frantz, author of **A Moonbow Night**.

"…Where Appalachia rests its foothills in the rolling meadows of Kentucky's outer Bluegrass—Todd Moberly grew up listening to conversations, touchstones of his book of short stories about the inhabitants of a fictional small village in central Kentucky."
    Byron Crawford in *Kentucky Living* magazine.

TRUE FICTION: Todd Moberly calls his manuscript "Pure fiction," but to me it rings true, a genuine portrait of country folk and their stories, humor, traditions, and unique ways of life in rural Kentucky.
    Billy Edd Wheeler

Notes on Cracker Barrel Napkins

Stories by Todd D. Moberly

Old Seventy Creek Press 2018

Notes on Cracker Barrel Napkins

Published By
2018 OLD SEVENTY CREEK FIRST EDITION

Published in the United States by:
Old Seventy Creel Press
Rudy Thomas, Editor & Publisher
P. O. Box 204
Albany, Kentucky 42602

ISBN13: 978-0-9982374-4-2

Ilustrations by Gay Thomas Agee

Baptism Picture, Ella Nunn in Old Seventy Creek 1907

For Lorene

…Blessed are the dead which die in The Lord from henceforth: yea, saith the Spirit, that they may rest from their labours; and their works do follow them.
(Revelation 14:13)

Acknowledgments

The author gratefully acknowledges: former English teacher, Julie Whitaker, and author J.B. Hamilton Queen; Sharyn Mitchell and Harry Rice of Hutchins' Library's Department of Special Collections at Berea College, and The Leonard W. Roberts Collection.

A special thanks goes out to Gay Thomas Agee, for the art work she produced for this collection.

Notes on Cracker Barrel Napkins

"Clay, if that thing could talk…" Granny said, pointing to the stone jug in the corner of the smokehouse; she then did the talking. "Aunt Mollie Moore kept dandelion wine in that jug…poor ol' thing." A typical teenager, I didn't know which "poor ol' thing" she was talking about--the jug or Aunt Mollie. The jug was cracked and I didn't know Aunt Mollie from a load of coal. But I learned.

More importantly, is that, I, Russell C. "Clay" Hall, learned to listen.

By age fifteen I learned that, *if* I listened, Granny would eventually tell me why Aunt Mollie was a poor ol' thing. Granddaddy would sometimes fill in the grittier manly details. I observed that older people would tell me things if I asked a few prompting questions along the way. If I watched their eyes with interest, their tales came to life. The old stories most of my peers regarded as the ramblings of Fordville's geriatric set came to be my own personal Library of Congress. There, I could "read" to my heart's content and the supply, though fading from view, was abundant.

I was raised by my grandparents and surrounded by a host of tribal elders in rural Kentucky in the 1950's and 1960's. I knew this was my proving ground. Stories were as much a part of life as bacon grease and occasionally even better. Many of those stories along with fragments of wit and wisdom were heard in the company of loafers, and sadly, since that time, loafing has become a lost art. The frequency of family meals has likewise suffered and the net result has been the loss of time and place for storytelling. By the time my own children were in school, the pace of modern life required no small amount of effort to bring the family together just for supper.

When our daughters married and began raising their own children, loafers were becoming an endangered species and family dinners increasingly difficult to plan, due to all the various schedules that had to be coordinated. Lamenting this sad state of affairs several years ago, my wife Sandy offered a brilliant solution: *Every* Friday evening at 6:30, we would plan to have supper at Cracker Barrel, even if it was only the two of us that showed up. It had always been our favorite restaurant and was on a practical level, convenient.

Happily, Sandy's plan worked for us…most of the time. Occasionally, one of the daughters or a son-in-law, or one of the grandchildren wouldn't be able to make it, but they knew we would come together again the following week at the same time and place. There seemed to be a genuine desire for everyone to be present for these weekly gatherings.

We still have holiday and special occasions at home, but the regularity of these weekly meals together filled in the gaps and cultivated some much-needed continuity in our lives

Here ends part one of this tale. Now for part two.

At one of our Friday night suppers several years ago, out of the blue our daughter Charity asked me where the red graniteware dishpan came from, the one that sat on our kitchen countertop for years, "that reddish looking thing that usually has bananas in it."

I told her that it had been my grandmother's, and explained how it came to be in the kitchen. She was surprised to learn it had been found on the dirt floor of the toolshed where for a number of years it held screws and other miscellaneous items.

Halfway through the story, and finding no paper in her purse, Charity handed me a napkin and asked me to jot down the bare facts of what I'd just told her. This I did...sort of, and returned it to her on notes scribbled with two different colored ink pens.

Coincidentally, the very next week our older daughter, Loren, asked about a wooden spice rack we'd given her that had also belonged to Granny, for whom she was named. Out came another napkin and I produced another scribbled note.

This became a regular thing at our Friday evening suppers, and something akin to a joke, when the daughters began to recognize that many of the objects they had grown up with had stories attached to them. For the first three or four note- taking sessions, nobody had paper to write on, and Cracker Barrel's napkins were readily available upon request. For better or worse, a whimsical tradition was born, and the napkin notes practically became a standing order. Our Friday night suppers and note-scribbling sessions continued mostly uninterrupted for about three years. As far as I knew, the napkins themselves were never

11

really taken that seriously. Much to my surprise, I later learned they had been tucked away here and there in purses and coat pockets. From there, most of them graduated to a desk drawer, and there they most likely would have remained were it not for my health heading south.

If I were to come up with a title just for the next part of this saga, it would be fittingly called "The Big C and Me."

We were about three years into our Friday evening Cracker Barrel ritual when I began experiencing lower abdominal pain which was determined to be colon cancer. That chapter in my life gummed up the works for our weekly suppers for several months, but for my daughters it served as a reminder that I wasn't getting any younger. Nor was there a guarantee of a rebound, even after the surgeon confidently said "he'd gotten it all." Just for the record, I've heard that line spoken in hushed tones at more than one funeral.

Keeping the road hot between doctor visits and the drugstore, I mended well, and our family was glad to resume our weekly Cracker Barrel suppers in the late spring. We synchronized our calendars for the Friday evening of Memorial Day weekend that year, to begin coming together again. Then and there, they presented me with the neatly pressed stacks of napkins, the very ones upon which I'd scribbled notes for three years. Miraculously, the daughters had kept them, stored for safekeeping in Wal-Mart bags.

They then informed me of what they wanted for Christmas: to take the incoherent napkin-notes home and actually write the stories I had roughly outlined on them. Charity said, "Daddy, you need to connect the dots for us. Nobody can make any sense out of these."

The daughters said I had plenty of time to finish their stories by Christmas. I was already tired from eating supper, let alone writing but I told them I would think about it and let them know. The stack of unfolded napkins was placed on my desk later that night awaiting my decision.

This would be a good time to say that old things had always been part of my life, and consequently, the lives of our daughters.

Over the years, to each daughter, son-in-law and grandchild, we had occasionally given an old dish, chair, tool, or object of curiosity from Granny's farm where I was raised. It was also where Granny was born and spent her turn-of-the-century girlhood. Little was thrown away over the years that couldn't be used somehow sometime by somebody somewhere. The numerous outbuildings, barns, sheds and especially the house had been crammed full to the rafters.

I did not realize it at the time I scribbled the illegible notes, but I was given what I only know to call "the gift of an ear." For reasons unknown to me, I can recall most of the stories and anecdotes I've ever heard from my elders, even some best forgotten. Call it a quirk, but it's real. I still hear their voices. I still remember the curiously turned phrases and old, forgotten words they used in doing so, their tones, gestures, and facial expressions. Not only the spoken words of my grandparents, but those of all my elders, as I grew from boy to man in mid-20th century Fordville, Kentucky.

Growing up, our daughters would ask me "Daddy, where did you hear this stuff?"

Daughters, I can only tell you I lived in a different time.

The already declining Fordville of my youth had no outlets. Little came into it, and little went out, except by the main road which led twelve miles to Harriston, the county seat. That isolation was strangely truer in 1960 than it had been in 1900. Fordville was both defined and limited by the muddy Kentucky River less than a mile away. The ferry that for more than a century joined it to the busier world beyond its guarding palisades closed before I was born. At least in those days, Fordville residents typically had more extended family just across the river in another county than they had in their own county seat thirty minutes away. It was a community possessed of some vague sense of its own history, a love/hate relationship with the nearby river, and an abiding spirit of cooperation among its dwindling inhabitants.

Fordville had its stories to tell, and I was there *just in time* to hear some of them before the curtain fell on its final act. Not that the community disappeared entirely from view, but in contrast to the present, it was like watching a fading sunset that could never, ever be duplicated. If it's true that sound by definition requires both a sender and a receiver, Fordville's last audible sound was a raspy whisper and I, the grateful receiver. Stories were told, old words were spoken…and I heard.

14

Sandy shook her head when the daughters made their Christmas present request known to us. She knows me too well. I still have second hand woodworking equipment in the barn I bought years ago to build the cedar chests both daughters requested as wedding presents. Come to think of it, they were actually supposed to be hope chests *before* they married.

I would like to say I was inspired to immediately begin fulfilling our daughters' request for their stories to be written. The truth is that although I did think about writing them from time to time, I never developed an action plan to make it happen. However, one valuable lesson I've learned is the healing, even transforming power of *just getting started.*

The following Labor Day morning I was positioned on my old recliner, coffee cup in one hand, remote in the other. Being an early riser, I was at my post in front of the morning news when my wife Sandy, my ever-faithful encourager, suddenly came into the living room and stood in front of the television screen like a cigar store Indian, blocking my view. Dangling the gray plastic bags of Cracker Barrel napkins in front of me she said, "Mister, are you going to do this or not? Because, *if* you're not, I'm giving them back to the girls on Friday." Yep, I would need to be shamed into getting it done.

I think that's when I tried to play the cancer survivor card, but you have to be careful not to overuse that one. Sandy had faith in me, even when I had none in myself that I could get the stories on paper.

We talked about the task ahead and in typical fashion she offered to do the typing if I would simply write two stories to the best of my ability, and she suggested I start *today* with just one napkin. "Take it slow and easy," she said. I'm all about taking it easy, so I accepted both the challenge and her offer. By Thanksgiving Day, after a series of revisions I had written two stories, one for each daughter--not a good dent in the napkin pile, *but a start*.

Fast forward to Christmas. We sat around the Christmas tree in our living room that morning opening gifts, and the daughters kept poking around under the tree, thinking just maybe I had complied with their request. Seeing nothing, hearing nothing to indicate otherwise, they drooped like sick chickens. As we sat down to our customary country ham Christmas dinner, I must say I was deeply gratified and honestly surprised by their obvious disappointment, for until that very moment I really had no idea the stories meant that much to them.

After eating, the daughters and their families began loading their gifted plunder and prepared to head home. My great-uncle J.B., once regarded as Fordville's premier practical joker, said "timin's ever'thing." Although not a skilled practical joker, I had maximized the day's surprise potential to my own satisfaction. It was at that moment I handed the daughters their requested stories, typed, double-spaced with title pages, and in clear plastic page protectors, no less. Soon unburdened and unbundled, they sat down in our living room and read them. Then they swapped. For fifteen minutes you could hear a pin drop. Even the grandkids were quiet. Then, both emotional daughters turned on the waterworks. They cried, they hugged--me, their mother, their kids, each other, and their old golden retriever lying happily undisturbed in front of the wood stove. In short, they appeared to be pleased.

As they prepared once more to leave, on her way out the door, our older daughter Loren said, "Daddy, you know I've got a birthday coming up. Would you write me another napkin story?" I indicated that I would *consider* it. Surprisingly, I found it a mostly pleasant and, sometimes bittersweet experience--to recall the old people, now all gone, and the lessons I learned from them. The relics of the past about which I've written are mostly from their lives-- those that I lived among as a visitor. Some of the chosen objects are old-very old, while others are no older than I am; to my knowledge, none of them has any real monetary value. Mostly, they are object lessons for me, representing the people that helped me grow into a manhood that took me from a fading Kentucky River village to the jungles of Southeast Asia and back. With other stories included in these pages, there's not really a lesson, only a memory I get to relive through the telling.

Consequently, you can see how this little collection of "old stuff stories" came into being. For each Christmas and birthday since, the daughters have requested that I write more stories for them. Ever so slowly, I've been able to reduce the original inventory of Cracker Barrel napkins-- still in gray Wal-Mart bags, except for the rewrites which, for the purpose of easy identification are transferred to their bright yellow, Dollar General Store equivalents.

The stapled, dog-eared stories that our daughters read, swapped and then shared with their friends resulted in yet another request, that I assemble them coherently for others to read. Once again with the able assistance and organizational skills of my wife, these stories were chosen from the collection to put into print. Although I remain skeptical as to their worth, they insist they will prove me wrong. It's okay either way. It seems the stories themselves *wanted* to be told.

Although it took me quite a spell to get started, Daughters, as you have requested, I have tried to come through for you with these stories. Some of them you know now by heart, while others will be strangers to you.

By the way, the now hoped-for chests you wanted me to build for your wedding presents are coming right along. After the grandkids were born, I decided to use walnut instead of cedar. But, take heart. I finally got around to planting the trees last fall. How's that for optimism?

See you Friday evening. I love you.

"Dad"

The blue bicycle

Biker Girl

By mid-afternoon the estate auction was down to sorted piles of worthless junk. Unable to coax a bid from the sparse pool of remaining bidders, the auctioneer finally reached into his pocket and playfully tossed a crumpled dollar bill onto the one item that drew my attention. Making eye contact with me as I nodded, his nasal chant rose to a fever pitch. As I made the lone bid, he cried "SOLD, for *one dollar*!" Amid the laughter, I retrieved the one meaningful object from the debris I had acquired, the rest of which I left behind.

In making my sentimental purchase that fall afternoon, I obtained a historical Fordville relic in the form of a faded blue bicycle frame. Its elderly previous owner was something of a local misfit and on a bet I had once pedaled her through Fordville on my own bicycle.

I never fully understood if the old codgers who comprised the membership of The Children's Hour realized what a tantalizing offer they had dangled in front of me that day. I'm not even sure they were serious about "the bet", but I soon put them to the test. Purchased at the Western Auto in Harriston, my new bike had been a Christmas present from my grandparents. It was joyously received due to the fact that I was forever walking down the winding three mile distance into Fordville, or to my great uncle J.B.'s shack on the river. I was quite pleased with the shiny, fire-engine red acquisition. Eager to use my newly found freedom to earn a couple of extra bucks, I embraced an opportunity that presented itself in the person of eccentric, elderly Josephine McQueen who lived at the edge of what could be called Fordville.

"Josie" had been a widow for as long as I could remember. After the death of her improvident husband, she had somehow scratched out a living by taking in laundry and occasionally selling homemade cakes and pies. Small built, she possessed a set of piercing brown eyes and a sharp tongue that was known to loosen itself on those who messed with her. She was a quaint old character, gruff and plainspoken—but good. Even though bonnets had long since fallen out of fashion, if you passed Josie walking to or from Perkins' Store, she could be seen wearing one of her many handmade versions, a long print dress and men's work shoes. She couldn't have been much older than I am now, but at the time she seemed ancient as the limestone cliffs above the nearby Kentucky River. My earliest memory of Josie is watching her walk home from Perkins' Store carrying a burlap bag over her tiny, stooped shoulders. By the time I was old enough to go fishing on the river by myself, I sometimes carried the bag for her as she headed home. We usually meandered along in silence unless she noticed something out of the ordinary that she might call attention to—especially, things she saw in the sky--shapes among the clouds. On those walks she sometimes imagined animals and even the faces of people whose features she could see in the sky over Fordville. On rare occasions a story might follow from one of the many she had read as a young woman who once yearned to teach. Of those shapes in the clouds, however, only one stands out in my memory. Not because I saw it—I didn't—but the story Josie told with it has remained with me ever since.

It had rained earlier that spring day and we dodged mud puddles on the way to the McQueen Place. Looking up, Josie untied her bonnet and pulled it back to take in the full view of the sky.

"Now look up yonder why don't you? Up there now…it's Mazeppa ridin' that wild runaway horse." I had no earthly idea what she was talking about as she happily pointed into the clouds and told the bizarre tale of a tragic young lover—a nobleman who was tied naked to the back of a taunted, wild horse and sent flying into the remote countryside, nearly killing him. It was his punishment for having an affair with an older and powerful nobleman's much younger wife. She kept staring at the clouds as we ambled along downhill toward the McQueen place, telling her story—one which had once captured her youthful imagination.

As we came within sight of her tired old house, she ended the tale by saying, "I've always wanted to ride in the wind." Then, as if she suddenly realized she'd been thinking out loud, she grinned sheepishly and said, "Well—maybe not *naked* on the back of a horse—but just out in the open, flyin' away in the clouds and not a care in the world." Then, as if closing a curtain on a school play gone bad, Josie pulled the loosened bonnet back up over her head and set her lined face toward the weathered farmhouse. I've never forgotten the longing in her eyes as she peered into the clouds that day, as if she dreamed of drifting away to the wild and distant setting for her story and free herself of the yellow Fordville mud that clung to her work shoes. Maybe she still dreamed of faraway and exotic places. Although at the time I thought it was a story Josie had made up for my amusement, I was astounded when one of my college English professors recalled the story in detail. At the next class meeting Dr. Rhoads gave me the musty little volume from his own vast library that contained the early 19th century poem entitled "Mazeppa." Written by the Romantic Era English poet Lord Byron, it was pretty racy stuff for the Josie McQueen I thought I knew. Maybe she *had* once been young.

Josie hardly seemed the exotic type. The words "hard-core plain" might be closer to describing the image I had seen in my youth as she occasionally walked into Fordville. Whether or not it was due to her modest circumstances or just the fact that she didn't want or need much, Josie didn't travel up the road to Perkins' Store more than once a week and she didn't tarry there long. She spoke no more than necessary to any loafers who happened to be there and seemed to have an uneasiness about her that bordered on paranoia where those men were concerned. She correctly understood that she had often been the butt of their jokes.

Until I was old enough to occasionally walk along beside her and carry her purchases, I, like the old men, came to assume that Josie was an unrepentant old sourpuss. "Old Acid Face," they called her. The old fellows meant no harm with their banter, and surely she knew that. However, Josie McQueen did not suffer fools, which she clearly thought them all to be. She would gather up her groceries into the burlap bag and begin her solitary journey home where she lived alone in two closed off back rooms of the old McQueen place, a neatly-kept two story farmhouse which had long before seen its better days. I didn't really encounter Josie on my own very often, however, until I acquired my own means of transportation and that didn't happen until I turned thirteen.

Although I had been given my shiny red bicycle as a Christmas present, it was probably March before I ventured all the way down into Fordville with it on my way to fish on the river with J.B. As I turned the corner by Josie's, I saw her sitting alone on the porch with one or two cats rubbing themselves on her legs and work shoes. She called to me as I made the turn.

"Hi-dee Clay! Whatcha got there?"

Josie appeared to be more than a little interested in the new bike. She rose from the porch to meet me at the old fashioned picket fence which was unpainted, and missing a few slats. She came through the gate and immediately focused her gaze on the bicycle as if she had never seen one before.

Noticing her interest in it, I said, "It's the bike I got for Christmas."

"It's a pretty thing," she said, admiringly. She ran her hand along the handle bars, and curiously bent down to examine the spokes and the chain that made it move.

"I've never got me a good look at how one o' them works," she said, still running her fingers along the freshly oiled chain. She couldn't take her eyes of it, even as I steered toward the river and looked back toward her. She was there on her porch when I was on my way home. She waved me down. "Clay, where you reckon I can get me one o' them?"

"Granny and Granddaddy bought this one for me at the Western Auto Store in Harriston."

"Hmmm," she mumbled. "Wonder what it cost 'em?"

Balancing the bike with both my feet planted on the muddy road, I said, "I don't know Miss Josie, but you can ask Granny when you see her at the store. She or Granddaddy one could tell you."

With a childlike giggle, she said, "I just might get me one, some day."

I thought she was kidding.

The next day I was on my way back from the river when I stopped at the Store and The Children's Hour was nearly

24

ended. I told the loafers about Josie admiring my bike. All the old men present cackled at the thought of the old girl riding one. Of course, Red Perkins was the first to chime in. "Now that'd be a sight to behold—Josie McQueen ridin' a bicycle wearin' a dress all hiked up to her Adam's apple-- and pumpin' them pedals with work shoes. Even ol' Mack here'd be put off women if he saw somethin' like that."

Granddaddy said in a low tone, "Now Red, Josie was a good lookin' gal back in her day."

Mack Perkins laughed, "That's right, Russell. You courted her a little didn't you? I'd forgot that."

"I did," he replied, solidly, "'til Bill McQueen came ridin' in on that big fine saddle horse his daddy'd given im."

Red nodded. "I'd forgot about that horse. It was a dandy…Josie would've been better off if she'd kept it instead of Bill."

Others present remembered a poor but bright-eyed wisp of a girl, one of seven children—her red hair plaited into braids. She loved to ride horses, they said—and the faster the better. She'd been smart, they remembered, and loved to read. She had once been the star of school plays in the old one room Ford's Branch School and seemed destined for some level of stardom that never materialized. Since Josie had never learned to drive, after her husband died she'd sold his car and became something of a recluse and far away from the public eye she'd once reveled in.

My debut at the store with my new bike was the occasion when Doc Wilcox leaned forward, looked at me seriously and said, "Clay, I'll tell you what I'll do. I'll give you fifty cents if you can get Josie McQueen to ride down here on it."

Red cackled his dry hacking cough, and said, "And I'll match it."

All the old men in the room guffawed at the very idea—either of them—that Josie McQueen would ride through Fordville on a bike or that Red would part so willingly with fifty cents. However, I now had one United States dollar riding on my ability to persuade her. The pressure was on.

That very next day, I pretended to go by Aunt Josie's house, on my way to J.B.'s shack on the river. She was on the front porch as I made the turn toward the river and she called out to me. "I saw your Granny a little while ago," she said. "She said your bicycle was parked at the Store and that you'd prob'ly be headin' this-away."

I said, "Yes, ma'am, I was just going down here to J.B.'s to fish." I then falsely admired the old girl's flowers, her dogs, her cats, her free-range chickens and her whatever I could think of before submitting my proposal that she ride on my bike all the way into Fordville.

With a touch of kindled anger in her voice, Josie said, "Now Clay, I want to ask you somethin'--and I want you to tell me the truth. Did any of those men down there at that store put you up to askin' me to ride your bicycle?"

I paused before attempting an answer.

She smacked the arm of her porch chair with her little open hand.

"I knew it," she said, defiantly. "I just knew as much."

"How much did they offer you to get me on that thing?"

Once again, I was caught in the middle. I couldn't lie to the old lady whose piercing gaze was now fixed upon me.

I just decided to come clean. "Fifty cents from Mack," I said, "and another fifty from Red if I can get you to ride all the way to the store and back."

She studied my hopeful expression. She said, "Hmmm. You're not doin' too bad if you can squeeze fifty cents from Red. I'd say you've done all right for yourself" then added cryptically—"that is, if **I** come through for you."

She sat back in her porch thoughtfully and fixed her eyes upon my shiny red bike. Leaning forward in the metal porch chair, Josie stroked her chin and said, decidedly. "Tell you what, Clay. If you'll wait 'til tomorrow, I'll do it, but I'm gonna make you an offer. I'll do it **if** you promise to teach me how to drive the thing—and then I'll give you another dollar. How's that sound to you?"

I will never forget how she laughed when she made her own counter offer. The joke, however, was on both of us, for little did we know just where Mack's little dare would lead.

I said, "Well, I *guess* I can."

"Good," she said, firmly, *"Trade made.* I'll be lookin' for you here tomorrow when you get in from school--and we can practice ridin' it around in the yard before we take it out on the road."

As I rode my bike home I came to dread the very thing I had so eagerly undertaken only minutes before. I prayed for an earthquake, monsoon winds or a sandstorm-- anything to keep me from facing my ordeal, but no natural disaster made a visitation on Fordville that night. I came in from school the next day, hustled up my afternoon chores—and tore out for Josie's as fast as I could pedal.

I pulled up to the front porch of the old McQueen house while Josie came down the steps beaming from ear to ear in anticipation. At least *she* was looking forward to it. I steadied my bike and waited for her to get situated behind me.

It was an awkward if unforgettable sight to behold: Josie McQueen climbing onto the seat of the bike in her print dress--and the trademark bonnet tied around her head. I held the bicycle steady while she fumbled around to get situated. Steeling my nerves for what lay ahead, I knew I would essentially be standing up and peddling our combined weight for nearly a full mile into Fordville. Finally, I girded up my loins and started peddling—and wobbling--downhill, and after about four circles around the fenced-in yard, I knew I was as ready as I'd ever be.

Suddenly, as an apparent afterthought, Josie said, "Wait just a minute. Hold this thing steady while I get off. I could use a couple of things at the store and I'll just call ahead and tell Mack to have 'em ready and waitin' for me. Then I'll tell 'im you're bringin' me down there on that bicycle. That'll bring them ol' fools out." In the house she went and shortly she returned beaming from ear to ear. "I gave my list to Mack—and then I told 'im you were peddlin' me down there. I hung up before he could say anything."

I turned to look at the spectacle for myself: Josie appeared to have a sinister but altogether satisfied grin on her face.

"She said, "Saddle up, Rowdy Yates. Let's ride!"

My solitary passenger was a natural and seemed to understand our delicately balanced seating arrangement. I pumped and peddled. Josie giggled, "Woo-wheed" –all the way up the long incline into Fordville until I was nearly out of breath. I still managed a grin when we got there and saw the old men on both benches in front of the store, leaning forward-- trying to look around each other to watch the spectacle unfold. I was part of Josie's magnum opus that afternoon, and I knew a little more about the eccentric old lady than I had *just* the day before—when I had made a bargain with the Devil. That knowledge came from a conversation I had with Granny the night before.

As we had washed up the supper dishes—shortly after Josie made her counter-offer, I asked Granny about the strange old lady's younger days. Like every other kid in the community, I knew well who she was but I had really never fully encountered her on my own terms—or hers.

I said, "Why doesn't anybody seem to like her?"

"Oh," she said, "That's not so. Josie's all right. She's just…different--keeps to herself. Your granddaddy's prob'ly never told you, but he courted 'er before he ever met me, and you know he had to see somethin' in her."

"Why didn't they stay together?"

"Well," she said, "the truth of the matter is she didn't want to be a farmer's wife. Josie loved to read and they said she wanted to go off somewhere and get her education to teach. She ab-so-lutely devoured books, accordin' to what her family always said. But, where she was the oldest daughter and her mother needed help with all them other children, all she could do was to squeeze in a little readin' here and there. Her mother and daddy didn't have the money to send her to school past the eighth grade. It's a shame, too. I think ol' Josie would've made a good teacher.

Your granddaddy said Josie was forever dreamin' of travelin' to other places. She wanted another life for herself and when she met Bill McQueen, she prob'ly thought he'd help her get it. His family had a little money at one time. They came here from the other side of Harriston and bought that place where Josie lives. Bill's mother and father had lost two little boys to typhoid fever where they'd lived before and that's why they came here. Bill was their only child to live— and they gave him anything and ever'thing he wanted. The first year they came here they bought 'im a big fine black horse, and he thought he was somethin' else ridin' around on it. It wasn't long before they bought 'im a new buggy when he started courtin' and all your granddaddy had was an old gray mule that he paid for hisself. Bill got to comin' around right regl'ar to see

30

Josie at her mother and daddy's place. When she saw what prospects she had with Bill instead of your granddaddy, she started courtin' him. They married before long and she moved into that ol' McQueen house down there with Bill and his mother and daddy. When the Model T came out, nothin' would do but for Bill's mother and daddy to go to the new Ford garage in Harriston and buy him one, and it brand-spankin' new. After that, most ever' mornin' Josie would get Bill all slicked up and he'd drive that Model T into town wearin' a shirt and tie like he had corn for sale. Poor ol' Josie'd iron his clothes and the creases so sharp you could cut yourself on 'em. That's about when she finally figured out she'd married a dreamer. Bill would settle into a job of some kind and for a while he'd go after it like puttin' out a house fire…and then he'd just let it fizzle. He tried his hand at a dozen different things and made a flop of ever' one of 'em. Finally, Mr. and Mrs. McQueen had to start sellin' off land to bail 'im out. Bill wouldn't stay with nothin' long enough to make a go of it. He was always full of big ideas about how he was gonna make him a fortune. At the last, his daddy sold off the biggest part of their farm to set Bill up in a furniture store in Harriston--but he wouldn't never stay in it. You'd go by there and he'd have a sign up on the door "Gone for Dinner." He'd go up to the Elks Lodge and spend half the day sittin' around playin' cards. When Bill's daddy died they had to close it down."

Granny chuckled, "I remember one time, years ago, hearin' Josie fuss about Bill. That was after he lost a job as a feed salesman. 'That husband o' mine couldn't grease a monkey's tail—*and it tied*.' (For the record, no one has ever attempted to explain why anyone would want to undertake the task.)

"The last straw for Bill's mother was when he got it in his head to run for county judge. He lost the election but she put ever'thing she had left into that race. Always before, when he'd would be in a hard place like that, his mother and daddy would just sell off another piece of land to come up with more money--but nothin' lasts forever. By the time ol' Mrs. McQueen died, all that was left of their farm was that ol' house on the corner and two or three acres. That left Josie havin' to start take in washin' and ironin' to earn what little extra money she needed to keep 'em goin'. There at the last, Bill just gave up on doin' anything, but even up 'til he died, Josie would dress 'im up in a white shirt and tie and off he'd go into town nearly ever' day lookin' like a Philadelphia lawyer."

Hearing the story made me feel bad for Josie. When I learned what difficulties she had experienced, I suddenly felt ashamed of my great-uncle J.B. and some of the old men that poked fun at the unfortunate old woman living in two rooms of what had once been one of the better houses in Fordville. I felt even more ashamed of myself for laughing with them at her quaint appearance and said nothing to Granny about my plan to drive the old girl through the middle of Fordville--or about teaching her to ride a bicycle. Those thoughts were clearly on my mind the next afternoon as the old loafers in front of the store came within full view of me peddling the venerable Josephine McQueen through Fordville.

As we rolled toward the old men she had known all her life--two of whom she had courted, Josie suddenly reached up with one hand and loosened her bonnet. Although at least some of her pinned up hair was now freed and blowing in the breeze behind me, I could only imagine the look on her face from the reaction of our onlookers. The old men suddenly seemed less like my old friends and more like "the others" as I conspired with the old lady who giggled and cooed like a two year old in butter. Caught in a puff of wind, Josie's old bonnet and a couple of hairpins blew off her head. If she noticed, it didn't seem to matter. I kept peddling.

I rode on past Fordville toward our road and stopped. I said "Josie, are you ready to go home?" "Yep," she said, "I'm ready…and I'm ready to learn how to ride one of these things." Although I had gotten a kick out of our brief journey, I was not looking forward to biking lessons. Our audience was still in front of the store waiting for our return trip. We did not disappoint. With added downhill momentum Josie tilted her head back in the afternoon sun, allowing the gentle breeze to waft over her. I couldn't see the expressions on the faces of the old men in front of the store, *but this wasn't about them.*

A couple of the old fellows tipped their hats toward her, laughing aloud, but after being an object of their amusement for years, the best I could tell she didn't even give them the satisfaction of looking in their direction. Pulling just past the store, I stopped and steadied the bike while Josie literally hopped off and entered Mack's store-- barefooted—to the absolute amazement of all who saw it, including myself. I had not noticed that she had taken off her pair of men's work shoes just before we began our steady uphill ride into Fordville. Grinning from ear to ear, she said, "I didn't want you to have to pedal me and them heavy shoes o' mine *both* up here." Somewhat awkward in her bare feet, Josie stepped across the uneven wooden floor like a burnt-toed chicken, fumbled in her apron and brought out the change to pay for a can of peas that Mack had waiting for her and a packet of sewing needles. I suddenly realized that she hadn't really needed anything. This was for show.

We were soon back on my bike and back at Josie's house and she still hadn't noticed her bonnet missing. Once again, I helped her climb off.

"Hoo-wee!" she sighed, happily.

"We had us a hell-rollickin' time, didn't we?"

"Yes ma'am we did. We made it." Truthfully, I was relieved I hadn't spilled the old girl in the middle of the road, on her bonnet-covered head. My knees were shaking.

I propped the bike up against her porch.

"Clay, I'm gonna go inside and get us a cold pop, and then...then, you're gonna teach me how to ride that thing." After we split the luxuriously tall, sixteen ounce bottle of Coke, we took the bike further up the road toward Fordville where she employed the gradual slope toward the river to her advantage. After a couple of downhill rolls, stops and starts, Josie had it down pat. She was surprisingly strong and nimble for a woman of her age, and she was even able

34

to nearly stand up on the pedals, pumping her way back uphill toward Fordville. For half an hour or more Josie rode up and down the hill and around her house, chickens darting to and fro out of her way. Finally, she parked the bike, fumbling at the kickstand with her work shoes before propping it up against her leaning picket fence. She reached into her apron pocket, handed me four quarters— and shook my hand. Together, we'd scored a great victory and I pedaled home two dollars to the good.

When Granny learned about me taking bet money, she brow-beat me into putting some of my newly acquired wealth into the offering plate at church--but I was still $1.50 ahead. Granny said it was "ill-gotten gain" and would do me no good. Her words proved prophetic. Two days later I rounded Josie's corner as I headed toward the river to fish and punctured a tire on a honey locust thorn. So much for my windfall.

The next time I passed Josie, she was not sitting on her porch watching the world go by, a handful of cars in a day. Wearing a pair of her dead husband's cut off work pants she was peddling *her own bicycle* into Fordville where she parked it in front of the store. How she managed to avoid getting her oversized pants legs from getting caught up in the chain, I have no earthly idea. This time, I was assembled with my male tribal elders near the cold potbellied stove. *I was one of them now.* Still, she came directly over to me, appearing not to notice the others.

"Clay, come out here after Mack rings me up. I wanna show you somethin'."

With two small brown paper bags in her hands, Josie nodded toward the door and I followed her outside. There she stood, pointing toward her new blue bicycle with as much joy as a sixteen year old would showing off a new red sports car.

Giggling mischievously she said, "My niece Vera took me to the Western Au-to store in town and bought it for me. Looks sharp don't it?"

She said, "I found me a basket for it at the ten cent store. That way, I can carry me a few things." The pride she felt in her newfound mobility was apparent. With gravity on her side, Josie mounted the bicycle and rolled slowly toward her home down the road. I never again saw Josie McQueen riding her bike wearing a bonnet. Wiry gray hair now overruled the red as the breeze blew it around her wrinkled smiles, but she was past caring. Movement of her own making was a thing to be savored and her hair could do what it would.

About two years later I was as surprised as everybody else to learn that Josie "had found her a boyfriend" in the form of Cecil Winstead, a widower who worked in the Western Auto Store in Harriston repairing bicycles and small engines. She had first met him there when she purchased her own bicycle. We came to learn that the gentle natured fellow was also a book lover and had purposefully saved his meager earnings for years until he was able to buy a tiny little house *next door* to the public library. Josie was in her seventies by the time she and Cecil married, and I don't recall ever seeing her on her bicycle again. Josie took it into town with her—along with her love of reading.

When the McQueen place was ultimately sold at public auction, with other contents from the house in town, the faded blue bike was put up for a bid along with an old mower that didn't run and a garden rake with a broken handle. I returned Josie's dollar to her that day by buying the whole pile. I rationalized the purchase with the idea our girls could ride the bike up and down the farm lane where we live. Although I did eventually repair and repaint the bike, it was not for riding. My wife Sandy decided it would look cute with flowers growing in little buckets hanging from the front and back. It is now purely ornamental and sits on the front porch—with us.

Looking back, I take some satisfaction in the role I played in Josie McQueen's autumn revival. Neither of us had the foggiest notion where life could—or would—take her on the basis of that one dollar bet. On the other hand, her willingness to take a risk played a role in the course she took at an unlikely, if not unpromising time of life. Maybe it had just been lying dormant all those years, like one of the flower seeds she kept wrapped up in a piece of brown paper—and waiting for spring.

The old crosscut saw hanging on the wall in the barn.

Mondays on the Moon

The thing was an instrument of torture in my youth, like something you'd expect to see in a dark dungeon alongside the chains and shackles to the left of the stretching rack. In this case, it was more like a dark toolshed, and chains were on the wall…log chains, not shackles. Just as regular as clockwork, if we experienced an unusually warm Saturday in the winter, I could expect to hear Granddaddy announce that it was time for us to cut wood. By the time I left home for Vietnam, the whole process was mine to manage, with him as a sidekick and helper—a reversal in our roles necessitated by circumstance. But first, *I had to learn* and as such, my introductory lesson came one Saturday morning when I was ten years old.

38

My grandparents didn't burn much wood at all, only what was used to heat the homemade stove in the stripping room of the tobacco barn above Polly's Point. But, since it was tobacco money that mostly paid the bills and helped put food on the table, a supply of wood to keep the stripping room warm during the fall and winter months was serious business.

Granddaddy would listen to the weather report, his own instincts, and choose the woodcutting day when he rose in the morning. For reasons of his own, he bucked the trend and forsook all modern wood cutting equipment, namely the chain saw. He had used chain saws helping neighbors, but was clearly not a fan. He preferred the old way: a pair of work horses, iron wedges, sledge hammer, and the ultimate weapon itself, *the cross cut saw*. This particular saw had belonged to his father and it was a safe bet that his only sibling, my ne'er-do-well great-uncle J.B. would never use it. In the sometimes contentious environment of dividing up family possessions, the sharp-toothed heirloom passed to Granddaddy without protest.

For as long as I could remember, the saw hung above the door in the toolshed with the saw teeth turned up and it took both of us to get it down and to put it back, without shedding blood.

After taking the saw down from its position on that particular day, I was mustered into service. In fairness to truth, that first day wasn't nearly as bad as it could have been. The homemade stove was intended primarily for burning coal, so the pieces of wood had to be chosen carefully and cut smaller. The kicker is that coal cost money and there were always free dead trees that needed cutting down in or near pastures. They were the chosen targets for our early Saturday morning labors.

Riding the tractor with Granddaddy, we pulled alongside a dead tree in the hayfield that had blown over in a summer storm. At some point earlier in the winter he had taken his chopping axe to cut away smaller limbs. He hooked chains to it, and we slowly dragged it over the field, pulling it in the direction of the tobacco barn above Polly's Point.

Every step of the day's work had a specific purpose and function which met yet a larger need. It all ended with the clothes on my back and food on my plate but I couldn't connect the dots at that point: *work was just what you did.*

I had never handled the cross cut saw before, and this was to be my inaugural event as the only other male on the farm. I think my grandparents had discussed the matter and agreed that it was time I learned.

Granddaddy unhooked the log at a strategic point on some locust posts near the barn which raised the logs above the ground so they could be more easily cut. After we unloaded the cross cut saw, he demonstrated how we were to begin cutting the bigger end of the log, loading the smaller sections onto the work horses.

Cutting wood with a cross cut saw is truly a partnership, and one requiring a rhythm shared by both. The way this works, one defective cutting partner is frustrating, but two can be disastrous. While not as potentially lethal as two novice chainsaw operators, it can still get you banged up.

"Me and J.B. had to cut ALL our wood when we was your age," he said. "Supposed to be both of us anyway."

I knew there had to be a back story if my great uncle J.B. was mentioned. There was ALWAYS a back story if his name came up. He was the fun brother. I was the oppressed grandson of the not so fun brother. Even as an old man, Granddaddy was strong and sinewy… and I was a skinny kid that didn't know jack diddly about cutting wood.

He would pull his end and I would push as he had tried to teach me. I thought the owner's manual had to be pretty clear on the subject. He coolly reminded me how to follow his lead and then, *pull* my way.

Maybe he was mad at Granny, the world in general, or me in particular that morning, for at some point early in the sweat slinging session he roared, **"DON'T YOU RIDE THAT SAW, BOY!"**

You need to understand that I can count on one hand the number of times I ever heard the man raise his voice. Being human, of course he had a temper, but it usually manifested itself in other ways. Yelling was generally not something I heard growing up. Actually, this came through as a gravel-throated squall, not just a frustrated announcement.

To make matters worse, I didn't know what he meant. He evidently assumed that I was just propping my hands on my handle and not pulling or pushing when I should've been. Maybe I had been. Regardless, I caught on quick and started using more muscle. It was a step in the right direction, but rhythm comes with experience and today was not going to be a good rhythm day. When he saw that I was at least trying, Granddaddy said, "Now you're cookin' with gas, let 'er rip". I don't know how much more we cut, but I remember how that little compliment made me feel-- like *a man,* doing his best, a childhood lesson not to be understated.

Maybe one or two other times in that day's wood cutting did he raise his voice somewhat and say, "You're ridin' that saw again!" By mid- morning, I must have learned the rhythm thing or the old fellow learned to put up with me, or maybe a little of both. We were cutting wood;   I was helping, and it was a good feeling.

As it was unusually warm for a winter day, about ten o'clock we took a little break. Granddaddy always had an army surplus canteen of cold water that Granny filled every morning before he left the house. He gave that to me, while he sipped on his quart jar of cold coffee. If he had ever known of a thermos, he didn't let on. Granny would pour the leftover coffee into the Mason quart jar which was of course cold as a cucumber within an hour, even in warm weather. He opened the stripping room door and let the rare sunshine in as we sat down on the long wooden work bench where the tobacco stripping took place in the fall. He took a swig of coffee from the jar which missed his mouth and trickled down his shirt. Wiping it away, he said, "I remember helpin' my daddy cut our wood and that's ALL we had to heat and cook with. This little pile here wouldn't have lasted us more'n a day or two."

I drank readily from the canteen and listened.

"When J.B. got up about your age, Daddy said he was turnin' the wood cuttin' over to us. J.B. had busted up a little wood with an axe, but not with the cross cut saw. Mama was always afraid J.B. was gonna overheat and get sick. She'd lost a baby boy between me and him and she never got over it. Then when J.B. was just a little fellow, he got down with… diphthery, I think it was, and she and Daddy thought he wasn't gonna make it. He got better, of course, but after that, she watched him like a loaded .45.

So me and J.B. go out to the woodpile and start sawin' some logs that Daddy already had layin' there. We hadn't been workin' thirty minutes before Mama came out there with a wet dishtowel in her hands and started wipin' the sweat off J.B.'s face. You'd have to know how partic'lar Mama was about her dish towels to appreciate it.

Mama looked right hateful at me, like I was J.B.'s keeper or somethin', and said to me and Daddy, 'Don't *YOU TWO* let him get too hot!'"

Granddaddy chuckled, "There wasn't nobody worried about ME gettin' too hot. We were there maybe another fifteen or twenty minutes and J.B. got to actin' like he was sick, and that did it. He went to the house and you can guess who got to cut the rest of the wood…so it took me twice as long.

Daddy fussed at Mama--that she was babyin' J.B. and it would hurt him in the long run. I think he finally gave up tryin' to argue with her. He knew how hard it was on her losin' a baby, and then very nearly losin' J.B. He just gave in to her.

43

He would help me every once in a while, but cuttin' and stackin' our firewood fell mostly on me. J.B. would split wood a little when Mama would break down and tell 'im to, but if he *ever* picked up that cross cut saw again, I never knew of it.

It wasn't just the sawin'. I got to do most ever'thing else. Even when he got grown, J.B. was just like a kid. I remember one spring Daddy sent him with the team down to that little piece of river bottom daddy rented below Babylon to plow, and when he got there it was too wet. Instead of comin' back to the house to see what else Daddy wanted 'im to do, J.B. and a couple of them Farris boys took the team and one of their wagons to haul up some of that wet river sand and then they spent the whole mornin' makin' 'em a croquet court. They had it all set up by end of the day, and even played a match on it, if I remember right. J.B. never said a word to Daddy about it bein' too wet to plow, and the next day he took the team back down there and spent that whole blessed day playin' croquet again, and they had 'em a big time. Mama got worried about J.B. not havin' any dinner and she fixed up the awfullest pile of food you ever laid your eyes on. Mama sent Daddy and me down there to check on him. I reckon J.B. never thought about Daddy comin' down there to see about things, and there he was with the Farrises, playin' croquet. Them Farris boys took one good look at Daddy's face and they hightailed it out of there, and J.B. right along with 'em. Daddy didn't do him a thing but hook that plow up and made a furrow right through the middle of their croquet court. That ended the croquet playin'."

Granddaddy looked at me as he rose up from where he'd been sitting and said, "You can guess who got to do J.B.'s plowin' for him. Daddy nor nobody else could do anything with him. He'd been drinkin' a little bit one evenin' at a dance somewhere, so he couldn't get out of the bed for breakfast the next mornin'. Daddy was plumb put out with him. He got his face right down into J.B.'s and told 'em that we were gonna be workin' down at the sawmill that day. They needed extra help workin' logs that was brought down on the river from up in the mountains. Daddy told J.B., he said, "Son, the least you can do is get your sorry hide out of that bed and split some wood for the fireplace. We'll be cold, and most likely wet when time we get back. You can bring in a backlog and at least have me and your brother a good big fire built by the time we get home for supper."

Granddaddy continued with a chuckle, "Daddy didn't know how right he was, about bein' wet…after dinner we was helpin' break up the log rafts on the river, down at the sawmill. He slipped when he went to put his foot on a log and it rolled out from under him…and right down in that ice cold river he went. Daddy was a good swimmer but that water was freezin'. We pulled 'im out all right and tried to dry him off. Of course, he had to come out of that wet shirt or freeze to death, but finally I got him bundled up in a smelly old horse blanket somebody gave us down at the sawmill and we came on home. The air was just as cold as kraut and poor ol' Daddy was blue as a fish hook and shiverin' all over.

We came through the door into the livin' room there where we lived at Babylon, and there sat J.B. He had not split the first piece of wood. All he had burnin' in that fireplace was a little gnat fire left from what Daddy had started before we left--and it was about played out. J.B. had bought hisself a second hand guit-tar just a few days before, and there he was sittin' in Daddy's chair strummin' away on it. There Daddy stood with ice formed on his coat, soakin' wet, and shiverin'...cold to the bone. He never said Boo—but he reached down and snatched that guit-tar up, busted it on the floor all over Mama's braided rug, and *kept* smashin' it, J.B. yellin' the whole time for him to stop. Then he gathered up the pieces and pitched 'em on the fire, strings and all. When Mama heard all that splatterment goin on, she came runnin' in there and told J.B. to leave the house. He stayed gone 'til after bedtime and then Mama worried all evenin' about where he was. She waited supper and when Daddy found where Mama had set it back for him and pitched it out to the dogs. Mama never said a word to him that time. I believe that was the maddest I ever knew him to be."

We sat in silence for a moment.

I said, "Did you *ever* get a break from working when you were growing up?"

"On Sundays," he said. "Mama was a strict believer in not workin' on Sunday, except for just what *had* to be done. Ever' once in a while Daddy kept us home to work if he thought the weather was fixin' to turn bad, and Mama didn't like it one bit. I remember one Sunday mornin' he told us to get our work clothes on, that we wouldn't be

46

goin' to church on account of it lookin' like rain and we had a field of hay cut and ready to stack. He was afraid we'd lose it to the rain if we went to church. Mama said, "John, you'll be like the man on the moon. If you work on Sunday, you'll have to spend *Monday*s on the moon carryin' brush for the fires in hell." Granddaddy said, "That's the only time I ever sassed her, but I couldn't help it. I said, "J.B.'s in good shape then, but I'll have to be in hell seven days a week—to carry his brush *and* mine." She twisted her mouth and made toward me with that open hand to slap me—and I knew I was in trouble. I had it comin'. I knew I'd done wrong and I just stood there, gettin' ready to take it. Right then I said, "I'm sorry, Mama." She had that hand up," he said, holding his own hand at eye level. "And she held it right like that for a second or two. Then she dropped it. She knew I had to do most of the work, what Daddy didn't do. All she said was, "Son, you know J.B.'s not well."

Granddaddy sighed as he emptied his cold coffee onto the dirt floor of the stripping room, and with a dry, raspy chuckle said, "So it was Mondays on the moon for me...*and J.B. got nothin' but Saturdays down here.*"

Break time ended with the story of my errant great uncle who was a constant source of amusement for Fordville in general, and for me in particular. By noon we had sawed the tree up and Granddaddy wanted to sharpen the axe again before we did the splitting.

We drove the tractor back to the house for dinner and returned in the early afternoon to the task of using the splitting axe, iron wedge and sledge hammer to split the bigger pieces in halves and quarters. I had to be eased into axe wielding much more slowly, but that's another story. *This was the day of the crosscut saw.* By the end of this introductory lesson, I was a tolerable apprentice. When fall arrived, we had an ample supply of wood for the stove and the work that waited for us in the stripping room where we sorted the cured tobacco leaves, preparing them to be sold. I remember the satisfaction I felt when I warmed myself in front of the fire I had helped fuel.

Granddaddy was not particularly fond of reading, but he was a decent philosopher. By suppertime that Saturday night, I was tuckered out. I remember he looked over at me as Granny began clearing the dishes away and said, "I read somewhere that Henry Ford said, 'If you split your own wood it'll warm you twice.'" America's leading mechanical genius in his day, old Henry was correct in that piece of homespun philosophy that resonated well with my grandfather who lived by that one maxim.

Only after Granddaddy's lifetime did I purchase and use a chainsaw on his farm. By the time I came back from Vietnam, the tobacco crop was being leased out to neighbors who did the raising and there was no longer a need for wood to be cut. Although others used the barn and stripping room for the same purpose, we were no longer part of that experience.

The crosscut saw is now an artifact. Although it still hangs from the same pegs in the same toolshed, I have made the smooth transition to a chainsaw with no regrets. While I am grateful for the lessons it has taught me, I remain just as glad to oil the blade every once in a blue moon and leave it hanging.

Having had several decades now to reflect, I think that first day of wood cutting with the crosscut saw was chosen deliberately. Maybe it's only wishful thinking. Maybe Granddaddy simply needed to get the wood cut, but I think his own upbringing and a lifetime of hard work compelled him to make sure that I learned *how to work*—to carry my load and *NOT RIDE THAT SAW*. Through small tasks and increasingly larger ones I had to learn to do my part of what it took to keep the farm running. Later, I was allowed to work for neighbors and earn my own spending money, but only after my primary obligation to the family was satisfied.

My non-sawing great uncle had been a lifelong source of irritation for Granddaddy, who was bound and determined that Fordville would not have another colorful character from the fruit of his own loins.

Nobody said life was fair. Granddaddy never told me as much, but I'm sure he knew I'd figure it out soon enough.

The red dishpan on the kitchen counter

Teardrops on Granite

Granddaddy died after my first year of active duty in Vietnam. I was unable to spend much time with Granny until after my enlistment period ended, but I tried to come home from college on weekends to help her with odd jobs around the house. During one such weekend visit in late September, Granny asked me to repair her kitchen cabinet door, the handle of which had fallen off. Recalling Granddaddy's large assortment of screws and other hardware, I set my face toward his old toolshed, dreading every step.

I hadn't been in the leaning tarpapered building since his death, and this would be the first time without him hovering nearby to make sure everything was put back in its place. I unlatched the plank door Granddaddy had made from the bed of an old wagon and stepped into the darkness and the familiar, musty smell of oily rags. I turned on the switch at the side of the single light bulb hanging just over my head, and surveyed Granddaddy's orderly inventory. Nuts, bolts and washers had been carefully stored in coffee cans, and leaky metal buckets that were too good to throw away. My eyes then came to rest on what appeared to be a grimy metal pan tucked under the workbench and, pulling it into the light I saw that it was an old dishpan--a type commonly known as "graniteware." Its red and white swirls housed a farmer's lifetime accumulation of miscellaneous odds and ends.

Emptying the dishpan's contents on the workbench, I picked through the pile until I found the right screws for my job. I then noticed that a tiny hole in the bottom had been repaired with a tiny bolt, and a single washer had been carefully beaten in place to follow the curve in the bowl portion, secured by a tiny nut. Granddaddy was known for his resourcefulness, but even that would've been a stretch for him. For whatever reason, there had been a serious attempt to save *that particular dishpan.*

After dumping the ancestral hardware collection into a lard can, I carried the rediscovered dishpan into Granny's kitchen. Evidently Granddaddy had used it numerous times to change the lawnmower oil, but after a thorough cleaning I found it to be in surprisingly good condition. Against the cream-colored oilcloth on Granny's kitchen table, the bright red and white object begged for attention.

In keeping with her summertime Saturday tradition, she had been working in her flowers, and entered the kitchen with a pitcher full of "fall roses," the old-fashioned term she used referring to zinnias. Her usual upbeat demeanor visibly changed upon seeing the old dishpan and she paused to stare at it. Then, with a quiver in her voice, she said, "Lord, lord…I wondered here a while back whatever happened to that ol' thing. It still hurts me a little to even look at it."

Granny wiped her hands on her apron, almost reverently in preparation. She picked it up, turned over and felt the beaten washer and nut that had been used in the repair. "I remember the day Mama got these. She bought a new cook stove from Mack Perkins' daddy down at the store and he gave her a whole set of this stuff—graniteware. I don't know what went with the rest of it, but I remember this ol' dishpan. Mama kept it on the back porch on a white table. She'd hang towels out there on a nail above it and poured water in it so Daddy and Harry Winston could wash up for meals."

Studying the dishpan's well-worn bottom, I said, "It looks like Granddaddy went to a lot of trouble trying to fix it."

Granny rubbed her bony finger over the the tiny nut that had held the beaten washer in place for several years. "He did…but it kept leakin'. He said he'd find somethin' to use it for. You know he didn't get rid of much."

I had moved into a small apartment near The University of Louisville and had taken only the bare minimum of furniture. Thinking about Granddaddy's long-ago attempt to save the dishpan, the thought occurred to me that I could set it on my kitchen table to put fruit in.

As if she had heard my thought, she said, "*You're welcome to it, but* I can't say as I've missed it." Then, she added, "Mama wouldn't even let the thing back in the house after The World War…not after Harry Winston got killed." Granny's references to the deaths of her only brother and only son in two world wars were understandably connected, and often veiled in moments of sadness.

She stood at the kitchen sink and began the task of trimming the zinnias with a heavy pair of kitchen scissors. I asked, "What's the dishpan got to do with Harry Winston?"

Sighing through her nose, Granny paused as she looked out the window just above the sink. "It puts me in mind of the day he left here…for good. Of course, it was practically new then. The caps on Mama's old stove had gotten bad and first one thing and another went wrong with it. If I remember it right, Daddy sold a cow and calf to pay for part of it, and bought it for her. We hardly ever bought anything new, so Mama was tickled to death to get it and some new pans at the same time. I reckon that dishpan's the only piece left."

"So, to answer your question, *that's* where it came from. Mama hadn't had them pans too awful long before the World War started up…the overseas part of it, before the U-nited States got into it. After Germany kept sinkin' our ships, why then, we didn't have much choice."

"I remember 'em talkin' about war when Johnny was born. That was at the end of January in 1917, and Harry Winston got his draft notice that summer. There were several boys around here that were drafted ahead of him and Harry Winston's best friend Clevie Walker was one of 'em. He died of typhoid fever in trainin' camp, fixin' to go to France just a few days before Harry Winston. I know you've heard me speak of them, the Walkers…they owned just about ever'thing in Fordville back then…the distillery and the sawmill both. Clevie was their only child." Nodding at the table where I was seated, she said, "He's eaten many a meal sittin' right there and we all just about grieved ourselves to death over him dyin' like that…for nothin' it seemed like."

53

Granny suddenly glanced at the screen door. "Right there," she said, nodding toward it, "Poor ol' Aunt Sue Fox stood right there that fall and told us somebody in our family would be dead within a year. She was what they called a fortune teller. She believed in readin' cards…she called it "cuttin' the cards." She'd give out secrets to make love charms and all such as that. She could be spooky when she wanted to be, but we never paid her no mind. Mama just laughed at the poor ol' thing and she'd try to help her when she could. Your Granddaddy and I were up here eatin' dinner that day. We hadn't much more than set down when Aunt Sue came to the door, plumb out of breath. She had climbed that hill from Fordville and she was a big, heavy set woman. She stood right there to get her wind and she said, "Oh Miss Annie, Miss Annie, you gonna be havin' some sad news."

And she meant it. Mama jumped up from the table to go to her and the door was standin' wide open. Aunt Sue pointed out in the yard there to this big ol' snowball bush Mama used to have—right there off the porch. It was nearly in *full bloom*, and that had to be in October. That didn't hardly ever happen. Aunt Sue said, 'Children, somebody in this house is fixin' to die.' That liked to have killed Mama, and come to find out Aunt Sue didn't even know Harry Winston was overseas. I don't know how, but she didn't know. Granny looked out the kitchen window once before she spoke. "I've thought about what Aunt Sue told us that day. Things were goin' good for us then. Harry Winston was still livin' and Johnny was just a baby. It was a good time for us. We didn't know at the time *just* how good. And

54

the spring after Harry Winston got killed, that ol' snowball bush died, too."

Granny resumed snipping the ends of the zinnias and placing them one by one into the Mason jar. After a few minutes she suddenly stopped and smiled. It was a slow, spreading smile—the kind I saw come over her when she would smell a fresh bouquet of buttercups in early spring. At that point, I was hoping for a good memory to lighten the mood. She said, "Before Johnny was born, the whole time I was expectin', Harry Winston kept pullin' for me to have a boy he could take with him huntin' and fishin' when he came back home." Granny paused for a moment and her welcomed grin faded as quickly as it had appeared. "But…they never got to go… and I—just---hate it. They would've sure had a good time together. Ever since Johnny got killed in '45, I can't think of one of 'em without the other, and Johnny wasn't but about eighteen months old when Harry Winston got killed. I sit here by myself sometimes and think about both of 'em dyin' for their country. I like to think they're both up in heaven right now. And, I know it sounds strange, but I wonder what they're doin' up there right now--*right this minute*."

Granny laid down her scissors and sat at the kitchen table with me, her eyes focused on the dishpan.

"Harry Winston thought there wasn't nothin' like Johnny. He was a little sickly when he was born, so we spent a lot of time up here then. Mama was afraid I wouldn't know what to do if he got real bad, and it was just as easy for us to stay here to keep her from frettin'. Harry Winston always liked it when we stayed all night. Johnny was Harry

Winston's namesake, you know. We named Johnny for him—John Winston. He'd sit and hold 'im sometimes when I'd help Mama in the kitchen. I think we'd pretty much gone back home by then, 'cause Johnny was doin' better but Harry Winston asked if we'd spend the night up here one last time before he had to leave. That's why we were here the mornin' Daddy drove 'em to Harriston to take the train to Georgia for basic trainin'.

He got up real early and I don't think he slept none. He helped out with the chores like he'd always done," and then turning to face the dishpan once more, Granny said, "*and he washed up in this dishpan*. We kept it here in the kitchen then. Harry Winston took his shirt off and washed his face and hands in that hot water Mama had poured out of the reservoir in the stove. He'd already shaved the night before. I remember that well because he'd complained about the razor bein' dull, so Daddy took it from him and said he'd sharpen it. He carried it out on the porch…set out there all by himself for the longest time, sharpenin' it on a whetrock, and when he came back inside, he had big tears welled up in his eyes, *and I'd never seen 'im cry before.*

We all dreaded Harry Winston leavin' that mornin'. Daddy took him to the train station in Harriston, so he had to say goodbye to Mama, and me real early. If she ever went to sleep, she was already up way before daylight to cook a big breakfast. She killed a chicken to fry and made cornbread muffins for Harry Winston, but none of us felt much like eatin'. We all tried not to dwell on it for his sake, but he put on a good face for us. After we cleared all the dishes away, he cranked up Mama's old Victrola in the dinin'

56

room there and took my little sister Ida May by the hand and tried to dance with her like he'd done since she was little. She'd stand on his shoes and he'd do the dancin'. Ida May was always *his* pet...and then *he* was Mama's."

Granny sat looking at the dishpan, her hand over her mouth. She shook her head. "I got so aggravated with Harry Winston...." She held a clinched fist to her lips and I could see the tears in her eyes. "Nothin' would do but for him to wake Johnny up to play with him *one more time* before he had to leave out."

At this point, I thought Granny had said all she could, or wanted to say, and by then I wished I'd never found the dishpan. She stood up from the table and resumed trimming the zinnias, and abruptly picked up where she had left off.

"Lord, we thought that was the saddest day ever was, but it got sadder. After Harry Winston waved goodbye to us as he and Daddy were pullin' out for Harriston, Mama just about fell apart, so I had to be the strong one. Poor little ol' Johnny cried all day long. He was nursin' and I prob'ly passed the worry onto him. He knew somethin' was bad wrong. The only thing that kept us goin' for the rest of that day was knowin' we had chores to do. Daddy came back from Harriston by dinnertime, but we never laid eyes on him 'til that evenin'. He and Mama both took Harry's leavin' real hard. All of us puttered around here doin' what we had to, but nobody had much to say. I think us bein' here helped some. Mama had little Johnny to play with, and Ida May was still at home then.

Just before Daddy came back in the house, Mama was tryin' to get supper together. She stepped out on the porch to empty that dishpan, to put some fresh water in it for Daddy. She went from about here to the window over yonder—she got that far in the yard, to throw it out. Then, all of a sudden, she stopped—right like this," Granny said, holding her arms out, "and never moved a muscle.

I hollered, 'Mama, what's the matter?' She stood there for prob'ly close to minute, and then she turned real slow, just like she was carryin' a newborn baby, and tiptoed back to the porch. As careful as you please, she set that dishpan— and it full of dirty water--way up on that shelf above the wash table. Then it dawned on me what she was doin'. *Harry Winston had washed in that water* early that mornin' and after he finished, he carried it out to the back porch. He was on his way to throw the water out when Mama hollered at him to come help her take that big hot skillet of gravy off the stove, where she was weak in that one hand. I just imagine he'd set it down, aimin' to come back for it and forgot. Mama didn't think anything about it til she looked down and saw it out there on the porch that evenin', and then it hit her: *That water* was her last memory of seein' Harry Winston…and she just couldn't stand the thought of pourin' it out.

We got a letter ever' week from him in trainin', and even after his ship made it to France, he'd write home just about that often, but the mail was bad slow in them days. In the last letter we got from him, he said they were just waitin' for their marchin' orders. For a while after that, we never heard nothin', not a word. Finally we got a letter that was

58

written by a nurse and she told us he'd been wounded and was bein' looked after in one of them big cathedrals they'd made into a hospital. That nurse was writin' for him, but the letter said it was the biggest church buildin' he'd ever seen--he could plant a field of corn inside of it. He was shot in the leg, but he healed up quick and he begged the army doctor to let him get back to his regiment.

The next we knew about him was when we got the telegram tellin' us he was dead...killed in action in what they called The Argonne. Seems to me like it was a big forest-like. It sounds funny to say it, but I'm glad he was in the woods somewhere. He loved to hunt. There was a bunch of men in his unit that didn't make roll call the evenin' he was killed. One of his two best buddies died the same day. The one of 'em that made it to the end of the war got sick on that transport ship as they were sailin' across the water to England, and he died before they could get him to a hospital.

Granny sighed. Shaking her head, she said, "All three of 'em were dead by Christmas that year...in 1918. Come to think of it, I've got a picture here somewhere of all three of 'em grinnin' like midnight possums. They were fixin' to sail to France and that picture was in the envelope with Harry's letter. If you'll remind me, I'll show it to you sometime.

But now, back to the dishphan, Mama left it settin' up on that shelf for prob'ly three or four days after Harry Winston left--*and the dirty water still in it*. I just left it alone, and we thought it was right funny. Then, when we were fixin' dinner after church that next Sunday, she reached up and

59

brought it down. I watched her like a hawk all the way to see what she was fixin' to do. She carried it outside and— real gentle-like, she took her hand and sprinkled it over her rosebushes, just like it was holy water or somethin'. Always before, she'd just pitch it out on the ground, but *that* water was special. Later on, when Johnny went overseas to fight the Japanese I got a taste of what she felt. I understood it then.

But, after word came that Harry Winston had gotten killed in France, Mama would not let that dishpan come back in this house. Before we got that telegram—even after he shipped out, I was always glad to see it. After The War, we kept usin' it around here for one thing or another, 'til it got a leak in it. Your Granddaddy spent a solid hour out there in the toolshed one day tryin' to fix it. He knew it was kindly special to me, but the thing kept on leakin'. Finally I just told him to take it out to the barn to feed the cats, or just anywhere he could use it."

Returning her attention to the flowers in the Mason jar, Granny handed the dishpan back to me upside down, as if to pour out the many tears that had been shed. After she had arranged the zinnias to her satisfaction, she placed them the center of the kitchen table. Pausing to take what was to be one last look at the dishpan, she said, "I'm kindly glad to see it again… *in a way*." As she cleaned the sink and gathered up a handful of the green cuttings to throw away, she said, "and in another way, **not**."

The shotgun in my gun cabinet with Colby's name on it

13 and 1930

Long had I understood the number 13 to be unlucky, but for me there was no dread of turning thirteen. Like most twelve year olds, I had looked forward to it for months. For me it meant I'd get my dead Uncle Johnny's much loved and cared for .410 shotgun.

As part of that rite of passage, Granddaddy had also given me the hope of a rabbit hunting trip with him on Thanksgiving Day. In his defense, "Maybe" was the word he'd used.

Granddaddy hardly ever mentioned hunting and when he did it was all past tense, referring to earlier Thanksgivings spent with his son—my Uncle Johnny, a naval pilot killed in World War Two. I'd been hunting many times with friends and their dads, but never with Granddaddy or Uncle Johnny's coveted shotgun.

Carefully enshrined in the small closet under the stairwell was the gun I had long admired in secret, for it had been promised to me when I turned thirteen and not a day before. Unbeknownst to Granddaddy, I once watched him clean it. This task he performed as tenderly as if he was using that oily rag to soothe the feverish face of an infant.

Because of snow, school had let out at noon that day, three hours early. As usual Granny was puttering around in the kitchen when I got off the bus and ran upstairs to change clothes. Strangely, my bedroom door was partially shut. Sensing something a little out of the ordinary, I peeked around to see Granddaddy sitting on my bed in Johnny's old room—a particularly vivid memory because he almost *never* set foot in there. After going downstairs for breakfast, he rarely even came back upstairs until bedtime.

I stood there for a moment, struck by the oddity of the situation, and deliberately coughed to make my presence known. He seemed startled when I entered, as if he'd been interrupted in prayer, and, perhaps he was. Granddaddy cleaned his other guns periodically, but that always took place in his shed, or on the side porch—some random time and place. But this was different. Over time, I came to have some vague notion of Granddaddy cleaning Uncle Johnny's gun. He sought solitude for the ritual, which he conducted *almost* in secret, and as if it was an intensely personal, even religious experience.

For as long as I could remember, Granddaddy had said the shotgun was mine when I turned thirteen. He'd bought it brand new for his son Johnny's thirteenth birthday just days after selling the year's disappointing tobacco crop in December. Uncle Johnny's thirteenth birthday wouldn't be until January 30, 1930, the beginning of a new crop year, leaning expectantly on a new decade. If only... Although the Stock Market Crash had taken place only weeks earlier, its crippling effects would have little impact on already hurting farmers. Most of them, like my grandparents, had chafed under an agricultural depression of their own since shortly after the First World War. Still, the crisp new calendar hung on their kitchen wall--coaxing from them a thin ray of hope for what lay ahead. With its January page came the tidings of a new year, even bearing the number of the coming new decade—and the illusion that the struggles of the 1920's were behind them. Just maybe, they thought, 1930 would be better.

As much as I looked forward to my thirteenth birthday, I noticed that as the day approached, the less Granddaddy wanted to talk about our first planned hunt together. I had asked him numerous times when and where we'd go hunting, and always got a vague response, if I got one at all. "Maybe," he'd say.

62

November 10, 1963…. My thirteenth birthday arrived, and although vested with the much anticipated shotgun, I fired it sparingly. Thanksgiving was right around the corner, which for many rural Kentucky boys at that time meant rabbit hunting, either before or after a big dinner. I could hardly wait for that day to arrive.

Already dressed for the inaugural hunt before breakfast, I was raring and ready to go when my feet hit the floor that morning. Not so, Granddaddy. Even as a kid I could sense that he was not looking forward to the occasion, and perhaps even dreading it.

As the early morning routine faded into busied Thanksgiving dinner preparations, it became clear we weren't about to go hunting unless it was in the distant adult "little while."

By 2:30 that afternoon, Thanksgiving dinner was done, the table cleared, and dishes put away. Wearing two pairs of jeans, two pairs of socks and my work boots, I sat down on my bed, forlorn and forsaken. Once again, I was ready for *our* first hunt, which at that hopeless moment did not appear likely. To this day, I don't know if Granny prompted Granddaddy to follow through with his vague promise, or if he felt the compunction on his own. I had resigned myself to a hunt-less fate when I heard him climb the steps and, finally—at long last, pull his heavy work boots from under the bed. It was a sign from God. I had already gotten ready twice—once before daylight and I'd defrocked before Thanksgiving dinner. This time, just maybe, it was for real.

Without the slightest trace of a smile, Granddaddy came to the door of my room and said almost sarcastically, "Are we goin' huntin' or are you just gonna sit there?" I jumped off the bed and hit the bottom of the steps before he could change his mind.

63

To this day, I remember how he held his shotgun coming toward the pickup--low to the ground in his long arm. Only once before had I seen Granddaddy carry his gun like that, when I was seven years old and followed him to the barn lot where he had to put down his old mule Julie.

We wound downhill toward Fordville in the pickup, in silence. I noticed Granddaddy was even quieter than usual.

Within fifteen minutes the truck turned onto a rutted, unfamiliar dirt road. We stopped several times for me to hop out to open the sagging gates which registered their protests with creaks and groans. We were soon parked by a dilapidated stock barn near the farm road, and Granddaddy pointed to the ridge on our right.

"We'll start here," he said. Hopping out of the truck, I was quarter of the way up the hill carrying Uncle Johnny's gun before I even heard Granddaddy's truck door slam shut. I thought maybe he'd gone the other way around the barn and stopped to "shed some tears" as he called it when he answered nature's call.

There appeared to be little joy in this outing for Granddaddy. I watched and waited for what seemed days as he plodded uphill. Loose tin on the rusted barn roof rattled in the breeze. A sagging barn door creaked and thudded as wind nudged it into a stubborn furrow of dried mud. Even for the neglected farm, it seemed our hunt was a thing to be dreaded.

Granddaddy never raised his eyes from the ground as he meandered wearily up the long hill ahead of him, as if he carried invisible, heavy sacks of feed on his stooped shoulders. He finally neared me with his long legged gait, a slow and sweeping stride, only looking up at me at the last second as if he'd forgotten why he came.

"Granddaddy, who owns this place?" I asked.

"My cousin, Doyle"

"Does he farm it?"

"Lord, no. He lives in Florida now. Used to be one of the head knockers with a big insurance company in Memphis…I forget the name of it. I doubt he's set foot on this place in the last five years."

Almost disgustedly he added, "He's rented it out since the first day he owned it."

We meandered uphill in our heavy boots on a gradual slope toward a distant ridge where we could see for a mile in any direction a sea of scrubby cedars, briars, and broom sage. If nothing else, it was a rabbit's paradise.

"We owned this place….once upon a time," he said. "Your granny and me."

This came as a revelation. I couldn't even imagine them living anywhere other than where they did then, and *where I'd lived* since I was eight years old.

"Why'd you move?"

*"Had to….*we lost it in the Thirties…the Depression."

Clearly it was not a favorite topic. I asked no more questions as we pulled our legs through inhospitable saw briars that clawed into our jeans and padded jackets.

As we zigzagged down the steep hill from the top of the ridge, Granddaddy pointed to a rabbit perched on his side of wild rosebush bramble. I took aim just as the rabbit jumped and fired my shot. It was true and I had my first rabbit with my own gun. It was the first time I had seen Granddaddy smile since getting out of the truck. He said "Looks like you got 'im in the head. Nothin' wasted thataway."

He picked the rabbit up by its hind legs, its limp head dripping crimson where he paused to ponder our course. Although he carried his own gun, he preferred I do the hunting while he did the "doggin'"--deliberately wading through the brushy hillsides to spook the rabbits. Granddaddy was going on this hunt just for my sake.

We plodded awkwardly down the same hillside, stubble and briars crunching under our boots. The dry, earthy sounds seemed louder in the momentary silences.

"When did you all move away from here?" I asked.

He paused, half bent over, looking distractedly into a bramble of wild rosebushes.

"We lost it at the end of '30.....didn't move off of it 'til '31 though," he said—"but it was 1930 that done us in."

As if he did not want to go into details, Granddaddy said "Fresh droppings right here." Sticking the end of his shotgun barrel into the thorny den, he said "I might just *get me* a rabbit." He chuckled, and under his breath muttered, "It would be the only thing this here land ever gave me, except for a hard time."

He led the way again—aimlessly, and carrying his shotgun as if he'd already run out of shells.

Abruptly, Granddaddy picked up where he had left off.

"It went up for sale when Aunt Molly Moore died in '21 and we'd saved up a little money to buy it, *or* thought we had. I reckon I just made the wrong move at the wrong time…and went caflunkus. Your Granny always wanted it since this was where her mother grew up-in a little house on the branch below that ridge there.

This was your granny's dream place…we sure thought we were set to make a good showin' here."

66

I was trying to listen and wasn't paying as close attention to the path before us. Granddddy held his left hand up again, motioning to my left. I took aimed and fired as the broom sage fluttered. He yelled, "I think you got 'im!" I had killed another rabbit, but smaller. "They're better eatin' when they're small," he said.

Boasting, I said "Two rabbits within an hour of getting out of the truck!" This place was good luck for me. It made me proud to think I would be putting food on the table. If he heard me, Granddaddy didn't respond.

By then we were nearly at the bottom of the hill where a wet weather branch cut a deep swath into the limestone. Pointing into the deepest of the shallow pools where water gathered, Granddaddy said, "We lost the best milk cow we ever had here in 1930…she fell into that hole and broke her neck. Tryin' to get to water I reckon. She gave more'n four gallons of milk a day."

"Where was the pond?"

"Our little pond dried up…like everything else did that year."

Another period of silence followed as we swished and crunched our way through whispering sage grass and biting briars. Granddaddy appeared lost in thought. Looking back, I have no doubt he was "thinking 1930" as he retraced painfully familiar steps.

"And you know what? I never had another kidney stone after that one, in '30."

Pointing to a distant field, he said "We set tobacco up there in pure dust that spring, on the ridge way over yonder above the creek. The soil in that patch was as dry as I ever saw it, like a bed of ashes. That's the only time I ever remember a spring like that.

We kept waitin' for rain…..hopin'. Finally on the 20th day of May I think it was, we set one little patch and I said to Johnny 'Time to quit!' We've gotta have some rain to set anymore'. We'd been haulin' water already just for the plants in the beds. That was on Saturday, and the next day was Sunday. We were at church that mornin' and it was just a little cloudy on the way there. Just about the time the preacher began his sermon, I heard a few big raindrops hittin' the windows," and then, pausing at that recollection of hope, he added, "*and I blessed ever' one of 'em.* Several of us men…we just looked around at one another, and one by one, we got up and left. I told your granny that Johnny and I *had* to get that tobacco in the ground while there was some hope there'd be enough moisture to keep it alive. We drove straight from church to the tobacco patch—never even changed our clothes.

But the way it turned out, I could drink all it rained that day. Your granny and the girls came out to bring us dinner and then they helped us. Still, it all dried up. We lost the tobacco, and then the corn. Puny little ol' stalks came up with just a few spotty kernels on each ear.

What ponds and wells there were then mostly went dry. When people around here went to the river to get water and hauled it off in barrels, it smelled rotten, like dead fish.

He mumbled, "Even the river stunk that year."

"Did you lose this place just because of the drought?" I asked.

"It sure didn't help us none.

The truth is…I paid too much for it to begin with. Your granny's daddy never let me live it down neither. He loaned us a little on it. This place was a lot closer to them than where we lived at Babylon, and your granny always admired it when we'd come to visit Big Granny or Aunt

Mollie Moore up in the big house. That was after her brother Harry Winston got killed in France and I knew she wanted to be closer to her mother and daddy. They weren't gettin' any younger. I reckon I thought it was the one chance for us to buy it, to get off Uncle Tobe's place and work for ourselves. We were so far off the main road down there at Babylon, the hoot owls hollered in the daytime. Our closest neighbor was over a mile away and you know how your granny loves company. Aunt Mollie's house here on this place was in pretty good shape and the barns were solid…good pastures and a sandstone ridge over yonder to raise tobacco. It had that spring near the big house that was never known by anybody livin' to go dry, 'til 1930, anyway. Buyin' this place just seemed like the right thing to do."

We crossed the branch and headed up the next ridge.

"By August everything dried up and that's when I got a letter from my brother J.B., out in Oklahoma. We hadn't heard from 'im in months. Somehow he got word we were just about to lose this place and he sends me a letter sayin' he had me a job if I could get out there in time, workin' in an oil field….makin' good money, he said.

And like a fool, I believed 'im. That's J.B. for you. Your granny sold a little ring her mother'd given her to buy me a train ticket out there, and off I went. By the time I got there, J.B. had already been gone *four days*. He said later he didn't think I was comin', and of course there was no job to be had and I was stuck out there with no money and no job.

The foreman on the oil pump crew where J.B. had been workin' felt sorry for me. Turned out, he was from Kentucky too, from over in Washington County. He found a few odd and end jobs for me to do so I could stay in a boardin' house, but even with that I was months gettin' enough money ahead to get home on.

Another period of silence followed. We walked.

"Your Granny and Johnny kept it all goin' the best they could while I was gone but finally, everything went caflunkus. We never got another rain until up after Christmas, early in '31. We had a big payment due on this place at the bank in Fordville. When we bought it, we messed up and put every penny we had on the down payment. We'd been limpin' along payin' the interest for the couple of years before that. And then we lost what money we had in it just to get out from under the debt--to keep from goin' bankrupt. Nobody could really help us. None of my people or your granny's either one had any cash money to spare.

That's when my cousin Doyle bought it. His mother's people were well off. She had a little money she let 'im have, and we had to let the farm go for next to nothin'— less than what we paid, not countin' what we put into it. The truth is if it hadn't been Doyle, it would've been somebody else. That part didn't matter. He was workin' for an insurance company in Louisville then—he's been in the insurance business all his workin' days. I don't think he's ever opened a gate on this place, let alone got his hands dirty doin' it. Things come easy for some people, and he's one of 'em. Everything that man touches turns to gold, but he's sure let this place go downhill from what it was when we had it. I'd never have let the pastures grow up like this. These old barns need work. He just rents it out and he gets a check every year when the tobacco's sold. Easy money. Doyle got this place for a song and sung it hisself. All he has to do is go to the mailbox and get the check."

He grew quiet again, and again, we walked.

Granddaddy was cleaning out the barn of memory that day, one with "1930" painted on its doors in big, black numbers. Although I was the only other human within a mile to hear him, it was almost as if he spoke to the overgrown hills, to the land itself.

Granddaddy stopped and bent over to remove a honey locust thorn stuck in the side of his work boot. He studied the thorn as he held in his hand and felt the sharp point that had pierced the leather.

"To Doyle this place was just a good deal—an in-vestment's *what* he called it…but it was our whole life…and I hated like everything to lose it."

We walked.

Granddaddy said "Sometimes I felt like if it was rainin' soup, I'd be outside with a fork in my hand. For a long time, it looked like everything I touched just turned to…ASHES." I remember the way he said it, as if their gritty residue was still in his mouth and had to be spit out with the word.

Since that day, I've never heard the word "ashes" spoken without thinking of that November afternoon, and a yearning in his voice for some undefinable thing.

"Doyle said he'd let us stay on this place rent free that next year—'31, if we wanted--but we'd be still tenants on land that had been ours. *I know* he meant well, but I just wanted out.

That's when we went back to where we live now. We had to move in with your granny's mother and daddy and look after them. And I can tell you one thing about *that*—there ain't no house big enough for two families. Your granny's daddy was a good man in his own way, but he wasn't the easiest fellow to get along with. He never let me live it down that I'd paid too much for this place, and then borrowed way too much. It didn't matter that I did it so's I could get your granny closer to 'em."

He was wheezing by the time we reached the top.

"I always felt like the Devil owed me a debt and paid me off with 1930. We'd a-been all right if the Crash hadn't come along when it did, *and then the* drought right behind it.

"IF" he mumbled… "IF a frog had wings he wouldn't bump his tail when he hopped." Managing a smile, he looked up from the ground and winked at me.

I was glad to see it, for it was one of only a few that whole day.

"*I told her* we'd stay with her mother and daddy for a while. But come spring we'd rent us a place of our own if I had to wade blood up to my neck to do it."

"Why didn't you?" I asked.

He searched my eyes sympathetically, as if to say, "You have *no* idea."

Granddaddy shook his head before he spoke. "Son, you can't hardly imagine what times was like; *everything* dried up--even after the drought. The Citizen's Bank in Harriston went under and your Granny's daddy lost what money he had in it—not no fortune, but it was his whole life savin's and his workin' days were about played out. Her mother took sick that fall so your Granny took charge of the kitchen, and I started doin' most of the farm work, me and Johnny. So there we were…just kinda stuck. Our luck took a bad turn, but we still had it better than a whole lot of people. I reckon that's when I learned that, a whole lot of the time, a man just has to play the hand he's dealt.

When we moved back to your granny's home place, I still had to work just as hard as I ever did, or harder, to keep it

72

all goin', and just to keep us fed. Your granny's daddy was up in years by then and couldn't work like he had. He couldn't do much to help me. It was all up to whatever I could do—and Johnny. He was about your age, come to think of it. My daddy was already dead by then, so I couldn't go to him for help, let alone money. I was on my own in a man's kind of way and it's a mighty lonesome feelin'. Tobacco got down to ten cents a pound and you couldn't give stuff away. We did have food enough to get by. Nobody had any money, but at least we had the land, and we could raise what we ate…most of the time."

We spent another hour or so dragging our feet through briars and scrubby cedars up one hill and down another as Granddaddy would point to some feature on the land and recall some nearly forgotten memory buried under the weight of 1930. Occasionally he would raise a large boot and bring it down on the heavy, menacing saw briars in our path, ready and willing to inflict pain. He seemed *to take* some kind of pleasure in keeping them away from me. Within sight of one of Granddaddy's more memorable briar-stomping episodes, we came to one unlikely spot below a tobacco barn. "There!" he pointed, "That's where Johnny shot his first rabbit. "That liked to have tickled 'im to death." Pointing to the shotgun in my hands, Granddaddy said, "He hadn't had that gun right there but just a couple of weeks."

We came toward another ridge top as Granddaddy looked up at a clear blue sky above the long field. He pointed upward *"Over there"* he said. "That's right where Johnny saw his first airplane. We were cuttin' tobacco and Harold Collins' brother Howard flew it from Harriston. Johnny stood there wavin' for all he was worth. Howard flew over us and tipped his wing our way a little. That was about the first'un anybody around here ever saw. Johnny just took on the funniest you ever saw. He was ab-so-lutely....hypnotized with watchin' that airplane--*couldn't take his eyes off it.* He ran the whole length of that field over yonder lookin' straight up, afraid he'd lose sight of it, 'til all you could hear was that single engine up in the clouds. I think the idea of him bein' a pilot started on that ridge the minute he saw that plane. From that day forward, that boy had his head set on bein' a pilot."

Granddaddy paused. "...and he finally got what he wanted......I reckon."

He didn't speak again until that particular long ridge was behind us and completely out of sight.

As we got halfway downhill, he said, "We're closin' the circle up here," pointing in the distance to his pickup, next to the barn where we'd parked. We were approaching it from another direction, and I could see the same hill I had practically sprinted up to begin our hunt.

"I reckon--I thought we'd get away from that place where we live now— before '31 was over and find us a place of our own, but it never worked out that way. Your granny's daddy never had sick day that I ever knew of, but he got down with pneumonia that next fall and died, just a day or two after Roosevelt got elected the first time. That left us to take care of her mother and she hadn't been well since Harry Winston got killed. That just about destroyed her. After we came back there to stay with them, it wasn't long before they gave the land where we live now to your Granny, and her sister Ida May got the rest of it...across the river. We finally got a place of our own, free and clear, but it wasn't the same. I'll just tell you, *I never felt like it was mine.* I just had to get over that, but it took me a while. For a long time I felt like I was a visitor eatin' in somebody else's house...workin' somebody's else land."

He chuckled and said, "My mother always said 'Pride goeth before the fall." It's in the Bible I'm a-thinkin'…and I had to learn that lesson the hard way."

Your Granny's mother was a fine old lady. I thought a lot of 'er. Prob'ly a year before she died, one mornin' there was just the two of us in the house. It was on a Sunday mornin' and Lorene and the children were gone to Church. I didn't go back to church for a right smart while after we lost this place. She hadn't been feelin' too good, so I came in from the farm to check on 'er while Lorene and the children were gone. She told to me sit down next to the bed where she was layin' and she propped herself up on one arm and looked me in the eye. She said, 'Russell, I've been layin' here this mornin' since daylight, just thinkin'…I don't know what we would've done if you all hadn't come back here to live. You've kept this farm goin' and it's mostly been on your shoulders ever since. I'm gettin' old and I don't feel good. Truth is, I'm liable to die most anytime and I know it—and it's all right. I just wanted to tell you this while I'm still able and I want you to know I'm real proud of you. '" Granddaddy cleared his throat and spit into the rust colored broom sage in front of us. He said, "It meant a whole lot to me…for her to tell me that."

Meandering along the branch and now within view of ending the hunt, we saw no more rabbits. For most of the afternoon, Granddaddy carried the two I'd killed. The land upon which he'd once toiled had yielded, if only a little. Bright red scratches stood out on his hands, inflicted by saw briars as he walked what had once been his own hillsides carrying *my* rabbits in his firm grip. Noticing that I saw his blood stained hands, he looked at them himself, unperturbed, and perhaps expecting it. In fact, from the look on his face, he seemed to understand that the land wasn't going to give up anything without taking blood in return. The constant breeze that had followed us for so long settled down in the stillness of the late afternoon. The rattling, loose tin on the barn roof and the groaning, sagging door that had earlier received us with indifference were now as silent as the lengthening shadows. The farm had given us the benediction. It was time for us to leave.

Returning home, the two of us set about the task of cleaning the rabbits, and I proudly carried them in to Granny in a dishpan—to soak overnight in salt water. They would be fried for supper the next day and served with leftovers from Thanksgiving Dinner. There was little need for more food. Still, Granny understood the significance of our one and only but at that time, inaugural hunt, and my need to celebrate the harvest. I'm certain Granny prepared them for supper the next evening for my sake alone.

I looked forward to that meal all the next day; I was beaming like a Cheshire cat for bringing in some of the food on the table. For once, I was a provider, thanks to the bounty of the Moore Place and Uncle Johnny's shotgun.

My aunt and cousin sat down to eat supper with us the next evening as Granny passed around the plate of fried rabbit. I eagerly bit into a piece, and heaped the hot gravy onto mashed potatoes and biscuits--along with the turkey hash.

Looking around the table a few minutes later, I noticed that I was the only one eating the rabbit meat; the blue platter was still nearly full except for what I'd taken. Although Granny and Granddaddy had each taken a piece, they remained on their plates untouched.

"Something wrong with the rabbit?" I asked.

Smiling, Granny said, "No, Clay. As my mother used to say about somethin' she didn't want to eat, 'if you're dividin' it in parts, you can have mine.' We ate enough rabbit meat around here in 1930 to fill this kitchen, and I've never cared for it since."

So much for putting food on the table. After eating my fill of it, the rest was irreverently fed to my dog Kelly, along with the other table scraps.

Perhaps it was ironic that Granny identified the humble platter of fried rabbit with the hardship and uncertainty of that painful year. After all this time I'm unsure if Granddaddy had mentioned something about our hunt to her. Regardless, by the end of that day, it became clear to me that 1930 had been no picnic for her either.

In my hearing, Granddaddy never again spoke of the farm they had lost, or the trials of that year.

For that matter, Granddaddy and I never went rabbit hunting again. When I learned the old folks had no taste for rabbit, and why, that understanding quenched my desire to be an intrepid game hunter. Those in the future would be confined to outings with friends and if I ate rabbit at all, it was in their mothers' kitchens.

On the plus side, I had celebrated a ceremonial rite of passage, one that took a scenic detour: Yes, I had at last gone hunting with Granddaddy, and along the way got far more than I'd bargained for. That insight into an adult world meant more than the rabbits or the gifted shotgun which, by the way, hasn't been hunted with since. It remains in my gun cabinet, mostly as a conversation piece. There it patiently awaits another generational transfer of ownership.

Even though I say that it's just for my grandson Colby's sake as its next owner, I take the shotgun out of the cabinet once in a while and clean it. Like Granddaddy, I get off by myself somewhere to perform the ritual, someplace where it's quiet. I take my time to do it, and like him, I remember.

77

The Hundredth White Horse

It seemed like a good idea at the time.

My wife Sandy and I had just gotten engaged and were locating furniture for our first apartment. When I came home to Fordville from college on weekends, I pilfered through the outbuildings and barns in search of furnishings we could use.

It was on such a mission that I returned to the old log smokehouse which had been cleaned out several years earlier. All I found there that might be useful was an old bed leaning against the side wall. Dusty and spattered with bird droppings, its four spooled posts pointed upward to a rounded point—except for one which appeared to be broken off. As I stood there examining the old bed, I saw possibilities beneath the dull black finish and asked Granny if I could have it.

"Why do you want the thing?" she said.

I said, "I think I can fix it up. And besides, that old sleeping sofa I have won't work for both of us."

Raising up from the kitchen table she said, "It needs a whole lot of work. But," she said wearily, "if you're sure you all want it, you're more than welcome to it. I'm just not so sure you know what kind of a job you're gettin' yourself into. It wasn't no count when it came here— several's tried to fix it but it never stayed fixed. I'm thinkin' my cousin Alta was the last'n to sleep in it. Me and

78

your granddaddy married in 1916, so it would've been a couple of years before that."

I wanted to surprise Sandy with it and made no mention of what I was undertaking. I set up shop in the barn to begin the refinishing which always looks worse in the early, messy stages—when the layers of black varnish come off, revealing the true wood grain beneath. The day I brushed on the first coat of finish, I was pleased to see the rich brown walnut grain fully revealed and congratulated myself for salvaging the old bed. As we ate lunch I asked Granny what she remembered about it.

She said, "Oh, there's not a whole lot to remember, other than Uncle Ned bringin' it here on the day he got married. He stayed with us a lot, and that's how come for us to have it." Between giggles, she added, "He broke it down on his honeymoon and it's here ever since."

Over the years I'd come to learn that Granny's old family home had been a laying in house for a host of relatives. Widowed or old maid aunts, bachelor uncles, orphaned cousins and other obscure relatives had often come to stay for weeks or months at a time when Granny was growing up. In this case, it was a great-uncle.

"Uncle Ned was Daddy's uncle, my great-uncle. After his mother died—my grandmother, he'd live with first one and then another of his people. That happened a lot back in them days.

Nobody would put up with him but my daddy. Uncle Ned was bad to drink but he was harmless—and one of the best carpenters around here when the notion struck, but as Mama would say, it just didn't strike much. He'd sit around when Daddy was little and tell them big tall tales. Of course, Daddy bein' a kid, he'd believe ever' word of 'em—til the end, when ever'body would bust out laughin'. When Uncle Ned stayed with us, he got his own room off the kitchen. He'd take his meals with us if he was around, but we never knew if or when he'd show up. He'd stay gone for weeks at a time, doin' carpentry work in Harriston or maybe across the river somewhere. Most the time, I don't think there was a job to take. We just didn't know where he was.

But then, he surprised us all when he up and got married. I remember that woman well, but I can't think of her name-- she didn't stick around long enough for us to call her aunt anything. Uncle Ned had been gone for a month or better and he showed up with her on the afternoon of their weddin' day, and they had that ol' bed and a feather mattress in the back of a wagon. Seems to me like somebody Uncle Ned knew gave it to him on account of it needin' work done on it, and he was a carpenter. Mama took one look at that woman he'd married and was she ever a dandy. Mama told Daddy, "I'm not keepin' *that woman* in my house. It's time you told Uncle Ned to find his own place."

Daddy knew she was right. He got Uncle Ned off to himself out on the front porch. I stood just inside the house listenin' to 'em. He said to Uncle Ned, "Neddy,"--that's what he called him-- he said 'Neddy, what on earth are you thinkin'--gettin' married at your age?' Uncle Ned got about

80

half mad and said, 'Son, I ain't dead yet—and I can pull my load workin' at anything I go after!" Daddy was plumb put out with 'im. He said, "Neddy, what are you talkin' about? You couldn't pull a greasy string out of cat's hind-end. How are you gonna keep that woman up? You don't keep yourself half the time!"

Daddy told him if he was a married man, he'd have to find another place to stay. Uncle Ned agreed with him, but the plan was for them to stay with us a few days 'til they got situated. In the meantime, here he came in carryin' that bed. Mama was halfway afraid of it comin' into the house and wiped it down with coal oil. She believed doin' that kept the bed bugs away—chinches, she called 'em.

On account of Uncle Ned bein' Daddy's favorite uncle, Mama felt like she had to do right by him, so she went all-out fixin' a weddin' supper for him and that Aunt-- Whatever She Was." Granny chuckled, "Come to think of it, from that time on, if any of us dared to bring up the subject of Uncle Ned and his honeymoon, that's what we called her—"Aunt Whatever She Was." We sat down right in here at the supper table, and with that woman not knowin' any of us, you'd a thought she would've held back a little bit, anyway, but she never shut her mouth from the word go.

Like always, Daddy bowed his head to ask the blessin' and she'd done helped herself to a biscuit and was lookin' around for the butter when she noticed we were waitin' on her. She just laughed about it and said, "Looks like you all are the kind that talks to your plate, ain't you?" I'm not kiddin', that's what she called a prayer at the table, "talkin'

81

to your plate." That didn't exactly get her off to a good start with Mama. I remember we hadn't much more than started eatin' when Daddy said somethin' to Mama about him needin' to talk to one of our neighbors about their cow gettin' in our tobacco patch. It was kindly a touchy subject because we went to church with 'em, but before Mama could even open her mouth, that woman butted in and said, "Well, it's like a turd in the sweet 'tater bowl--there ain't no use dancin' around the subject. You just have to tell 'em. That's the way I see it—*I just tell it like it is*." And of all things, Mama had baked sweet 'taters in the oven with one o' her pretty meringues on top of it. That there big bowl sat in the middle of the table and after hearin' what that woman said, nobody wanted to eat 'em. Mama was ready to dump that whole big bowl in her lap."

I said, "What else did she talk about?"

Granny grinned, "My lord, what didn't she talk about? She'd lived in several different places—all of 'em somewhere in Kentucky, but it sure sounded like it'd been a poor livin'. She claimed that she'd faked bein' deaf and dumb on a train one time 'cause she didn't have no money--so she could ride for free. The conductor suspected she was lyin' and stuck her with a pin to see if she'd holler, but she said, "I never made me a squeak—I showed 'em.'" She was a dandy, let me tell you."

"How did they even meet?"

"You know, that was one of the strangest things I think I've ever heard, or at least it's in the runnin'—how she latched onto poor ol' Uncle Ned. She didn't tell me and Mama this part of it until we got up from the table. While we were doin' the dishes, she said she'd been workin' as a cook at the boardin' house in Winchester where Uncle Ned stayed while he was doin' some carpentry work. The first mornin' after he stayed there, this woman was on her way to buy butter the next street over and she saw him drivin' a wagon load of lumber for the job he was workin' on and it was bein' pulled by two white mules. She had waited on Uncle Ned at breakfast and waved at him real big. He saw her and waved back. Well, later that evenin' when he came back to that boardin' house for supper, he said she gave 'im the prettiest smile any woman ever had. Um-um...it's a good thing he couldn't half see, or he'd known better." Granny shook her head. "Her teeth were so crooked she could eat corn through a picket fence.

After supper, she got Uncle Ned off to hisself at the boardin' house and says, "Mr. Clark, you're the man I'm supposed to marry." Well, you can imagine how that caught Uncle Ned off guard. She went on to say, "When I met you pullin' that load of lumber this mornin' *I saw my hundredth white horse*." Granny sat with her arms crossed, still shaking her head, "If I never live to get up from this table, that's what the woman said. There'd been this old colored lady there in Winchester that read tea leaves, and if you paid her ten cents, she claimed she could tell your fortune. I don't know a thing about it, how she did it or what, but this woman read the tea leaves for Aunt Whatever She Was. Then she said, 'Oh yes, Honey, you'll marry again one day, but it won't be no time soon. From this day onward, count ever' white horse you see, and after you've counted ninety-nine of 'em, look out! The man you

83

see drivin' that hundredth white horse will be your future husband.'

Mama just stood at the sink listenin' to all this foolishness and never said a word, not one. She stopped all of a sudden and said to that woman, "I thought you said just a minute ago that it was supposed to be the hundredth white horse—and now you're sayin' it was two white mules you saw Uncle Ned drivin' that wagon with." That woman leaned over toward Mama, grinnin' like a mule eatin' sawbriars. "Oh," she said, "I must've left that part out—that old colored woman told me that one white mule was equal to ten white horses, but I was already up to eighty-one anyway." Granny giggled, "Then, to beat it all, she had the nerve to say, 'I didn't tell Edward this at first'—that's what she called Uncle Ned—"Edward"—she said, 'But after that preacher married us, I told Edward I cheated just a little bit on my countin'. I was visitin' my sister last fall in Irvine and saw a dead white mule on the railroad tracks. He hadn't been dead long, so I figured it ought to count for five white horses, anyhow.'"

Well, I thought Mama would fall through the floor when she heard that. She was washin' and rattlin' them dishes to beat sixty anyway, and the more that woman carried on, the madder she got. We didn't know it, but Daddy was standin' in the doorway that whole time and he'd heard it, too. He said to that woman, "Sounds like Ned's load of lumber moved things right along for you, didn't it? You got the white mules and him in the same deal." Mama shot him a look to kill, but he didn't care. So, I reckon that's when

Uncle Ned and her started courtin' and in the space of two weeks, they was done married.

Daddy just thought the whole thing was funny. Here this old man was gettin' married to a woman he hardly knew, and she was a hum-dinger. We never did know for sure where she came from—or where she went to--*but she was ours that night.*

Mama put me in charge of hullin' lima beans while she and that woman put fresh linens on that bed they'd brought with 'em. Come to think of it, Mama even sent me to cut a bouquet of roses for 'em. We hadn't no more gotten that little room fixed up a little and the bed made before Uncle Ned and his woman came in there and flopped down on the edge of it—and the headboard fell right down on top of 'em. Harry Winston was standin' in the kitchen when that happened and he said if it'd killed 'em both, it was still funny. Uncle Ned claimed he'd worked on the rails and got it fixed, and he was mad as fire. He got up from the floor, rarin' and pitchin' and I can hear 'im now. He said, "I'll conquer this here bed-stead, if it's the last thing I do," and he made a bee-line for the barn to get a hammer and some nails. Harry Winston helped him get it propped back up and he went to work nailin' the rail into where it joined the headboard. After that we all sat around the kitchen, listenin' to Uncle Ned's big tales for a long time. That woman was just about a match for Uncle Ned though— only I don't think hers were big tales. I believe she was in the middle of ever' one of 'em, accordin' to the way she looked.

I couldn't help myself. I said, "And how did she look?"

Granny rubbed her furrowed brow with her fingertips, as if to coax a long-forgotten image from her memory. "This is awful, but Daddy said she had a face like a bucket of mud and Mama said her language was right in there with it. Best I could tell, they were both right.

But, anyhow, Uncle Ned and Harry Winston got the bed all set up and Mama straightened the covers. She had just about had her fill and was hopin' they'd turn in early so we could all go to bed. Now, Daddy on the other hand, he didn't care. He could set up all night and swap tales if we had men here, but Mama was tired and she told us kids that it was time for bed. Daddy took the hint and told Uncle Ned and his woman that he and Mama were ready to call it a night. So, ever'body went to bed-and we hadn't much more than blown the lamps out before we heard this great big crash downstairs. There was dead silence for just a few seconds and then we heard Uncle Ned holler, 'This dang bed's fell down again!' Said it like that woman was a mile away, and her right there with 'im. Then the two of them started hollerin' at each other so Mama and Daddy jumped up and ran downstairs to see what the ruckus was. Me and Harry Winston ran to the top of the steps and Mama was standin' at the bottom in her nightgown, mad as a wet hen. She gave us the evil eye and yelled, "Y'all git on back to bed!" That's all she said, and that was enough. Of course, that woman took off and hid somewhere while Daddy and Uncle Ned got the bed propped up against the wall. Uncle Ned said he'd have to wait 'til daylight to work on it. That little bracket of a thing the bedrail fit into had come loose and the whole bed came down. So, the newlyweds spent the rest of that night on the floor and before mornin' I reckon she told him they'd be gettin' their own place or she'd be headed back to wherever it was she came from.

Nobody slept much that night, but Mama dragged herself out of bed and got me to help cook breakfast early the next mornin'. She said, "Lorene, I've had my fill of them two. Let's get breakfast and put 'em on the road." When we all sat down to eat, Harry Winston was grinnin' like a basketful of possum heads. He opened his mouth to say somethin' and I just knew it was gonna be about that bed fallin' down but Mama shot him a look and he hushed. We all knew what that look meant.

The whole time we were eatin', Uncle Ned hung his head like a sheep-killin' dog and that woman was quiet for the first time since she'd been here. After breakfast, they crept around gettin' their clothes together, and all Mama could say was "Good riddance." Harry Winston winked at Daddy and said, 'I hate to see 'em go. We ain't had this much fun since Little Granny got her teeth in upside down.'

We stood on the front porch out yonder and waved 'em goodbye and that was the last we ever saw of good ol' Aunt Whatever She Was. Mama said she never wanted her name mentioned again. I reckon it worked, too, because I can't think of it now to save me.

I said, "Did you ever see your Uncle Ned again?"

"Several times. Uncle Ned's woman never came back--and he didn't either, for a long time. Daddy got so mad at him after that, he could've killed him. Uncle Ned had let on to that woman that he had part interest in a farm—this one right here, as a matter of fact. And, at one time he'd had a child's part in it, sure enough, but he'd sold it to Grandpa years before, and drank up what little money he got. That woman was a gold-digger, but she found out that mine didn't have nothin' but Fool's Gold in it. I think Uncle Ned discovered later on that she'd already been married before and had tried to court different men to see what she could get out of 'em. She drove her ducks to a bad market with Uncle Ned, though…he didn't have two nickels to rub together.

Uncle Ned was back here to see us a month or two later, after that woman left him. I don't know where he went next because he'd just about worn out his welcome ever'where else. Mama said, "I'll feed him supper, but after that, he's back on the road." Then, about a year later he came ridin' back here on his horse one evenin'--and he looked like the end of a hard winter. He'd gotten thin and had a real bad cough. Daddy helped him get down off his horse and I remember him sayin' to Mama, 'Neddy's a mighty weak pattern. Like always, he says when he gets to where he can, he'll pull his own weight again, but right now he couldn't pull a sick granny-woman off the pot. He won't live 'til this time next year.' Mama took pity on 'im and fixed his old room up again—and got Daddy and Harry Winston to hammer another nail or two into that ol' bed so he could sleep in it.

Mama and me both waited on 'im hand and foot for a while. But, by and by, he got some better. Mama hadn't no more than gotten a few pounds back on 'im before he started takin' a little carpenter job here and there. Then,

88

first thing you knew, though he was back to his old ways, drinkin' again. I'll never forget the last night he came in drunk—and it *was* his last'n here. Mama saw to that. Up around dinnertime one day, he told us he was goin' into town to see about a job an old friend wanted him to do, but Daddy knew better. He watched him ride down the lane yonder, and I remember hearin' him tell Mama that Uncle Ned was grievin' over that mud faced woman leavin' him and that he was prob'ly gonna go drown his sorrows in a bottle of whiskey. Mama decided to clean his room while he was gone, so when she was in there sweepin', she found a pair of his suspenders on the floor under that ol' bed. She handed 'em to me and said, "Just tie 'em around the top of one of the bed posts and he'll find 'em whenever he comes in."

So, way up in the night, after we'd all gone to bed, Uncle Ned came home stewed to the gills drunk. He lit the lamp on the kitchen table and staggered into his little room there and saw them suspenders wrapped around the bedpost and thought it was a big blacksnake. First thing you know we heard gunfire and Uncle Ned cussin'--he'd killed a so-and-so snake. He killed it alright…blew his suspenders to bits—*and* the bedpost. Mama just had put up new wallpaper in there and she was ready to kill him. She sent him packin' to Aunt Laura's after breakfast the next mornin' and he was stayin' there when he died.

We kept his bed in that room off the kitchen for a long time, but it fell down again when my cousin Alta was livin' with us, and Mama said it was gonna get somebody hurt.

She had Daddy and Harry Winston to haul it out to the smokehouse…been there ever since.

Just so you know, then, there's already been one honeymoon spent in that bed, and it didn't turn out too good. I hope you know what you're doin'."

Despite Granny's warning, I set about finishing what I had undertaken with the old bed. After hearing the black snake story, I couldn't bring myself to replace the top of the damaged bedpost, but I repaired the iron fittings and refinished the rails. After working on it for several weekends, I was proud of the finished product. The freshly finished walnut gleamed—and even the shot-off bedpost didn't look so bad.

Ready for the unveiling, I took Sandy to the barn for the viewing. When I removed the sheet I'd draped over it, she stood there expressionless. I thought she would squeal with delight, but the first words out of her mouth were, "Clay, have you MEASURED this bed?"

I had not.

A tape measure soon indicated that I had devoted my labors to the restoration of a *three-quarter bed*, several inches narrower than a full size version. A new mattress would have to be special ordered. I ordered one, and it wasn't cheap. I then hauled both bed and mattress set two hours down the highway to Louisville—to the apartment we were preparing to begin married life in. We set the bed up and then attempted to place the box spring on the new slats I'd made for it.

It wouldn't fit.

Sandy folded her arms and said, "Clay, did you measure the LENGTH of it?"

Once again, *I had not*. This was my somber introduction to the fact that people, and consequently their beds, were shorter in the 19th century, when the old poster bed was made.

So, the honeymoon bed--wasn't. We propped it and the ill-fitting box spring and mattress up against the wall until we could haul them to Fordville—and back to the smokehouse. I had totally lost interest in the project at that point. Sympathetic to my plight, but no less amused by it, Granny said, "Clay, if you and Sandy will go to Murphy's Furniture Store in Harriston and find a bed that's good and solid, I'll buy it for you as a wedding present—and a mattress set to go with it."

We found a new bed, well-made and well-equipped for modern times. It's the bed we still use, and maybe one day a member of our family will treasure *it*. After all, every heirloom has to begin its journey as something new.

When I could stand to look at the Uncle Ned bed again— several years later, I lengthened and altered the rails to accommodate the special-ordered mattress. We placed it in our oldest daughter Loren's bedroom. It's still there, covered with several of her stuffed animals-- but unlikely to ever again furnish a honeymoon suite.

The strawberry pattern bowl in the china cabinet

Strawberries in the Snow

Every May Granny fetched the familiar strawberry
patterned bowl from her china cabinet, and served her
freshly sliced and sweetened strawberries in it. When the
season was over, the special bowl was *always* returned to
its rightful place. This was a rite of spring I always looked
forward to.

I was nearing high school graduation this particular May,
and as I picked the first ripened strawberries, I couldn't
think of anything else. That afternoon, I carried two
buckets of the ripened fruit into the kitchen. Granny and I
went to work, capping and slicing some for her famous
strawberry shortcake. She had already conscripted her
strawberry bowl into service for the task and I said, "There
must be some kind of law that says you've got to use that
bowl before you can have the berries."

Granny grinned as she propped her eyeglasses with the
back of her hand. "No, I don't *have* to use it, but it puts me
in mind of Mattie Terrill. She gave it to me one Christmas.
The Ladies Circle used to draw names and she got mine.
We bought berries from her for several years before we
started raisin' our own, and I'm guessin' that's why she
picked it out for me."

I remembered Mattie Terrill—"Mrs. Mattie"—the tiny soft-
spoken old lady who sat by the church window. I remember
how strange it seemed when her accustomed seat was
vacant because no one else would sit there. "Mrs. Mattie"

hadn't been in church for several months when the preacher announced one Sunday morning that she had died.

Older than my grandmother by several years, she was also a lifelong member of the same church. For as long as she was able, every Sunday morning would find the tiny woman sitting by herself in the same seat by the window. In my memory, Mrs. Mattie was veiled in white. Wispy, white-skinned, wearing a white sweater, her tiny little head crowned with white hair, she looked as if she'd been baptized in buttermilk and cleaned up with a wadded tissue from the bottom of her purse. The morning sun in the church window only highlighted her whiteness with the result that Mrs. Mattie gleamed like a tired little angel St. Peter had forgotten, still waiting to get her wings.

My grandparents once gave Mrs. Mattie a ride home from a church potluck dinner in their pea green 1952 Dodge and I rode with them. There, she sank into the back seat, little more than a slightly filled print dress attached to a black pair of open toed shoes, her head barely even with the window. She seemed much older than the few years that separated her from my grandmother, and exuded a spirit of stoic, battle-wearied resignation.

On that solitary ride, I sat next to Mrs. Mattie in the back seat. Looking toward her garden spot on the right, Granddaddy said, "Mattie, how long have you raised strawberries?

She leaned forward in the back seat so he could hear her.

"Forever, it seems like. Fact is, Russell, one of my first memories is pickin' strawberries *in the snow*."

She leaned back and looked over at me, smiling. "I bet you've never heard about that, have you?"

I guess she saw the skeptical look on my face.

She patted me on the knee with a chuckle. "It *is* hard to believe. I'll always remember it because it was *my birthday* and we ate snow crème with fresh strawberries-- the twentieth day of May in 1894. I was eight years old— and it's never happened since then, neither. Nobody could believe it—we had several inches of snow on the ground and it was still fallin' early that mornin'. We'd never seen a late snow like that, and come to find out none of the old people we knew had, either. We jumped up and ran to the garden with our heavy coats on—"and here she mused **"to—pick--strawberries—in—the—snow.** Mama was afraid they'd freeze and we'd lose ever' one of 'em. We picked 'em 'til our hands and feet both was numb and hurtin', but we knew there wouldn't be any berries if we didn't. We couldn't wear gloves so we just had to pick as long as we could stand it. We'd put our hands under our arms to warm 'em up, and then go right back to pickin'." To no one in particular Mrs. Mattie said, "We nearly froze our fingers off but it was all kind of fun in way. But, it's like this: w*e had to have the hurtin' to have the berries."*

Mrs. Mattie and her husband John lived in an austere two story frame farmhouse that looked as if it hadn't been painted since ration stamps were used to buy the paint. Cracks in the upstairs windows were taped over with cardboard and the tin roof was brown with rust. After we arrived, I helped her get her potluck dishes from the trunk. Afterwards, as we backed out of the Terrill's muddy, gravel-less driveway, I could see the front door standing wide open. It occurred to me that there wasn't even a screen in the screen door, nor a spring to hold it. As we drove away, Granddaddy pointed to Mrs. Mattie's garden spot and said, "I'll bet she's walked one and one half million miles between there and the house."

Granny quickly added "And a whole lot of that was *on her knees*—right there *in* that berry patch.

Mm-mm…it's hard to imagine now, lookin' at this ol' rundown house, but Mattie was well-set at one time… when she and John first married." Backing the car out of the rutted Terrill mud, he turned in his seat looking past me as we turned around in the yard. He said, "I don't remember seein' John when he wasn't drunker'n a boiled owl, but poor ol' Mattie's hung right in there." That was essentially all I knew about John Terrill. As we sat at the kitchen table, capping and slicing strawberries Granny told her story. I remembered some of her comments about Mattie's hard life from that Sunday afternoon drive to the dismal Terrill Place.

She said, "Mattie's children left home as quick as they could when they got grown. They figured out if they were ever gonna have anything, they'd have to get it on their own. Mattie kept 'em fed and clothed the best she could, but for anything extra they just had to… root, pig, or die."

95

While the rain fell that afternoon, we sat together in the kitchen where Granny continued her berry-capping, the work of her wrinkled hands evidenced by the blood-red dishtowel beside her.

"Mattie had a green thumb like no other. Anything she put in the ground did well. Years ago, somebody at church gave her a coffee sack of strawberry plants they'd dug up— runners from plants they already had. Mattie planted 'em that spring, and the next year when they bore fruit, she sold what she had extra. I've seen her carry dried manure to that berry patch in big cream cans, but I reckon it paid off, too. She had the sweetest tastin' berries of anybody around here and people wanted hers first, if they could get 'em.

At church one Sunday she brought me a bucket of 'em she'd picked *early* that mornin' just for me. Her vines were bearin' extra heavy and I asked her what she was gonna do with all that money she was makin'. She was beaming from ear to ear and said she was savin' up to put a bathroom in her house. She said she had always wanted to be able to take a bath in a real bathtub and have a toilet in the house. John didn't care if he ever had one or not, but she determined she was gonna get one. Poor ol' Mattie…she saw them berries as the one way—maybe the *only way,* she'd ever get to have a bathroom. Ever' single berry she could sell put her that much closer to havin' it. She never ate many of 'em after that, either—not for jam, or nothin'.

She'd found a way to get a hold of a little extra money with that first little berry patch, and it just took off from that.

96

"The next year, Mattie ordered a bunch of new plants and she had John plow up more garden space. I bet she turned half or more of that big garden spot into a strawberry patch, but John Terrill never set his foot in it that I ever heard of—leastways, not the back-breakin' part of it.

"Did she ever get a bathroom put in?"

Granny shook her head, with something like a look of disgust on her face.

"*No. Not really*. She kept that strawberry money, savin' it up bit by bit ever' year. I reckon she did that for, prob'ly seven, maybe eight years or more. Her kids were mostly up and gone, and she was able to hold on to what little extra she made. Mattie was smart and a good manager. If she hadn't been, her children would've done without.

Then, late one Saturday night John blew in from a card game somewhere. Mattie had already gone to bed. He'd been drinkin' and woke her up to tell her he wanted that strawberry money she'd been savin'. She told me later that he just flat demanded it, *all of it*. He told her he'd lost money in a poker game--money he didn't have, but he said he'd make it all back that night and more besides…and he wouldn't take 'no' for an answer.

Poor ol' Mattie…she got that money from wherever she had it hid. I think she said it was a little over six hundred dollars, and she just handed it over to 'im.

He didn't come home 'til after daylight that Sunday mornin'. Mattie never made it to church that day and she hardly ever missed. We had a telephone by then, so I called

97

her up in the evenin' to see if she was all right. John must've been sittin' close by, for all she would say when I asked her that question was one word—"trouble". I knew not to ask her anything else, so we just spoke for a minute. She told me later that John had lost ever' last penny of her strawberry money in a card game and it ab-so-lute-ly broke her heart. She couldn't hardly tell it without cryin'. All the poor ol' thing wanted was a bathroom and all that time, she'd been workin' and scrimpin'--and it was all gone in one night. Makes me sick to think about it now, but we'd drive up there and she'd be brown and red from the waist down, where she'd crawled around on her knees pickin' them berries.

It seemed like losin' that money killed poor ol' Mattie's spirit, and she just let the berry patch go after that. She just let the weeds take it over and John or somebody finally plowed it all up.

"Did he ever pay her back?"

Granny smirked.

"Well, not really, but somethin' did happen along that line. It's kindly funny-- and pitiful at the same time. Mattie finally did get a *piece* of a bathroom put in that ol' house. I reckon that's what you'd call it. When Mattie got down sick, a couple of years before she died and John saw that she wasn't gettin' no better, he changed--a little. I don't know that he quit drinkin' altogether, but he did *better*. He drove to town one day and bought Mattie a new bathtub. When I heard it, you could've knocked me over with a toothpick."

98

Totally confused, I asked her again, "Didn't she get the whole bathroom?"

"No, not hardly," she said.

Granny giggled as she tried to suppress her laughter.

"It's not funny, but I can't help it. John Terrill wouldn't hit a lick at a snake… never hardly had a cent to his name, but he owned a rifle of some kind that ever' man around her tried to buy from 'im—for years. I don't know nothin' about guns, but this'n had come down through the family. He broke down and sold it so he could buy Mattie a new bathtub, but there wasn't nowhere to put it without closin' off a bathroom. Mattie always wanted to add one on the side of that ol' house beside the kitchen but John didn't have the money so he just stuck that bathtub in the corner of their bedroom. Didn't hook up no plumbin' to it nor nothin'…he just cut 'a hole in the floor and let the water run out under the house.

Mattie showed it to me right after he put it in, and I declare, it was the awkwardest lookin' thing you ever laid your eyes on. Nothin' around it—no toilet, no sink, water faucets, no nothin'. When she wanted to take a bath, John would pump the water at the kitchen sink and he'd set two big kettles on the stove to heat it. She was so proud of that tub she could bust--and it as ugly as a mud fence daubed with tadpoles. I reckon she took a bath in it ever' night or two, 'til she had to go into the hospital.

We stopped by not long before that, and I said, 'Mattie, is John *ever* gonna put in the rest of your bathroom fixtures?'

Well, I got right tickled at what she said. She held my arm right like this," Granny grabbed my hand, and laid her other hand on my forearm, gripping it firmly, "and then she said, "'Well, Lorene,'"—"she said it real slow, like she'd thought about it for a long time,"…"'I'll just tell you—I don't know if he'll get around to it or not but, it's like this: **half of somethin' is better than all of nothin.'** That was the last time I laid eyes on her, and she was plumb tickled…just like a two year old in butter. As sick as Mattie was, I believe to my soul she was the happiest I'd ever known her to be.

Granny chuckled as she recalled her old friend's battle-hardened philosophy.

Maybe sensing that she needed to lighten her own mood, Granny forced a smile and said, "I remember hearin' Big Granny say one time that she'd dreamed about strawberries the night before, and she was laughin' about it. I'd never heard it, but she claimed if you dreamed of strawberries, it meant you'd have a happy courtship and marriage. By that time, Big Granny had been a widow for years—and wore black 'til her dyin' day. I guess that's why she thought it was funny. I don't know if Mattie ever dreamed about strawberries, but I'd like to think she still had her dreams. Sometimes they're all we've got…and all we ever have."

Years later, I drove by the Terrill place which had been sold by then at public auction. The new owners gutted the old farmhouse and completely remodeled it, maintaining the exterior as it was, most of which was built at the turn of the century. Mattie's home of many years finally looked like the house it should've been, but never was. The field to the east of the house containing the large garden spot where Mattie had toiled to feed her family was sold separately from the rest of the farm which was divided into tracts. A *new* house was under construction where she had once crawled on her knees down the muddy rows of a strawberry patch just so she could have something of her own.

On the day I drove by, the builder was installing very expensive, state of the art bathroom fixtures, plainly visible through the newly framed up walls. Recognizing the utility truck parked in the newly cut driveway as belonging to someone I knew, I tiptoed through mud puddles, scraps of plywood and pieces of sawed off two by fours, to speak to him.

My friend gave me a brief tour of the impressive new structure, pointing to all the modern features it would have when completed.

Just before climbing into my truck afterwards, preparing to head home, I wondered what Mrs. Mattie would've thought of the scene before me. As I looked back toward the new house rising up from the mud, I noticed that the newly installed luxurious bathroom on the first floor stood directly *over* the site of Mrs. Mattie's strawberry patch. Only someone who knew her story could appreciate the irony of that moment.

Granddaddy often said, "Life ain't fair. Some you win, some you lose—and some get rained out." That was a lesson that I had yet to learn, but I later came to understand the truth behind that maxim, in so many ways.

I eventually established a strawberry patch in my own garden and in a time-honored tradition, my wife Sandy produces Granny's special bowl from the same oak china cabinet every May. When Mrs. Mattie's May 20th birthday finds me on my knees eagerly picking the ripe fruit, I pause to consider the angelic little figure bathed in the light of a church window--who once upon a time picked strawberries in the snow. But mostly, I remember the story of her gratitude for the *half of something* in life that she had finally been given.

The old metal button I carry in my pocket

Confessions of a Step Counter

From where Cousin Andy lived on the hill above Fordville, I never knew him to travel more than three miles in any direction. He simply walked everywhere he went.

Actually, he *shuffled*--as if in pain, but I'm getting ahead of myself.

For that matter I never even saw the man in an automobile until the day Coley Pepper's long black hearse delivered him to the Fordville Cemetery. It was said at the time that he hadn't left sight of the Kentucky River foothills of his birth since he was an American Doughboy returning home from the trenches of France in 1919.

Among the peculiarities for which I remember Cousin Andy is the fact that he counted every step he took every single day--and kept a record of it. Maybe that accounts for the way he shuffled his feet with a predictable one-two rhythm.

103

For as long as I could remember, it was said that Cousin Andy had been "gassed" by the Germans in The First World War. At the time I knew nothing of chemical weapons like mustard and chlorine gas that had been used for the first time in warfare. Although I didn't know what "bein' gassed" meant, I knew it couldn't be good for you if you wound up counting every step. Perry Guinn Taylor ran a gas *station* but he seemed normal enough for Fordville. I began to understand the science behind the gas connection when somebody successfully dared three-time eighth grader Harold Gene Hoskins to ignite one of his own farts in the locker room after basketball practice, using the new Zippo lighter he'd won shooting pool. Unlike Cousin Andy, the only adverse effects of *his* gas encounter appeared to be scorched underwear and singed body hair in unmentionable places—plus the fact that Coach Hart made him run laps until he dropped.

Cousin Andy generally spoke but little. I remember sitting around the (cold) stove during The Children's Hour one summer day when the old fellow shuffled over to the cooler to get a pop. Mack Perkins winked at Granddaddy and asked, "Hey Andy, what's the count up to *today*?"

Without missing a beat he answered sharply, "sem'teen hundred and eighty, now *two*" as his feet stopped their rhythmic shuffling and he laid the pop opener on the cooler. I remembered the number only because it sounded like a year, possibly the one in which he'd been born, for I could not imagine him ever having been young. When he was once asked when he had started counting his steps, Cousin Andy said, "Armistice Day, in nineteen and

104

eighteen—the day them big guns stopped." Cousin Andy had the habit of speaking a year like his one-two step pattern, with a two-and-two approach in referencing any particular year. Upon hearing his answer, and in his usual overbearing manner, Red Perkins said, "Andy, what did you do about that big ocean 'tween here and there—you can't count walkin' on water—unless you're Jesus."

The quirky old soldier studied Red's expression for a moment, and while all eyes were upon him, he reached for the dime store reading glasses in his shirt pocket, then into the front pocket of his overalls. Bringing out a worn five cent tablet, he turned to its cardboard backing and gave us the name of the US Navy vessel that brought him home and the number of steps he had taken on that transatlantic voyage. For once, Red Perkins was silenced, and even he was forced to produce a grin in the midst of the laughter that followed.

For decades, Cousin Andy kept a small work counter in the back of Pop Ed Richards' adjoining barber shop, where he sometimes repaired clocks and watches. About the time I turned twelve, I began helping him a couple of times a week to carry his small bag of purchases home from Mack Perkins' store—and on rare occasions, a troublesome clock he had been tinkering with. Until nearly the time he died four years later, for at least five days a week, I was climbing the hill above Fordville with him to what we knew as The Old Walker Place.

Those walks with Cousin Andy could get interesting. I recall an unusually warm afternoon in early April when I escorted him up the hill above Fordville. We stopped at the little rise before the lane turned toward the Walker Place and The Little House behind it where he lived. The surrounding fields were turning green after their winter slumber and the red bud trees were in full bloom. Cousin Andy stopped and turned to take in the full view of the awakening landscape as it sloped toward the nearby Kentucky River. He closed his eyes as if meditating and whispered something that sounded like *"Main-gawt."*

I'd almost forgotten the words when, that fall, I heard them again. It was in October when the fireworks display of fall colors was highlighted by a brilliant sun beneath a clear blue sky. We were climbing the hill in silence and at the very same spot as before, he stopped abruptly. Turning around slowly, he again took in the full view of Fordville and its surrounding hills, closed his eyes and mumbled— another-- barely audible "Main-gawt."

Then came yet another day in early summer. As we climbed the hill to the Walker Place, the air was heavy with the fragrance of honeysuckle and locust blooms when a lone butterfly made its way to Cousin Andy's arm. He stopped, gently raised his arm to examine it more closely and, as before, he appeared to close his eyes in solemn meditation. I watched and waited for him to mutter the mysterious incantation when he opened his eyes and said, "Wait here a minute... I'm needin' to pee." As the old veteran with an enlarged prostate strained for five minutes to relieve himself in the nearby bushes, I pondered the two strange-sounding syllables and repeated them over and over again in my mind.

The next time I remember hearing the elusive phrase was early the following spring when Fordville received an unexpected blanket of snow during the relatively short time we'd been in Perkins' Store for The Children's Hour. Once again, I helped Cousin Andy get back home. We made it all the way to the Little House with his small bag of provisions when he stopped suddenly and turned to take in the aerial view of Fordville freshly veiled in white. Scattered, big puffy flakes were still coming down all around us when Cousin Andy said, "It looks like the old woman's shakin' out her feather bed again." Surveying the landscape, he closed his eyes and extended his open hands to feel the snowflakes as they touched his skin. And, once more he whispered, "Main-gawt." Maybe it was just quieter in the stillness of that afternoon-- in the hush of an early evening snowfall, but the words—if one could call them that--were more distinct than I'd ever heard them.

Emboldened with this sudden clarity, when he opened his eyes this time I finally had the nerve to ask, "Cousin Andy, just what **does** Main-gawt mean?" He seemed surprised, as if uttering those syllables was something as natural to him as breathing, and as if no one had ever heard him--or *should* have.

Studying me briefly with his ruddy-faced, ever-present smile he said, *"It's German…*"Mein Gott"…'My God.'

It was as close to an explanation as I got that day.

Spring melted into the heat of summer, and one sweltering August afternoon I carried Cousin Andy's single sack of groceries *into* The Little House. Ordinarily, I stopped at

107

the door and set the bag down on the bench in front, for it was generally understood that Cousin Andy was not a particularly good housekeeper and you entered what was primarily a dog's domain at your own peril. By the time we'd climbed the hill from Fordville, we were both sweating bullets and Cousin Andy propped the front door open and left it. He was very much a creature of habit, and followed protocol by emptying contents of his pockets onto the kitchen table. Picking through the change, he gathered up three nickels, handed them to me and said, "Here, go buy yourself a cold pop when you get back to the store." I watched as he sat down at his tiny kitchen table and entered the day's step count in the open spiral notebook he kept there for that purpose. That portion of the ritual I had observed many times before. However, this was the first time I stuck around for the second step, for normally I would've taken my leave of the old fellow at that point, but something told me to stay put. You never knew when another Cousin Andy quirk might surface, and on that particular day the very one that seemed to define him was at least—partially—revealed. He seemed not to mind my presence as he very methodically took off his right shoe, then the sock, which he folded. Removing his left shoe next, he shook it just a little, producing a small object which rolled into his hand. The retrieval process was smooth and efficient—and for him, clearly, nothing out of the ordinary. Before my eyes could focus on the unknown object taken from his shoe, he quickly placed it on the kitchen table along with his pocket knife and loose change. I then observed what had *not* been there only moments earlier: what appeared to be just a dull, brownish, coin-like object with a crown stamped on its surface.

Cousin Andy apparently took notice of my interest.

Nodding toward it, he said, "You know what that is? That right there's a German soldier's button…from The World War—the first'n. I brought it home with me from overseas…in nineteen and nineteen."

Avoiding the obvious question as to why it had been in his shoe, I tried an indirect approach. I asked, "Did a German soldier give it to you?"

He studied my hopeful, perhaps even innocent expression for a moment, and said matter-of-factly, "Nossir…I killed 'im."

His response caught me off guard.

"Why do you carry it?" I asked, hoping he would expand the answer to include its placement in his shoe.

He said, "For good luck, I reckon. When I was a kid, Mama used to say if you found a button, and carried it in your shoe, it'd bring you good luck."

After an awkward silence, I suppose he felt some sort of explanation was due. "I've studied on it a right smart since I was overseas," he said, "and I'm thinkin' that German soldier could've been what some of the In-dians called a *con-trarian.*"

"A what?"

I searched Cousin Andy's eyes. He pursed his lips before offering up an explanation, one to which he had clearly devoted some thought.

He said, "When I was just a kid—prob'ly about your age, my cousin Ed and me slipped off to Harriston one time with our Uncle Jake to see a freak show. We didn't have money for a ticket, but he let us poke our heads in under the tent where he was standin' and he could be our look-out. We got right up and under his feet between two hay bales where he'd let us look without gettin' caught. The people runnin' that freak show had 'em a In-dian there from way out west somewhere, and they claimed he was a holy man o' some kind. I forget what tribe he was from but he was what they called a con-trarian. He was the *one* member of their tribe that did *ever'-thing* the exact opposite, to kindly balance things out. Instead of him sayin' "Goodbye," he'd say "Howdy-do?" or instead of sayin' "Howdy-do?" he'd say, "Goodbye." He even walked backwards and by Ned, he could do it as well as me or you walk straight ahead." He claimed that by him goin' about ever'thing backwards like that, it evened things out for his people. That was to please The Great Spirit or god or whatever it was they called it."

Andy chuckled and said, "The next thing we saw that night was "The Wild Man from Borneo." Tell you what he done--he tried to eat a live chicken, bones, feathers and all, and then puked it up--right in front of us. Women and kids all went to screamin' and hollerin' and somebody got Sheriff Tate to come and shut the whole thing down." Andy grinned as he recalled his long-gone adolescent misadventure. "By jacks" he said, "you couldn't *give* a chicken away in Harriston for six months after that." Sharing the memory seemed to provide Cousin Andy the steam he needed to finish what he had to say about the old button—slowly distilled thoughts representing nearly a half's century's reflection on human destiny—fate, that somehow included an Indian of questionable authenticity, a freak show gone bad, and a dead German's button. I kept waiting for a smile, a guffaw…something that might let me know he was joking. He was not. Nor for that matter was he ever a joker. Cousin Andy was as serious in his contemplations as a hog on ice.

He said, "The way I got it figured, that German could've been some kind of a con-trarian for *his* people, just like that there Indian was." Cousin Andy held out his hand at eye level and, tilting it from side to side, he said, "Maybe some things in this ol' world have to balance theirselves out that-away. Maybe some of his *bad* luck became my *good* luck."

It might've been rude, but I couldn't help myself. I suppressed a laugh unsuccessfully and tried to pass it off as a cough.

Halfway miffed at me for my obvious skepticism, Cousin Andy said, "You laugh, but when them bullets gets to flyin' around a man's head, he can start thinkin' some funny thoughts. That button come off the uniform of that German I killed… in the shell hole we was in. After it fell out his hand, I reached down and grabbed it…stuck it in my pocket when I climbed out of there. I hadn't gotten from here to the road down yonder when another big shell hit right close by and throwed me five foot in the air. It didn't hurt me

111

too bad, but it addled me some. I finally 'bout halfway came to myself… and raised up out of the dirt, kindly in a daze. I looked around and saw our boys runnin' past me. Right then I felt somethin' under me and there I was, layin' on top a dead German that shell'd blowed up.

I've studied on it some. If I hadn't taken the time to bend over to grab this here button in the mud just a minute or two before that, I'd-a-been blown to bits just as sure as you're livin'. So, after I made it out of there alive, I remembered what Mama used to say and I got to thinkin' that German boy's button might be lucky for me. That next mornin' I started keepin' the little feller in my shoe, and he's been with me ever' day since."

"Doesn't it hurt your foot?"

He picked up the old button--his shoe-bound traveling companion for untold thousands of steps and inspected it. Licking the end of his thumb, he gave the button a quick spit bath and polished it on his sleeve. He said, "Oh, it kindly did at first, but I reckon I just got used to it."

I felt as if something sacred had passed between Cousin Andy and me on that sultry August afternoon: I had been given a rare glimpse into the tender heart and unsteadied mind of a step counter. So far as I ever knew, no one else among Cousin Andy's extended family and friends had been so privileged. Although he did not request confidentiality, it somehow didn't seem right to share his story with anyone else. Doing so would've been a breach of honor in my mind, and I never spoke of it to anyone while he was living.

What Cousin Andy said that day about killing the German soldier has stayed with me ever since. Although I sensed he didn't want to talk about it, I was curious as to the details of what had happened in that shell hole and waited for him to mention it again. As unlikely as it was, that opportunity actually did present itself the following week.

I was once again walking Cousin Andy home and we were at the base of the hill below the Walker Place. I just came right out and asked him, "Cousin Andy, were you ever gassed when you were in France?"

Ominously, he said "Nossir, I wasn't…but I saw what it could do to a man."

Emboldened by his response, I decided to venture further into his mysterious phrase. We were nearly at the top of the hill when I decided that this was the moment and I'd better seize it. "Cousin Andy, why do you say that all the time— those two words, Main Gawt?"

He at first acted as if he hadn't heard me, and I figured I'd asked too much. We kept walking, and were soon at The Little House, which stood in the shadow of the old Walker house. Within a couple of awkward minutes, he answered, "I promised myself that if I lived to get out of there alive, I'd never forget them words." Another, longer period of silence followed and I assumed that was as much as I'd ever learn about Main Gawt, whatever it meant. I placed Cousin Andy's bag of groceries on the bench at his front door, and out of the blue, he began telling the story—and as a rule, stories were not part of his makeup.

Sitting down beside the grocery bag which had fallen over and spilled a half dozen cans of Vienna sausages, he leaned his elbows on his knees and folded his hands before he spoke. "We was in France when I killed that German…The Second Battle of the Marne. Me and him was about the same age. I reckon he'd lost his rifle and side arm both, but I didn't have no way o' knowin' it. I couldn't take a chance and I fired soon as I laid eyes on him. I searched him for a weapon, and never found one. When I saw he was fixin' to die, I got down closer to him and he grabbed a-hold me—like this—with his fist, and the last words he spoke was, "Mein Gott." He'd been holdin' that uniform button in his hand. He'd just about been cut in two by machine gun fire before I ever saw him. He was already dyin', and…I reckon I finished 'im off. When he breathed his last, that there button rolled out of his hand. I don't know what made me pick it up, unless it's on account of Mama always sayin' it was good luck to find one.

We took heavy machine gun fire for a right smart while, and I had to stay put in that shell hole with him…that dead German boy." He said it again, slower and louder this time, "Mein Gott."

Although I already knew what the words meant, I was beginning to understand them.

At the time of this revelation, Cousin Andy's daily routine had already begun to change. He was moving much slower, and counting fewer steps with each passing month. Over the summer, his barber shop clock repairing and loafing became less predictable. By early fall, he had grown noticeably thinner and was only coming down off the hill

114

from The Walker Place maybe twice a week, and even that was uncertain. Like his favorite old clock on his living room mantle, Cousin Andy was visibly winding down. Not only had he failed to wind his clock as he had done for years—every eight days, when I glanced down at the ten cent tablet on his kitchen table one afternoon, I noticed that he hadn't kept record of his step-counts for at least two weeks.

Probably six weeks later, Cousin Andy and I again climbed the hill in silence and although it took us twice as long this time, we made our way to The Little House. I carried with me his sack of groceries in one hand and an old mantle clock in the other--that rattled and chimed all the way. He wanted to take it home to work on. I had never known of him to carry one home but a couple of times before. Perhaps Cousin Andy had some sense of his own time drawing to a close. It was to be the last clock he ever repaired.

As I rested the bag on his kitchen table, Cousin Andy said, "Clay, wait right here a minute. I've got somethin' I've been meanin' to give you."

I placed the clock on his kitchen table and waited for him. The loose change and other miscellaneous items that usually adorned the table were, for the first time, not there—not even his open spiral notebook, his "step-log."

Shuffling back into the kitchen from his bedroom, he said, "Here, go back down there and get you a cold pop, and there's somethin' else here for you."

I opened my hand to see two dimes, a nickel, and the old German uniform button, worn smooth as the pump handle in Granny's kitchen sink.

He said, "They called me up to go overseas in nineteen and sem'teen. There's this other thing we've got into now overseas. I can't think of it, but that little country over close to China where France got into a mess and we tried to help 'em out."

"Vietnam," I said.

"Yessir," he said, "Viet-nam…that's what they call it, and I can't remember it from one day to the next. They're callin' more of our boys up for it, too. I hope you don't go, Clay, but if you do, maybe that ol' button'll be a good luck piece *for you* like it was for me." Ironically, he had no way of knowing it, but I was already thinking about enlisting when I graduated from high school. At that time, it was a secret I kept to myself.

"So far as I know," he said, "You're about the first'n outside of my mother to see it." He turned the television on to a snowy screen and motioned for me to sit down on the other end of the worn sofa. We both sat there for a moment in silence. He said, "I think you're a lot like me that-away. Those ol' fellers down there…them ol' loafers like Red and Mack…even your Granddaddy, Russell…they're not like me and you. They look all day, and don't never see nothin'." I've often wondered exactly what he meant by that, but I never got the chance to ask him. I was already pushing my luck that day with questions.

116

Rolling the smooth metal button between my fingers, I was still hoping Cousin Andy would tell me more. I sat there with him, waiting…and waiting, but the only sound in the room was the constant back and forth motion of the pendulum clock, the age and accuracy of which Cousin Andy was always so proud. "See that ol' clock up yonder?" he said. "It's so old, the shadow of the pendulum has wore a hole plumb through the back of it—open the door of it and take a look, if you don't believe me." The old fellow was grinning from ear to ear. I had done this probably a half-dozen times before, but he always forgot, and he enjoyed the joke so much I hated to disappoint him. When you opened the door, there truly was a hole in the back of it which had been papered over years before with the cartoon image of a little boy dropping his drawers to "moon" the viewer. Visitors were infrequent at Cousin Andy's place, but checking out the shadow-battered clock was the one common experience they all shared. To humor him, I rose from the couch to examine the clock and noticed that the time was off by half an hour. This was so not him. He turned up the volume on his television set upon which he now focused his attention, effectively killing any chance for another war story, and within five minutes the staccato sounds of his snoring filled the room.

By the beginning of my senior year, I had finally learned the truth about the kinsman I had walked so many miles with during the previous four years. To this day, I've never heard man or beast snore like that as we sat together on the dog hair-covered sofa--late in the day, and late in the life of Corporal Andrew Merritt Venable. My most important, longest-pondered question had at last been answered: No,

117

he hadn't been *gassed* in the First World War. For sure, that dead German's button in his shoe might've explained his peculiar walking pattern—and possibly his step-counting. Whatever wartime injuries Cousin Andy had sustained, his *lungs* had not been affected. That much was obvious, both to me *and* the old hound at his feet that raised his head when the snoring reached a skull-jarring crescendo.

The following spring of my senior year, the old fellow failed to make his planned appearance for The Children's Hour. During that year, his daily visits during The Children's Hour had dwindled to maybe one a week. "Feelin' puny," is all he said when Mack Perkins called him, and two weeks later, on the very day he had finally— reluctantly--agreed to be taken to the doctor in Harriston, Granddaddy and Doc Wilcox found him dead, sitting on his sofa—with his devoted but hungry Walker hound at his feet. To the utter dismay of his friends who had so often speculated on it, Cousin Andy's final step count was never tallied. With no explanation, during those last weeks of his life, he had mysteriously burned the carefully archived horde of ten cent tablets wherein all his post-war steps had been accounted for. All that remained were the dozens of fire-blackened wire spirals found in the ashes of the coal grate in his living room. The dirt on Cousin Andy's grave was still bare by the time I landed in Vietnam in 1969, but recalling the story of his own wartime experience and as a remembrance of home, I carried his gifted German button with me—in my pocket, not in my shoe. It's nothing short of a miracle that we both made it back.

Not long before my tour of duty in Vietnam ended, I once dropped it in a rice paddy while on patrol. I was switching it to another pocket and only the keen eye of another 19 year old in my unit allowed *it* to come back home even though *he* didn't. There came another day when our unit split up to patrol a relocated village. My right leg was sore from a boil just under my front pocket. From the heat and sweat—and the friction caused by the German button—infection had set in and I was constantly digging at it. Another soldier in my unit told me he'd hand me some kind of ointment he'd carried with him for the same kind of sore. The boys in my unit decided we'd take the short route around the village for the two of us to drop our drawers and doctor ourselves. While we were thus engaged less than a quarter of a mile away, friendly fire decimated the location we would have been in the thick of on our patrol. We later learned that no one was killed…not even injured, in the village. Maybe Cousin Andy was a little bit right. You might actually call his button *my* good luck charm.

As I've grown older, like Cousin Andy, I often find myself pondering remarkable coincidences… the mysteries of life and death, and unexplainable things. I consider the youthful faces of my fellow soldiers who didn't make it back home. I still sometimes imagine the shadowy and shapeless Vietnamese that I shot at with everything I could send them. I'm glad I didn't see *their* faces, which may well have haunted me as they had Fordville's only known step counter.

As Cousin Andy discovered, I've found that walking every day is not only therapeutic, but a good way to stay in touch with the wonders of nature. On these solitary walks along the ridge tops above the Kentucky River, I stop often…to look, and to take in the stillness. On these occasions, I am very much aware of Cousin Andy's button in my pocket. Its comforting presence reminds me how lucky I am to be alive, even for another walk—even one more (uncounted) step. I'm getting older now myself—the same age in fact that Cousin Andy was when I first came to know him. Sometimes during these morning ritual walks, I close my eyes and breathe in the natural world around me--in all its seasons. Remembering Cousin Andy and the very real but invisible wounds of war, I sometimes find myself whispering to the wind a *very* grateful *"Mein Gott."*

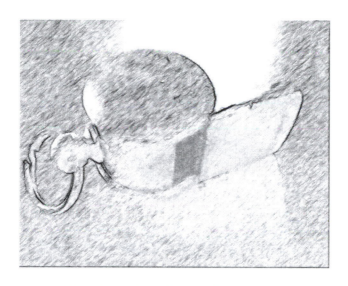

The tin whistle in my desk drawer
(the one I used when coaching).

Distant Kin

"They're *sisters*."

Granny spoke in the present tense as we approached a cluster of graves, nearly hidden in the tall weeds.

"Daddy's sisters...my aunts are buried in here. My uncles are, too."

I was now beginning to understand why she wanted to come here, to this lonely knoll: we had just left the grave of her only sister, Ida May, who though ten years younger had died unexpectedly the previous winter. Now it was Memorial Day—the solemn day of remembrance she knew as "Decoration Day," and we had been to The Fordville

121

Cemetery. Now she stood here, on a mission it seemed, to glean something unspoken from other, silent stones.

Granny leaned over to touch the grave marker closest to her. "This is Aunt Vi here, and Uncle Joe. They wanted to be together on one marker." Careful not to step on the actual grave site, she moved behind it to reach the other stone. "Aunt Jessie's buried over here next to her," she said, straining to touch the dull marble with her fingertips—"beside Uncle Bill."

Standing on that spot, I suddenly recalled my ten year old self looking across the river at a distant farmhouse, and seeing what appeared to be a woman hanging bed linens on a clothesline. I wouldn't have even noticed, but for the billowy white sheets that looked like ship sails in the wind.

"Who lives over there?" I had asked.

She looked in the direction of the faraway figure and stood there for a moment, taking in the scene.

"Some of your kinfolks," she said, blandly. "That woman is my *sister*, Ida May."

No explanation was given as to why I had not—knowingly—ever met her. Sensing that I was somewhat puzzled, she added, "It's a far piece from here over to her place." and yet, from where we stood we could watch the woman hang bed sheets. Granny's explanation was more than I could fathom.

She drifted her gaze toward the bottom land directly across the river from her own farm, and the hill rising above,

122

where Ida May lived. Their father's property had been divided between them many years before, but in Granny's tone, even a ten year old could tell there was more than a river that separated the two sisters.

She went on to explain that her father had run the two farms together, as one—something made possible by the nearby ferry. "BUT," she said, "after it sunk in that '37 Flood, it took nearly an hour to get there."

Now grown, and standing on the same spot as then, I recalled the memory of that strange introduction to my great-aunt. And now as then, Granny stood looking at what had been her father's land across the river--and who or what she might be able to see on it. By sheer coincidence, there were sheets blowing on the same clothesline, but this time they were not Ida May's.

The all-but-forgotten graveyard was located at the high end of a long hayfield that gradually rose in elevation, narrowing at the point where we now stood. Looking all around me, I could understand why the site was admired, for it offered an unequalled view of Fordville and the surrounding fields on both sides of the river. Dotted here and there with Black Angus cattle, the landscape appeared pristine—unspoiled, and interrupted only by rows of freshly mowed hay drying in the sun. As if nature had even attempted to be equal in its treatment of Granny and Ida May, the broad river bottom lay perfectly--evenly divided by its sluggish waters. Consequently, each sister's part of their father's land remained an island unto itself—each now carefully guarded by ancient, pale sycamores.

Looking around me from that lonely vista, I could see several crude, nameless stones—grave markers, some barely visible. Granny pointed to one that had all but disappeared beneath the sod. "These were poor people buried over here on this side... day workers, mostly, back when Fordville was boomin'."

Granny held onto my arm with one hand, and a water bucket with the other, containing what remained of the pink peonies she brought from home to place on the graves. Thus equipped, we moved ever-so-slowly among the markers of uncles and aunts, unnamed, stillborn cousins, and others whose initials triggered foggy memories of a Fordville in its heyday. Unlettered fieldstones spoke as a reminder of dead day laborers, their wives and small children, now as gone and forgotten as the distillery and sawmill jobs that once beckoned.

I looked across the freshly mowed pasture that surrounded the little graveyard as Granny laid the last of her peonies on the graves of "the sisters," her aunts and their brother-husbands, Bill and Joe Johnson.

In doing so, I observed that she would stop and look toward the distant farmhouse, hoping, it seemed, to catch a glimpse of Ida May.

Recalling that the land across the river from us had once belonged to her father, I said, "When your parents divided up the farm, why did Ida May want that land across the river?"

Her answer came quickly, and with an uneasy chuckle. *"Because I wanted it.*

After we lost The Aunt Mollie Place in '31, Daddy decided it was time to wind up his estate while he was still livin'. I thought movin' over there—across the river-- would be a fresh start for us—new friends and neighbors…and your granddaddy felt the same way. Since I was the oldest, Daddy offered me first choice and I told 'im I wanted it. Well, when he and Mama told Ida May, she threw a pitchin' fit…said it wasn't fair because the house over there was better than the home place where we grew up. Well, it really wasn't, but I felt like Daddy was dividin' up mostly on account of me, so I told 'im to let Ida May have it—just to keep the peace. So, they deeded me the home place where we live now, but I got Mama and Daddy along with it, takin' care of 'em. Daddy died right sudden-like, but Mama needed a lot of lookin' after and that whole time, Ida May never much more than raised a finger to help me."

Granny pointed across the river to a ridge, a hundred yards or more above the house where Ida May had lived.

"And to beat it all, Ida May and Carl—well, you prob'ly don't remember him, but he was her husband—they tore down the old house that stood on that ridge--and there wasn't a thing in the world wrong with it. He got a principal's job at the Rosstown School and they built that'n you see yonder. Nothin' was ever good enough for her. She was spoiled rotten and I reckon I'm partly to blame for it. Where she was so much younger than me, I treated her just like a doll-baby. Ever' one of us spoiled her. She was Harry Winston's pet and when he got killed in The World

125

War, it nearly killed her. She quit eatin'…and pretty much lost interest in ever'thing for a long time. Ever'body was worried about her. I was married and gone from home by then, and I've sometimes thought that dotin' on her is what kept Mama and Daddy goin'."

She sighed heavily through her nose, something she usually did when recalling some unpleasant event. "I never thought but what she'd outlive me. Somehow, someway, I always thought things might get…better, but…" her voiced trailed off.

Having seen what she came for, she was now ready to move on. With me holding one arm, she navigated around the stones as she pointed with her cane to other names she could recall.

I said, "You miss Ida May, don't you?"

Theirs had been a relationship so distant, so odd that her name seemed foreign to me even as I spoke it. I think Granny understood, since it was equally strange for her to hear.

She stopped and turned to face me.

"I do," she said. "You know, it's hard to miss somethin' you didn't have, but…just the same, you miss the *hope* that you *might* get to have it."

Sensing the need to lighten the mood, and recalling the curious name given to the familiar location, I said, "Granny, why's this called The Peddler's Field?"

She nodded over her shoulder, "Well, really it's on account of those aunts of mine buried back there. Lord, what a pair."

Granny still had family—sisterhood, on her mind. I said, "They're buried close together. Were *they* close?"

She paused.

"Off and on," she said, smiling, "but I know they loved each other."

As we headed toward my truck, Granny nodded toward a solitary grave in the enclosure, fenced off by strands of barbed wire hanging loosely between tired fence posts and dead trees.

"You were askin' about why this is called Peddler's Field, *right over there's where that ol' peddler's buried*." I helped her across the soft, uneven ground to see and touch it. "He used to come to Fordville back when I was a girl…ever' spring and fall, seems like."

There was no name inscribed on the marker, only crude undecipherable initials, hidden beneath hardened brown moss, which I attempted to scratch away with my pocket knife.

"What was his name?"

She bent down, trying to trace the dead man's initials with her finger. She shook her head. "It's been too long. I can't think of it right off, but ever' kid around here loved 'im. He'd spend the night with some of his customers, the ones he'd known for a long time. Fact is, he died over there in Willie's house—Aunt Vi and Uncle Joe owned that place back then. "

Granny nodded toward her left. "Aunt Jessie's house was way down yonder. I was stayin' there the night that ol' peddler took sick. Aunt Vi and her girls, my cousins came over the next mornin' to help Aunt Jessie get ready for a big quiltin' party--and I can remember 'em fussin' over who was gonna to look after 'im.

Aunt Jessie was real partic'lar about how ever'thing looked. If Aunt Vi got anything new—Aunt Jessie had to out-do her. Maybe that's where Ida May got it. She's just like Aunt Jessie for the world. Aunt Vi was the oldest, and Daddy claimed that when she started courtin' Uncle Joe, Aunt Jessie set her cap for him--just because Aunt Vi wanted 'im first. Grandpa Clark put a stop to it, and she turned right around and went for his younger brother—Uncle Bill.

Uncle Joe had kindly a withered arm. He was a good worker, but of course, he never could do as much as Uncle Bill. He got by, though…raised a family, and Aunt Vi worshipped the very ground he walked on. Uncle Bill worked like a mule, but he never could make enough to please Aunt Jessie. She was never satisfied with nothin'…always had to have somethin' better." She paused. *"And Ida May's just like her."*

Every time Granny spoke of her dead sister that day, I noticed she had not yet made the transition to speak of her in the past-tense.

"People around here loved to visit Aunt Vi and Uncle Joe. You never hardly came to see 'em that they didn't have company. I'd stayed with 'em when I was a kid, so I could play with my cousins. Aunt Jessie was a good woman, too, but she had a different turn—a little stand-offish. She had nicer things, but…Aunt Vi had a better time…and a whole lot more friends."

"What happened to the peddler?"

"Oh, I don't know…he was just old and wore out, I reckon. He always claimed Fordville was his favorite stoppin' place and Mama believed he came back here to die. I can see 'im now comin' down the road from Harriston…a little old man with a long white beard…and carryin' a pack on his shoulders nearly as big as he was.

Ever' time he passed through this country, he'd come up here on foot, just to take in this view. He told Daddy when he first came to Fordville, there wasn't nothin' to it but two log houses and a blacksmith shop—and a tanyard--and it had grown from that to a 'happenin' little place.'

Granny chuckled, "That's just how he said it—'a happenin' little place.'

Mmm-mm…I'd sure hate for 'im to see it now. Of course, the sawmill was goin' strong then—and the distillery. When I was a girl, you could stand on any hill around here and see the smoke from thirty some-odd chimneys. He'd watched a lot of the people around here grow up…Daddy…and then Harry Winston and me…and Ida May.

I remember how the ol' fellow loved to play tricks on us. He'd act like he was gonna reach into that big pack and bring out some kind of a treat for us. Then he'd say, 'Let's see here now, would you rather have a see-saw snake or a sun-burnt cake?' and if a kid hadn't heard it, why of course they'd say 'A sun-burnt cake.'

"What's that?"

"Lord, that's an old'n. A sun-burnt cake's a cow pile that's all dried up in the sun.

Struck by the oddity of it, I said, "Then what's a seesaw snake?"

She grinned. "I can't say as I know. I don't think I ever got that part of it, but he was plumb full of jokes and riddles like that." Granny smiled at the childhood memory and grew quiet as the breeze made a peaceful, swishing sound in the tall sage grass that marked the end of the field.

"I was down yonder at Aunt Jessie's when the poor ol' fellow took sick. Aunt Vi had come over real early that mornin' to help get things ready for the quiltin' party. My oldest cousin on that side was fixin' to get married and all the women around were comin' with quilt blocks to start a quilt for her. Aunt Vi brought her two girls, my cousins, and we all sat down to eat breakfast together. We laughed about what happened all day long…'til the ol' fellow got real bad off and it wasn't funny no more. I remember we just had said grace, and I looked across the table at him and I could tell somethin' was wrong with 'im. He was right gray-lookin'.

He'd gotten hard of hearin' and spoke real loud. I can see 'im now. He was settin' over here at the end of the table right next to Aunt Jessie and he cleared his throat and says, 'Now Mrs. Johnson,' —and you could've heard 'im all the way from here to your truck, he says, 'I gotta tell you—I had a misery on my stomach last night, and before I could make it to the outhouse, I got a little shit on your bed—not hardly none a-tall worth mentionin', *just a little shit.*' Well, I thought Aunt Jessie was gonna drop through the floor. She was right prim and proper, and she kindly fussed at 'im for sayin' that at the table. The rest of us thought it was funny, but we knew better than to laugh.

Direc'ly, he said, 'Mrs. Johnson, I'm still feelin' a little puny and if you don't mind, I think I'll go back upstairs and lay down for a spell before I head out." He hadn't no more than left the room before Aunt Jessie started fumin' and fussin'. She said, 'On top of ever'thing else I've got to do, I'll have to go wash his nasty bed sheets.'

Aunt Vi wasn't as partic'lar a housekeeper, but she was plenty clean enough. She said, 'Jessie, he's an old man. He can't help it. You remember how Grandpa Clark got to be.' Aunt Jessie kept goin' on and on about havin' to look after him and finally Aunt Vi said, 'Just hush up about it. If he doesn't get better, I'll take 'im home with me this evenin'.

Aunt Jessie sniffed and said, 'Well, that's fine by me, and you can take his nasty bed sheets with you. I've got all I can say grace over here.' Sure enough, when Aunt Vi got ready to leave, she gathered up the ol' fellow's dirty bed covers later and took 'em home to wash. Me and my cousins stayed that whole day at Aunt Jessie's, and when none of the grownups could hear us, we'd say, '*It's just a little shit,* not hardly none a-tall worth mentionin'.'

The ol' fellow laid in the bed 'til after the quiltin' party and Aunt Vi was ready to leave. Uncle Bill tried to take 'im some dinner and he turned it away. I remember the look on his face when he came into the kitchen with his plate. He told Aunt Jess, he said, 'The poor ol' feller's too weak to pull the foam off his own pee. Just let 'im stay here.' Well that didn't suit her, but Aunt Vi did exactly like she said. She took 'im home with her…fixed 'im broth and such as that but ever'thing kept goin' right on through 'im. The next day, they sent for ol' Doc Witherspoon and I was back over there when he came through the door. He took one look at the ol' peddler and listened to his breathin'. They'd known each other for years. He says, "Mister—he called his name, 'Mister,' he says, 'your peddlin' days are done. You best get word to some of your people to come and take you home.'

And I'll never forget what the ol' fellow said. He looked at Doc Witherspoon and Aunt Vi and said, 'Fordville's as much family as ever I had. *I reckon I am home.*'

Doc stepped out on the porch with Aunt Vi and we tried our best to hear what was said. I don't know what else he told her, but I heard a little of it. He said, 'Well Vi, I'll say this much for Jessie: she knew when to be shed of 'im. It looks like he's all yours now, but I'll do what I can to help you. Send for me if he gets any worse.' Then he turned to face her and said, 'What I mean is, *when* he gets worse.'

132

Aunt Vi sent me home to fetch Mama to come and help with him. She'd sent for Aunt Jessie, but she said she was all whipped out from her big quiltin' party. She said she wasn't signin' up to take care of an in-valid, but that she'd send food over, later.

Well, I didn't tell you this part of it, but this field here belonged to the Tiptons then. It laid between Aunt Vi's place and Aunt Jessie's. I think there's forty some-odd acres in it. Old man Tipton died and neither one of his boys wanted it, so it went up for auction to settle the es-tate. I was there that day and I won't forget it if I live to be a thousand.

The ol' peddler stayed with Aunt Vi and people brought food for him and such, the way neighbors used to do. Mama took a turn, and I went along to play with my cousins. Aunt Vi's youngest girl and I were in the room when he and Uncle Joe started talkin' about old man Tipton and I reckon that's how come the subject came of this field here, and that it was gonna be sold in a few weeks' time. The peddler said, 'Joe, that's the prettiest piece of ground in Fordville. You and Vi ought to buy it." I remember how Uncle Joe laughed. He said, "Uncle Jimmy—that's it...that's what we called 'im...Uncle Jimmy Potts.

I'm glad I finally thought of it. Anyway, Uncle Joe said, 'I couldn't no more buy that field than fly, but I'd sure love to have it. The way it is, I have to rent pasture from the Harrises.'

And I can remember Uncle Joe sayin', 'I just imagin' Brother Bill will wind up with it. He's got the money and it joins him all the way to the main road.'

No more was said, and Uncle Jimmy drifted off to sleep. Me and Minnie were scared half out of our minds when Aunt Vi would send us in to check on 'im. We just knew we'd go in there and find 'im deader'n a hammer. Along about suppertime, then, Aunt Vi brewed some kind of tea for us to take to 'im. I was just a kid but I remember thinkin' the ol' fellow had lost ground since breakfast. Direc'ly, he raised hisself up in that little bed and said to me, 'Honey, go tell Vi I need to see her —*her and Joe both.*"

I could tell from the look on his face it was somethin' important, so Minnie and I waited for Uncle Joe and Aunt Vi to come in the room. He cleared his throat like he was fixin' to make a speech and he said, 'I need for you and Vi to bring my big pack here to me, and lay it down here beside me.' I think he gathered up what little strength he had left just to empty it. He looked at my cousin Minnie and me and said, 'Girls, get one of Vi's quilts and put it down on the floor here --and lay these things on it as I hand 'em to you.' Well, here he commenced emptyin' that pack---just as slow as Christmas…one thing at a time. He had ever'thing in the world in it--- spices…little tools, bottles and jars. He pulled odds and ends out of there for fifteen minutes or better and had us sort it out in little piles. The very last thing he brought out was a little ol' tin can, somethin' like you'd see paint in now, where you have to pry the lid open.

134

Uncle Joe had to use his pocket knife and finally opened it. Lo and behold, if there wasn't a wad of cash big enough to choke an ox—all rolled up, real tight. I'd never seen that much money in one place in my life.

Uncle Jimmy said, 'Joe, my eyes are bad. I need for you to help me count this money out.'

"I can't remember exactly how much it came to, but seems like it was seven hundred and some-odd dollars. Aunt Vi put it all back in that little can and started to hand it back to 'im. He waved her away, like this," she said, demonstrating. 'Keep it' he said, 'There's somethin' I want you to do for me. I'm fixin' to die and I want you all to see that I'm buried at the end of that field--up yonder, under that big white oak. I've loved that spot since the first time I saw it."

He said, 'Vi, you and Joe have looked after me, so when that field's sold I want you to buy it. From what Joe says, there ought to be enough money there to do it after you pay for my coffin and a headstone. This is what I want for you all to do: I want you to buy that field for *me*, but put it in *your name*.' Then he kindly laughed, and said, 'I won't be needin' no deed to it, where I'm goin.'

I could tell Uncle Joe didn't really want to do it. He turned to look at Aunt Vi and shook his head back and forth—like this. Aunt Vi could tell what he was thinkin' and told Uncle Jimmy that they'd see to it that his money got to some of his people instead, but then, Uncle Jimmy said it again-- that Fordville *was* his people. And you know, to this day, I

135

don't know where he came from or if he even had any family.

I think he thought they were gonna turn 'im down and the poor ol' feller started to tear up. I think that's what changed Uncle Joe's mind. He said, 'Children,' he said it just like that—'Children, you surely won't deny a dyin' man his last request.' Aunt Vi was tender hearted and she was about to cry by then. She shook her head and says, 'No, Uncle Jimmy, we'll do it.' He said, 'Well, good. And I ain't done, neither--I got one more favor to ask you…Joe,' he says, 'When you all bury me up there, I want you to step off a piece of ground for a graveyard—and put me in the middle of it. I'm thinkin' about an acre ought to do it. That-away, anybody around here can be buried there if they want to be. Fordville's been good to me and I want to return the favor.'

After that, he said, "Let's shake on it, then.' I remember how he reached up for Uncle Joe's hand— put one hand over top of his, like this—here. Then he reached up for Aunt Vi's hand and said, 'Pray for me, Vi.' Well, she was a mess after that—tried to cook supper and nearly burnt ever'thing.

Then Uncle Jimmy asked Minnie to find a piece of paper and he had me cut it up into ten or twelve little pieces. He called out the names of some of his old customers and had me write 'em down on the pieces of paper, and told Minnie what little piles of goods to lay 'em on.

He handed me a shiny little child's drinkin' cup with a little rabbit on the handle, a tin whistle and I'm thinkin' a little music box of a thing that didn't work no more…then he

136

reached a couple more things to my cousin Minnie and she laid 'em in the same pile I'd started. Direc'ly, he said, 'Go get the other children and each one of you can go through this last pile here and pick out a play-pretty or somethin' else you want." Well, I wanted that whistle so bad I could taste it. When I reached for it, Ida May decided she had to have it. *Anything* I wanted, she had to have.

She started cryin' and Aunt Vi came back in the room and whispered, 'Lorene honey, you're too big for any of this stuff here.' It kindly made me mad. I wasn't too old to blow a whistle. She said, 'Let the younger ones pick what they want. Ida May can go first since she's the youngest, and then the rest of you take your turn.'

Naturally, Ida May took my whistle. I was the oldest, so I went last and wound up with the tin cup and it galled me for the rest of that day. Just for spite, ever' chance she got, Ida May would blow that whistle in my face. The more I thought about it, the madder I got and when she went to sleep that night, I tiptoed over to her dresser in our room and grabbed the thing. I hid it, hopin' she'd be mad as fire the next mornin', but she never even noticed it was gone. If I hadn't wanted it, she wouldn't have given it a second glance."

Once more, Granny said, "That's just the way she is."

Since my ten year old observation of my distant great aunt across the river, I'd come to an adult understanding of that complicated relationship, one born of a thousand small injuries. Whenever Ida May's name was mentioned—

which wasn't often, the words "spoiled rotten" were usually close by.

Granny continued her story of the dying peddler.

"We left Aunt Vi's house after supper that evenin' and they said Uncle Jimmy died early the next mornin'--just as the sun was comin' up. Uncle Bill and Uncle Joe made his coffin and Aunt Vi lined it...stayed up half the night doin' it so they could get 'im buried. They didn't have embalmin' here then and on account of it bein' warm weather, they needed to get 'im put in the ground right quick. I remember ridin' with Daddy over to see the Tiptons to ask 'em if they'd let Uncle Jimmy be buried here—and took 'em two little bags of peppermint sticks. That's what Uncle Jimmy had put in their pile. He said that peppermint candy was the first sale he made when he came to Fordville—to the "Tipton boys"—and they seemed like old men to me. He'd never forgotten that, 'So this here's on me,' he said...bless his ol' heart. He never forgot anything anybody ever did for 'im.

The auction was prob'ly a month or so after Uncle Jimmy died, and I went with Daddy since I knew my cousins would all be there—Aunt Vi's and Aunt Jessie's. And the way this land lays, there weren't too many people that could benefit from it. Uncle Bill thought he was gonna get it for a song--and sing it hisself. Nobody knew Aunt Vi and Uncle Joe had the money to buy it. They'd kept quiet and dared us kids to breathe a word. I didn't know this part of it 'til the auction day came, but Aunt Jessie had been pesterin' Uncle Bill about buyin' it and buildin' 'em a new house—right here where we're standin'. She was the kind that wasn't never satisfied...always had to have somethin' better.

So, the day of the sale finally came, and I remember the auctioneer climbin' up on the back of a hay wagon at the bottom of the field near the main road. He read the deed description of it—how big it was and who all joined it. He started cryin' the sale then, and direc'ly somebody made a bid and for a little while it looked like it was gonna go for nothin'. Then Uncle Bill and Aunt Jessie kindly stepped forward to make a bid. They were standin' right together, side by side. Well, then here comes Uncle Joe and Aunt Vi, standin' right across from 'em—just like they were fixin' to have a square dance, and Uncle Joe makes a bid. I can see Uncle Joe holdin' up his one good hand—way up high—like this here—kindly wavin' it back and forth. Oh my land o' livin', he was proud to make that bid. Then Uncle Bill made another bid, and so on. Well, the biddin' kept goin' back and forth between 'em—just them. I can't remember now what Daddy said this land was worth, but they went past that amount—and kept goin'. The bid got way up yonder, and I remember several old men shakin' their heads at Uncle Joe and Uncle Bill, like they were both foolish. There they were brothers, and standin' there with their arms crossed like they were fixin' to fight. I don't know why the two of 'em couldn't have worked somethin' out. Uncle Joe didn't need this much pasture. And so far as that goes, Aunt Jessie didn't need that much land for a new house.

It was hot as blazes that day so the auctioneer stopped to take a drink of water. All of a sudden Aunt Jessie hollered over at Aunt Vi. She says, 'Vi, just how much more are you all gonna bid?' Aunt Vi said, 'Not much, Jess—just a dollar more than you.' Well, ever'body there got a big laugh out of that. To tell the truth, I think it kindly embarrassed her and Uncle Bill got plumb mad over it. He said. 'Jessie, we're goin' to the house' and off they headed back home in a big huff. When the auctioneer got goin' again, there wasn't another bid made, not one. Uncle Joe and Aunt Vi bought it fair and square, and that was big talk around Fordville for a while. Ever'body wanted to know how they got their hands on that much money…"and him a cripple," they'd say. When word got around where the money come from, some of their neighbors were jealous. For a while there, a rumor went around that they'd just taken it from Uncle Jimmy when he died. But…like all things do, it passed. The gossip died down, but it was a sad time for us kids, after that auction.

Aunt Jessie was so mad about not gettin' to build her a new house that she quit speakin' to Aunt Vi or Uncle Joe either one…even quit goin' to church for a long time. She wouldn't let my cousins go over there anymore to play with Aunt Vi's kids, and I hated it so bad I quit goin' to see 'em."

Looking at the sisters' graves situated so close together, I said, "It looks like they made up, eventually."

Granny nodded, "They finally did."

"How?"

Granny sighed wearily.

140

"Well, it's sad to say, but it took somebody dyin' to do it. Aunt Vi had some kind of problem with her bowels…I can't think now what they called back then, but nobody thought it was real serious. Whatever it was, she'd had a bad spell with it and Aunt Jessie knew, but she still never went over to see about her. There was a woman that went to church with us…Effie was her name…Effie Wilburn. She had a son named Forrest that was in my grade at school. Their family ran a dairy and she was a great big stout woman…milked I don't know how many cows ever' day of her life. I think she'd already given birth to eight or ten children and they nearly filled up two whole pews at church. Anyhow, she got in the family way about the time most women were goin' through The Change, and nobody thought much about it. Well, she went into labor too early. It was late one night and they said she was doin' fine but then she had a heart attack —and died. The baby died, too. She and Aunt Vi were just a few days apart in age and early the next mornin' the church bell started ringin' down at that little Methodist Church in Fordville—tellin' ever'body there was a death. When that happened, people would stop what they were doin' to count the tolls: one ring for each year of the person's age—and it stopped at the exact same age that Aunt Vi was at the time—forty somethin'. Aunt Jessie was bakin' a cake when the tollin' started—just had shut the oven door, and when it stopped she said to my cousin, Hallie—that was her daughter, 'Oh my Lord, it's Vi. *She's dead.*' Honey, they tore out of that house in a dead run, headed through this field here toward Aunt Vi's-- and it was wintertime. Hallie said Aunt Jessie never even grabbed a coat. What made it worse was that when she got

141

closer to Aunt Vi and Uncle Joe's house she saw three or four men standin' on the porch, talkin'. I forget what they were there for, but it she was sure that Aunt Vi had died and the neighbors had started gatherin' in.

Hallie said by the time they reached the house, Aunt Jessie was plumb out of breath and bawlin' like a baby, all the way up to the front porch. Uncle Joe saw her comin' toward 'im in a hurry, so he took off, runnin' toward her, hollerin', 'Jessie, what on earth's the matter?' She said, 'That bell's tollin' for Vi ain't it?' Uncle Bill said, 'Lord no, Jessie—she ain't feelin' the best, but she's putterin' around in the kitchen. We ain't heard who they're tollin' the bell for.'

Well, I reckon Aunt Jessie ran into the house and nearly knocked Aunt Vi down huggin' her.

'I want my sister back, I want my sister back,'…where she was out of breath, that's all she could say—over and over."

Granny grew silent, looking at the distant farmhouse of her dead sister. She produced a forced smile, but I knew the sound of pain in her voice. "I'm not gettin' mine back."

There was nothing I could say. Thinking the tale was told, I placed my hand on the ignition, preparing to leave.

Granny cleared her throat. With a chuckle, she said, "They got back together, them two. We were all glad of it.

Aunt Jessie stayed there with Aunt Vi the rest of that mornin' and the cake she'd left in the oven burnt completely up. She'd forgotten all about it. Uncle Bill came

142

in for dinner and the house was full of smoke. Hallie said that burnt smell never left Aunt Jessie's kitchen 'til spring, but she got her sister back. The two of 'em made up that day, and when they got word about Effie Wilburn, the two of 'em went to work—together, cookin' food to send to her family."

"Did they get along all right after that?"

"Well, for a while—'til a year or two after that-- when Grandma Clark died and they had a fallin' out over her dishes...or were *fixin' to*."

Puzzled, I said, *"Fixing to?"*

Granny nodded. "Now that was funny. The mornin' Aunt Vi and Aunt Jessie came to divide 'em up, that big old two piece hutch Grandma kept 'em in fell over and broke the biggest part of 'em. Mama was out on the porch talkin' to Aunt Vi, waitin' on Aunt Jessie to show up. Daddy was tired of bein' in the middle of their bickerin', so he and Harry Winston tried to pull the hutch away from the wall without unloadin' it first, and where it was topheavy and the floor wasn't level, it just pitched right over. You never saw such a mess...two bushel baskets of broken dishes."

Granny chuckled, "To tell you the truth, I always felt like Daddy done it on purpose to teach 'em a lesson."

It was a story that put a welcomed smile on Granny's face, one that I was glad to see that day.

She said, "You know, I came across Mama's old sewin' box last year. I was goin' through it and found that whistle

I took away from Ida May, the one she claimed out of Uncle Jimmy's peddlin' goods. I put that sewin' box away in the attic after Mama died in '44, but I have no idea how that whistle got in there."

And then, in a rare nod to something bordering the supernatural, she said, "I know I've gotten things out of it since then, but when I saw that whistle, it was almost like... Mama was tellin' me to..." Granny didn't finish the thought.

 As I started the truck, Granny's eyes were still fixed on the scene across the river. She sighed, "Now, I'd give anything if I could give it back to her."

I could count on two hands the number of times I ever saw my great-aunt Ida May—and that includes my childhood sighting of her from across the river. Still, Granny's words stung.

As I backed the truck into the field to turn, the thought occurred to me that I couldn't even remember the two of them talking on the phone, though she said they had—only to relay news of a death in the family. "You were prob'ly at school when I called her."

I said, "I know it takes an hour to get to Ida May's from here, but both of you had telephones...for years. Why didn't you call each other every once in a while?"

A look of horror came over her. "*Clay, it's a long-distance call over there. You know we ain't made of money.*"

I had learned by then that forgiveness is a work in progress—a journey. Some days it's two steps forward and one step back. Other days, it's just two steps back.

In coming to terms with loss—with forgiveness and regrets, Granny traveled over a lot of emotional territory that day. Decades of baggage had been opened. Some of it was clean, pressed and ready to be put away. Dirty laundry had been sorted. Clearly, some things never made it to the washing machine.

The stone gallon jug above the kitchen cabinets

A Harvest of Dandelions

It is a thousand wonders the stone jug survived that cool April morning.

But I'm glad it did.

Because it did survive, I experienced an awakening of sorts-- something akin to puberty, without the awkward locker room comparisons. You might call it a puberty of awareness...of history, of people mostly dead and forgotten and the dust-covered objects they left behind.

Although I learned something about the jug that day, I have learned a great deal more *from* it. In the way only a cracked, forgotten stone jug could, it spoke to me. I know this sounds weird, but it's spoken to me ever since.

For Granny, April meant spring cleaning. However, this spring cleaning detail was to be no ordinary "haul everything out of the room, top to bottom scrub down." This was to be a cleaning tale of epic proportions, and for me, containing elements of a Greek tragedy: the emptying of a century-old farm building and the destruction of most of its contents.

The focus of our attention was the old log smokehouse on Granny's farm, located behind the house and above the garden. Unpainted, its earth-tone shades of gray made it appear less man-made and as much a part of the natural world as the sky above it. For easy access to the garden, we hung our hoes and rakes beneath its overhanging roof, but I had never seen most of what was inside--not that it was forbidden, just forgotten. If Fordville ever had its own version of King Tut's tomb, Granny's smokehouse was it, minus all the valuable stuff.

Eager to be done with the dreaded chore, right after breakfast Granddaddy started a small fire in the field just behind the smokehouse. My job was to keep the fire burning with debris carried from the shadows of the old building's dark and dank interior. Granny somehow got the idea that it could collapse at any time and leave yet a bigger mess to clean up. It stood for another twenty years.

The windowless structure had an aura about it-- an unwelcoming presence that seemed to whisper, "I'm old and tired. Let me rot in peace." The pungent musty smell of smoked fat meat and decay met us at the plank door, green with mold and rotten at the bottom. Unable to guard its colorless inventory any longer, the old door pulled loose from its top hinge and fell off to the side, as if to say "I surrender."

To an unknowing fourteen-year-old, the rotting logs housed a wall-to-wall assortment of nondescript junk that now would be a treasure to me.

By noon, the building's interior was emptied of anything combustible except for what I now call the Smokehouse Survivors: the walnut four-post spool bed, one of the tops of which had been shot off by Granny's drunken great-uncle, and an unusually wide, homemade ladder back chair suspended from pegs in the eave near the roof. The bed only *survived* because it started raining after lunch and we propped its headboard and footboard against the one non-leaning wall. The handmade chair was luckily out of reach. Hung upside down, high-up against the back wall, it required a ladder from the barn to reach. Granddaddy said we'd bring it on our return trip from the house after dinner. Its future then tied to that of the condemned bed, both pieces were granted a stay of execution by an unexpected turn of the weather.

A gentle spring shower began as we ate our noon meal, and Granny decided that the mission would have to be interrupted. She said we'd return to it later that afternoon when the weather cleared. Thankfully, the rain set in for the day, and the rest of the burning was postponed indefinitely. But still remaining was the task of cleaning the inside of the smokehouse.

While the rain reduced the fire to a smoldering heap of gray ashes, I tossed buckets of hot soapy water onto the walls and floor for Granny to sweep out using a stubbled straw broom that was too good to throw away just yet. Although she was concerned about the old log structure falling in, she felt compelled to see that it was clean and presentable when it chose to do so.

Sweeping the water from under a low shelf against the wall where it pooled on the sagging floor, I felt the broom hitting something in the dark corner.

That's when I discovered the stone jug.

It was nothing special, just an old stone jug covered in dust and cobwebs. Part of a snakeskin had gotten stuck to Granny's broom-stub as I pulled the jug into the dim light and its former resident was nowhere in sight.

"What about this old jug?" I asked.

Granny gently took it from my hands and took it to the doorway where she could see it in better light.

Wiping away the dust, she said, "That was Aunt Mollie's. She used to keep dandelion wine in it, bless her ol' heart."

Pointing toward the house, she said, "Just take it to the kitchen, and I'll find a place for it direc'ly."

As she returned to sweeping the walls down, Granny said, speaking to no one in particular, "…Poor ol' Aunt Mollie."

I'd heard her make that kind of comment many times before and would've thought no more of it had the jug not found its way next to the coal heat stove in the kitchen.

By suppertime, Granny had washed the sole survivor of the smokehouse purge and set it down on the floor temporarily, awaiting placement elsewhere. Elsewhere wound up being on the floor next to the dresser in my room to save pennies in.

We were finishing supper when I asked Granny about her Aunt Mollie Moore. More to the point, I wanted to know just why Granny wanted to bless her heart every time she held the jug.

Granny sighed as she began gently turning her coffee cup in its saucer, using both hands. I observed that she sometimes did so as she was thinking, recalling people and events; the more bittersweet the memory, the more the cup turned. If the tale had elements of personal shame or embarrassment for her, the turns either picked up tempo *or* stopped altogether.

"Aunt Mollie was Mama's oldest sister. I loved her dearly, and she loved me…but she was prob'ly the saddest one woman I ever knew.

But she loved company. My lord, how she loved company--and people…..but nobody much went to see her. My mother, her own sister, didn't want us to be around her, but I'd still slip off once in a while and go over there anyway.

She'd be so glad to see me she'd tear up a little. And then, she cried again when I left."

Granny stared at the jug.

"Aunt Mollie made dandelion wine, and she drank a right smart lot of it." Nodding toward the jug, she said, "There was still some in it when she died. It was settin' on her kitchen table that very day, and got left in the house. After we bought that place, I found it on the bottom of a big cupboard she had on the back porch, where one of her stepson's wives had put it.

When I was just a girl and we'd go over to Big Granny's, sometimes I'd slip off and go up to Aunt Mollie's. Mama didn't let us go, but sometimes there were so many of us to gather at Big Granny's, she never missed me. In the springtime, she'd get a big basket and say, "Lorene honey, come help me gather up some dandelion flowers." Granny chuckled, "She meant the blossoms—that's what she used to make her wine, but she'd call 'em flowers. And to this day, even after they've bloomed and turned white, I still can't bring myself to dislike 'em. I think of Aunt Mollie...and I just let 'em be."

The turning of the cup stopped briefly as Granny looked straight ahead--out the kitchen window as if she expected Aunt Mollie Moore to pull up in the driveway. In a few seconds, she began turning the cup again slowly, but in the opposite direction.

Listening to Granny tell the story was like watching her unfold one of her beloved quilts. Carefully, respectfully,

151

she explained each "pattern" and "stitch" with appropriate, almost reverent pauses. And, in a figurative sense, she painfully revealed some bad stitching and a few permanent stains.

The cup stopped turning.

"It's a complicated story," she said.

"Aunt Mollie…was the prettiest woman I think I ever saw…and maybe the saddest. Your granddaddy got halfway mad at me when Lucy Taylor and I paid a dollar apiece years ago to see *Gone With the Wind* at the State Theatre in Harriston. And let me tell you, as pretty as she was, Scarlet O'Hara didn't have a thing on Aunt Mollie. The fact is she reminded me a lot of Aunt Mollie. I'll show you her picture sometime."

I wish she had done so then. To this day, even after Granny's glowing description, I'm not sure what Aunt Mollie looked like.

"Aunt Mollie was the oldest in the family and there were six children. Five girls, and then Uncle Archie was the baby and the only boy. My grandfather and my grandmother—we called *her* 'Big Granny'--were poor people. He was a great big man—any way you could measure him, and could work as much as any two men. They were tenants on Uncle Cy Moore's place. I never laid eyes on my grandfather but from what I've always heard, he was a good man. They just struggled to survive but they got lucky when Uncle Cy and his first wife asked Grandfather to come to their place to work for 'em. There was a good solid tenant house way down on the branch below Uncle Cy's place, and that's where they lived. It wasn't very big, but it was a far cry better than what they were used to. Grandfather worked on the farm and Uncle Cy was good to him and that whole family. His first wife was some kin to Grandfather, but I can't remember just how. Then one day in the fall, they had what they called a bush-hackin', a workin' I guess you'd call it, in the woods on Uncle Cy's place where he was clearin' off a piece of new ground. Men and boys brought their sleds and wagons to clear brush and cut wood to burn. Women brought food or cooked things outdoors while the men worked. They said when it came to the splittin' part, Grandfather was runnin' way ahead of the rest of 'em, even younger men. Then all of a sudden he told Uncle Cy he needed to go set down in the shade and rest for a minute. Uncle Cy handed 'im a water jug and Grandfather set down under that big maple— I've seen that old tree many a time. Anyway, he set hisself down in the shade with his axe across his lap this-away to rest. Then they said he yelled at Uncle Cy and some of those younger men sayin' he'd catch his breath for a few minutes and they still wouldn't be caught up. Them was the last words he ever spoke. After fifteen or twenty minutes they said Uncle Cy hollered at Grandfather and he didn't answer. He ran over to where Grandfather was and there he sat, deader'n a hammer with that axe layin' across his lap. My cousin Norris has the axe.

That was a big shock to the family, but Uncle Cy was good hearted and he let Big Granny and her children stay right where they were, on his farm. He told her they could stay on 'til he found another tenant and then he'd try to help 'em find another place. Then, it wasn't long before Uncle Cy's first wife got sick and needed help in the kitchen. Lavinia! That was her name—it finally come to me. Uncle Cy came down on horseback to that little tenant house on his land and asked Big Granny if one of the older girls might be willin' to come and stay up at the big house with them and help in the kitchen with the housework and such.

I don't know that Aunt Mollie knew any better. She was just about sem'teen or eighteen, and pretty as a speckled pup. She had no more idea what she was gettin' herself into than a hog knows when Sunday comes. Big Granny knew better, but I reckon...maybe...she was just tryin' to survive after Grandfather died and the only way she knew how was to help Uncle Cy with whatever he wanted.

She shouldn't have, but Big Granny allowed Aunt Mollie to go. She gathered up what few things she had to take with her, and moved up to Uncle Cy's house to look after Lavinia. They just had one child at home by that time, the youngest son. The other two were grown and on their own, when she took sick.

Aunt Mollie thought a whole lot of Lavinia, and she took a likin' to Aunt Mollie. They got along real well. Lavinia showed her how to run the kitchen to suit her and really showed her how to cook the way they were used to eatin'. Better than Aunt Mollie and Mama were raised on, I can tell you. By and by, though, Lavinia kept gettin' weaker...and sicker, and the day came when she took to her bed...her death bed, as the sayin' goes.

I think that's when Uncle Cy's eye started wanderin', if it hadn't already." Granny paused here as she was dancing around the edge of the *Forbidden Subject.*

Now don't get me wrong. Uncle Cy was a *good* man. He spoke the truth, honest in his dealin's. He was a hard worker, and a good provider. I reckon most people would've called 'im an upstandin' citizen. He was deacon in our church and such as that. But, when it's all said and done, *he was still a man.*

By and by, Aunt Mollie was tendin' to Lavinia, and runnin' the kitchen, and Uncle Cy got struck on Aunt Mollie. Well, Lavinia died and after the funeral, Uncle Cy's daughter in laws came in and took over the kitchen and helped out thataway. Aunt Mollie packed her few things and went back home, down to the tenant house where Big Granny and the rest of the children lived.

Mama was just a girl but she was old enough to figure out what was goin' on. She said Aunt Mollie hadn't been home for three or four days when Uncle Cy came ridin' up on his big bay horse, dressed in his Sunday best, and Lavinia hadn't much more than gotten cold in the grave.

He asked to speak to Big Granny first, and then he talked with Aunt Mollie and asked her to marry him. There he was old enough to be her father and then some. All three of his sons were older than Aunt Mollie, but there he was, well-set with that good farm. And, there Big Granny was--no man, nowhere to go and six children to feed. She had family around Fordville, but they weren't any better off than she was, and some of them weren't doin' *as well.*

Truth be told, Big Granny kindly forced Aunt Mollie into marryin' Uncle Cy, just to take care of her family. Old Judge Turley married 'em in his front parlor and Aunt Mollie moved into Uncle Cy's house as his lawfully wedded wife. His sons and their wives like to have had a conniption fit over him marryin' so soon, and to a poor tenant girl on top of that. But, I reckon Uncle Cy just told 'em he'd do as he pleased. I think the words Mama used was that he told his boys that he was "free and twenty-one and didn't have to answer to nobody."

So, Big Granny finished raisin' her family right there in that little house on Uncle Cy's place. On account of her bein' Aunt Mollie's mother, Uncle Cy just let the family stay there right on. He was good to Big Granny's family…butchered two or three big hogs for 'em every fall. He saw to it that they had plenty of firewood split and put away in the woodshed. Now that is the truth. Uncle Cy kept 'em all fed and saw to it that my youngest uncle, Aunt Mollie's baby brother, Uncle Archie, got a little education. That's where Big Granny lived when I was born…lived there 'til she died. It's untellin' what would've become of 'em if Aunt Mollie *hadn't* married Uncle Cy, but she sure paid the price--in more ways than one.

Uncle Cy never had but one fault that I ever heard tell of, and it's a bad'n to have; *he was insanely jealous*--crazy jealous. I never heard this 'til I was grown, but Uncle Cy's first wife, Lavinia, had a sister that was married to an old man we called Uncle Taylor. Uncle Taylor and Uncle Cy, his brother-in-law at the time, was gettin' ready to go fox huntin'. The sisters, their wives were sittin' on that front porch there where Uncle Cy and Lavinia lived. I heard Uncle Taylor tell this out of his own mouth when he was a white bearded old man. He said he and Uncle Cy were just gettin' ready to go on the hunt, walkin' toward Uncle Cy's barn to saddle their horses. He went to the porch to kiss his wife goodbye and her sister, Lavinia, was just jokin', and said, 'Why Taylor ain't you gonna kiss me too?'" Uncle Cy had stepped onto the back porch to get hisself a drink from a bucket of water and was comin' up alongside the porch when he saw what happened next. I don't think Lavinia knew Uncle Cy was standin' that close by or she wouldn't have even joked that-away, but Uncle Taylor just played along, leaned over and gave Lavinia a peck on the cheek.

I reckon Uncle Cy didn't like it one little bit but he didn't do nothin' right then. They walked over to the gate. Well…they didn't have gates much in them days, just bars or poles across the lane. They got to that bar in front of the house where the lane came up from the barn, and Uncle Cy hauled off and hit Uncle Taylor without ever sayin' a word—sent him to the ground with one blow. They got into a regular knock down-drag out, right there in front of the house. The sisters came runnin', hollerin' like everything to get 'em to stop. They did quit, finally, and Uncle Cy said if Uncle Taylor ever did anything like that again, they'd have to lay him out in two pieces at his funeral.

Well, that ended the foxhunt. But, so far as anybody around here ever knew, that was the only episode like that. And it seemed so odd that, when most people heard about it, they just gave Uncle Cy the benefit of the doubt.

But then, by and by, Uncle Cy's sons married off and had their own farms to work, so he needed another tenant, a man to help him on his place. After Grandfather had died a few years before, when Uncle Cy's boys were still livin' at home, he'd hired day workers to help him, first one then another. Then somebody told him about Frank McWilliams. Frank had worked for some of Uncle Cy's people that had died and he was needin' work. So, Uncle Cy hired him on. Frank was about the same age as Uncle Cy's middle boy, and he started eatin' dinner every day with Uncle Cy and Aunt Mollie. Um-mm…she was too young to be married to Uncle Cy. I reckon you can kindly figure out the rest of it."

Granny paused again.

"Well, maybe you're too young to understand what I'm gettin' at, but there was a big difference in their ages…Uncle Cy and Aunt Mollie."

Uh-oh. The *Forbidden Subject* was near again.

The cup began another slow rotation. This time, in the other direction.

"Ten or fifteen years'd gone by since Aunt Mollie and Uncle Cy married, and he was gettin' along in years by then. Frank McWilliams and Aunt Mollie was about the same age, had the same friends and such…so the first thing you know, they started talkin' a lot. Aunt Mollie just loved people, and I don't think she ever pushed herself on him, but somethin' got started between the two of 'em. Uncle Cy got suspicious, but from what Aunt Mollie told me, it didn't take much for that to happen.

Uncle Cy confronted Frank with it one day down at the springhouse. Aunt Mollie'd made some of her fresh oatmeal lemonade and it sounds awful, but it was THE best stuff to drink when you were hot and thirsty. Too much trouble for me to fool with, but it's good. She took a big glass of it down to Frank at that old springhouse where Uncle Cy had him workin' on the shingle roof. Uncle Cy'd let on like he was goin' to Fordville and would be gone all afternoon; but then he came back shortly to see if he could catch 'em together. Then, sure enough he came upon 'em, and heard 'em laughin' and carryin' on. They were just talkin' and havin' a good time. Uncle Cy and Frank had a big ruckus and then Aunt Mollie said she came between the two of 'em. I reckon Uncle Cy ran Frank off, and told 'im to never set foot again on his property. But, as those things go, there was somethin' between him and Aunt Mollie. Uncle Cy suspicioned it, and he sent word to Frank's mother in Fordville that if she wanted her son to live, she'd better get him to leave this county AND QUICK. Frank wasn't no coward, but I think his mother just flat-out begged him to go somewhere. A few days later, he told her and some of his friends that he was headed out to Missouri. He had kinfolks out there, he said, and he was gonna go live with them for a while.

Ever'body in Fordville heard about what happened between him and Uncle Cy…and Aunt Mollie. But the thing is, Uncle Cy *was well thought of, all over this county.*

Nobody here would ever question him runnin' off a man that tried to takin' his wife away from 'im."

Granny propped her glasses, and said, "I don't know how many times I've heard that sayin' over the years--that some man took another man's wife away from him, and it never seemed to matter if *she* wanted to go.

But anyway, Frank left, and I reckon he went someplace. Maybe it was to Missouri or in that direction anyway. I never knew that part of it. Some people said he never went any further than you could swing a mule by the tail. Others said he stayed in Fayette County with some of his daddy's people.

One way or another, things cooled down for a while-six months, maybe longer. Then one day Uncle Cy was handed a letter to read that he shouldn't have.

Old man Thompson Wilkins was the postmaster in Fordville at that time. He and Uncle Cy were big buddies. They were both Masons, deacons in the church and such as that. One day he saw a letter come through addressed to Aunt Mollie, and to beat all if he didn't open it, and him the postmaster! It was a letter from Frank McWilliams tellin' Aunt Mollie what day and time he'd be comin' back to Fordville, and for her to meet 'im behind the distillery warehouse.

Mr. Wilkins gave that letter to Uncle Cyd so on that particular day, maybe a month later when he came in to Fordville, Uncle Cy was there to meet Frank instead of Aunt Mollie. Uncle Cy was waitin' for him, armed and ready, and had been nearly all day. In broad open daylight, Uncle Cy met Frank in the middle of the road in Fordville. There in front of where Perry Guinn's gas station is now, he shot Frank right between his eyes and he fell on his back, right in the road—and then kept shootin' 'til he emptied his revolver.

Uncle Preston was there when all this happened and saw ever' bit of it. He'd tell that tale and it's hard to believe any man could've been that cold-blooded. Frank's own mother came up on the little crowd that gathered around him, and she thought he had gone out to Missouri. Some of the men held her back, to keep her from seein' Frank like that. I've heard Mack Perkins say his daddy sent him out there with two big buckets of water to wash the blood out of the road, there was so much of it."

Granny grew quiet as we finished our coffee. A part of her quilt had been unfolded, the corner with permanent stains that she didn't want displayed.

"What happened to Mollie's husband?"

"They took Uncle Cy to jail but his friends posted his bond that very day, 'til he was held over by the grand jury. They never even handed down an indictment against 'im. I was just a young girl when all that happened but I remember very well—Big Granny, Mama, and all of 'em, cryin' and carryin' on over how Aunt Mollie had ruined the family name.

Frank's mother and several other people blamed Mr. Wilkins, the postmaster. He knew better, and by rights he should've lost his job over that. If he hadn't opened that letter, Frank might've lived. It's hard to say what might've been, but my Daddy always felt like Mr. Wilkins had some of Frank McWilliams' blood on his hands.

I think life pretty much ended that day for Aunt Mollie. But...she lived on just the same." Granny sighed heavily through her nose.

"She just dropped out of livin'...quit goin' to church— pretty much quit comin' around Fordville altogether. So far as I know, she never darkened the church door again. Uncle Cy went ever' Sunday just like nothin' had happened, but Aunt Mollie stayed home. Ever'body talked bad about her, about what a bad thing she'd done to disgrace Uncle Cy and her whole family. They said Uncle Cy took Aunt Mollie in, and looked after Big Granny and the other children when they didn't have a pot to...pee in, or a window to pitch it out of. They said that's how she thanked him--by takin' up with another man. "

She sighed, "But...as bad it was for her, I reckon it could've been worse;
Uncle Cy didn't run her off--or her family--and a lot of men would've, back in them days. And strange as it sounds, Aunt Mollie stayed right there by his side. With just the two of 'em there in that big house, I don't know how they stood it. But, she took care of him when he got down sick, and stayed with him 'til he died. And Uncle Cy took care of Aunt Mollie in a roundabout way. I think the words he wrote in his will were that Aunt Mollie could live on that farm 'as long as she remains my widow and lives discreetly'. And Uncle Cy's grown sons were to make sure

she did. Aunt Mollie couldn't hardly raise a turnip in her garden, without them givin' her permission. They watched her like a hawk, accordin' to what she told me—their wives more than the boys. Women are funny that-away. Aunt Mollie never had children of her own and if she did remarry, she had to move off the farm, and take Big Granny and the rest of the family with her. Uncle Cy's boys couldn't stand Aunt Mollie's family, so I have no doubt they would've run 'em all off if Aunt Mollie had remarried. I remember one time helpin' her pickin' dandelions in that big front yard. She had this big willow basket that she gathered 'em in—the flower part of it now, not the greens, and *that's* what she used to make her wine with. After we'd filled her basket all the way up to the handle, she held it up at eye-leve—like this here-- and she said, '*Some people call 'em weeds, but these dandelions are the only things on this whole place I can call mine.*' And it *was* the truth. Prac'ly ever' move the poor ol' thing made was controlled by somebody else and always had been. First, it was Big Granny, then Uncle Cy, and his boys took over after he died. Aunt Mollie had no life what-so-ever after Uncle Cy killed Frank McWilliams…none a-tall.

After all that happened, her own mother, Big Granny, wouldn't even go around her, and if it hadn't been for Aunt Mollie she would've been in a world of hurt. She gave up livin' her own life just for them. Big Granny and her other children that was still at home lived on Aunt Mollie's farm 'til the day she died, and never wanted for nothin'.

I know for a fact Aunt Mollie kept an account at Perkins' Store and *anything Big Granny needed* went on her bill…I've been with her and heard her tell ol' Mr. Perkins' to 'put this on Mollie's account.' She and both my aunts did that and sure enough, Aunt Mollie'd go down there to pay the store bill ever' fall when the tobacco was sold and Uncle Cy's boys paid her so much for her part. One time, I remember hearin' Aunt Mollie say that her store bill had gotten up higher than it ought to be, so she'd do without certain things to make up the difference on account of it bein' a bad crop year. Uncle Cy's boys only gave her so much money ever' year, accordin' to Uncle Cy's will, and that's *all* she got to live on. And you know, to this day, I don't ever remember hearin' a member of Aunt Mollie's family give her any credit for all she'd done for 'em. It was just expected.

Even when we were children, Mama wouldn't take us to see Aunt Mollie, but if we had a big Sunday dinner at Big Granny's and there was a lot of people there, I'd slip off and go anyway. But then, when I got grown and could do as I pleased, me and your granddaddy would stop by there ever' time we drove from here back to Babylon, where we lived when we first married.

I think she was the most lonesome person I ever knew. She was so glad to have anybody visit, her face would light up like a candle every time we stopped there; she would nearly beg us to stay and have dinner. Aunt Mollie was kindly a…marked woman. Hardly anybody came around to see her unless they had to. She didn't go anywhere much, but when she did go into Harriston, or even into Fordville, there were some women that wouldn't even speak to her, people she had known and loved all her life. I've been with

164

her and I saw it with my own eyes: some women would walk across the street to keep from havin' to say anything to her. You can just imagine what some of the men folks thought."

I think this is one time Granny really forgot herself. Lost in the tale, she unfolded a soiled part of the memory quilt she otherwise wouldn't have.

Granny said, "Aunt Mollie and I were close, and I never asked her about Uncle Cy, but ever' now and then she'd talk about how jealous a man he'd been, a controllin' kind of man. That's the one thing she warned me against before I ever married, or even started courtin' your granddaddy. Nobody else knew it like she did. Maybe his first wife, Lavinia, did but she was dead and gone. Not too awful long before she died, Aunt Mollie told me that Uncle Cy was so jealous of her when they first married, that he'd mark her in a certain way before he went out into the fields to work."

"*Mark her*?" I asked

Then, Granny sort of came to herself, caught herself, you might say.

She was embarrassed, *and I loved it.*

"Well, he just *did somethin'*...to her body...so he'd know if...any other man had (longest pause here) been around Aunt Mollie while he was gone."

She dropped her head.

"No!" she said to herself.

"No, no, no. I swore that I'd never repeat such an ignorant and nasty thing as that. I'll not let that one pass my lips. I've said too much."

I kept waiting, hoping for her to break if I sat there quietly, and stared at her. She jumped up and started clearing the table. I was clearly disappointed, but the show was over.

For the rest of that evening, my imagination ran wild. I tried to think of any conceivable way that a man could "mark" his woman. On the farm, knowledge of the birds and the bees came fairly early on because you're right there in the midst of it. Cows produced calves, sows produced pigs and hens produced baby chicks, and if anything interfered with the process, you ran out of meat. But for 8th grade boys such as myself knowledge of the human female anatomy was limited to selectively censored back issues of National Geographic, stealthily pilfered from Miss Nancy Halcomb's desk in the back of the school library.

As Granny's health declined and she was on a walker, and limited to the space of two or three rooms, I shamelessly put my wife up to asking her—-one last time, to break her silence. She dearly loved Sandy, who became her primary caregiver. But, even that close bond would not loosen Granny's lips to reveal the secret of "the mark."

Correctly sensing that I had conspired to do so, her final word was, "Sandy, I told Clay-and now *I'm tellin' you*: I ain't budgin'. That foolish business will go to the grave with me." She didn't, and it did.

166

As to poor old, bless-her-heart Aunt Mollie…at supper the next evening, Granny did finish her story, which had ended abruptly with the revelation of her Uncle Cy's mysterious marking process.

"Aunt Mollie held on there by herself a long time after Uncle Cy died, ten or fifteen years I guess. Then one day, one of Aunt Mollie's neighbor boys came flyin' up here on horseback. Mama and I were right here in this kitchen, cannin' beet pickles. We dropped everything and got Daddy to take us up to Big Granny's house. It just so happened that Mama's youngest sister Aunt Mildy, was there with her first grandbaby. Aunt Mildy hadn't been there but just a few minutes when Big Granny went to empty a dishpan of water out the back door and had a stroke at the same time. She fell right out into yard with the pan of water. My aunts sent for Dr. Washburn. He finally came and hadn't been there five minutes before he told my aunt to hold that baby up, Big Granny's newest great-grandchild, where she could see it from her bed. He said if Big Granny's eyes followed that baby, she'd prob'ly live, but if they didn't, she wouldn't make it. Aunt Mildy was a great big woman," and here Granny raised her hands up even with her eyes to explain, "and she held that baby way up like this, in front of Big Granny, and walked back and forth across the room with it. Aunt Mildy and the baby both started cryin'. Big Granny's eyes never moved the whole time, and sure enough, she died late that evenin', just like Dr. Washburn said.

We buried Big Granny that Friday in the pourin' rain, and Aunt Mollie died *the very next Monday mornin'*. Emily

167

Scrivner lost a milk cow and she sent her youngest boy to find it. He thought it had gotten over on Aunt Mollie's place and he rode over there on his horse to ask her if she'd seen it. He's the one that found her dead, right there in the kitchen floor. He ran to fetch his mother, and got word to my aunts down in the little house. Aunt Mollie had been makin' an applesauce cake and she even had the batter poured into the cake pans ready to put in the oven. There was nearly a full glass of her dandelion wine on the kitchen table where she'd been sittin', and that stone jug was sittin' there beside of it. It was early in the mornin' and she had already started in on the wine, bless her old heart. People were shocked to hear Aunt Mollie was dead. My aunts hadn't even gotten the neighbors' pots and pans back to 'em where they sent food for Big Granny's funeral.

Poor ol' thing...Aunt Mollie never had much a life and I think she felt like she just had to live, to see that Big Granny was taken care of...and when that part was over with, she was done through livin'. We buried Aunt Mollie on a Wednesday right next to Big Granny, not even one week later. It hurts me to say it, but that was as close as they'd been to one another for many a day. I dearly loved Aunt Mollie's old farm, sad as it was...and it got sadder yet, for us after we bought it. "

I knew the subject of the Mollie Moore place to be an unpleasant one, for I never heard either Granny or Granddaddy speak of it over a handful of times, for as long as I knew them.

Aunt Mollie's stone jug helped me save up pennies for years. The last time I emptied the thing I nearly dropped it and decided then to retire it as the family penny bank. It's a dust collector now, but safe, above the kitchen cabinets. I commune with it briefly every morning as I meditate over Corn Flakes and coffee. No one living has ever seen its one time owner Mollie Moore. I know her only by the jug and one of three unknowable female faces in Granny's big red box of age-dimmed family photos, none of which looks like Scarlett O'Hara, as Granny remembered her.

Still, because of the stone jug, I began listening more, and I asked more questions. I thought about life as it had been, and sometimes still was. Although other old things have spoken to me, Aunt Mollie Moore's jug is perhaps the most important because it was the first to do so at a crucial moment in my own journey to adulthood. From its strategic position atop the kitchen cabinets, the old jug continues to speak. It has both whispered and shouted, but it has consistently urged me to listen.

In recent years, the stone jug is politely *asking me* to do something, and there is some reasoned sense of urgency in the request. It's the same feeling I get when I look at our faithful old golden retriever as he lies on the sun room floor to warm his bones. His sunken eyes look at me knowingly in the stillness of early morning, and he still swishes his tail when I call his name.

Now, in my autumn years, The Aunt Mollie jug is quietly asking *me* to speak as *my* elders did. It patiently nudges me to begin unfolding my own quilt for the family to view, before it too, is folded up and put away in the cedar chest of mist and memory.

The Homegoing

"When Aunt Pud gets here..."

This was a household phrase I grew up hearing...so much that I still use it myself to describe anything good that just seems destined *never* to happen.

I still remember the first time I heard Granny utter those hopeless words. She said, "Russell, I'd give the eyes out of my head if we could take us a trip to Garrard County and spend the day with Ella Turner. When do you think you could take me?"

Granddaddy mumbled some vague response. Granny sighed, "I reckon I know what that means; we'll do it when Aunt Pud gets here." In context and following similar exchanges over the next few years, I came to understand the sarcasm—mingled with despair, in those few words.

Any event or undertaking that was hoped or even longed for, but unlikely to result in action, was relegated to the distant memory of Aunt Pud, an obscure relative I knew only by that unhappy association. That is, in addition to a relic she left behind in the form of an antique rocking chair with a broken rocker. Tucked away for decades in the corner of an upstairs bedroom, unloved and unrocked, it waited patiently to be understood.

To the best of my knowledge, the old piece was only mentioned in my hearing twice—when it had to be moved to wipe the walls down for cleaning and painting. At least on those two occasions, the never-used rocker was referred to as "Aunt Pud's." After hearing her hope-deadening name for most of my childhood, when Granny pointed to her rocker for the first time and connected the two, I felt like the long-dead aunt and I were being formally introduced.

I had returned home from Vietnam after two years of active duty and was moving a couple of hours away to attend The University of Louisville. There I found a tiny two room apartment in an old house not far from campus. The week before classes started in August, I had set about getting some things moved into it that were given or loaned to me by family and friends. You've got to admit a rocking chair isn't exactly bachelor pad furniture, but when you're young and broke, you take what you can get.

In surveying the miscellaneous pieces of furniture tucked away here and there in the farmhouse where we lived and in which Granny had been born and raised, she pointed out the ugly duckling, deliberately hidden away it seemed, upstairs.

"There," she said, "You can take Aunt Pud with you. It don't favor much, but I reckon it's a place to sit down."

With that practical suggestion, I loaded the old rocker in my pickup and tied it down for the journey. With a few other mean pieces of furniture and a box of culled dishes and bent silverware, I began my journey as a college student.

Aunt Pud's lone surviving artifact is nothing special…just a gimpy-legged old rocker with scrolled arms, long flat slats in its back and a plain, scalloped headrest. The sturdy maple piece was heavily stained and varnished when it was made in the early 1900's. By the time I took it to Louisville with me seventy or so years later, the best way to describe its overall appearance would be "gnarly black."

The semester after I got settled in school, I brought Granny to my apartment in Louisville to spend the weekend with me. It only happened once. She had wanted to cook supper for us but that was an epic failure without her utensils and pantry. Then she couldn't sleep that night for worrying about her garden and the barn cats going hungry. Then she realized she'd forgotten about the Fifth Sunday potluck at her church and she would have major cooking to do. By Saturday morning at sunup she was packed up and ready to head back to Fordville.

When I woke up bleary-eyed and entered the living room, Granny was perched in Aunt Pud's rocker. Although she was making perceptible movement, any attempt at rocking on the deep shag carpet was purely nostalgic on her part.

I said, "You're up early!"

She smiled as she continued rocking mostly just her body, "You know I always get up early. I laid there on that couch all night and fought the covers. I don't see how on God's green earth you can sleep in with all this racket--at all hours…cars honkin'…people walkin' and hollerin'—and cussin', some of 'em. And it never gets good and dark here neither. When daylight finally came, I just got to studyin' Aunt Pud's ol' rocker here." She spoke the words approvingly this time, as she patted the scrolled arm of the

172

unloved rocker like the shoulder of an old friend fallen on hard times.

For some reason the oddity of the long-dead Aunt Pud's name hadn't enlisted my interest until that particular moment.

I said, "Granny, what kind of name is Aunt Pud?"

She grinned and said, "I don't know, but I reckon it sounds ever' bit as good as Uncle Fud...that was her husband."

Great. As if my family tree wasn't compromised enough with a few dotted lines and arrows pointing here and there, somewhere in it was an Uncle Fud *and* an Aunt Pud.

In terms of visual appeal, Uncle Fud and Aunt Pud at least look like rhyming equivalents on paper, but with my family nothing could ever be that simple: Granny pronounced Fud as you might expect—as in cartoon character Bugs Bunny's nemesis Elmer Fudd; Aunt Pud, however, sounded like the "pud" in "pudding."

Granny said, "Uncle Fud's name was sp'osed to be Frederick Lee...Snodgrass, but he always said packin' around a name like that's enough to wear *any* man down; ever'body in our family called him "Fud." He was my great-uncle--Big Granny's oldest brother, but the poor ol' thing couldn't say "Fred" on account of her not bein' able to pronounce her "r's", so when she tried to say "Fred" it came out "Fud."

She shook her head sympathetically, "Big Granny couldn't get a word out right to save her. On top of that, she never had but one tooth in her head—and as the sayin' is, *it needed pullin'.*"

I said, "Okay, I understand the Uncle Fud part but where did Aunt Pud come from?"

"You know," she said with a thoughtful sigh, "I don't reckon I ever heard 'em say. Or if I ever did hear, I can't remember it now. She was just always Aunt Pud. The only word I know that even comes close is "puddin,'" so maybe there was a puddin' there somewhere—like "honey," or "sugar pie." It's doubtful anybody knows. Nobody around Fordville, anyway."

She smiled, and said, "You know, I laid here for a right smart while when the sun come up and I got to lookin' at this ol' rocker and thinkin' about the time when Aunt Pud was comin' to see us. We had us a big homecomin' planned for her when I was just a young girl."

I said, "Homecoming? Where did she live?"

"Arkansas. Aunt Pud and Uncle Fud lived in Hardy, Arkansas. That's where she was raised. Uncle Fud moved down there a long time before I was ever born and that's where they both lived when they married.

Now Uncle Fud…he was from Fordville—*born, bred and buttered*, as the sayin' goes. The funny thing is that Aunt Pud was born in Kentucky too, but her people moved to Arkansas when she was just a set-alone baby--about the same time Uncle Fud and his first wife went there. By and by, she took sick and died...left him with two children still at home. Aunt Pud told Mama the story about the first time she ever saw Uncle Fud.

A travelin' salesman came into the store one day tryin' to sell Uncle Fud some fertilizer. Nobody much knew what it was back then, when it first came out. We called travelin' salesmen "drummers" back when I was growin' up. Uncle Fud kept ignorin' this drummer when a customer would come in and I reckon he finally decided it was high time to leave, sale or no sale. He was gettin' tired of bein' put off ever' time somebody came through the door.

Uncle Fud was prob'ly just as tired of listenin' to him yammer on about his fertilizer and finally he says, "Mister, I just ain't interested. Farmers around here use "FIZZLE-IZE" to put on their land." Well, I don't reckon you've heard that before, but that's just what some people used to call cow manure. The drummer gets mad and gathers his satchel up and commences to storm out the front door. He gets halfway to it and throws up his hand to Uncle Fud and says, "The back of my hand to you, Sir!" Uncle Fud turned his backside to him, and yelled right back, "And the crack of my be-hind to you, Sir!"

"Aunt Pud was in the store that day and when she heard Uncle Fud say that, she busted out laughin', and the two of 'em struck up a conversation. Uncle Fud was prob'ly fifteen or twenty years older than she was. Anyway, that's how the two of them met. She hadn't never been married or had children, but she raised Uncle Fud's youngest two children like they was her own. Before I was born Mama took Big Granny down there on a train and stayed a whole month. Mama thought a lot of her, so years later when she

175

got a letter from Aunt Pud sayin' that she was comin' back to Kentucky for a homecomin' visit, we all went to work cleanin' and gettin' ready for it. Uncle Fud was dead by then and she was gettin' on in years. Seems like to me she sent that letter in May and told us she was comin' to Fordville in July.

Uncle Fud had done right well for hisself in that store in Arkansas. Had money in the bank and such as that--and he'd built Aunt Pud a big new house with all new furniture in it. Mama was always a little embarassed that we never had much new or shiny stuff--mostly just what was passed down or what somebody around here made. Ever' now and then maybe she'd order somethin' from the Wish-Book, that's what we called the Sears & Roebuck catalogue. Anyway, for the next few weeks that's all we heard: we gotta get this cleaned and polished before Aunt Pud gets here; we gotta get this fixed up and painted before Aunt Pud gets here; Oh, I've got to find that recipe for when Aunt Pud gets here. We cleaned every room in our house extra early on account of her comin' to see us.

Mama took inventory of everything she had to cook all the best dishes for Aunt Pud comin' in on that train. She was gonna invite her brother and sisters and all the nieces and nephews and their families and we were gonna have a big to-do here at the homeplace. Then there was some of Aunt Pud's own people still in Kentucky she hadn't seen in years, so Mama wrote and invited them to come. Of course, Big Granny was still livin' then, so she'd be there to help Mama with the cookin' and such.

Then about a month before Aunt Pud's train was to come in, Mama gets to studyin' that spare bedroom where you sleep now. Aunt Pud was an old woman and Mama got to thinkin' she might need a rockin' chair in there to sit in. Well, the only one we had was homemade and the truth is I think Mama was halfway ashamed of it. I don't reckon we had a store-bought chair on the place and she didn't want Aunt Pud thinkin' we were poor. She walked down to Mack Perkin's store and his daddy, Joe, was still livin' then…and she ordered a brand spankin' new rocker straight from the catalog. The only problem was that she didn't have the money to order it, so she decided she could sell some of her layin' hens. That whole next day we spent chasin' down chickens, tyin' 'em up and puttin' 'em in a big crate of a thing that Daddy spent all mornin' tryin' to build. Now--all this, mind you, was just to buy a rockin' chair for Aunt Pud's homecomin'.

Mama made the trade with Mr. Perkins and got her a rocker ordered. Every day or two, she'd be in Fordville and ask him when it was comin' in. It got down to within five days of Aunt Pud's train comin' in on the sixth day of July, and Mama got plumb worried over it. I remember it was the sixth because that was my brother Harry Winston's birthday. Mr. Perkins said not to worry, that the rocker would get here in time.

The very day before Aunt Pud's train's came, Mr. Perkins gets a call that the rocker was put off the train by mistake over at Speers, but there wasn't another train comin' through in time. Daddy and Harry Winston were cuttin' and stackin' hay on the land across the river so Mama and I had to take the wagon across the river on the ferry and find them to drive all the way over to Speers to pick up Aunt Pud's rocker.

I reckon Mama and Daddy had a big fuss over it right there in the hayfield in front of the work hands and ever'body else. Finally Mama told Harry Winston to come with her, she'd go to Speers without Daddy if that's what it took to have somethin' nice for Aunt Pud to set in. We got all the way to Speers and the man at the train station said, "Ma'am I hate to tell you this, but we can't find hide nor hair of that rockin' chair. I think it must've got put back on that train somehow." Mama was fit to be tied. Then he said, "But I tell you what, there's a new store that's just opened up down the road at Hargus that carries some furniture, and if you hurry, I think you can get there in time."

Mama was mad as a wet hen by then and the three of us rode hell-bent for leather to Hargus. Mama still had all these chores for us to do at home, she was mad at Daddy, and we still didn't have Aunt Pud's rocking chair.

Daddy didn't know it but Mama had a little wad of money she kept hid. Not much, just what she had from sellin' butter and eggs—her "mad money" as she called it. She paid for this rocker--almost to her last nickel and we loaded it in the wagon and commenced headin' home.

Nobody'd given a thought about it, but the ferry was done closed down for the day by the time we got back to Fordville. There we were, stuck across the river. Mama was afraid to let Harry Winston take us across in one of Bob Ulyss Whitfield's little john boats that he kept on that

178

side on account of her not knowin' how to swim. Harry Winston could swim and I could dog paddle a little, but Mama would no more cross that river in a john boat than she could rise and fly. She sent Harry Winston in the wagon to find the man that helped run the ferry, but he'd gone to a revival meetin' at Knock Buckle. His wife told Harry Winston to go find her feeble-minded brother Lem who had a john boat, and he probably wouldn't care a bit to take us across the river, *and the rocker* of course. Sure enough, Lem got us across the river in his john boat and this thing was in our faces the whole time—or the rockers pokin' into our ribs. Mama held onto it for dear life while poor ol' Lem and Harry Winston was tryin' to paddle.

It was about dark when we finally got home. None of us had eaten any supper and we were nearly starved to death. Daddy was still in a foul humor about the hay business and Mama hollered at him and asked if he'd bring the rocker in out of the wagon. Well, I reckon nothin' had gone right since midnight that day—and it got worse. Daddy was fumin' anyway and he goes to pick the rocker up out of the wagon and marches up the porch and into the front door with it--but he didn't turn it the right way and he broke one of the rockers off of it, *clean as a hound's tooth*. I thought Mama was gonna bawl like a baby right there in front of God and all of us. Her face turned beet-red and she just walked off and left Daddy standin' there with it at the front door.

Daddy never got him *any* supper that night. He drove down to Fordville in the wagon and got my uncle, "Big Hetch," we called him, to find these two flat pieces of iron down there in his blacksmith shop to fasten the rocker together on both sides and some screws and them two long bolts to hold 'em on. Daddy went to work and set the clamps on it, and then screwed them iron pieces on both sides of that split rocker down there. Daddy packed it back in the house about midnight...but, bless his heart he hadn't done the best job fixin' it. You can see it down there—the iron pieces was too long and too wide and they couldn't follow the curve in the rocker too good. They stood out like a sore thumb when it was brand new. Not so much now. Poor ol' Mama just looked at it and shook 'er head—never said another word. And you know, I never saw her sit down in it...*not one time.*

That next afternoon of course was when Aunt Pud's train was supposed to come in. Mama was up before daylight and Aunt Maud had gotten permission from the Walkers to spend the night with us so she could get up early and help. Big Granny and my Aunt Rhoda came up and they all started cookin'. It was on Ju-ly the sixth and I'll never forget it if I live to be a thousand. We'd been plannin' on that day for weeks. Bob Ulyss Whitfield told us he'd ferry us all across the river at no charge. He knew how hard Mama had worked to prepare for Aunt Pud's homecomin' and we were all gonna take the ferry, then drive the three miles to Speers to the train depot and be waitin' for her to get off the train. Then we'd all come back to our house for the big dinner. Of course, Aunt Pud was gonna be stayin' with us.

We sat there at the depot all afternoon, just waitin' for Aunt Pud--and it was so hot that day a bird wouldn't fly. The first train finally pulled in—and it was runnin' thirty minutes late. Lafe Johnson had tied his old red mule to the track, they said, tryin' to get it killed so he could collect a few dollars for it. Anyway, Mama and Daddy hollered for us all to gather around that train to welcome Aunt Pud. We all jumped up and waited. We thought ever'body had gotten off, and finally, here came one ol' lady steppin' off the train and Harry Winston hollered, "There she is!" We all went to clappin' and to this day I don't know who that old lady was. It wasn't Aunt Pud but I think it made her feel right proud to have that kind of welcome, 'cause she waved at us and hugged a couple of my aunts like it was old home week. Then we thought maybe Aunt Pud might be on the next train--in two hours I think it was. There we all sat, fannin' and waitin'. Suppertime came, and by then my uncles were sayin' they were hungry and tired of waitin'. All of us kids was just playin' and entertainin' ourselves the best we could but I could tell Mama was gettin' worried. When dark came, the train depot closed up and there we sat. Aunt Maude and Uncle Henry took all of us kids on home in the wagon while Mama and Daddy stayed behind. I reckon they finally left around nine o'clock that evenin' and the next mornin' Mack Perkins got a telegram in the post office in his store that was sent from across the river. He sent an ol' one-armed man that hung around the store named Wash Johnson up here to give it to Mama. It was from Aunt Pud's stepson in Arkansas tellin' us that she'd died the day before she was to leave. He said she'd already had her trunk packed up and ready to go. He wrote in a letter that after they'd eaten dinner that day and put the dishes away, Aunt Pud and her daughter-in-law

181

went out on the front porch to cool off and Aunt Pud says, "I'm feelin' mighty tired. I think I'm gonna go lay down for a minute." The daughter-in-law sat there on the front porch for a little while and then she said to herself that she'd never known of Aunt Pud to take a nap in the middle of the day. She goes upstairs to check on her and found her dead at the top of the steps."

"That's sad," I said.

Granny looked at me thoughtfully and nodded.

"Did you like her?" I asked

"Who, Aunt Pud?"

"YES, Aunt Pud."

"Oh, from what Mama always said I prob'ly would've--*if I'd known her.*"

"What?"

Granny said, "I wouldn't have known Aunt Pud if she was settin' on that no-account cook stove of yours in there. Mama and some of my aunts met her that one time, but I wouldn't have known her from buckshot. I've got a picture of her somewhere upstairs, but I never laid my eyes on her."

I said, "So you mean to tell me Aunt Pud's rocker you're sitting in right now *DIDN'T* belong to Aunt Pud?"

Looking down at the rocker suddenly as if a mistake might've been made, Granny said, "Well, I reckon it did in

182

a way, but *she* just never got to sit in it. We always called it Aunt Pud's rocker, and I reckon it *is* funny, if you think about it."

She chuckled, "Daddy was about half mad about the whole thing for a week. When he allowed Harry Winston to go with me and Mama to Hargus to buy it, he couldn't finish cuttin' the hay and it came the biggest rain you ever saw that evenin', and rained on it ever' day for the next week. That whole big field of hay across the river wasn't hardly fit to stack. Then he'd busted the rocker and had to fix it. Mama just hated the way it looked—with them big pieces of metal holdin' the rocker together it was ugly as homemade soap. And then to top that off, poor ol' Mama had promised that foolish Lem a blackberry pie for ferryin' us across the river with it. He said he wouldn't think of takin' a cent from Mama for doin' her a favor, but he said he'd sure be glad to have one of her blackberry pies. Early that next Saturday mornin', Mama said to me and Harry Winston that the three of us had to go down to the river bottom and pick us some blackberries to make some jam— and a pie for Lem. We hadn't gotten halfway down there before Mama slipped in the wet grass and skinned her leg all the way up to the knee. She sat there on the rocks and dobbed at the cuts and scrapes with her dress. She didn't do it often but that time she teared up a little bit and handed me *her* bucket to fill with blackberries. She went back to the house limpin' all the way like a burnt-toed chicken, so me and brother Harry Winston got to do all the berry-pickin' and wouldn't you know it? We fooled around and got chiggers. Neither one of us'd ever gotten 'em before and we'd picked a hundred gallons of berries between us if

183

we'd picked one. The berry-pickin' didn't turn out so good: Mama hobbled around for a week on account of that fall, and me and Harry Winston both scratched our legs blood raw from the chigger bites—but we saw to it that Lem *got his pie.*

She said, "*Ever'thing about* Aunt Pud's b-i-g homecomin' went caflunkus. We'd turned our lives inside out to get ready for it…so after all that, nobody had much use for her busted rocker."

Granny sat there still attempting to rock in it a little and leaned back. With her eyes closed she shook her head slowly from side to side. "It sure wasn't much of a homecomin'. Bless her ol' heart, for Aunt Pud, it was a *home-goin'* …to the Gates of Glory, I reckon."

My poor daddy…a long time after that when he got to movin' slow and his joints were hurtin' him so bad, one day I told 'im I'd bring this rocker down to the livin' room for 'im to sit by the fire and he said, 'Nothin' shakin'. After all the clatterment that thing caused, I'd just as soon fling it to the furthest fork o' hell.' After that, I never mentioned it again…to him or Mama either one."

Granny and I were on the road headed home before eight o'clock that Saturday morning. She was tired from lying awake all night and she soon drifted off to sleep once we got on the open road. About half an hour into the journey she abruptly raised herself up in the passenger seat of my old Dodge pickup and declared, "**PAULINA—URSULA-- -DAVIS**".

Startled and in an early morning stupor myself, I nearly ran a red light and said, *"WHAT?!"*

Granny held up her hand, "Hold on here a minute! It just came to me--Aunt Pud's name--the name she had before she married Uncle Fud...her full name was *Paulina— Ursula--Davis*. She'd embroidered her initials—P-U-D--- on one of her old pillow cases when she was just a girl, down in Arkansas. Before Mama married, she and Big Granny took a train to visit Uncle Fud and Aunt Pud and they stayed a whole month with 'em. One day Mama was helpin' Aunt Pud with her ironin' and she saw the letters PUD sewed on that old pillowcase and asked who *PUD* was. Mama always said Aunt Pud was a jolly, good-natured old woman and she laughed out loud and said, 'Honey, that's me...*I'm PUD*.' Mama got so tickled over it that Aunt Pud gave her that ol' pillow case as a keepsake when she left. Fact is, I remember seein' it--and I might even still have it upstairs in some of Mama's things. It has to be bad old-- Aunt Pud would be a-way up over a hundred and then some. If she made it when *she* was a girl, why Lord, that thing's as old as Methusalem's housecat."

Granny sighed, "It's an ever-lovin' wonder her name finally came to me. It just popped up in my head all of a sudden like it was in four foot neon letters...I was takin' a cat-nap and wasn't even thinkin' about her or the rocker. When we were growin' up we all just called her Aunt Pud when her name came up in conversation. Mama'd get a letter from her ever' so often and she'd tell us about it and the relatives in Arkansas. Like I said, I wouldn't have known her from a load of coal."

Had there really been one, Granny had solved the mystery of Aunt Pud's name—now attributed to the initials on an embroidered pillowcase. In terms of historical accuracy, it was safe to assume that no pudding connection had ever existed for the aunt she never saw, the busted rocker the unseen aunt never sat in, or in her own despairing sigh for any unattainable good thing.

Within minutes of her unexpected revelation, Granny once again closed her eyes as we rolled down the highway in the warmth of the morning sun. In that time of life when her world was drawing close around her, maybe she was just resting—awaiting the welcome sound of my old truck on gravel, as we turned homeward to the familiar.

Before Granny died, she showed me a picture of the celebrated Aunt Pud of rocker fame, seated prominently in front of a group of people standing behind her. Only a faintly penciled note on the back identified the matronly old lady wearing black taffeta in a big whicker rocker. From her wide front porch adorned with ornate 19th century gingerbread trim, the portly Aunt Pud exuded a spirit of hospitality and good cheer. Judging from her age, the photograph was apparently taken not long before her homegoing train to Fordville took an unexpected detour--to The Other Side.

When my wife Sandy was pregnant with our oldest daughter Loren, I refinished the rocker intended for the ample haunches of good old Aunt Pud. I am happy to report that it was used almost daily during the infancies of both our daughters as we rocked them to sleep. Remembering Granny's tale of woe and with a sympathetic nod to those things in life that go wrong from the start, I decided to leave the unsightly iron braces put there by my great-grandfather in a noble attempt to render it useful. Since then it has also been used to rock our grandchildren; and now, after a century and five generations of ownership, the much-maligned rocker has at last been restored to favor. *Rock on in Glory, Aunt Pud.*

Note to the reader: The ancient pillowcase embroidered with the initials "PUD" did in fact surface after Granny's death--in an old steamer trunk in the attic, and as she would've said "it came within one red hair" of being thrown on a burn pile. Although moths had devoured some of it, they had spared what I assume were the unappetizing—but helpful, identifying initials of Granny's long-departed aunt.

The Big Chair

bab tism 19-10

"Do you believe in ghosts?"

It sounds like a question I might've asked Granny when I spent my first Halloween with her and my grandfather when I was eight years old—not a twenty one year old army veteran with two years of active combat duty under his belt.

It was exactly 12:00 noon and for many years, the time for Granddaddy to make his trek to the house from wherever he was on the farm—usually a long legged, slow and steady gait from the barn "coming in for dinner." She knew I'd seen her, still looking for him—or so it seemed.

Breaking the momentary silence, I asked, "Do you?"

She sat down at her usual place with her favorite kitchen knife in her hand. It was the one Granddaddy had made for her and sharpened so many times that the blade was nearly worn in two down close to the handle where she'd used it for a million and one tasks—in this case, spreading her homemade pimento cheese onto slices of salt rising bread. Pausing, she glanced once more out of the kitchen window toward Granddaddy's quieted tool shed where for the first time, unwelcome weeds now grew at the doorstep.

She composed herself before responding. "No…no, I don't. But, I sit here and catch myself lookin' out the window for Russell to come in for dinner and he's been gone three years nearly. Whether I feel like eatin' or not, I still have it ready at noon just like he's gonna be comin' through that door. In my mind I can still hear him whistlin' like he always did when he came up the back porch. Bedtime's the worst, though. Sometimes, I lay awake at night, listenin' to the voices I've heard here in these ol' walls--and I hear him speak to me, *plain as day.*" Looking again toward the barn, she said, "And if I'm not real careful, I catch myself talkin' right back to him."

But then, she quickly added, "But now, that's not his ghost. That's just from us bein' married fifty-five years nearly. His soul, his *spirit's* in heaven."

I said, "You've been around a lot of sickness and death. I just wondered if you had seen any ghosts."

With an affirming nod she said, "Been around it my whole life--but I don't believe in ghosts. But now, I will tell you this: I was in the room when Aunt Peg died and we saw her spirit leave her body. I don't call that no ghost, but Mama always believed Aunt Peg communicated some way or another with Uncle Crutch."

Amused at hearing names long forgotten, I said, "I've heard you speak of *him* before. And now that you mention it, what kind of name is 'Crutch?'"

Grinning she said, "Well…that was just his nickname. I don't remember doin' it, but I reckon I'm the very one that pinned it on 'im. Ever'body else around Fordville knew him by "Will," but his real name was William. He was Grandma Clark's brother, so he'd be my great-uncle—Aunt Peg was his wife, my great-aunt by marriage. Uncle Crutch was the biggest cut-up I reckon I've ever known…loved to play pranks and tell jokes, such as that. Poor ol' feller didn't have but one leg—he was wounded in the Civil War, in a battle on that big mountain down in Tennessee or Georgia somewhere and his leg had to be taken off, right here above the knee—and one of his favorite jokes was to tell people he'd met Aunt Peg at a dance, just to see the look on their faces. He was a great big heavy-set man the first time I ever saw him, but 'til I was prob'ly eight or ten years old, he still got around a little usin' a pair of homemade crutches. One time when I was just a kid, I called 'im Uncle Crutch and he got the biggest kick out of that. From that day on, he was Uncle Crutch to me—even called himself that.

He stayed here some, with us," and nodding toward the back porch, Granny said—"and died right over there in the ol' log part of the house we tore down in '47. I've still got his great big chair down yonder in the smokehouse—special made just for him, on account of him bein' so heavy. After Aunt Peg died, he came here to live." Here was yet another name, another character to add to the list of relatives that had once took lodging in Granny's old house.

I remember the pride with which she spoke when she said, "Them days, we *always* had family to look after here, young and old alike. Wasn't no old folks homes and such as that. You stood the best chance in the world of dyin' in your own bed back when I was growin' up. I'm not so sure it didn't work out better for ever'body, to tell you the truth.

Uncle Crutch had been a school-teacher way back—before my time…smart as a whip. As he got older, he kept gettin' fatter where he couldn't get around as well. Finally, he got to where he couldn't hardly move a-tall and, I reckon by the time he died, Uncle Crutch prob'ly weighed close to four hundred—even with that one leg gone."

Granny opened the top of a small metal can where she kept potato chips, scattering the few good ones onto my plate, and emptying the remaining crumbs onto hers.

As she nibbled at half of a sandwich, she said with a smirk, "I know you're courtin' pretty heavy these days, but now *right there* was a true ro-mance, Uncle Crutch and Aunt Peg. I've thought about 'em over the years. 'Specially since Russell's died, I've thought about 'em a *whole lot*—and I believe they were about as close as any couple I've ever known. They grew up together… started courtin' when they were real young, before he went off to war. He wrote these long letters to her when he was a soldier. Aunt Peg kept showed 'em to me once. But--when he came back home from the war with a leg gone, he quit goin' around her. As the sayin' goes, Aunt Peg's people were poor as

191

Job's turkey and her daddy didn't want her to marry Uncle Crutch, thinkin' he wouldn't be able to work and support a family. He got a job teachin' at the Clear Creek School and so they did marry and set up housekeepin'. Then, about a year after they married, Aunt Peg lost a set of twins at birth and never had no more children after that—and she very nearly died herself. Grandma Clark and Aunt Peg both always believed that's what made Uncle Crutch turn against God the way he did. And, well—I never heard 'em, but he told Daddy things that he had seen durin' that— Civil—War, that was just awful. The only thing he told Daddy that I heard was that one of his buddies was killed right in front of him. I don't know where it happened, but they made a charge—they were both infantry soldiers and got separated from one another. The last he saw of him, he was wavin' him on to come toward him and I reckon a cannon ball took him out of this world in a second. Daddy didn't want me to hear what they were talkin' about, so I just caught it in bits and pieces like a kid would. But I remember Uncle Crutch said he ran right straight to that spot as hard and fast as he could get there, and his friend had marked his shoes in such a way that they stood out. I can't remember just how it was, but Uncle Crutch found that pair of shoes right there on the battlefield with his buddy's feet still in 'em—and the laces tied. I reckon that cannon fire had just blasted him out of his shoes. Grandma Clark always felt like the war made him like he was…and then losin' the babies. For most of the time I knew him, I reckon he was what you'd call an in-fidel."

It was an old term, especially the way Granny spoke it, in-fidel. The word atheist was not one I ever knew her to speak. Knowing that would've been unusual for his time and place, it also seemed strange that a family with such strong Christian faith—like Granny's, would've taken an unbeliever into their midst, let alone give him a place to live and care for him.

"Uncle Crutch never made a big fuss about NOT believin'…he just never went to church nor made any profession of believin', or in Heaven or Hell—or nothin'. I know it made Aunt Peg awful sad—and my Grandma Clark, too. They'd both beg and plead with him to read his Bible and go to church. Oh, he'd read a lot of books…and I believe he read the Bible through twice, cover to cover. He had a memory like an elephant and could quote Scripture about as good as most of the preachers around here--*but readin' ain't the same as believin'.*

I recollect one Sunday when Grandma Clark had Brother Ross here for dinner. He was young then--a great big, strong sort of fellow that kindly puts me in mind of a lumberjack. He'd just been called into the ministry and didn't hardly look old enough to shave. I think the preacher we had before had told him about Uncle Crutch not bein' a believer and he made it his job to convert him. His heart was in the right place, but he kept pesterin' Uncle Crutch about what he believed—*or didn't*, right there at the dinner table. Lookin' back, the way Uncle Crutch answered him, I think it made Brother Ross not so sure about what *he* believed." Granny chuckled as she held some imaginary object in her hand sticking it toward my face, "I remember he held a piece of fried chicken in his hand, like this, pointin' it toward Uncle Crutch as he spoke to. He said,

'Mr. Clark, do you *want* to go to Heaven--or Hell?' Uncle Crutch got just as quiet, and laid his fork and knife down, wiped his mouth with the back of his hand. He leaned over his plate this-away, lookin' at Brother Ross and said, 'Son, what do YOU know about Hell?' **I've** been there.' After that, he motioned for Daddy to help him get up and leave the table. I think he was afraid he'd say too much if he stayed."

Granny sat quietly for a moment, still looking out the kitchen window from the table where we sat.

"*But then*, I've learned that The Lord can get our attention in ways we can understand. Mama always believed Aunt Peg communicated with Uncle Crutch after she died. I've been in prayer meetin's and she'd ask for us all to pray that he'd come to know The Lord before she died, but, *he didn't*. Bless her ol' heart, Aunt Peg went to church ever' time the doors were open. She taught our Sunday School class and might nearly ever' Sunday she'd bring children home with her. Uncle Crutch never made a fuss about it— he loved children. The only thing I ever heard him say he'd ever believe in was Aunt Peg and Grandma Clark. Aunt Peg was a little bitty short woman, but she was nearly as big around as Uncle Crutch. Ol' Dr. Washburn was her brother-in-law and he told Uncle Crutch and Aunt Peg they were diggin' their graves with their teeth, and they did. The day Aunt Peg died, she had her cornbread batter all stirred up, ready to pour into the skillet and she fell right there in the kitchen where she stood talkin' to her sister—hit her head on the open stove door and made a big place right here," Granny pointed to her temple. "They sent for Dr.

194

Washburn, but there wasn't nothin' could be done for her. She lived through the rest of that day, and the family all gathered down there, poor ol' Uncle Crutch grievin' himself to death. By then, he'd gotten so big he couldn't sit in a regular chair—they'd have to pull up a straight chair of some kind and put in front of him just to hold his stomach up whenever he left his house—and that wasn't often. Aunt Peg paid that colored preacher down at Babylon, Matt Campbell, to make that great big chair for him—the one that's hangin' up in the smokehouse." Stretching her hands out, she said, "I reckon it's ever' bit this wide. Um-um…Uncle Crutch was a big'n all right.

The day she died, Aunt Peg stirred a time or two after they carried her to the bed and she just spoke a handful of words. I was in the room with Grandma Clark and Mama and when Aunt Peg took her last breath, I'll *always* believe we saw her spirit leave her body." Granny glanced out of the window at a passing bird. "It's kindly hard to describe, but it looked to me just like an old withered hand bein' shed of a glove that didn't fit it no more.

That next spring after Aunt Peg died, we had a big revival down church and thirteen people came forward to be baptized. They'd all agreed to wait 'til May when it warmed up a little to have the baptizin' but then we had heavy rain most of that spring and early summer so they held off. Durin' that time, Grandma Clark would sit with Uncle Crutch and ask him to come to the "Big Baptizin'" they were plannin' for. She kept sayin' she wouldn't take 'no' for an answer. It wasn't about a week before we finally had it when Grandma Clark died--right sudden-like.

She hadn't had a sick day so far as any of us ever knew…just died in her sleep one Saturday evenin' after we'd canned corn all day. They found kernels of corn stuck in Grandma's hair when they got her body ready for buryin'—you know it goes all over the place when you're cuttin' it off the cob that-away.

Well, Uncle Crutch thought the moon rose and set in Grandma and he took her death hard, just like the rest of us. I remember settin' there at our big dinner table after the funeral and Brother Ross was tryin' to talk to Uncle Crutch into joinin' the church. I'll say one thing for him—he didn't give up easy.

Uncle Crutch told 'im, "*Preacher, never you worry--if there's a Heaven*, Peggy will find a way to let me know." He'd lost her and Grandma Clark, his sister, in the space of just a few months and he just wasn't the same. If there's one thing Uncle Crutch loved as much as his food, it was a good laugh. They said when he was a young man, he was one of the biggest pranksters in Fordville, and he knew more jokes and tall tales than anybody I've ever heard of. A week or two after we buried Grandma Clark, Brother Ross and the deacons planned a big baptism service for the first Sunday in August. And…Lord, what a day that turned out to be."

We finished lunch and as Granny cleared the table, I made my way down the overgrown garden path to her old smokehouse to search for the big chair she'd mentioned. Finding it still hanging there—but out of my reach, high up on the wall, I brought a folding ladder from the barn and brought the old chair down from the two pegs that held it in place. Plastered with cobwebs and mud dauber's nests, I carried it to the back porch where Granny could see it again.

I called for her through the screen door and with the aid of her aluminum cane she carefully stepped out onto the back porch and admired the old family relic.

I said, "Granny, how did this thing wind up in the smokehouse?"

"I thought I told you--Uncle Crutch brought it here with him when he came to live with us. Come to think of it, he was *baptized* in it."

I said, "Baptized?—I thought you said he was an atheist?"

"No, not always," she said. "He finally came to be a believer before he died. Fact is, *on the very day* of that big baptism. Right down yonder in Copper Creek—in what we used to call "the cat-hole" about a half mile back up the road above the church.

I said, "He must've had a change of heart."

She answered with a smile, "That he did, I reckon. And you know after all these years, I ain't for sure if the Devil didn't get somethin' started that the Lord took hold of and finished—for Uncle Crutch's sake."

The church went ahead with the baptism service and dinner, but L-o-r-d, what a day. The women had a big long table set up on saw horses in that clearin' above the creek where the baptism was to take place and it was plumb loaded down with food. The church women planned that big dinner weeks ahead of time.

But, nobody planned for the meanness them Snodgrass boys would get into, though. They were the terror of Fordville when I was growin' up. If any devilment took place, they were likely to be in the middle of it. Nothin' really to hurt nobody much, just pranks and such. All the boys around here used to fish down there at the cat-hole and a day or two before The Big Baptizin', they'd spied a big hornet's nest way up high in a dead tree limb. Well, you can imagine what they decided they were gonna do with it when Sunday came.

Ever'body started gatherin' down there on the creek about eleven that Sunday mornin'. Mama and some of the women were way back at the table lookin' after the food while most the rest of us went down to watch." Granny suddenly cackled, "Oh, I nearly forgot about poor ol' Mag Arvin. She was one of the thirteen to be baptized.

Mm-mm...I hadn't thought of Mag in many a day. She didn't have the best name ever was, but the men that worked down at the sawmill felt sorry for her and built a little shed kitchen onto the foreman's shop for her to cook dinner for the workers. The preacher and a couple of the deacons had already baptized five or six when it came Mag's turn. The deacons had led her out into the water and the preacher put his handkerchief over her mouth and nose, took her under and brought her back up. Well, Mag had made biscuits at breakfast and she put jam and butter in a couple that was leftover and stuck 'em down in her dress pocket early that mornin' thinkin' she might be hungry later. She told some of 'em she felt out of place stayin' for dinner, 'specially with some of the women that was bad to gossip. So, when she waded out into the creek, them biscuits floated up—out of her pockets and on top of the water." Granny chuckled at the memory. "We had this simple minded ol' fellow in the church we called Uncle Mundy. We all just learned to look over 'im like we did most anybody we thought was kindly "off" a little. But when them pieces of poor ol' Mag's biscuits came floatin' by, he yelled to the preacher, "Dunk 'er again Brother Ross, *Mag's sin is comin' out of her in chunks!*" You could've heard 'im a mile away and ever'body there nearly busted a gut to keep from laughin' at the poor ol' foolish thing—includin' Brother Ross.

Anyway, one of the women sent me back to Mama to get another armload of clean rags to dry ever'body off with and *just about the time* she handed 'em to me, here came the awfullest hollerin' and carryin' on, you ever heard in your life. The Snodgrass boys had climbed up in that tree before the baptizin', just waitin' for ever'body to get there. Once they got about halfway through with the baptizin', that oldest'n took a big stick and started punchin' holes in that hornet's nest and finally knocked it down on the creek bank. Lord, it was awful. Ever'body took off runnin', and the ones in the creek started slosshin' through the water tryin' to make it to the bank, tryin' to get away from the hornets. It wasn't long before peoples' faces was swelled so bad you couldn't tell who they looked like, they'd been stung so many times.

Mama and the rest of us was far enough back to where we didn't get stung, but we could see 'em flyin' all around. Mack Perkins' mother sent him runnin' down to open up the store and bring some clean rags, and bakin' soda and a big jug of vinegar so they could fix poultices to put on the stings. Daddy swelled up fit to burst on one side of his face and the preacher was worse off than any of 'em. Well, Uncle Crutch had been settin' there with us that whole time—in this big chair—he had it up near that long dinner table. Grandma had done ever'thing but beg him to come to the baptizin', and then she up and died before they had it. I believe he got to thinkin' about her and Aunt Peg both wantin' him to make his peace with God so he told Daddy that he'd come for their sake. When he heard all that commotion and saw ever'body runnin' back up the bank and them hornets eatin' 'em alive, there he was with a front row seat, takin' it all in.

Poor ol' Brother Ross was one o' the last'ns to come up out of the water and he saw the Snodgrass boys climb back down the tree and take off. He was a great big stout man and when he got mad, his voice could sound like a clap of thunder. He came up that creek bank hollerin' at 'em, shakin' that big fist—right like this—and he said, 'If you boys was grown men, I'd take God's hammer right here and maul the time out of you with it!" Oh Lord, was he ever mad.

Well, I reckon Mrs. Snodgrass was afraid that her husband, Slim, would beat them boys to death when he got wind of what they'd done. When Brother Ross came to the top of the clearin', he hollered, 'Them hell-fired little heathens has killed me!' Mrs. Snodgrass thought he was talkin' about *her boys*—and in a way, I reckon he was. So she lit into him for cussin' her little darlin's—and then, here came Brother Ross's wife—she'd gotten stung, too--and she said, 'Kate Snodgrass, if you say one more word to my husband, I'm gonna knock you Hell-western crooked!'

I said, "Now what does that mean?"

Eager to get on with the rest of the tale, Granny said, "I never did know--maybe that's why I remember it. Whatever it was, it didn't sound too good comin' from the preacher's wife. Them two was fixin' to square off if some of the men hadn't separated 'em.

Anyway, Uncle Crutch was sittin' off to the side of us, just takin' it all in like it was a Christmas pageant. I was watchin' those women and him both, and all of a sudden he let out a squall you could've heard all the way to the river, and a laughin' fit like I'd never heard. Ever'body stopped rubbin' at their stings and just looked at him like he'd lost his mind. And he kept laughin'. Brother Ross and my daddy walked over to where Uncle Crutch was sittin'--in this chair here. Uncle Crutch said to him, "Preacher, I didn't think you were supposed to get mad."

Brother Ross wasn't the best preacher I've ever heard, but I'll say this much: he was honest. Uncle Crutch was just waitin' on him to make excuses for himself, and Brother Ross said, 'Well, you're part of the way right, Mr. Clark. But it's like this—I'm hurtin' like the devil. I said what I did to those boys before I thought,' and then he hesitated for a second and said, 'And then, I thought *and I said it again.'* Well, I'll tell you--the dry and droll way Brother Ross said that tickled Uncle Crutch to death, and they came to be good friends later on. All pretenses fell by the wayside when them hornets started stingin'.

But, after ever'thing settled down, Brother Ross and the deacons decided to go ahead with the dinner, the ones that wanted to stay and then they'd baptize the rest of 'em. Some of the church people went on home, some stayed. Brother Ross went right back over there where the tables were set up and sat down on the ground close to Uncle Crutch--tryin' to eat with one hand and hold that bakin' soda poultice to his hornet stings with the other. I saw Uncle Crutch lean over and say to him, 'Preacher, I asked for Peg to give me a sign if there's a heaven, and I reckon she has. I've not laughed this much since she died. If you'll still do it, *I want you to baptize me.'*

Well, that pleased Brother Ross to no end and he always claimed that Uncle Crutch was his first real convert. I've heard him nearly preach a whole sermon on how he brought an unbeliever around. He took the credit for it, but by rights I reckon the hornets did their part.

But--when the deacons and Brother Ross took a good hard look at what a big man Uncle Crutch was, they started scratchin' their heads as to how they were gonna get 'im baptized. They got to studyin' on it and the only way they could do it was to tip 'im back in his chair here. So after dinner, they loaded Uncle Crutch—and the chair--onto Daddy's wagon and ever'body headed back down to the creek bank, swelled faces and all. I don't remember seein' any hornets, but we kept our eyes open.

People around here talked about that day for years. "The Big Baptizin' is what old the Old Timers called it. I was there, of course, but I wasn't much more'n a girl. And believe it or not, one of them Snodgrass boys became a preacher.

Granny sat out on the porch with me and watched as I scrubbed the chair with warm soapy water, and allowed it to dry in the October sun. Wiping with an old rag where I dug and picked at a mud-dauber's nest imbedded in its underside, I said, "There's not a thing wrong with it that I can see."

She said, "Your granddaddy said it was the worst settin' chair on the place. He said the arm rests are too far apart for a skinny man—two men his size could've sat in it. We stuck it out in the smokehouse when we tore down that ol' log part of the house and didn't have nowhere else to put it.

Referring to my then fiancé, Sandy, she said, "You all are needin' a few things to set up housekeepin' with when you tie the knot. You can have this ol' chair if you want it." Although I did enjoy cleaning the nearly forgotten family relic, washing away years of dirt and grime to reveal its sturdy construction and a beautifully hand woven hickory bark bottom--it wasn't exactly practical for a newlywed couple in a tiny apartment. The old chair remained in the farmhouse where Granny found a place for it and enjoyed retelling its story to any passing visitor who happened to take notice of it.

Returning to the question that had prompted Granny to tell her story in the first place, I said, "So, you think your Uncle

203

Crutch's wife sent him a message from Heaven with a *hornet's nest?"*

Granny stretched her legs out in front of her with her arms folded, studying her feet. Grinning, she looked up at me. "Oh, I don't know as that's how it was, really. But...*who's to say?"*

Nearly a decade after I sat on the back porch with Granny on that October afternoon, an old photo surfaced in an abandoned farmhouse near Fordville. The structure was donated to the county fire department for a training exercise and during the preliminary walk through, one of the more curious firefighters forced his way through a scuttle hole into the tiny attic space, searching for anything that might be hidden there. Legs in the air, lying upside down on its top like a dead cockroach was a small, rustic table with a drawer full of old pictures--which, upon examination, spilled onto the floor below. The only item salvaged was the largest photo—a very old one on heavy cardboard backing with one corner broken off. Written in purple ink at the bottom were the crude, almost childlike letters spelling out "**bab Tism 19-10**."

After passing through several hands, the photo was presented to Granny, who instantly recognized the event as "The Big Baptism," which, she confirmed, took place in 1910. She was also able to determine the probable origin of the photo, for she recalled that once upon a time the dilapidated tenant house in which it was found had once been occupied by the much-maligned Mag Arvin, one of the thirteen people baptized. At what was to be Granny's very last church potluck, she sat down with the only other

204

living person who was present at the time, to identify the people in the photo—which included the only known image of sin-floating Mag Arvine.

As you know, I eventually acquired the old photo, but that's *another* story.

The Dinner Bell

A Mockingbird on the Window Sill

Nodding toward the old dinner bell just off the back porch where we were sitting, Granny said, "I still don't understand why in the world you took the clapper out of it."

I did. I was able to recognize that it was a childish, fear-induced response to a silly dream. I was twelve years old when I had removed the rusted metal clapper from Granny's dinner bell, mounted on a tall cedar post. At one time, it had summoned the men of the family for a hearty midday meal, but those days were long gone. Granny's father, husband, and only son were both dead by this time, along with a host of uncles, cousins and other day laborers who had once welcomed its beckoning call.

At daybreak on that cold October morning, I'd untwisted the heavy wire that attached the clapper to the bell using a pair of Granddaddy's pliers. Not only did I remove the clapper from the bell, I ran barefooted across a frosty field and hurled it into the woods. I hoped I'd never see it again.

By age twelve I'd already been living with my grandparents for four years and I was used to helping them with chores around the farm. It was nothing out of the ordinary when Granny handed me a small bucket of thick black paint left over from painting the barn and directed me to brush a coat on the dinner bell. It was on a Saturday in October and although the evenings had been seasonably cool, this particular day was warm and sunny, and by late morning an ideal time for any outside painting.

It was an annoying task, for I found there was no way to avoid ringing the bell while trying to paint it with a brush way too big for the job—and hold the paint bucket with my other hand. I would tilt it this way and that and still manage to achieve numerous nerve-wracking clangs that echoed all over the farm.

Later that evening Granny and I sat on the back porch after supper when the shadows grew long—and when the last rays of a brilliant fall sunset cast their dying glow on Granny's now shiny black dinner bell. Looking at it glistening like a blacksnake in the sun, and proud of the transformation it had undergone, I asked, "Granny, how long's that old bell been here?"

Stretching her legs out from the porch swing where we were sitting and looking at her feet, she said, "Your

207

granddaddy set that bell and post on your mama's first birthday, and that would've been in…1932. Your Uncle Johnny wrapped his hand around hers to pull the rope, and it rang so loud, it liked to have scared her to death. Bless her little ol' heart, she just cried and cried. That was the first time that bell was rung—here."

I said, "It seems big for a dinner bell."

Granny smiled and said, "That's not no reg'lar dinner bell. It used to be in that little Methodist Church down in Fordville."

"When did you all get it?"

She stared into the sunset. "Let me think. Well, it was after we bought the Aunt Mollie Place and that was in 1921. A storm blew that little steeple clean off of the church house and that bell came down with it. Your granddaddy said there was more bell there than there was steeple and it was too heavy. By then there wasn't a good handful of members left—just Jerusha Bowles and a few older people, women mostly, and they decided to close it. They asked Daddy if he'd come and get it for our church and he did, but the deacons decided it was gonna be too costly to build the steeple. Daddy kindly got stuck with it, so he and Russell hauled it out yonder to the smokehouse and it stayed there 'til we moved here in '31. We'd had us a dinner bell since we were married—your granddaddy always liked havin' one in case we needed help—for a fire alarm or such as that. I never used one to call for dinner 'til we moved to the Aunt Molly Place. The farm where we lived when we first married belonged to your granddaddy's uncle at Babylon.

At Aunt Molly's we had a brass dinner bell set in concrete and I started ringin' it to call your granddaddy in for dinner—did it for ten years, 'til we had to move. After we came here—and decided we wouldn't be leavin' anytime soon, Russell hauled this bell out of the smoke house and Daddy helped him set it up here in the yard."

Granny started to speak and paused. She was holding something back. By this time, I'd already learned if I held eye contact with her and didn't interrupt, there was a chance she would finish the tale. This was one of those occasions.

Her eyes fixed on the setting sun and her arms crossed against the fall chill, she said. "But now... before it came here, I reckon it was mostly used for a *death* bell."

"A what?"

"To ring when somebody died. We didn't have no bell in our church, so when anybody around Fordville died--before the Methodist Church closed, somebody would ride up to see ol' man Gabe Harris and get him to toll the bell—one ring for each year of the age of whoever it was that died. Judgin' by the number of times the bell rang, you gen'lly knew who it was. People would stop what they were doin' and listen to the tollin' of the bell. That's what they called it."

It all seemed odd to me at the time, hearing that the bell in our back yard was once used to inform the community of a death. I don't think I'd ever even heard it ring unless it was me attempting to paint the thing.

"Mr. Billy Bowles was the last'n to toll that bell--*and died doin' it.*"

Her words enlisted my attention.

We rocked gently back and forth in the porch swing as dried brown leaves blew playfully around our feet, caught in a gentle breeze.

"Did you know him?"

"Yes indeedy," she said, "knew 'im well. I was raised up with his boys Willie and Luther."

"How could anybody die ringing a church bell?"

"Well," she chuckled, "I reckon you can die most anytime—and doin' most anything. It ain't against the rules to die in church, neither. Come to think of it, I've known of two people that's done it. Ringin' a church bell's as good a way to go as any, but it was mighty strange when we heard about Billy Bowles--and the more we heard, why, the stranger it got."

There was an uneasiness—an uncertainty present in her voice that evening. The way Granny inflected her tone on the word "strange" piqued my curiosity. As we sat in the lengthening shadows, I asked her what she remembered about the long-ago ring of the death bell. Thus began The Dinner Bell saga.

"Now this was back before my time, but I've heard my daddy say Billy Bowles came here on foot from Virginia. I reckon he was just passin' through, on his way to see his

210

sister up in Indiana, and was needin' to earn a little money to get him there. Daddy said all Billy had to his name when he came to Fordville was the clothes he wore on his back, and he died a rich man.

It was fixin' to rain that day Billy came through here lookin' for work and my uncle Preston told him ol' man Gabriel Harris was needin' help to get his hay stacked. The Harrises owned most of that whole country through between Fordville and Babylon. Billy walked out there, and sure enough, Mr. Harris hired him to work for the day. He was a good worker and I reckon they let 'im sleep in the barn of a night--'til the hay was all cut and stacked. He started takin' his meals with Mr. and Mrs. Harris and Jerusha--that was their only daughter. We called her "Rusha."

She was the sweetest ol' thing but she was hare-lipped real bad," Granny said, touching the ridge on her upper lip, just under her nose. "People had a hard time tryin' to understand her because she couldn't talk plain, and she kindly kept to herself. Little Granny said when she was a girl people thought it was a curse from God for anybody to be hare-lipped--like a little baby could do anything to help it. Fact is, Little Granny was the midwife that brought Rusha into the world. She never believed it was a curse, but seems to me like it'd **be** a curse sure enough to live with."

Rusha prob'ly thought she'd never marry on account of her havin' that split lip and I'm a-thinkin' she was close to thirty when Billy showed up. I remember him well--a tall man, and thin as a whippoorwill. He had that *horn* of thing

211

up here on the side of his face and when I was little he'd scare me into the sawdust with it."

I said, "A *horn?*"

"That's what all the old people called it. It wasn't a thing in the world but a growth of some kind. Nowadays a doctor'd take it off in ten minutes, but back then there wasn't no way to do it. My daddy said when Billy Bowles first came here, that horn wasn't no bigger than the end of a baby's little finger and had a head of a thing--a point on it just like a little baby horn—but it kept growin' 'til it was plumb scary lookin' --to a kid.

Billy stayed up there that whole summer workin' for Jerusha's daddy. Then he commenced courtin' her. They said ol' Gabe Harris and his sons wasn't much in favor of him since he didn't have a nickel to his name. No--now, wait a minute—I've told you wrong; I reckon he did have somethin' when he came here. My daddy said Billy came totin' two sacks. One of 'em was full of sausages wrapped in corn shucks and the other'n was full of goose feathers. I'd done forgot that part of it. Rusha told me herself one time that when he left Virginia, all he had was ten cents in his pocket and a pone of cornbread and by the time he came into Fordville he'd had his room and board along the way and traded up to the sausage and goose feathers. People used goose feathers back in the old times. Now, I've never seen sausage put up in cornshucks, but I've heard of 'em doin' that back in Little Granny's day."

Granny chuckled and said, "and after workin' the first day for the Harrises he traded them sausages and goose feathers

212

to Gabe Harris for a sickly pair of twin calves that he'd given up for dead. Some of the old people thought it was a bad sign to have twin calves born. I don't know why, but that's what they always said. Anyhow, Billy thought he could save 'em and sure enough, he doctored 'em back to health right there in Gabe Harris's own barn. Now that was goin' some—to get the best of Gabe Harris in a trade. That hardly ever happened. The Harrises always claimed Billy had a magic touch about 'im where tradin' was concerned. The sayin' was that Billy Bowles could out-trade the Devil hisself from hell to breakfast. Then he married Rusha, and he traded the twin calves to my daddy for a good jersey milk cow. But, I will say this much: the Harrises were all in agreement that Billy Bowles was a worker. But the plain truth is that up 'til that time he was the only beau Rusha ever had. I've heard people talk about how hard he worked for ol' Gabe, just to win the family's approval. They said Billy had gone hungry when he was a boy in Virginia and hadn't known nothin' but hard work since he'd left home. Rusha told me one time that his mother died in childbirth and the daddy was a drunk. She said Billy's sister was a few years older, and late one night she lit some twisted corn shucks late and they ran off to live with a neighbor, just to work for their keep and have somethin' to eat. That neighbor had a son that married Billy's sister later on and they moved out to Indiana and bought a farm there. That's where Billy was headed when he came into Fordville that day. I was born in 1894, so that must've been around 1890.

From what Rusha told me, she fell head over heels in love with Billy that summer and they married that winter. People said he married her for her daddy's money, knowin' she'd come into plenty one day. I never believed it, but he was a cravin' man—a jealous man. Daddy thought he was just plain greedy, but I kindly thought like Mama did. She said Billy never felt like he was good enough for Rusha's family since he came here with nothin' and he just set his mind to out-do 'em—and have as much or more than any of the Harrises—with no help from them. But, it's sad to say, he earned a name for bein' hard-nosed and hard-hearted a man as ol' Gabe Harris. As Billy got older, that horn of a thing on the side of his face kept gettin' bigger but seems like I just got used to it. He always petted on me, on account of me and his son Willie bein' the same age and playin' together in school and such. Especially after the little feller took sick and died, Billy always made it a point to say somethin' to me and smile.

So, no…I never believed he was just sittin' around waitin' for Rusha to get her daddy's money—he just wanted to make a good showin' and was willin' to do might near whatever it took to make it happen. Pride might've been his downfall, but I never felt like he was greedy just for the *sake* of money. My daddy would joke and say that Billy had made a bargain with the Devil and that horn on his face kept gettin' bigger ever' year he had to wait for Gabe Harris to die. But even he said Billy was one of the few men he ever knew that prob'ly worked hisself to death. "

"What *did* he die of?"

"Prob'ly a heart attack, but Dr. Washburn examined him and said he looked like the *picture* of health. "In his prime," he said. That's all I ever heard said about it. But, *the way* he died…it was all…mighty peculiar." The

214

uneasiness in her mind was evident in her voice, even after all those years. She grew quiet.

Perhaps sensing that she needed to lighten the mood, Granny chuckled, "But, talkin' about their courtin' days, I've heard Daddy say, "Rusha was love at first sight for Billy, 'cause he just looked right past that split lip and into them big blue eyes of hers--and saw her daddy's herd of Shorthorn cattle." I don't believe it myself but I know this much: if *anybody* ever thought they'd ever come into easy money foolin' with the Harrises, they had another thing comin'. Gabe Harris drove a hard bargain—a *mean* bargain, at ever'thing he did. He'd catch people in a bind, hurtin' for money and instead of helpin' he took advantage of 'em. They claim he bought a lot of land that-away, and livestock too. People used to say you couldn't trade nickels with the Harrises and come out right.

Rusha told me one time that after she and Billy first married, he wanted to borrow her daddy's yoke of oxen to get his hay loaded and moved down from the hillsides where he'd cut it. Her daddy said he'd let Billy use 'em, but that for ever' single day he had that team of oxen, that he'd have to work FIVE days to pay him back. Now can you imagine that? There Billy was, married to his daughter and you would've thought he'd been glad to help 'em, but the Harrises was all for theirselves.

Now I will say this for Gabe Harris…he *had* furnished Rusha and Billy a place to live. He didn't deed it to 'em outright, but it was to be theirs when he died. That was a good thing to do, but Mama said the Harrises held it over Billy's head, like he should be beholdin' to 'em. That didn't set well and I don't know who'd blame him. Gabe Harris gave each of his boys a farm—but he didn't keep remindin' 'em of it--and on top of that they married Silas Howard's daughters, and they had more land than Gabe Harris. All Billy had was his own two hands and a *lot of pride...maybe too much.*

Rusha said Billy wasn't gonna be outdone by not havin' the use of her daddy's team of oxen. He told her that he wouldn't trade that way with no man and that he'd make do without 'em. He had Rusha to sew 'im up a big canvas bag of a thing with leather straps on it and he filled it with hay and carried it on his back--all the way from the top of the hill to the bottom until he'd moved all four of them big hay stacks. It's untellin' at the number of trips he made up and down them hillsides to move that hay, but he did it. Then it turned off dry that year and there wasn't much hay to be had and Billy Bowles sold them big stacks of hay for twenty dollars apiece *in gold.* He was so proud of what he'd done, he had Rusha to sew an extra pocket on his britches just so he could feel them gold coins against 'im...and he held onto 'em 'til his dyin' day.

The Harrises went to that tiny little Methodist church in Fordville, the one that closed down back in the Twenties. Gabe Harris was one of the deacons and for years, when anybody in Fordville died, he was the one to toll the bell for 'em. By and by, though, Gabe got old and feeble and one of his sons lived closer to the church, so he started doin' it.

I remember when I was just a child and when we heard the first bell strike, we'd all stop in our tracks to listen—and

216

then start countin', to see who it was that'd died. Ever' now and then, it'd be a young person...a child. Fact is, Billy and Jerusha Bowles lost Willie when he wasn't but twelve years old-- Little Willie they called him. We all heard about it but I just remember thinkin' how short the tollin' was compared to Little Granny's. It didn't seem fair to me. She was over a hundred...poor ol' thing had been wantin' to die for a long time but I reckon she just didn't know how. Then there was Little Willie—same age as me, with his whole life in front of him, dead, just like that. He complained with a bad stomach ache at school that Friday at dinner. I reckon he had a twisted bowel and by Tuesday evenin' he was dead. That's when the notion struck me that if Little Willie Bowles was dead, *I* could die. I didn't have to be like Little Granny—over a hundred and tryin' her best to do it.

After the bell tolled for Little Willie, I came to dread hearin' it. At the beginnin', the first strike caught people off guard unless they already knew, or knew of somebody that was bad off. When it got up to sixty tolls or more, most ever'body knew who it was, if they'd been sick for a while. I remember one time when Little Granny took a bad turn and we all thought she was fixin' to die. She was already over a hundred and could still thread a needle without her spectacles. She didn't get out of bed one mornin' and we couldn't wake her. Mama told us then she was as much in the next world as this one. We sent word to all the family, and here they came. By dinner, this house was full of people waitin' on Little Granny to die. That's about when Gabe Harris started tollin' the bell for Miss Betsy Taulbee, our church piano player. She died earlier that mornin', and

217

didn't none of us know it 'til then. Come to find out, she'd dropped dead in her barn lot right about sunup, wringin' a chicken's neck. Word got around that Little Granny was failin', and neighbors started bringin' food since there was so many of us. Miss Betsy was fixin' to fry that chicken to send up here to us, but then *she* up and died.

I think we'd all given Little Granny up for dead, but when she heard that bell, she started stirrin' some. She opened her eyes just a little and said, "Children, who are they tollin' the bell for?" Mama leaned over and said, "It's for Betsy Taulbee, Granny. She died this mornin'." Little Granny just laid there for the longest time, listenin' to the bell toll--and never said nothin'. She'd been a midwife for years, and she said, "I brought Betsy into this world, but I'll be joinin' her up yonder, directly." Poor ol' thing thought she already had one foot inside the Pearly Gates, but it didn't work out that-away. Up around suppertime that evenin', while Mama and one of my aunts were upstairs gettin' Little Granny's buryin' clothes laid out, she opened her eyes and asked for a glass of water. And by bedtime she was sittin' up, eatin' a piece of the applesauce cake that somebody brought us for her funeral. She lived two more years after that--and was mad about it the whole time. God love her heart, Little Granny wanted Gabe Harris to toll the bell for her—and the sooner, the better.

The mornin' Gabe Harris died, I remember Mama sendin' some salt and bakin' soda to their house. Rusha sent her daughter in law up here for some, since they'd used up what they had on Gabe Harris."

Confused, I said, "To cook with?"

Granny said, "No, there wasn't no embalmin' goin' on around here then. The old people believed if they put salt on the stomach of whoever died, it would help keep the swellin' down, especially if they'd been sick a right smart while. They used sody-water to clean the bodies with. When Big Granny died, Mama took a white cloth she'd soaked in it and laid it over her face. It was a strange sight to behold."

As the evening shadows seemed to suddenly grow longer— and darker on the porch, Granny's mood grew somber.

"Early in the mornin' on the day Gabe Harris died, Rusha told Billy Bowles she wanted him to ride down to the church house and toll the bell for--eighty-five tolls I think it was. Might've been eighty-eighty, but it don't matter. Her brother had taken over the job of doin' that from Gabe when he got old, but Rusha didn't want him to have to toll the bell for his own daddy. He was gonna take her to their place to change clothes and after he'd done the tollin', he was to come home and get ready before they rode back to the Harrises.

I've heard Rusha tell that, I bet half a dozen times. After Billy left, she was pourin' hot water into a dishpan to clean up. She was in the house by herself then and she kept hearin' this peckin' sound. When she got to lookin' around to see what it was, there was a mockingbird on their bedroom window-sill, flappin' its wings and flyin' up against the glass. She put her coat on and grabbed a broom to shoo it away, but she left the door standin' wide open and it flew into the house. And if that wasn't strange enough, it got into their bedroom and perched on Billy's pillow. Rusha said she had a time tryin' to get it out of the house, and that later on she wished she'd killed it. Back then, some people believed that a bird flyin' into the house was a sign of death—a death omen, they called it. She told me that after that day there was never another *live* bird to leave her house, and I know she spoke the truth.

On the mornin' this happened, my Uncle Preston was at Perkins' Store and saw Billy ride up into the Methodist church yard on his horse. After he tied it up, he stepped inside and commenced tollin' the bell—real slow. That's the way they did it, and that first one would just about make your blood run cold. Most people around Fordville knew Gabe Harris was fixin' to die, so when Billy started tollin' the bell for him, people started countin', thinkin' for sure they'd hear eighty-odd rings.

Then, all of a sudden, he stopped right at *forty-nine tolls*. I remember us all stoppin' to count 'em. Ever'body did. It was in the dead of winter...one of them cold, nasty days after a big snow had melted and ever'where you stepped, you'd sink shoemouth deep in mud. The leaves were all down, so we could hear that bell all the way from here— three miles. We stood around, just waitin' for it to strike fifty and keep goin', but we never heard another sound, *not another tink*. Uncle Preston and a couple of other men down at Perkins' stood around waitin' for ever' bit of five minutes. Finally, he said, "Boys, somethin's not right. Let's go up here and see what's goin' on." Two or three of 'em headed up to the Methodist church and they found Billy Bowles dead, just inside the door.

Some of the other men from Fordville came up the hill with his body in the back of a wagon. Uncle Preston rode ahead of 'em to the Harris Place to tell Rusha. I watched it go by but Mama wouldn't let us go to the road and look at Billy. She said it was bad luck. They took him home and the neighbors went to work cleanin' him up to get him ready for his funeral the next day—and Gabe Harris was bein' cleaned up for buryin' at his place.

Early the next mornin', there was prob'ly a dozen men or more that rode down to the cemetery to dig the graves. Them days, all the old people around here thought it was bad luck to leave a grave uncovered. You always dug the grave the same day as the buryin'. To make it easier on Rusha, the Harrises decided to have both bodies laid out in Gabe Harris's house way up on the hill there above Babylon. So that evenin' they had Billy and Gabe Harris both laid out in the parlor. I remember seein' 'em both layin' in their coffins with shiny new nickels on their eyes, to keep 'em closed. They had to do that you know, before undertakers came along. That was a scary-lookin' sight to me, seein' 'em that-away. It was like they weren't even human—just cold metal--coins in place of their eyes.

Uncle Preston sat up all night with Billy and Mr. Harris. Just before daylight, he said he looked over at Billy's face and said to his wife, my aunt, "I want you to look--that horn on Billy's face has might near disappeared." He told that and I never knew of the man to lie. He sure did. His brother-in-law was there with him and I've heard him tell the same tale—that Billy's horn--that growth on the side of his face finally gave out." When I was a kid we'd hear that

221

and it would scare us to death. As I got older I thought it prob'ly had somethin' to do with the blood flowin' to it, and when Billy's heart stopped, that growth prob'ly just lost some of what made it look so big. *But I don't know.* They closed the lid on both coffins when daylight came and none of us laid an eye on either one of 'em—ever again.

Both funerals were held down at that little Methodist Church. Since Gabe was the oldest, they buried him first-- in the middle of the mornin' and it was up close to dinner before they got Billy in the ground. They might've been buried two hours apart,"

As Granny finished the tale, I started thinking about Granddaddy and my Uncle Matt, my Aunt Irene's husband and what it would be like if they both died on the same day. I thought about Granddaddy's first heart attack, and the second one a few years later. The doctor had said he likely wouldn't survive the next one and he said ominously there *would be* a next one. The infamous Hall family heart would one day claim yet another victim.

I said to Granny, "That's the saddest story I've ever heard."

"Well, I haven't told you the strangest part." she said.

"Billy Bowles didn't have but the one sister and she lived in Indiana. When she got word Billy had died, she took a train down here to stay with Rusha for a while since she couldn't get here in time for the funeral—nobody did, them days.

I remember seein' her in Fordville, the sister. She was a widow by then. It was prob'ly a month or two after Billy and Gabe Harris had both died. Rusha hadn't put up a grave marker yet. Said she wanted to pick out a real nice gravestone for Billy and she wanted his sister to go into town with her to have it made.

When Billy's sister came to visit, she brought their mother's Bible that had his birth date recorded in it and the rest of the family's dates and such. She and her husband didn't have children and she wanted Billy's boy Luther to have it. Then I reckon Rusha showed her the dates she'd written down to take to the monument works. The sister looked at Billy's birth date Rusha and corrected her. She said, 'Rusha, Billy's not no fifty-three—it's in Mama's Bible right there where she wrote it down. He's five years younger than me and I'm fifty-four. *Billy wasn't but forty-nine when he died.*'

Well, I reckon Rusha fainted dead away when she heard that. Her son Luther's wife told me about it. They hadn't been married but just a few weeks and she was standin' right there beside Rusha when all this happened.

They got her up and carried her to the bed, fannin' and goin' on. When Rusha came to herself she was white as the drippin' snow and the first words out of her mouth were, "*Billy tolled the bell forty-nine times.*"

Billy's sister opened up that Bible and showed it to Rusha. Sure enough, the sister was right—and she had no way in this world of knowin' that he'd tolled that bell exactly forty-nine times. Nobody'd spoken a word about it since it hadn't really meant anything--'til then. And the strangest

223

part of all was that Billy wasn't even the one that was supposed to be tollin' the bell.

I never understood why, but I reckon Billy had lied about his age all that time. The only thing Mama could figure out is that he didn't want Rusha to know he was that much younger than she was—nine years. It shouldn't've made any difference but maybe he felt like it might give people reason to think he was after Rusha's money. My daddy said there was somethin' shameful about a man hidin' his age, but maybe he had his reasons."

Granny grew quiet after finishing her story, as nightfall was upon us. The brilliant sun we'd enjoyed all evening had dropped below the horizon and only orange-tinged clouds remained momentarily. Standing up from the porch swing, she reached for the straw broom that stood in the corner and swept the dead, dry leaves from the porch. No doubt I'd heard it many times before, but that night I remember hearing the dry, scratchy sound they made. She said, "After word got around about the sister bringin' that Bible back here from Indiana with his birth date in it, people didn't know what to make of it. Some people said it was a judgement on 'im. My daddy believed it was, but Mama didn't. All I can say is that nobody around here had ever heard the like. Billy Bowles was the only man they ever knew—or even heard of--*to toll his own death-bell.*"

Granny propped the broom up again in the corner and stepped inside the house where the kitchen light was burning, bright and cheerful. I stood on the porch staring at the orange horizon which now resembled the glow of a dying ember. The big sycamore leaves Granny had just

224

swept off the porch were suddenly caught up in a devil's whirlwind that dropped them, clawing and scratching playfully at my feet. As the wind picked up and whipped some of the leaves around me, I stepped inside and fastened the kitchen door shut.

Maybe it was because of the Halloween stories that prevailed during that time of year and the fact that Granny told this tale on a shadowy, fall evening as she would say, "when it was colorin' for dark," but I thought about it all night until I went to bed. Those thoughts bore fruit later during the pre-dawn dark in the form of the nightmare that sent me running to silence the dinner bell.

With the images and thoughts of Granny's story in my mind no doubt, I dreamed that Granddaddy died ringing the bell. It was so vivid I can still remember hearing the bell make its last ring, the noise that woke me. It had gotten cold in the night after Granny and I had left the porch and there was frost on the ground. I didn't even wait to put my shoes on and my grandparents weren't up yet. I grabbed a pair of pliers from the junk drawer in the kitchen and using the ladder I'd left from painting the dinner bell, I climbed up and removed the clapper. It took me fifteen minutes of twisting the heavy wire to do it while holding the clapper with one hand to keep it from making a racket. But when it come loose, and with my feet already freezing I ran with it as hard and fast as I could go to the edge across the small pasture on the west side of the house and hurled it out of sight. I heard it make a satisfying knock against some tree hidden from view in the woods.

For a long period of time, my grandparents appeared not to notice the clapper was gone and I lied about it when questioned. I told them I had taken it loose to do a better job of painting but had misplaced it. It was a credible defense because I was forever misplacing or losing things—and still do. I got fussed at a little, but the bell hadn't been rung in years—intentionally, and nothing more was ever said about it.

Long after both my grandparents had died--after my wife Sandy and I remodeled their old farmhouse, a summer storm blew down a dead walnut tree in the same woods where, as a frightened twelve year old, I had hurled the bell clapper. I waited until late winter to drive the tractor and wagon up there to cut it up for firewood. At the base of the stump in the loosened dirt, what should appear before my eyes but the clapper itself. In my fanciful memory, I had thrown it at least a hundred feet. In reality it had gone no further than fifteen. I brought it back to the house, cleaned it with a wire brush and even repainted the thing.

It lay on my workbench in the barn for a few weeks and then looking at it with sudden clarity early one morning, I remembered Granny saying that when the bell had been moved there, its days of tolling the death knell had already ceased. It fact, on the very day it had been moved from the smokehouse, it *had* in fact been rung by my fourteen year old uncle Johnny for my mother, when she turned one year old, in 1932. Thereafter it became a family tradition to ring the bill for the children's birthdays---Uncle Johnny, Aunt Irene, and my mother, that is until Uncle Johnny was killed in World War Two. He had enjoyed that tradition so much

226

so that it was evidently discontinued after he could no longer be part of it.

After musing on the recollection of a childhood fear, and recalling that it had not always been used as a messenger of death, I soon restored the clapper to the bell. With the next family birthday dinner, we made a big deal of ringing it once again. My children and happily, my grandchildren, now only know to associate the old bell with a celebration of life. I prefer to keep it that way.

The double screen doors to my workshop

The Rainbo School

There's something about old doors that fascinate me.

Over the last forty-odd years, I've taken hundreds of pictures of them—of all shapes and sizes. In Joshua, Texas, and Jonesboro, Tennessee. Whether it's been in Robertsdale, Alabama, or Roberts' Cove, Ireland, I've looked for doors with personality--those that can either welcome you with open, rusty hinges--or shut you out with cold, polished brass.

I've photographed the crudely made doors of log cabins that once kept out Indians--and others of indescribable beauty that were once opened before kings. Those I appreciate most, however, are a pair of seventy-year-old screen doors from Perkins' Store in Fordville. Kentucky. Offered to me when the old building was torn down, I gave them a new purpose in the workshop I built onto my barn.

Their only noteworthy feature is the faded "**Rainbo** is Good Bread" logo. In fact, I still have to think about how to spell the old ad's first orange-lettered word that caused me to get it wrong on a spelling test. My third grade teacher was matronly Miss Maude Hoskins. I still remember our brief exchange on the matter as she sat grading the tests at her big wooden desk. Seated on the front row, I was in her direct line of fire for interrogation. She peered at me over her chained, horn-rimmed eyeglasses.

"What on earth's wrong with you, Clay? You *know* rainbow has a "w" in it. Why did you miss it?"

I said, "Miss Hoskins, I don't believe anybody in Fordville knows how to spell that word."

Her eyebrows knitted. "And why is that?"

"At Mack Perkins' Store, the screen doors say it's "R-A-I-N-B-O-and there ain't no "W" in it."

A grin worked its way across her broad face making the wart on the end of her chin stand at full attention.

"Well, I declare, so *t-h-a-t's* where you got it—and don't say "ain't, Clay."

Miss Hoskins made me rewrite the word five times, correctly, beside the misbegotten version.

She said, "Well, *now* you know. If it makes you feel any better, I've been in that store a thousand times if I've been in it once...but *I* learned to spell before Rainbo Bread was ever thought of."

Imperfect as it was, Perkins' Store became one of the "schools" of my youth, and a vital part of my journey to manhood. When "class" began, there was no bell. After the screen door ceased splatting against its wooden frame every weekday afternoon, it was yet time for another session of "The Children's Hour." No books, no paper and pencils were required. All I had to do was *listen.*

Although loafers might appear most any time of day, it wasn't until around four-thirty in the afternoon that most of the "faculty" showed up—these Fordville residents, mostly men, from whom I learned some of life's most important lessons.

Let's expand this particular gathering to include those that likely never all appeared at exactly the same time. For that reason, seating is crowded—standing room only. We will stay close to the front—inside the double screen doors where I will introduce you to the "teaching faculty" of The Rainbo School.

We begin on my left with rotund farmer, Willie Ross. He loves to eat, and feeds anything and everything around him anytime, anywhere. Some say it's because he knows what hunger is, from a youth barely mentioned. Only once do I remember him referring to his childhood. He was speaking about hard times he'd known. He said, "We were so hungry there at one time, by Ned, Mama thought about boilin' the dishrag," and this time he wasn't laughing. Sharing the same bench and a special bond with him is *white* Willie's closest friend: *black*, tall, and rail-thin "Delb" Shearer, whose slave-born parents, against all odds, came to own several small farms through their own extraordinary effort and resourcefulness, noble traits they instilled in a worthy son; next is "Red" Perkins, a hardworking but miserly old codger who owns run-down property all over our part of the county, and to quote Delb, will "squeeze a quarter 'til the eagle hollers." In terms of religion, Red seems to be a scoffer-possibly an agnostic, but the way he admires the beauty of a freshly fallen snow, you wonder. He says he "don't believe in nothin' or nobody." Still, for decades he has come to these daily gatherings, seemingly in search of something he doesn't have and that the comfort of his horded money cannot give him.

Usually sitting next to Red is my hard working, good-hearted granddaddy, Russell Hall. Clad in clean but patched overalls, Granddaddy sits quietly with his long legs crossed, twiddling his thumbs. If he's amused at what's shared before the stove, Granddaddy lightly taps the coal bucket next to it with one of his work shoes. The funnier it is, the harder he taps.

Although they rarely sit next to each other, for this "class" I will position beside of Granddaddy, his alcoholic brother J. B. Hall. Willie Ross once described him as a genius, "sharp as a rat's turd, but so dad-blame lazy, dead lice won't fall off of 'im'." Still, I could never get enough of my great-uncle, for there is adventure--fun to be had, if he's around. The self-described "river rat" possesses an inventive mind, but one unfortunately marinated in liquor most of the time. By common agreement, Fordville's most naturally talented son who can do anything... doesn't.

Next to J.B. sits his rarely-if-ever-paid landlord and drinking buddy--short, plump veterinarian Doc Wilcox, who gave up his dream of becoming a sportswriter to follow in the footsteps of his only brother, who drowned in the nearby Kentucky River when The Titanic was still front page news. The brilliant, soft-spoken bachelor prefers to be at one with his unsophisticated brethren and speaks in the same southern drawl about the same topics, yet in one sitting can complete The New York Times crossword puzzle with an ink pen—and makef no mistakes.

Beside Doc, let's place soft-spoken handyman Terry Moses (Pronounced together as "Turr-Mose") Taylor, a quirky mechanical genius whose new bride Bonnie Little died the same month they were wed during the 1919 Flu Epidemic, not even long enough for her to be remembered by her married name. Although Terry Mose builds and rebuilds engines as a hobby, he is afraid to drive anything with one in it. He rides around Fordville with his employer--one-eyed carpenter Dan Jacob Little—his onetime brother-in-law, who drives him to visit Bonnie's grave *every* Sunday at 2:00.

Over from Mr. Little we see Andrew Venable. Distantly related to me, "Cousin Andy" repairs clocks and watches at a counter he keeps in the back of Ed Richard's adjoining barber shop. The old bachelor always smiles, and shuffles his feet when he walks, counting every step he takes in a day's time. This trait, among others, is reportedly due to him being gassed in France during the First World War, although storekeeper Mack Perkins says he was like that before the Germans ever laid eyes on him.

Sitting beside Cousin Andy is Terry Mose Taylor's older brother, Perry Lee Taylor, (pronounced "Purr-lee"), who owns the gas station and garage across the road. The gentle man who speaks with a coarse whisper has given away several tons of bubble gum to local kids over the years, one handful at a time. It is said that six year old Perry Lee nearly choked to death after swallowing shelled corn a neighbor fed to her chickens, some of which lodged in his vocal cords. J.B. always said "Hunger can drive a monkey to eat red pepper," and it *had* driven young Perry Lee to crawl around on the neighbor's frozen barn lot to pick up loose kernels. He was attempting to carry food home to little brother Terry Mose—later found cold, naked and eating raw eggs in the same neighbor's chicken house. Perry Lee's life was spared when the quick-thinking neighbor yanked him up by his feet and shook him until the swallowed corn dislodged. On that day, the hale and hearty neighbor, a childless blacksmith's widow who took in washing and ironing also took in Perry Lee and Terry Mose to raise as her own. The brothers whose birth name was Purvis, eventually honored the memory of Moll Taylor by adopting *her* last name.

Sitting quietly beside Perry Lee, we see "Brother" Simpson, the elderly, illiterate preacher of a tiny church he built with his own hands, one of which was missing two fingers shot off in Cuba during the Spanish-American War.

Sitting close to him and wearing an old-fashioned bonnet is his devoted, wife, "Sister" Simpson whose features cannot hide the scars of an unspoken childhood. She gazes at the little man sitting next to her as if she can never quite get enough of him, and affirms everything he says with an approving nod.

Last to appear, for he closed at 5:00 daily, might be local barber Ed Richards, a much-loved fatherly figure to me and every other kid around. Arriving late in the Children's Hour, "Pop-Ed" usually comes through the door sharing a lame joke of some kind he's picked up that day in his adjoining barber shop. He is usually the last to leave, and always with a smile on his face and a lunchbox strapped on his shoulder—special made so he can read the newspaper on his long walks home, and he insists on walking. Despite personal tragedy and the crippling arthritis that often made his work painful, Pop-Ed *habitually* looks for the good in people—and most often finds it.

There are others who frequently seek fellowship behind the Rainbo doors, but with less predictability. However, if there is a headmaster of The Rainbo School, it is stocky, white-aproned storeowner John McWilliams Perkins—"Mack." His father opened the store in 1902, and at his untimely death, a young Mack vowed to stay put—to run the store. In so doing, he not only cared for his mother and blind sister, but in his own unassuming way, the very heart and soul of the declining little community.

In The Rainbo School, and from these people—my "teachers," I learned many things--not all of them positive and uplifting. But, since this is my way of introducing you,

234

let's keep this lesson on the lighter side with the subject I prefer to remember most: laughter. There is no film footage that can be seen, no surviving sound recordings to be heard. However, if I could, for this lesson I would have you see Delb Shearer with a wizened smirk on his face as he playfully throws his cap on the floor. I would have you hear Terry Mose Taylor's joy-filled laugh and Willie Ross's thick hands as they clap —all for tales well-told, and worthy of praise.

The first lesson in humor inflicted upon me in that classroom was the seemingly heartbreaking story of the bloody mule's back—at least, that's the image Willie Ross used to lure me in. It was by no means the first, but it was the first one I learned well enough to repeat. I must've been about ten years old at the time and during that day's session of The Children's Hour, the discussion came around to the subject of mules.

The conversation had waned when Willie Ross turned his bulk toward me as his young and innocent victim. I am sitting on a metal porch chair that storeowner Mack Perkins has dragged in for the winter. It's a cold January afternoon and the old men draw near to the fire in the pot belly stove. Unknowingly, I am the primary focus of today's lesson.

Willie looks at me through his heavy, black rimmed glasses.

"Clay, did I ever tell you about my *first* mule?"

"No sir."

Willie shakes his head and looks down at his shoes as if the subject was almost too painful for him to continue.

"I wasn't much older'n you are now when I got 'im—that's how come for me to think of it. Lord, he was good'n, but to tell you the truth, he was about half-dead the first time I ever saw 'im."

What Willie was telling was an incredibly old and stale joke—one so old and told so many times that its teller couldn't keep his account of it straight, even as he attempted to tell it. I, however, was unable to frustrate the man's efforts. I had unknowingly taken the high road, and the bait.

"What happened to him?"

Willie's answer was not to be given up that easily. This was something to be savored.

"Well, we had us a neighbor up on Grizzard Hill that moved in there when I was a kid. He was uh, uh…what *was* that old man's name, Delb?"

Delb was seriously engaged in cleaning the mud out of the treads of his work shoes with his pocket knife. Without raising his head, he answered, "Bowman."

Willie continued. "That's it. Old Man Bowman. He was a mean ol' sum-buck, too—and poor as Job's turkey. Didn't have but one poor ol' red mule to work that rough land of his with, and, Lord, he was pitiful."

He knew I loved animals. "What was wrong with it?"

"Oh, he was old and wore out to begin with, and Old Man Bowman just about starved 'im to death—my lord, you never saw such an animal in your life. He was so thin Old Bowman had to tie a knot in his tail to keep 'im from slippin' through the collar. Why, I could've hung my hat on his hip-bone, and Delb there can back me up--that ain't no lie. But now, the first time I ever saw 'im, his back was bloody as a butchered hog."

I was being reeled in, but slowly. Fortunately for Willie, I was the only young fish picking at the bait.

"You mean Old Man Bowman starved AND beat 'im--both?"

Willie lowered his head, probably to bite his lip and reassemble a straight face.

He nodded.

His composure regained, he raised his head and continued.

"Yeah, Ol' Bowman nearly beat 'im to death ever' time he plowed. He knew just when to quit, though. I was walkin' home from school one day and he was flailin' away at 'im in the middle of the pasture. It was up close to Christmas where he'd been pilin' a load of rocks on a sled to haul 'em off...and--

I interrupted, "Mr. Ross, did he have a name—the mule?"

Willie never missed a beat. "Why, yeah...lemme think now. "Ted," he says, "Poor ol' Ted. Anyhow, I hid behind a tree while Ol' Bowman beat on Ol' Red and he—

I said, "You mean *Ted*?" Willie couldn't keep the details straight, but he could keep a straight face.

"Ted's what I meant," he said, "I think Red was the name of that last mule Ol' Bowman had—wasn't he, Delb?"

Delb avoided eye contact as he took his long hand and swept up the crumbs of dried mud from his boots. Tossing them into the coal bucket in front of him, he mumbled. "That's right, Willie. You're *plumb right.*"

"Well, Ol' Bowman kept beatin' on Ted 'til I reckon he finally he got the devilment out of his system. Direc'ly, he tuckers out and just leaves 'im all beat and bloody, still hitched to the plow in the middle of that cornfield and—

I interrupt again.

"Mr. Ross, I thought you said he was *pulling a load of rocks—in a sled?*"

Willie seemed just a little flustered, but he pulled himself together admirably.

"Well, I think I saw Bowman beatin' on 'im another time and I think he was plowin' *then*. Anyhow, he goes off to the house and I slip up there and that poor ol' mule's back looked plumb awful from where he'd been whipped so hard. That blood runnin' all down his sides made me want to cry. So I says to myself, "Ted ol' buddy, I'm gonna unhitch you from this sled and get you away from Old Man Bowman. I'm gonna take you to our barn and take care of you."

That sure sounded like Willie. Always helping people and known for being good and kind to his animals.

I was reeled about two thirds of the way in by now. This was w-a-y too easy.

Curious, I asked, "What did you do to help him? Ted, I mean."

"Well, I'll just tell you—that poor ol' mule was so weak he couldn't hardly stand up and I was afraid Ol' Bowman was gonna come back and catch me tryin' to take 'im. I had to hurry. I happened to look down by the sled about that time and he'd left a chain and a piece of rope layin' there so I tied me up a bridle and slipped it over 'im and we hadn't no more than cleared the woods than here come big snow flakes fallin' and I mean big'ns.

I never felt as sorry for an animal in my life as I did ol' Bud that day.

"You mean *Ted*?"

"That's right--Ted's what I meant. Bud's the one he got after ol' Ted—wasn't he, Andy?"

Cousin Andy was tallying his step count for the day in his tablet, but took the time to raise his head in support.

"Yessir, I believe that's it."

"Well, before I could get ol' Ted to our barn, there was an inch or better of snow that fell on me and him both. It was bad enough that his back was raw and bloody from where

239

Ol' Bowman had whipped 'im, but now he was near froze on top of that."

Delb Shearer added his two cents' worth, "Mm-mm. I sho-nuff remember Ol' Bowman. He was a bad'n, alright."

Reinforcements had arrived.

The other old men nodded in agreement. Even Perry Lee Taylor, who could barely speak above a whisper joined in. "Yessir, Ol' Bowman was the meanest one man God ever put a breath in, he was for a fact."

Willie says, "Well, we had to hurry so I slipped through that little patch of woods between The Bowman Place and ours and I finally got Ted to our barn. I put 'im in the stall and fed 'im some corn."

"What did you do about his bloody back?"

"Well, now…that was tricky, see. I wiped all that snow off of 'im the best I could with a feed sack, and it right red and bloody-lookin'. He was pitiful…plumb pitiful. I ran to the house right quick and got some coal oil and kindly dribbled it all over his back to help 'im heal up. Anytime any of us kids got a cut or scratch, that's what Mama or Daddy put on it."

"Did it make Ted get better?"

"Well, some…but the ol' feller was shiverin' in his tracks, he was. He was as pitiful a sight as you ever witnessed. Poor ol' Ted." The others joined in the sad chorus. "Poor ol' Ted," they moaned.

Willie said, "The coal oil helped ease his pain some, but now, it was that sheepskin that done 'im the most good."

"Sheepskin?"

"Why, yeah. Just about ever'body raised sheep around here back then. We had this big ol' sheepskin hung up on a nail in our barn and Ted was shiverin' and shakin' from the cold, and as weak-eyed as any dead mule I'd ever seen. So, I grabbed that there sheepskin and I laid it over his back and you should've seen 'im."

"Why? What did he do?"

"Well, in just a few minutes he just laid them ears back like he never felt no better in his whole life—all good and warm. He did for a fact. Then I got hold of a ball of twine Daddy had hangin' up there on a nail and I tied that sheepskin on 'im real good and tight so it wouldn't fall off.

Now Ted's eatin' this whole time, see—eatin' like he hadn't never seen an ear of corn in his whole life, but I get to worryin' about Ol' Bowman comin' out into his field and findin' his mule gone. So I start to lead 'im out of the barn to take 'im back to that sled and I look toward the house and you know what I see?"

"No, what?"

"It's Ol' Bowman hisself, beatin' on our door, that's what. And mad—his face was so red, you could've lit a match off of it. I could hear 'im hollerin' clean to the barn. Daddy opens the door and asks him what his business is and he tells that somebody saw me run off with his mule and it still hitched to the plow in the middle of his cornfield.

"You mean *the sled*, don't you?"

"Yeah, well, that's what I meant—and him still hitched to that sled. Daddy and Ol' Bowman see me comin' out of the barn with Ted right about then and here they come. Bowman was cussin' up a storm. Daddy was about to put 'im on the road, but then he sees what a sad shape Ted's in. He tells Bowman that he'll give 'im two dollars for Ted and he'd better take it since he was fixin' to die anyway. And about that time, sure enough, ol' Ted laid down right there in the middle of that barn lot—and in the snow. We thought he was gonna die, sure as two and two's four. Ol' Bowman was in a fix. He looked back and forth 'tween Daddy and ol' Ted, and direc'ly he says, "Sold.""

Daddy draws out his pocketbook to pay 'im and he leaves. But then Daddy turns around and says to me, "Son, I've paid Bowman, but now you owe me two whole U-nited States' dollars—and for a dead mule, looks like."

This was sad. "So what happened to Ted?"

Willie puts his heavy hand on my shoulder and softened his voice. "Well, don't you know--ol' Ted was puttin' on that whole time?"

"Really?"

He was for a fact. Ol' Ted was a smart'n. About the smartest old mule ever I saw—ain't that right, Brother Simpson?"

Even feeble old Holiness preacher "Brother Simpson" joined in for the slaughter. "Yessir," he said, "the smartest one mule that's ever lived in these parts, Ol' Ted was."

I asked Willie, "Did he live?"

"Live?"

"Son, what are you talkin' about? Why, I led 'im back into the barn and put 'im up in a stall out there and he healed up the best you ever saw."

I started to think how hard it would've been for a boy back in Willie's day to earn two dollars. That was a lot of money for me, even then.

"Did you ever pay your dad what you owed 'im?"

"Lord, I reckon."

I thought this happy story of a redeemed old mule was now complete.

It *nearly* was, but my education wasn't.

"How did you?"

"It wasn't easy. Remember that sheepskin I was tellin' you about?"

I nodded.

"Well, that sheepskin stuck to ol' Ted's back, where it was bloody, and *it dried*. I tried ever' way in the world to pull it off of 'im and it wouldn't budge...not one bit, so I just left it on 'im and when the weather warmed up real good and the pasture greened up that spring, I turned him out to graze on it and he done the best ever was. We had 'im for a long time after that."

"But how did you earn the two dollars?"

"Oh, that part," he says.

"Well, you know, that was the funniest thing ever was, right there. Where I tied that sheepskin onto ol' Ted's back, he commenced growin' the purtiest coat of white wool you ever laid your eyes on. Delb there knows I'm tellin' the truth—ain't I Delb?

Delb grunted.

"So here's what I done: I sheared the wool off ol' Ted that spring…sold ever' bit of it—and paid Daddy his two dollars back. Fact is, I sold enough wool off of 'im ever' year 'to pay his keep."

In something like a staggered chorus, the straight-faced old men once more joined in moaning "Good ol' Ted."

By then, the pressure was too great. Either portly Willie broke wind or I heard a split-second suppressed cackle from one of them, but it would've been about the count of three before the old codgers busted out laughing—at me, not an old joke they had heard for the better part of a century, and at Willie, who had told it so many times that he couldn't remember if the mule was Ted, Red or Bud, or if he was pulling a sled or a plow.

Having been hooked and reeled in without much effort, I was now being held up on the scales for weighing. The relatively painless hook had been removed. For old men in a dying little community, fresh opportunities for tired old jokes didn't come along very often.

After the laughter died down, Willie bought me a cold pop for being a good sport. For his part in the conspiracy, Delb Shearer handed me a "Pay Day" candy bar while he munched on one himself, eating the peanuts first which he picked off one at a time.

Although there would be many other such tales told and retold, some would be at my expense, and others not. Without exception, all who assembled for that gathering of Fordville's tribal elders had in some way at some-time been the butt of (generally) good-natured jokes. Conveyed to my young mind in hundreds of such sessions of The Children's Hour was a simple message: Life is hard enough, so don't make it any harder by taking yourself too seriously: *You are not alone.*

In my second-shift "classroom", in a country store in the middle of dying little Fordville, more or less in the middle of Kentucky, I learned the value of humor . From these old men over time I learned both how to tell-and take—a joke.

Early on—and perhaps most importantly, I learned to laugh at myself.

A Chairmaking Love

Sister turned Brother gently over on his side. She'd done it for weeks now to keep him from getting bedsores. Patting him tenderly, in a near whisper she said, "He's always been my hero."

She looked tired--more tired than her seventy years or more. She wasn't sure just how many more, since she didn't know her exact age.

We sat there in silence looking at the quilt that lay on Brother, barely rising under his light breathing. From where I sat, shrunken and withered as he was, Brother looked for all the world like a child tucked in for a good night's sleep.

Beside Brother Cain Simpson's bed stood the hickory bottom chair Sister had labored months earlier to convert into a homemade toilet. Hand painted daisies decorated the top slat of the simple ladder back chair she and Brother made together as newlyweds, fifty-odd years before.

Off and on for two days Sister tugged, pulled, sawed and hacked her way through the tough bark bottom, finally replacing it with a toilet seat taken from their nearby outhouse, redeployed and repainted with leftover brown floor paint found in the root cellar. Matching, pleated brown curtain material bought in town was tacked along the edge of the chair, concealing the white metal pot directly under the seat--the toilet part, known as "the slop jar."

But by now Brother was past needing a bed pan, let alone help getting to the outhouse.

246

The smell of the brown floor paint still lingered near the converted kitchen chair which stood beside the bed Brother and Sister Simpson shared.

Nodding toward Brother's potty chair, Sister said, "Lord, I had me a time takin' the bottom outta that old chair...I still remember me and Brother goin' to the woods to cut the hickory to bottom it with, and the rest of that set. I reckon we outdid ourselves-- I sure never thought about cuttin' it out. We made it to last, Brother and me--went to housekeepin' with that'n and four more just like it...and we've got three left countin' that one."

Sister grew quiet in the dark, gazing into the flame barely rolling over the coals in the grate.

It was probably just nervous energy that made her talkative. I don't really think Sister's mind was on the chairs she and Brother had made. For some time now her constant thought had been the loosening silver chord that was barely still holding him in the land of the living.

To Granny, she said, "We would've had the whole set but then the Colsons had that fire a few years back and when Brother heard it burnt up everything they had, nothin' would do but for 'im to take 'em two of our ol' chairs. Said he'd make us two more come spring, but I knowed right then Brother's chair makin' days was done."

It brought a smile to my face to hear it, but no one who knew them could be surprised. Brother and Sister had been known for such acts of kindness for many years. I was hoping Brother wouldn't die while we were sitting there watching him--waiting for it to happen. Hearing Sister chuckle lightened the mood a little. I thought to myself, "Nobody can die if there's laughter in the room."

247

I was hoping there would be more. More of anything than what we were part of at that moment, what was clearly the dying process. Granny and Sister Simpson had been around it their entire lives, for young and old alike.

Still thinking about the simple set of chairs that had been such a part of their lives together, Sister said, "It was just the two of us sittin' at that table most the time anyway. Just me now." She grew quiet again as we alternately watched the dying coals in the grate--and Brother. I placed a chunk of black on it, hoping for bright red flame, for any sign of movement—life. Sister said, "So, when Brother got sick, I took a notion to make Brother a toilet out of one of the three of 'em we still had, one he could use without hobblin' around outside like a frostbit chicken."

Sister dropped her head with the same vacant smile. "Brother didn't like to use that chair in here. He said he didn't like the idea one bit of eatin' in the same house his bowels moved in. But, I reckon he finally got used to it. But, time and again he'd still fuss about it. Said even a bird had sense enough not to dirty its own nest. I sure wish he had strength enough right there in that bed to raise hisself up and fuss about somethin', and I wouldn't care a bit what it was."

As on a blustery March day when high, dark clouds gather, a passing darkness would settle upon Sister when I asked questions about her youth. Even as a kid, I came to understand those questions should be handled carefully. When topics of the dim past arose, I learned to watch Sister's face before I continued. Still, as we sat there, something compelled me to ask about her earlier days, and the simple homemade chairs, one of which was now a toilet.

A tear-dimmed eye glimmered as she spoke of her younger life with Brother. She could never speak of the man without smiling.

"We were livin' on Bullskin Creek then. Brother 'd already cut the maple and I helped 'im with the bottoms after he made the chairs. We spent the day cuttin' the hickory bark into strips. Brother'd roll 'em up and put 'em in a tub of water in the wagon. I always loved goin' to the woods with Brother for he knowed ever' tree and bush there was. He'd cut white oak and we'd make baskets to sell when we went to housekeepin'. Brother'd cut round pieces of tin and put in the bottoms, to make 'em stronger . All the women around Bullskin wanted his baskets, and when we come here people kept wantin' 'em for a long time. We made about ever' basket here on this place and a good many of the ones people still has-- all around here." It was true, and to this day I encounter his trademark tin-bottom baskets at farm auctions.

Nodding in Brother's direction, Sister said, "With Brother just havin' three fingers on his left hand, he would-a had a tough time of it by hisself. We had to work together--just like a team of mules. He might lead this time, then me the next, but we pulled the same load most the time. We built this whole house and the outbuildin's together--and dug out the cellar...just me and him."

I stayed many nights with Brother and Sister Simpson after he "took his bed" with smothering spells. Although it was the 1960's, the couple had never owned an automobile, television set or radio. They rose and went to bed with the sun, and during the day they planted and cared for their farm animals strictly by the cycles of the moon and "the signs."

Married for many years, there was a clearly understood ritual the old couple observed every evening. The supper dishes cleared away, Sister would retrieve Brother's Bible from their bedroom dresser and with his receptive hand extended, he would receive it without comment, flip through a few worn sections and point to

249

a passage. Sister would then read aloud to him as best she could, in fits and starts.

Until I went to church with them one Sunday night a couple of years earlier, I didn't realize Brother couldn't read. I told Granny about my observation and she seemed surprised that I didn't know. She said, sympathetically, "The poor ol' feller wouldn't know his own name if it was lit up in four foot neon letters in the courthouse square." Then she added quickly, "but don't let that fool you. Ol' Brother's as smart as they come. He just never had the *chance* to get schoolin' like young people do now."

At their church services, Sister would read from the Bible. Brother would preach. It was a perfect partnership. When he was ready for more reading, Brother would look over his store bought glasses at Sister, saying, *"Read on, Sister Simpson."* I nearly bit my lip in two because the first time I heard this, it seemed funny and cool at the same time...and it worked. Brother carried his well-worn Bible and couldn't read a word in it. Yet, as Sister would read to him at night, Brother could quote entire passages almost perfectly from memory. He was convinced Jesus spoke King James English and quoted New Testament verses as if he was using the very same words two thousand years later. Everything the couple did, and had done was in partnership. Sitting in front of the fire that evening waiting for him to die, Sister detailed every addition she and Brother had made to build their simple four room home, beginning with just one room and a chimney, gradually adding a room or outbuilding on the seven acre hillside until there was more outbuilding than house: an outhouse, a henhouse, a barn, a coalhouse, a washhouse and a toolshed, and finally, a dozen or more of Brother's little bee houses, or "bee stands," as he called them.

Two nights before Brother drew his last breath, as we were sitting there, I unknowingly asked Sister how they came to be known as--Brother and Sister. We sat together in silence for a moment as I watched the dark clouds gather over her face. I honestly didn't think the question had any connection to her early life or I wouldn't have raised the subject.

"Well…" she drawled, "I reckon it's 'cause we was always over here at the Church, doin' somethin' to keep it goin' and it just kinda stuck. Members called us Brother and Sister so it just took, and before long everybody was callin' us that." As I later came to learn, that was only partly true, perhaps a façade, for the larger part of the story was simply too painful for her speak.

Sister said "At Christmastime years ago, one of the Sunday School children made a Christmas card for me and at the top it said, "Merry Christmas Mrs. Sis*ter."* True enough, nearly everyone around Fordville knew the aged couple as Brother and Sister. No other couple I've ever known has shared those terms of endearment with an entire community.

It wasn't until after Sister died that Granny shared another story with me that stands as testimony to the love shared by the old couple, heavily seasoned with irony.

Granny didn't particularly want to share what she knew of Sister's distant past, but by that time I was in college and had served two years of active duty in Vietnam, Brother and Sister were both in the Fordville Cemetery.

She said, "After Brother and Sister ran off and got married, they lived near some of his people on Bullskin Creek up in Clay County. Word got around there that Brother's mother came to him after he married Sister and said they couldn't stay together, because her dead husband was Sister's real father. And of course if that was true, it meant that Brother and Sister were

251

half-brother and sister. I've never said me a word about it to nobody…and I tell you the truth, even after all this time it just about makes me sick to even tell it. She said I was the only one she ever spoke it to, but…sometimes I wished she hadn't.

Sister did say that what her mother- in-law told her—that Brother's daddy had kinfolks that he'd go visit, on Cutshin Creek where Sister was raised—that part was true. She said Brother never thought there was any truth to it, but over time, people kept whisperin' about 'em behind their backs.

After Sister never had a baby to come along, the rumor went around that they were afraid to have any because they were half brother and sister. People started carryin' tales, and even callin' 'em "Brother "and "Sister" behind their *backs*. That went on for several years. They were hurt over not havin' any children and that gossip floatin' around made it that much worse. You know how meek and mild poor ol' Sister was. It had to be bad for her to want to leave.

Brother came up here and took a job at the saw mill in Fordville. He knew a man that worked there—they'd rafted logs together, down on the River. So, he bought that piece of ground on Slabtown Road and built 'em a little one room house. Then he brought Sister up here with everything they owned--in one wagon. He left his own people behind to come down here, so they could have a fresh start. After Sister told that story, she never spoke another word on the subject, other than she said she didn't believe what her mother -in-law had said. I reckon the ones that knew the real truth are all dead and gone, so it don't matter no more."

I had once heard Sister speak of the man she believed to be her father, but never had she made any reference to the ugly rumor— or the ugly reality behind their nicknames of Brother and Sister, which I only knew as terms of endearment. I had known the couple for so long I'd just about forgotten their real names until Granny reminded me.

"Cain and Betty," she said.

Tightening her sweatered forearms to warm them in the cool fall air as we sat on the porch, Granny grew quiet and reflective for a while as we watched a flock of geese fly overhead in the October sky.

She asked, "Do you remember hearin' about the Simpson Flood?"

I shook my head, "No, never heard that one."

"It's kindly funny--and sad, both. Sister was always lookin' for the end of time. She was convinced that it was right around the corner. I tried tellin' her I didn't think God wanted us to fret over it, but she would just study her Bible and watch for signs.

Granny said, "It was about the time that Harold Collins started fixin' up his mother's old place. We were in the middle of a long dry spell—not as bad as some I remember, but dry enough. Harold decided to clean out that big old pond he had there at the back of his place above Slabtown Road. That pond was old…dug before I ever married, and they claim it was deep enough for team of horses to swim across. It was spring-fed and held water when most these little ponds were mud holes—even in the droughts we had in the Thirties.

The bulldozer man cut deep into that pond bank and here came the water. Untellin' how many thousands of gallons came rushin' down that ridge and down into the holler—and it put Tattler's Branch clean out of its banks. Washed Sister's little garden away, buckets they'd been carryin' water with…and the hoes they'd laid down that mornin'." With a chuckle, Granny

253

pointed down at her feet and said, "Even carried away a pair of Sister's shoes. You know how she'd take 'em off sometimes and work in her garden barefooted.

Poor Old Sister...and the funny thing was--you could not see one single, solitary cloud in the sky. We hadn't had a drop of rain in weeks, and there comes a flood washin' everything away. She came runnin' out that road as fast as them little feet would take her, all the way to Perkins' Store. Just like the other time, somebody had to go find Brother and bring 'im home to get her settled down. After that, people would kid with Brother and call it the "Simpson Flood." Sister just knew it had to be a sign of the end times. I don't know what her life would've been like without good ol' Brother. I've never known another couple like 'em."

I thought about the sad tale of Brother and Sister that Granny reluctantly shared. She had been sworn to secrecy. I said, "Granny, if they left the mountains for being called Brother and Sister, how did they wind up being called that *here*?"

She sighed, "You know, now that they're both dead and gone, I've thought about that. I reckon what Sister told you was right, more or less. After Brother came through that ol' flu epidemic, the one right after the World War ended, he promised God he'd go to preachin' if he lived through it. And he lived—Sister never caught it and she took care of 'im. People would take food to Sister's front porch and then they'd fire a pistol in the air to let 'er know the food was there. People were afraid of catchin' it, and still tried to help each other the best way they could. After he came through the flu, Brother got lumber donated and built that tiny little church there on his land; he and Sister worked on it forever. Men at the sawmill and around the community would help out and maybe give some tin for the roof and what not. Over time, they had it up and runnin', and then people all around started callin' 'em Brother and Sister. It does seem kindly funny —especially after they came here to get away from it.

The funny thing is I don't think folks here ever knew the tales that were told on 'em up in Clay County. If they had, it prob'ly wouldn't have been one bit better here—maybe worse. Sometimes people just want to get away—not to any one place in particular...they just want to be away from where they've been."

Granny got up from the porch swing to go in for the evening.

She stopped as she started across the threshold, turning toward me. "Maybe by that time, it just didn't matter anymore what people thought...or said. Ever'body here knew Brother and Sister by the way they lived and they touched a whole lot of people in their time. When Brother was buried, even Humpy John the Bootlegger showed up. Didn't none of us know it at the time, but he'd done paid a man to dig the grave. Humpy didn't set foot in the church for the funeral, but he was there when they buried Brother. Nearly ever'body had left the graveside by then... just a handful of us standin' around. It was right cloudy all that day and about then it started sprinklin' a little and I was tryin' to get a sweater around Sister so she wouldn't get wet as we were walkin' back to the car. Humpy had been standin' back, under a tree smokin' a cigarette, but direc'ly he came up to Brother's grave with a shovel in his hand, waitin' 'til Sister was gone before he started throwin' dirt in on top of the casket. He took his hat off—like this here--and held it against his chest. I'll never forget that. Ol' Humpy stood still for just a second, starin' down into Brother's grave and I heard him say, *"Blessed is the grave the rain falls in."*

I said, "What did that mean?"

Granny answered, "Old people used to say if raindrops fell in an open grave, it was a sign that whoever was bein' buried made it to heaven."

A decade or more after that cool fall evening when Granny shared her story, I bumped into an old high school buddy in Harriston pumping diesel fuel into his tractor trailer hauling a bulldozer. After a brief visit, he told me he had been hired to "clean up" the hillside where Brother and Sister had made their home for over five decades. The good old couple had left their small estate consisting of the several acre hillside and its dilapidated buildings to the struggling little church they'd started in 1919. A neighboring landowner eventually bought the property for its road frontage, affording the small congregation the chance to move to a better location.

At his invitation, I followed Billy's truck and trailer down the winding road past Fordville, then onto Slabtown Road to the old homestead. Brother's outbuildings and the little house he and Sister built had nearly fallen in. Bushes and briars had reclaimed the poor hillside soil. I had to go in one last time to view whatever remained of the house where I'd spent many nights growing up. Stepping carefully from beam to beam in the rotted floor, I stood in the old kitchen and looked beneath me to see what was left of the little cellar the couple had labored to dig out by hand. From there, looking into their old bedroom, I beheld Brother's reconstituted potty chair. Treading lightly along the rough-sawed floor joists, I ventured into the room whose walls were still lined with old newspapers, now barren except for the homemade potty chair, shoved in a corner. The white enamel slop jar that Sister had kept underneath of it was still there, and after swiping away the cobwebs, I carried both pieces out of the house and back down the steep hillside.

After placing the chair and pot in the bed of my truck, I paced up and down the overgrown hillside lot, retracing the steps Brother and Sister made between their home and the garden patches along Tattler's Branch. In the distance I could hear Billy's dozer whirring and clacking its way through the leaning gray buildings which offered little resistance. Knowing how hard Brother had labored to build them, I didn't have the heart to stick around to witness their demolition. In a relatively short period of time, all traces of its former habitation would be erased.

I saw the hillside a year later and it looked like the first day of its creation. A tall, full stand of green pasture grass was waving and swirling in the wind, like the wheat fields of Kansas. Amazingly, it looked pristine-- as if no one had ever set foot upon it.

Now, when I look at the potty chair, I like to imagine that early chapter in the lives of Brother and Sister Simpson— when they looked up at that Fordville hillside for the first time, sitting in the wagon that contained their few worldly goods. And, among them were the chairs they had made together.

The framed drawstring bag and scrapbook page

In the Shadow of Pigeons

At ninety-six, Bob Ulyss Whitfield was by far the oldest of the men who gathered at Perkins' Store for The Children's Hour. On this particular cold, January day, he cupped his ear toward the others, trying desperately to listen.

I can still hear his dry-mouthed words, almost in the form of a plea.

"What? What now? What's that you say?"

Perhaps unintentionally, the near-deaf, semi-centenarian had been left out of the conversation—one surely beyond his understanding, for it was as new as 1964—specifically, The United States mission of putting a man on the moon in the wake of recently slain President Kennedy's initiative. Storeowner Mack Perkins was full of such up-to-date information, having spent most of the afternoon re-reading the Sunday paper. Finally, he turned to speak to Mr. Whitfield—with whom communication was a challenge.

Raising his voice to a near-roar, he said, "Bob U-lyss, I got a scien-tif-ic question here for you!"

The lanky older man leaned forward, eager to be included.

Mack folded the paper back and held it up to the light. "Here, let me read it to you. It says, *"What hap-pens when a force that can-not be stopped comes in-to con-tact with an ob-ject that can-not be moved?"*

Mr. Whitfield stared blankly at Mack as though he failed to even grasp the question. Clearly disappointed, he leaned back in his chair and shook his head. The old fellow seemed genuinely saddened by his inability to give an informed answer.

Red Perkins nudged my grandfather. "Watch 'im, by jacks. He's studyin' on it." Winks were exchanged among the other men while Mr. Whitfield tapped with his cane at the curled-up end of a floor board next to the stove.

All of a sudden, the tapping stopped with a determined thud. Mr. Whitfield raised his white head.

"W-e-l-l, boys" he drawled, "it sounds to me like A-L-L H-E-L-L's fixin' to break loose."

Laughter echoed from the store's dingy walls, forever earning the statement a place in the annals of Children's Hour history.

Mr. Whitfield may not have been up to speed on the subject of gravitational pull, or Einstein's Theory of Relativity, but on that day he opened up his own storehouse of knowledge, to reveal a previously hidden room, one that both saddened and intrigued me.

After the guffaws and laughter died down, the topic of conversation shifted from space and satellites to hunting dogs and guns. Due to his hearing, Mr. Whitfield was slow to grasp a subject, but once seized, he could summon extraordinary details from his far-reaching memory. Mack yelled, "Bob-Ulyss, I been meanin' to ask if you still have

Grandpa's old shotgun—that'n he traded to you for a mule way back yonder?

(Note to reader: communication with Mr. Whitfield was rarely this easy: each question had to be repeated at least twice in a near shouting match—a wearisome struggle omitted here as an act of mercy.)

Dogs and guns. Now here was a topic the old man could sink his teeth into.

He nodded enthusiastically.

"Yeah, boy. I still got it." He paused for a moment. "You want it?"

Mack chuckled. "No, No, Bob Ulyss. Ain't no rue-back now…that ol' mule's been dead sixty years--I just saw a shotgun the other day that put me in mind of Grandpa's." He winked at the others. "You ain't no old man yet, but you're gettin' there. You still have some huntin' days left!"

Mr. Whitfield grunted, "Uh-uh--No, I ain't, neither. " His tone was serious. "Truth is I couldn't tell you the last time I went huntin'."

J.B. chimed in. "Come to think of it, Bob-Ulyss, I don't *ever* remember you huntin'!"

"No, I reckon not," he said, his voice trailing, "I gave up huntin' before you was weaned."

The comment drew another round of laughter, for J.B. was nearing seventy. Something Mr. Whitfield said, however, caught my attention. His choice of the words "gave up" struck me as odd.

I said, "Mr. Whitfield, what made you quit hunting?"

His answer surprised me.

"I reckon I just lost interest in it," he said, suddenly drawing the attention of the other men, "way back yonder…when that last pigeon died."

"When that last pigeon died." I can still hear the sadness in his words, for they reminded me of other old men in recalling the death of a favorite plow horse or hunting dog.

What's more, I was confused by the words "*That last pigeon.*" I had seen plenty of them in barns and along the tops of Harriston's two story brick buildings and the bell tower at the courthouse. Mack indirectly answered my question.

"You mean them ol' wild pigeons, don't you, Bob Ulyss?—the ones there used to be so many of?"

Mr. Whitfield nodded. "That's what they was…wild pigeons…*Passenger Pigeons.* I recollect that somebody brought me a paper to read down to the ferry. There was news in it about that First World War breakin' out overseas, and that's when I read that the very last one of them wild pigeons was dead. It was a hen-pigeon and they packed 'er in a six foot square block o' ice and sent it off to a museum somewhere.

261

They gave 'er name in that paper, but I can't call it. She'd been in that big zoo in Cincinnati about all her life and hadn't never laid the first egg. They couldn't even find 'er a mate, a tom-pigeon."

The other loafers recalled stories from their elders of the great feathery waves that once darkened Kentucky's skies. Mr. Whitfield leaned back in his chair, seemingly lost in memory, and from force of habit, he gazed out of the window in the direction of the river where he had spent most of life running the ferry.

The conversation among the other men had just about run its course when, reenergized by some triggered recollection, Mr. Whitfield made a public confession.

Clearing his throat, he said, "I believe to my soul I killed the last wild pigeon in this part of the country." His words rang loud and clear. "It hit me on the day I read about that last hen-pigeon dyin' up in the zoo. And that'n I killed— that tom-pigeon I shot could've been a mate for her if I'd caught 'im instead of killin' 'im."

Even Mack seemed surprised to hear it. All eyes were now fixed on this last eyewitness of the extinct species whose numbers were once too many to count.

"Me and my brother in law, Georgie Moss, went dove-huntin' over yonder in The Babylon Woods and I fired into a few of 'em at the edge of Tom Hoskins' wheat field. Got over there to 'em and Georgie hadn't never seen a wild pigeon. He said, 'Bob-Ulyss, what is this?' I looked and by grannies if it wasn't a wild tom-pigeon--and he was a pretty thing, too…had kindly a wine colored breast, and this'n had 'im a waddle down here on his neck like a tom turkey does, but… I killed 'im deader'n a hammer. We brought 'im home with the doves and dressed 'em. Mama cooked 'em for supper, but I couldn't hardly eat for thinkin' how pretty the little feller was. We hadn't seen none of 'em in a long time, but we never give a thought to 'em playin' out like they done. I told Mama it looked to me like they was gone for good, and she said, 'Gone? *They can't be.* There was so many down yonder at that big roostin' place, their droppin's was as deep as my hand is long.' Mr. Whitfield held up his own long hand, marking the depth of it as his mother once had in describing the scene.

Mr. Whitfield had a long-established reputation for exaggeration. Skeptical, Red Perkins leaned forward to yell, "So that's when you give up huntin', Bob Ulyss?"

"Oh, no. I still hunted a little…for several years, I reckon— up 'til I read that newspaper ar-ticle. I kept thinkin' surely them pigeons couldn't all be gone, but…they was. They sure was. That was 'long about 1894, somewhere in there, when I killed that tom-pigeon, and I never saw me another'n, nowhere.

My uncles and some of the other old timers thought that maybe they'd changed their mi-gratin' habits or somethin'. I never studied on it no more 'til I read about that'n up in Cincinnati. I recollect they'd offered a big re-ward for anybody that could find a mate for it—that last hen-pigeon. It was a good'n, too…enough for a man to buy 'im a piece of land, but nobody ever come along to claim it.

263

After that, I started askin' around, could anybody remember the last'n they saw. Best I could make out, nobody could remember seein' one in this whole county after 18 and 86—and the only reason I remember it's 'cause that's the year my daddy died. It was about eight or maybe nine years after that when I shot that pretty little tom, down yonder at Babylon.

The more I got to studyin' on it I just kindly lost interest in huntin' altogether."

The others were silent in the face of Mr. Whitfield's confession.

"Tell you what else," he said, nodding in the direction of the river. "Way back yonder before my time, my grandpa saw a great big flock of 'em roost in the woods back this side of the McQueen Place—a flock so big they knocked 'em out of trees with clubs, shot 'em and ever'thing else. Old man Nin Perkins—now, that was Red's and Mack's Grandpa—he herded a bunch of hogs down there to feed on what was left of 'em after ever'body took what they wanted. My daddy saw some big flocks in his time, but they wasn't as big as the ones Grandpa told us about. Then, by the time I come along they was gettin' to be few and far between."

Mr. Whitfield turned to look out the window again-- in the direction of the river, where the legendary roosting had once taken place.

Just then, he said, "What I wouldn't give to hear that wild pigeon call again."

264

Even the usually quiet, coarse-whispering Perry Lee Taylor was interested enough to attempt a question at Fordville's rememberer: *"What did they sound like, Bob-Ulyss?!"*

The old man was in his element. Werner von Braun could do what he pleased with rocket science. Not only was the topic old days, we were now dealing with old sounds, and in this case, those he alone had heard. Said Mr. Whitfield, now the confirmed authority, "Their calls wasn't all the same, you know. They was kindly like people that-away."

To this day, I remember how he leaned forward, with both hands on his cane, and looked down at his shoes to recall sounds now lost in a world saturated with the manmade noise--radio and television. As he did, a hush fell across the room...and we waited to hear the call of a bird forever silenced. And waited. For a moment I thought he had forgotten and was afraid to admit it.

Finally, he raised his bright eyes and delivered a comically high pitched "TWEET!" "TWEE" "TWEET."

The other men laughed at the spectacle, but in the oldest man's face I could see pure joy associated with that memory.

He said, "You all can laugh, but now, that's what them wild pigeons sounded like. And the way they made that call, see, that first TWEET was the loudest. The next'n wasn't as strong, and then that last'n was softer yet," and then as if to remind himself, he did an encore performance, "TWEET! Twee... Tweet."

Mack said, "You speak their language pretty good, don't you Bob-Ulyss?"

The others laughed.

"I reckon so," he said, "but I come by it natural. *I was born on pigeon feathers.* My uncle Rueben come down here below McQueen's Place to that pigeon roost in 18 and 65—that was the last big'n, and he killed a big lot of 'em. My mother and daddy was fixin' to get married and my uncle told her, he says, 'Betts'—that's what he called 'er, he said, 'Betts, if you'll make the tick for your bed, I'll give you all the pigeons you want for the feathers.'

Well, Mama made Daddy help her, and they pulled the feathers from one hundred and for-ty-two DOZ-EN pigeons. I don't even know how many that is without puttin' a pencil to it, but that's how many it took to make a feather mattress when they went to housekeepin'. And then--after the feathers was pulled, my uncle fed what was left of 'em to his hogs…he fed 'em to the dad-blame hogs, and it kindly makes me sick now to think about it.

Daddy and Mama had that bed and mattress when they went to housekeepin' at Christmas in 18 and 65, and I was born on it in 18 and 67. When I was a sprout, people used to say you couldn't die on pigeon feathers, but there ain't nothin' to it. Daddy got pneumonia and died on that mattress when he was forty-three years old and Mama wouldn't never sleep on it again. It's on their old bed in that upstairs room. Ain't nobody slept on it since, so far as I know, unless it was one of my nephews when they would stay the night.

But, now, talkin' about them Passenger Pigeons, they had 'em a friendly call that they'd make, too. When they'd be feedin' in the woods--eatin' mast is what the old timers called it--if another flock of 'em flew over, they'd raise up and make another tweet-call, tellin' 'em it was all right to land there. But now, if they thought danger was close by, they'd make another call that told 'em not to—'cause it wasn't safe. They did now, for a fact.

Uncle Reuben netted two or three dozen of 'em one time down below Babylon, but that wasn't a patchin' to what they once was. And when they was caught, why, they never hollered like they did when they was roostin'—it wasn't even a coo--more like a grunt. I never heard it more'n a time or two, but it sounded kindly pitiful."

Having heard his words, I felt cheated—deprived somehow of "that Wild Pigeon Call," and, once again, I couldn't help myself but to probe a little deeper into this extraordinary recollection.

"What do you think happened to 'em all, Mr. Whitfield?"

His eyes seemed to dim, as his thoughts now returned to the present.

"They was as pretty a bird as God ever' put breath in."

At first, I thought he hadn't heard my question.

"My grandpa saw a flock of 'em one time when he was headin' towards Washington County in a team and wagon. He had a sister and brother in law that moved out there and he was takin' her a chest and spinnin' wheel that their mother had give to 'er. He claimed he heard this gurglin' sound comin' from the south and it kept gettin' louder til, directly, here they flew over on both sides of 'im. He said there was prob'ly a mile wide front of 'em in that one flock and it made a dark place on the earth as far as he could see it…a big shadow. Couldn't see to the other side of it, nor the back, and here in a few minutes, he heard what sounded like big drops of rain spatterin' and it wasn't a thing in the world but them bird droppin's hittin' the ground. I reckon Grandpa cracked the whip on his horses, tryin' to get across as fast as he could, past where they was flyin' over.

Grandpa said he drove for a mile or better *in the shadow of pigeons*—just as hard as he could go. When he made it to the other side, the stuff he was haulin' in the back of the wagon looked like somebody had spattered white paint on it--from all the pigeon-poop—and some of it hit him, too. He decided to turn and follow 'em as they headed north, for just a few miles. In one place he saw 'em swoop down to feed in a big woods and it looked for the world like a big waterfall—millions of 'em just pourin' out of the sky. When Grandpa told me that story, they just had finished buildin' the dam down here on the river. He said the way them pigeons landed looked like water spillin' over that dam. One man he talked to said it took might near half a day for that one flock to fly over--and there wasn't no break in it. Best they could figure, it was ever' bit of a hundred miles long.

In the space of time from Grandpa's trip 'til I was about the same age he'd been, the wild pigeons had all died out. They was gone…*all gone.*"

The old man grew somber and reflective upon saying those words and turned his gaze in the direction of the muddy old river that he knew so well. Then, as an afterthought he jerked himself around to face his friends.

He said, "Tell you what, at the house I got me somethin' that drawed a whole lot of attention, way back yonder."

Mack was interested. "What's that, Bob Ulyss?"

"It's a little-bitty oiled silk bag that belonged to my aunt-- no bigger'n the end of my two fingers here, and she tied it to the foot of one of them pigeons that carried it all the way from here to Michigan."

The men cackled at the very notion. Perry Lee Taylor said, "It's gettin' deep in here now, Bob-Ulyss!"

The old man planted his cane on the floor. "It ain't no lie, fellers. I'm tellin' you the truth. I got the letter from the man that found it--and newspaper clippin's tellin' about it."

Judging from the skepticism, perhaps Mr. Whitfield's long history of tall tales had caught up with him.

He then turned to me. "You want to see it?"

I was intrigued. "Yes sir, Mr. Whitfield, I sure would."

"Well then," he drawled, "I'll have Jincy help me hunt it up and next time we head this way, I'll bring it for you to look at." Miss Jincy was Bob Ulyss's soul mate, whose legal relationship to him could best be described as his common law wife.

Mr. Whitfield seemed especially eager to establish credibility with his fantastic story. Before his audience turned away and moved on to another topic, he said, "I know you don't believe me, but I'll tell you how it come to be. My Aunt Esther was down yonder in the river bottom with their brother, Uncle Norris, where he used a de-coy, one o' them stool pigeons, to trap some wild'ns. I was just a kid-- just barely can remember it, so it must've been about 18 and 75, or right along in there. He caught a dozen or more of 'em and Esther got the notion to tie a note to the foot of one of 'em in a little draw string bag, and for whoever found it to write her back. She done that in the spring of the year and then, around the first of November, here come a package with that little silk bag and a letter in it. This man that wrote the letter trapped that very same pigeon up in Michigan somewhere. He told who he was, where he lived and such as that. He was gonna send Esther a picture of hisself, but he never done it. He was a school teacher about her age and just had lost his wife. Esther hadn't ever married and I think she felt like she might get her a husband out of that deal, but she never heard back from 'im. It was in her box o' keepsake stuff when she died.

J.B. couldn't resist. "You still got time to hatch a nest of your own, don't you, Bob Ulyss!"

The other old men cackled, but Mr. Whitfield seemed to appreciate the vote of confidence.

With a chuckle, he said, "Nossir, fellers, my nestin' days is done. My tail feathers is drooped."

While the conversation of the others turned to more relevant, farm-related topics, Mr. Whitfield returned his half-blind, watery gaze toward the river, the old roosting site of the once plentiful pigeons. That day's session eventually came to an end and the other men helped get Mr. Whitfield transported home to Miss Jincy, who ordinarily traveled with him.

Due to his advanced age, Mr. Whitfield didn't make it to The Children's Hour on a regular basis, but surprisingly true to his word, he came by the store later in the week with Miss Jincy—just to drop off the items of which he had spoken. He had brought them just for me to see, for at least one person to know his story was real. Unfortunately, I was in school and wouldn't be there until late in the afternoon.

When I came through the door later that day with my grandfather, Mack said, "Clay, you ought to be proud. Bob Ulyss was bound and de-termined to see that you got to look at his bird-stuff. Let me go back behind the counter and get it." As he handed me a brown paper bag, the older men were eager to see its contents. "You know how Jincy is," Mack said, "She fussed and fumed at 'im catchin' cold, but she said he wouldn't hush 'til they brought this stuff by for you to take a look at."

To properly credit his old friend, Mack brought the items around for a Children's Hour version of "show and tell." The small silk bag with a leather draw string was passed around, along with the yellowed note that its Michigan finder had penned, and the two newspaper articles dated October, and November, 1874. The three paper relics had been glued onto an old piece of cardboard, representing

271

Fordville's lone archive dedicated to the memory of the passenger pigeon.

Every man there that afternoon marveled at that story, and examined the evidence. As I held the little bag and tugged at its leather draw string, I tried to imagine what that one pigeon saw—what it would have been like to fly over the vast stretch of fields and forests between Fordville and Michigan. All in an attempt to find a nesting site, along with millions of its kind, the same luckless bird had been captured--twice. I carefully returned the silk bag and the paper items to the refolded brown paper bag they had been delivered in, and which Mack placed behind the counter.

He said, "I'll give 'em back to Bob Ulyss next time he's in here."

I was taken by surprise with the next turn of events.

It was close to spring when I next saw Mr. Whitfield, visibly thinner and more frail than from the previous January encounter when he had confessed to killing the last wild pigeon. He and Miss Jincy were sitting with the others and she held the familiar paper bag in her lap with both hands folded on it. Mr. Whitfield was in the middle of a story, and I tried to slip into a chair on the other side of him, so as not to interrupt. Upon seeing me enter the room with my grandfather, he pointed at the bag in Miss Jincy's lap.

"Did you like lookin' at that ol' pigeon stuff ?"

"Yes sir, I did—a lot."

The old fellow beamed. "I thought you just might. *Tell you what*," he said. "Why don't you just take 'em with you?"

I think the matter had already been decided upon. Before I could even thank him, with both her hands, Miss Jincy held up the bag and its contents for me to take.

"He's right, honey. You keep this. He's got more stuff now than he knows what to do with. You ought to take these things to school with you tomorrow and show 'em to some of your teachers."

Stuffing some loosened strands of hair back under her baseball cap, Miss Jincy smiled up at me from her folding chair. "Good, then. That's settled."

Before returning their earlier conversation, Mr. Whitfield nodded toward the crumpled and rubber-banded paper bag I held, "I want you to be sure and tell me what your teachers think about that ol' stuff there."

I was fascinated by what I had been given, but I didn't honestly think anyone else would be. I remained skeptical, but I had promised Mr. Whitfield I would share their response with him. Surprisingly, when I casually mentioned the pigeon-artifacts to my English teacher, the thing took on a life of its own. She told our geography teacher about it at lunch, and she in turn developed a map lesson activity out of it. Not to be outdone, our biology teacher assigned us a special project based on other endangered species, not unlike Mr. Whitfield's much lamented wild pigeon.

When my teachers got their heads together, they decided to ask me to help bring the near hundred year old Bob Ulyss Whitfield to school as a guest speaker. It turned out to be a coordinated Fordville effort with Mack Perkins and Mr. Whitfield's "handler" Miss Jincy driving him to the county high school in Harriston. Once there, our building principal Mr. Moore and I guided him along the long hallways and into the music room, so students could hear from one who had heard—that Wild Pigeon call. With the same bright eyes, he performed the calls as he remembered them, to a surprisingly receptive teenage audience. And, once more, he shared with my peers his confession that he had killed the last known passenger pigeon seen in the county. He had not come equipped to teach a formal lesson on the subject of ecology for he knew not the word, but he did so indirectly. In his sad lament for the wine-breasted birds of his youth there could be heard an unmistakable sense of loss that would rival any scientific efforts to do so.

After Mr. Whitfield "gave his little talk," and with great difficulty heard and answered questions from students, the bell rang to switch classes and our high school principal, Mr. Moore, told everybody to stay put. Pointing to Mr. Whitfield, he told all of us what a privilege we had been given to hear what our ears couldn't—ever, and he had questions of his own to ask.

"You won't have this chance again to hear from somebody like him," he said.

Mr. Whitfield beamed from ear to ear as he sat in front of the classroom full of surprisingly curious eyes—and found meaning in the most unlikely of places.

Thinking perhaps he could get one over on old Mr. Whitfield, one of the sharpest students in my graduating class—who went on to become a college physics professor, asked him, "Mr. Whitfield, sir, what do you think about The United States going into space—putting a man on the moon?"

Perhaps it was out of habit, but once again, the old man looked out of the large classroom window at a lone bird flying into the wind, lofting and pitching.

He said, "Well, now that's somethin' to study on…it sure is, and I 'spect we'll get there some of these days. I won't live to see it, *but you all will*. But, I'll just tell you—it couldn't mean no more to me than seein' my first airplane. Now that was a sight to behold. Man's always been wantin' to find a way--like that bird yonder, to get hisself up in the air. Once we done that—the notion o' reachin' the stars don't seem so far off, now, *does it?"*

The whiz kid science student chuckled. "No sir. I never thought of it like that."

Nor, for that matter, had I.

Eventually, Mr. Moore sent us all on to our next class, and I remember how happy Mr. Whitfield seemed to be, perhaps an extra spring in his step, as he was led tottering on his cane, Miss Jincy in tow, back down the polished hallway floor.

Not only had he been involved in the conversation, he *was* the conversation that day.

My teachers talked about his visit for days afterward, and from time to time they asked me about him. This took place in my sophomore year, and until I graduated two years later, on several occasions several of them asked to borrow the Passenger Pigeon Archive Mr. Whitfield had given me.

From this unlikely, youthful stage, Robert Ulysses Whitfield took his final bow. Only once more did I even see him—for what would be his final appearance at Perkins' Store. His old friends there teased him, starting with J.B. "Bob Ulyss, I hear you had to go back to school." Always the joker, Pop-Ed said, "Accordin' to what I hear, Bob Ulyss, you've been all hugged up with some of them good-lookin' cheerleaders up at the high school." There were other jovial comments, and the old man loved every one of them. For one last, glorious day, he had found relevance…meaning, in a world he hardly recognized outside of Fordville. Although Mr. Whitfield was in high spirits that day, we could all recognize that our feeble old friend was losing ground. We had no way of knowing this would be his last Children's Hour session. I remember that he spoke at length of the weather that day, which was fitting, for it had always been one of his favorite topics.

A few weeks later, perhaps inspired by his near-celebrity status as the last hearer of The Passenger Pigeon, Mr. Whitfield requested that his parents' old feather mattress be brought downstairs and placed on his own bed. He said it's where he'd taken his first breath, and if he had his way, it's where he'd take his last. Mercifully, he had his way.

Pneumonia. Ironically, I once heard Mr. Whitfield call it "The young man's enemy and the old man's friend." When it had claimed the life of his young father—a married man with dependent children, it was a tragedy. Now, nearing the century mark, it had returned for the father's son, benevolently—peacefully, and as easily as blowing out a candle.

Having long expressed a desire for an outdoor observance of his passing, graveside services for Bob Ulyss Whitfield were held in The Fordville Cemetery. Mr. Moore, our high school principal, had been so impressed with Mr. Whitfield that he drove all the way from Harriston to pay his respects. He said that Mr. Whitfield had taught the teachers and him as much as he had the students on the day of his celebrated visit. For all his age, his words had proved as modern—as relevant as the wispy moon hanging over us in the clear October sky.

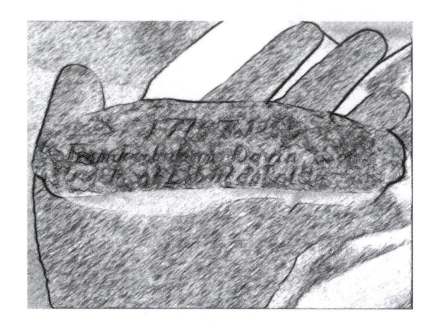

The whet stone on my desk

In the Sign of the Water Man

Where and when I grew up, there was something special about old men and their pocket knives. Fordville, Kentucky, wasn't the only place, but it's where I came to that understanding.

It's also where I began to ponder the mysteries of life and death as seen through the eyes of an old knife collector, a childless widower coming to terms with loss—a lament for the past as much as a future.

Like Mr. Dan Jacob Little, practically every old man I knew had his own preference for a brand, or a specific model of pocket knife. These men spoke admiringly of this knife and that one as a cowboy might eulogize a favorite horse he'd ridden the trail with. Some were reliable, battle-scarred survivors, with nicked or broken blades. Some were traded or given away, and others misplaced or lost—gone, to be lamented forevermore.

Perhaps with that longstanding tradition in mind, one of the occasional loafers for The Children's Hour gave me a shiny new Case pocketknife as a gift for my high school graduation, still a few months away. I remember on that occasion that old Mr. Little asked to see it. Holding the knife to the light, he examined it closely, turning it over several times, and opening every blade. With an affirming nod, I knew the knife met with the old carpenter's approval. I think he was looking at me when he said it, but with him it was hard to tell. Handing the new, still-in-its-box knife back to me, Mr. Little said, "Clay, the way you take care of one, it'll last you a long time. I've seen how good and sharp you keep that little Barlow that Mack gave you when you was just a little feller."

Little did I know he had taken notice. During many afternoon sessions of The Children's Hour, I'd used Granddaddy's small, slender whet rock to sharpen my knife, just the way he showed me. I valued a well-honed blade as much as a sharp pencil when I did my homework. As I came to learn, keeping a sharp, clean pocket knife was a trait Mr. Little admired, and for some time I had unknowingly been the subject of his keen but incomplete observation. It was difficult to tell when he took visible interest in anything because of the green ten cent store spectacles he wore to conceal a disfigured eye, the result of a childhood slingshot accident.

One gloomy winter afternoon, he said he had something he wanted to show me--after the others left just before the store's customary 6:00 closing time. Granddaddy must have known something about Mr. Little's plan, because he told me to meet him there for that weekday gathering of The Children's Hour. Usually we rode down together unless I had basketball practice or an away game.

I knew Mr. Little wasn't in much of a hurry to get home in those days. His wife, Minnie Lou, had died the previous fall, and as a widower with no family left, he had no schedule to follow and no home-cooked supper waiting for him. Still, on this particular day, he was clearly on a mission, and when the last straggler made his way out the door he said, "Mack, do you care if me and this soldier boy sit here for a spell?" I had just announced my intention to volunteer for military duty when I graduated.

"No, not a bit," he said. "There's some stuff that needs puttin' on the shelves--and I've got some bills to make out. You boys stay long as you want." At the time, I didn't know exactly why Mr. Little wanted this occasion to be private, or as it unfolded, even intimate. Many years have passed since that day, and now, as a father and grandfather—and an old man, I'm beginning to understand.

Mr. Little always wore a green union suit, which despite his trade as a carpenter and fix-it man, he kept as clean and neat as his own pocket knife. He motioned for me to sit down beside him as the other voices trailed away amid the mixed chorus of departing truck engines.

Reaching into his right pocket, he produced a brownish colored stone that appeared to be more or less rectangular in shape, maybe three inches wide, two inches thick and about seven inches long.

Extending his hand toward me, he said "You know what this is?"

I held it just as Mr. Little had with the stone's smooth side up.

"That's pretty neat," I said. "It's a whet rock, isn't it?"

The old carpenter smiled. "You've seen one before, ain't you?" The light of late afternoon came through the store window at just the right angle for me to see the twinkle in Mr. Little's one good eye, hidden behind his green lenses.

The whet rock Mr. Little handed to me had a very noticeable blade-worn "dip" down one side that was as smooth as glass, the result of many years of sharpening knives and farm tools. Coincidentally, Children's Hour regular Delb Shearer had shown me the one his enslaved grandfather had used to sharpen tools in order to purchase his freedom, a herculean effort that took him six years.

Nodding toward the whet rock I now held in my hand, Mr. Little said, "Now, look at the *other* side." Literally carved into its soapstone surface was an almost immaculate, if not poetic verse containing the whet rock's *human* history. In three lines, the cryptic message read: *"From Jacob's*

281

Jacob's David's son, Dan Jacob Little's rellic come."
Dates above the inscription read "*1776 to 1929.*" Great care
and attention had been given to the sharp, stylized points on
the letters and numbers. Not only that, an economy of
space required that thought and care be put into carving
those names. For someone, doing so had clearly been a
labor of love.

I said, "Mr. Little, I've never seen anything like this."

He seemed pleased as I turned it over again, examining
each of its smooth, well-worn surfaces. "No, I reckon not,"
he said. "Nobody else has, neither. I showed it to an
antique dealer from Lexington one time, and he wanted to
buy it. I was standin' in a crowd of people at an auction
sale in Harriston, waitin' on Minnie Lou. They were sellin'
off her aunt's stuff and this man was standin' beside me
when I reached in my pocket to get it and started sharpenin'
my knife blade. Direc'ly, he asked me if he could look at it
so I handed it to 'im. He studied it over real good and
offered me *five dollars* for it. That may not sound like
much to you now, but back then that was a full day's pay
for carpentry work. But I told 'im, I says, 'Mister, if you
knew what all went into this little rock, you'd know I could
no more sell it than I could rise and fly.'

Before handing it back to Mr. Little, I ran my finger across
the lettering, so carefully and painstakingly carved into the
smooth stone. The hand worn patina on its sides and edges
bore the evidence of nearly two centuries' use.

I said, "Did it come down through your family?"

"Yes sir. From this first Jacob right here—my great-grandfather. They called him "King Jacob," and then it was passed down from him to my grandfather, "Little Jake." His oldest son--my uncle, Nelson took it with 'im to Kansas and died out there. He never married so it went to my daddy—that's the David you see right there. He gave it to my brother, Woodson and then it came to me. My name's the last'n—you see it there, don't you?"

I nodded, although a couple of the names he mentioned were missing and I wondered why.

"There ain't room for no more." he said. "They might as well call me "Caboose," 'cause I'm the end of the line." It was a phrase I'd heard Mr. Little say before, and although it was intended as a joke, one could detect in his voice a tinge of sadness.

Fascinated by the earliest date, 1776, I said, "What happened in that year?"

Mr. Little's face brightened.

"That was the year it came into the Little generations."

The old carpenter and fix-it man was armed and ready with his family history—though to what end I had no way of knowing. It was almost as if he had rehearsed his lines from a well-studied script that was never used.

"That first Jacob you see here, my great-grandfather "King Jacob" was an orphan boy, and I never knew much about him. His parents was killed by Indians in Virginia when he was about four years old. Then they scalped him and left

283

'im for dead. The story Grandma told was that the father and mother hadn't even built 'em a cabin yet—they were livin' in a lean-to that was open on one whole side where they kept a big fire. There was another family within a couple of miles that saw the smoke the next mornin' from where the Indians had burnt 'em out. They got a party of men together and they found Jacob's daddy and mother dead and what the Indians hadn't taken, they set fire to. They got to lookin' for survivors and walked into the woods all around there and didn't find nothin'. The next day, a man by the name of Little came ridin' through the woods close by there, and he saw green flies swarmin' somethin' in the bushes ahead of 'im, so he got down off his horse to take a look, and it was Jacob. He was might near dead where the Indians scalped 'im and the flies gathered on his head where that blood dried. I never saw 'im of course, but he made a leather skull cap to cover the scars—and was buried with one. When he enlisted to be a soldier in the Revolution, this officer asked Jacob how old he was and where he was born. Well, he was an orphan and said for all he knew, he could've been born the king. That officer laughed at 'im and said his skull cap would have to do for a crown 'til he could prove it. One of the soldiers standin' close by laughed real big, callin' 'im "King Jacob," so that's how he got his nickname. Ever' other soldier in that regiment started callin' 'im that—and it stuck.

Anyhow, that Little man took 'im back to the settlement where he and his family lived and they nursed him back to life. When he got older, they told 'im his mother and daddy were Irish, but how they knew, I don't know. They didn't know their names and nobody else did, neither. They never found another dead body but Jacob always claimed he'd had an older sister or maybe an aunt the Indians took with 'em. The man that raised 'im gave 'im the Little name, but after he died his widow bound 'im out to a tanner to learn the leather trade. Nobody knows King Jacob's real name but it don't make no difference. We've been Littles for a right smart while."

I remember how Mr. Little spoke the word, "*We,*" as if the other long- dead Littles whose names were etched in stone were sitting there with him. Maybe, for his purpose that day, they were.

"Grandma said when Jacob was about seventeen he ran off from that tanner. Jacob hadn't done somethin' to suit 'im, and the tanner hauled off and hit 'im. He'd done it before but Jacob was grown by then--a great big hulk of a man, and with one blow, he "laid 'im in the shade," as my daddy used to say. He figured he'd be in trouble with the law on account of it, so he took off some distance away from there and made for a soldier. I'm thinkin' that was in Virginia, but I ain't for sure. Anyway, he ran off to join up in the militia that was fightin' the English. That's as far back as Grandma knew. Now, where the rock comes into it was in' his soldierin' days durin' the Revolution.

Jacob got it from another soldier. I forget what battle it was, but Little Jake told my daddy that Jacob and this other soldier got separated from their regiment somehow, and went so long a time without food, they were dang-nigh starved. I don't know how come for 'im to find it, or where he found it, but Jacob got hold of a dead turkey and said he

285

had to fight the maggots for it. That tells you how hungry they was.

Jacob and this other soldier didn't have but one knife and one gun between 'em. All that other fellow had was this rock. He was older than Jacob, and he'd fought in a war that came before the Revolution—and I can't think of it. But there was a battle he'd been in, and they'd surrendered to the French. While he was held prisoner, he found it somewhere and made a whet rock out of it. I never heard what battle, and I don't think Little Jake even knew that part of it. This older soldier had kindly took Jacob under his wing and looked after 'im, but he'd gotten wounded and Jacob tried to take care of 'im, what little he knew to do. This other man handed 'im this rock to sharpen his knife, so he could get to cuttin' on that turkey. He built 'em a little fire under a rock cliff and cooked a piece of it as quick as he could on the end of his knife. They ate some of it, but that older man kept gettin' weaker and he knew he was dyin'. Jacob set up with 'im all night long and he died just as the sun was comin' up. Somewhere along in there before he died, he gave the rock to Jacob…said he might need it if he ever came across another dead turkey. They said even when Jacob was an old man he would might near tear up ever' time he told that tale, and he said to his dyin' day that ol' half-rotten turkey was the best meal he ever ate. They claimed Jacob asked that other soldier, "How come for you to own a whet rock and no knife?" The man knew he was dyin' but he was still able to laugh, and he said, "Little, ain't no man can have ever'thing." I've heard my daddy quote that a hundred times--mostly when things weren't goin' to suit 'im. That's always been a Little family sayin'." Mr. Little repeated the phrase as if to pass on that bit of family lore that might otherwise be scattered to the four winds: *"Little, ain't no man can have ever'thing."*

It was about at this point in overhearing his old friend's historical narrative that a solemn Mack Perkins came to understand the nature of our meeting. I later learned he knew the rock well, and at least some of its history. Mack tiptoed behind the store counter to retrieve his clipboard for me to use as a writing surface, and then grabbed a small package of notebook paper from a nearby single shelf of school supplies. Handing them to me with an ink pen from his own pocket, he leaned over and said, "Here, you might want to write down what he's tellin' you. I've known the man sixty years and this is the first time I've heard some of it."

I thought to myself, "Write it down?" I was trying to figure out what this was all about—why we were meeting like this, just the two of us.

Mr. Little turned to look at Mack, "Yessir, a man ought to put this kind of stuff down on paper for the comin' generation, but... I ain't no good for such as that." Then he added, "It don't matter no-way, Mack...there ain't no more Little generations."

He ran his fingers along the whet rock's smooth side. "When I get to thinkin' on it, might near ever' bit of our history's tied up in this little feller right here. It ever' bit ends with me—the good and the bad...and sometimes I get to wonderin', *what's it all for?"*

At that moment Mr. Little looked at me—as youth, I think—and then at his old bachelor friend. He seemed to be searching for an answer that neither the hope of youth nor the wisdom of age could offer.

I said, "Aren't there some other Littles *somewhere* that go back to this King Jacob here?"

Still looking down at it, Mr. Little shook his head gravely. "No…there ain't. I've traced 'em as far back and down as I can—and I'm it. King Jacob was married three different times but my grandfather was the only boy that lived past infancy. His mother was the third wife and I think King Jacob was fifty-nine then. The rest was girls, three of 'em. One died the night before she was to marry—got bit by a rattlesnake. She'd been hoein' corn with her daddy and brother and was on her way back to the house to help her mother with cookin' to feed the weddin' party. The other two girls married brothers—Tacketts, and they moved way off somewhere. Several different times I tried to find out, but I never was able to learn what become of 'em."

It was beginning to dawn on me: *This was about the end of The Littles.*

Mr. Little pointed to the whet rock, lightly tapping the second name inscribed on it—the second Jacob Little.

"I never saw my grandfather, Little Jake. His first wife died in childbirth and he didn't marry again 'til after his mother died, so he was past fifty when my daddy was born.

Accordin' to what my grandmother told me, he was leavin' Kentucky for good, headed out to Missouri. Said he was gonna start all over. He just had forded the river into Lee County, when he heard screamin' and he looked up and here come these two young women runnin' toward 'im. They'd been pickin' blackberries and saw a panther sleepin' down in a swag...layin' on his back. They woke 'im up as they took off runnin'. Little Jake got down off his horse and told 'em to run and hide in the bushes and he'd be waitin' for that panther. Sure enough, here it came, followin' their scent.

Grandma said, 'When it throwed its head back to holler'-- and that's just how she said, 'When it throwed its head back to holler, Jake shot it in the throat and kilt it.' These girls took Little Jake home with 'em for dinner, and he wound up marryin' the oldest'n. That was my grandmother, Sarah Jane. She was a right smart younger than my grandfather, and she outlived 'im by forty some-odd years.

Then Little Jake gave the rock to Uncle Nelson as he was leavin' out for Kansas to work on a cattle ranch...stayed there several years and then froze to death in a blizzard tryin' to save the family of the man he worked for. They had already made it home safe and he didn't know. Daddy rode all the way out there to get my uncle's belongin's and went to work for the same people. He did that for a year or two, but he got homesick for Kentucky and by the time he made it back, his mother had remarried. Daddy couldn't get along with her new husband, his stepfather, so he came down here to Fordville to work in the sawmill. He met my mother here and they married and went to housekeepin'. Daddy wanted 'em to go back out west to start a new life out there somewhere—Kansas or maybe Texas.

It was hard for Daddy to stay in one place long. My grandmother claimed he was like King Jacob—they say he had a wanderin' spirit in 'im. I'm more like my mother's people—the Harrises. They came in here with Daniel Boone and stayed put. It's hard for a man to prosper if he's always packin' up and movin'.

"When did your daddy give the whet rock to you?"

Mr. Little dropped his head.

"Well...by rights, it really shouldn't *never* have been mine. It was supposed to go my brother, Woodson, and did for a while...'til he died. We called 'im "Woods." There was just the three of us: Woods was the oldest, me, and then my sister, Bonnie. Then about the time I turned eighteen Mama died in childbirth with our baby sister. Daddy buried the baby with her in the same coffin. And of course, you know Terry Mose... my sister Bonnie died less than a month after she married 'im.

After all that, Daddy got restless like he'd done before, and it wasn't long before he got it in his head to move again. If it hadn't been for my mother, he would've done moved a dozen times by then. Then one evenin', Daddy's cousin came up from Mississippi to visit his people and talked 'im into movin' down there. This cousin had bought land from the railroad and offered to sell 'im a part of it on good terms.

Woods nor me neither one was interested in leavin' and that's when the rock here changed hands again."

I looked at the whet rock again—closely—as Mr. Little held it. I didn't see the name Woods in the inscription so carefully etched on its surface.

The thought struck me, yet again--The death of another Little, his hopes and dreams.

"Daddy felt by rights that Woods ought to have it, him bein' the oldest. He told us if we wanted to stay here, we'd have to buy the homeplace, since he'd be needin' money to start over in Mississippi. Woods and me was both courtin' heavy and fixin' to get married, so we were gonna divide it between us.

That was in 1912, and Woods took a job that winter helpin' down yonder at the saw mill. He wasn't no log man...he was a natural born farmer like my mother's people, but we needed the money any way we could get it. They had 'im down there movin' logs by hisself just at the water's edge and I'm thinkin' he hadn't told nobody he couldn't swim...not a lick. Maybe he thought they'd let 'im go if they knew it. There was one other man supposed to be down there helpin' 'im, and he didn't come back one day after dinner...he fooled around and got drunk so Woods was there by hisself to do the job."

Mr. Little caressed the surface of the whet rock as he spoke. "And if it hadn't been for this little rock, we'd would've never known what happened to 'im. They found his body all the way down in Mercer County about six weeks later. Some young boys found 'im in a creek bottom when they was coon huntin', and it liked to have scared 'em to death. He was all bones, but he still had his heavy

291

work coat on 'im-- and this ol' rock was still in his pocket. They called for the sheriff and he sent word upriver about a man's body bein' found with a whet rock in the coat pocket. That's all they had to give a description. Old Sheriff Tate heard about it and drove down here hisself to tell Daddy that it looked like we should to go to Harrodsburg to the funeral home, and he'd go with us. It was Woods, of course, and that undertaker there in Harrodsburg brought 'im all the way back here and wouldn't take a cent for it. We buried 'im up in our graveyard beside our mother and our little baby sister that died." Holding the whet rock with one hand at chest level, he shook it a little and said, "It's a thousand wonders this thing hadn't sunk to the bottom of that river, but it was still in Woods' pocket…right where he'd left it."

It was hard for me to imagine that the rock Mr. Little had been holding all this time was once in the pocket of a dead man.

"Daddy stayed on with us for a week or two after we buried Woods, but he'd bought that land down in Mississippi and was head over heels in love with a young widow with four children. Right before he left, he asked me where his old whet rock was. I'd put it up on the mantle at our house on the same day we buried Woods. Nobody'd touched it since. I told him, I says, "Daddy, it's yours. You can do whatever you want to with it." So, he put it in his pocket and took it with 'im." To tell you the truth, I didn't give two hoots about it. Not then. Not 'til after he came back."

"Is that when he gave it to you?"

"Well," he said, thoughtfully, "kindly—maybe the best part of it, he did. To tell you the truth, by the time he came back here to live with us, this little rock was all he had left to his name—(Mr. Little shook it around in his hand for emphasis)--and the Little Family Bible. And I finally found it a home last summer."

I thought the story was now ended. I had written down what I could as fast as I could, but I knew I'd have to rewrite the notes the very minute I got home and could still remember the details. However, the story had one, final chapter yet to go.

Mr. Little cleared his throat, and continued.

"I never studied much on it 'til I brought Daddy back here."

Curious, I said, "Why did he come back?"

Mr. Little knitted his bushy eyebrows as he spoke.

"Daddy's second wife wasn't very good to 'im. They hadn't been gettin' along for a right smart while, and here comes that big flood on The Mississippi River. That was in 1927. Daddy had already sold his place for less than he gave for it, and by the time he paid his debts, there wasn't hardly nothin' left. His wife up and left 'im one night and took what little bit of money they did have. Some volunteer for The Red Cross wrote me a letter that Daddy was in a camp for people that had lost out on account of the flood and if that wasn't bad enough, he'd had a light stroke. This fellow was a preacher. He and his wife took Daddy home to look after 'im, so I bought a train ticket down there to get 'im.

Daddy didn't have nothin' much to bring back, but I paid that preacher man a little for takin' care of 'im and bought our train tickets for home. That was one long ride, let me tell you. And when we came through the door, he laid this rock in the exact same spot where he'd picked it up before he headed out the door for Mississippi. After we got 'im put to bed, I got to lookin' at it and I thought to myself, "This ol' whet rock is all that's left of our family. It had ever' bit come down to me."

Daddy lived for a little over a year, but in that time we talked a whole lot—more than we ever had, especially of an evenin' after supper. He'd talk about all the things he'd seen out west, in Kansas, Missouri—Mississippi, too for that matter. He'd talk about what he'd done wrong—how he'd messed up by goin' out west, or in comin' back here…and then again when he left here for Mississippi.

He was a smart man, but he was just like his grandfather-- King Jacob, accordin' to what they always said about 'im-- like a chicken on a hot rock. He couldn't stay put in one place long enough to accumulate anything, but I'll tell you what—Daddy knew how and when to do anything and ever'thing. He had the sharpest eye for nature of any man I've ever known. He'd study the signs and tell us when to plant the garden, when to render lard. He'd even tell me when to do certain kinds of carpentry work by the signs— like puttin' the weatherboardin' on a house to where the boards wouldn't curl up, such as that. He sure enough believed in the signs. You put your cucumbers out when the sign was in the arms. You didn't cut your bull calves or boars until the sign was in the knees—he believed there was signs for ever'thing."

Mr. Little went on for at least another ten minutes about signs for every imaginable undertaking--plants that could be grown or animals that could be tended to—weather lore he had learned and memorized from his long-dead father, David Little. I lost track of the jumbled recollections in my note-keeping—something I still regret, but I said, "Mr. Little, did you ever hear of a *bad* sign for anything?"

He just laughed. It was a laugh that started as a chuckle and matured the more he thought. He said, "Daddy always said that *nothin' would ever grow that was planted in the sign of the water man.* They call 'im by another name now. I forget what it is.

But let me tell you this--after Daddy died I got our old Family Bible to put down the date of his death, and when I got to lookin' at it, ever' one of us men of the Little generations was born in November—*ever' last one of us.* I knew Daddy and me, and my brother Woods was born in the same month, but I never thought about Little Jake, and my uncle Nelson that died out in Kansas. Now ain't that a wonder? And when I took the Farmer's Almanac and got to countin' back nine months, that's when it struck me: *we was all be-gat in the sign of that ol' water man.*"

In my mind, I can still see Mr. Little as he paused for a moment and leaned back into his chair. Holding the whet rock firmly with both hands, he turned to face me with a feeble grin and said, "I ain't never studied much on it, but maybe that's how come the Little's seed's run out." It was a forced laugh, but he said with a raspy chuckle, "We was all planted in the wrong sign."

He was near eighty. I was eighteen. There was no consolation I could give him for being The Last Little. Still, I couldn't help but feel some of the sadness I heard in his tone as much as his words. Not knowing what else to do, I wanted to bring the narrative to some kind of conclusion or possibly even change the subject. I said, "Was your father sick for a long time before he died?"

"W-e-l-l," he drawled, "I'd say long enough, if it was me. The trip we had back here on the train from Louisiana, now that was hard on 'im. We got home late in the night from the train station in Harriston, and Daddy slept for days, seems like. He was whipped out…ever' way a man could be.

It took him a few days, but he got a little of his strength back. I think he liked bein' near Mama's and the baby's graves at my place, and then Brother Woods and Bonnie bein' right down the road here in Fordville. Daddy came back here with just enough money in his pocket to have his gravestone made—one for him and Mama and another for the baby they lost. That seemed to comfort 'im, and as long as the weather wasn't too bad, he'd have me walk with 'im up to their graves after supper most ever' evenin'.

I reckon it was about a month or two later, I saw him out back, under a shade tree one afternoon. He was all hunkered over somethin' workin' on it. I says 'Daddy, what are you doin'?' and he showed me our old whet rock here--where he'd started puttin' the history—this letterin' on it…had it on a piece of stump he'd rolled out there under the shade tree. I had his old tools, the ones he'd left here when he went down to Mississippi. He didn't have no strength much in his left arm but he could use that left hand to steady the rock while he carved on it.

Seems like it gave him a reason to get up ever' mornin' for a right smart while. It was hard on his eyes, and if the light was bad, he'd lay off til the sun came out again. I think it just gave him somethin' to do, but he took a heap of pride in it, and I'll never forget the day he finished it. He'd gotten to where he didn't have no appetite much, but that evenin' he came to the supper table and ate like a field hand. Right before Minnie Lou started to clear the dishes away, he handed it to me all wrapped up in a piece of wax paper with a piece of twine tied around it—like it was a Christmas present or somethin'. There it was, just like you see it here, with all the letterin' and such carved on it. He didn't make much of a speech about it, but he did say to me, "Son," he says, "I ain't got nothin' left to give you now but King Jacob's whet rock. It's the only thing I've got that belonged to my daddy—and by Ned I had to travel halfway across the U-nited States to get it. But, I've added *somethin'* to it," he said. "Leastways, the history won't get away from us now."

Mr. Little paused. "That's what Daddy said, but it's gonna get away from us just the same…"

He was not just giving me an old whet rock. This was about the Little family history…he was letting go of their past as well as their future.

"Yessir, Daddy put a whole of work into that carvin' there. He still had the use of his right hand, and he was always a good hand to whittle. So, the way he'd done it, he got 'im a little piece of paper and a pencil and traced the rock onto it. Then he practiced writin' out what he wanted to put on it—sizin' up the letters and such. He was afraid he'd get into carvin' the names and mess it up if he didn't measure out ever' letter. He said he had to find just the right words to make the spacin' come out right, but when he figured it out, he said there wasn't enough room for brother Woods and me both. It's kindly sad that-away, but it's like he said: Woods was gone and there wasn't no bringin' 'im back. Daddy said there just barely was room enough for my name, *but no more.*

He finished it on Easter Sunday and then, as the sayin' goes, he took his bed on the first Sunday in May. I remember we planted corn that very next day. Then, he died on the thirtieth of June. That was in 1929, and I've held onto it ever since--'til now…" Mr. Little's voice trailed away. With a grin that was not yet a smile, he nodded toward the sacred stone in the upturned palm of his of his hand which he extended to me. "And now, I want *you* to have it."

I was dumfounded.

"I don't know what to say, Mr. Little…I…"

He waved his hand to cut me short—"There ain't no need, son, none a-tall. Ever' since you was just a little jasper, you've been listenin' to us ol' timers. When Nick McCart came in here a while back and gave you that little Case knife, I thought to myself, "Now right there's a young man that'll appreciate *our old rock*." Seems like all most people care about is what's goin' on right now, but a man starts to see things different when he gets ready for the graveyard. You're young and all you can think about right now is what's ahead, but a man my age spends as much time thinkin' about the past as he does tomorrow—maybe more. It's kindly like crossin' that road out yonder—you look both ways." I followed Mr. Little's expression as he looked up and waved a hand in the air, as if pointing to the peeling paint on the ceiling, its curled edges tinged in soot. "The way I see it, there's a whole heap of stuff behind us, kindly movin' us forward—surely it can't all dry up and blow away because we don't pay no mind to it… *no more than we do when we're dead and gone.*"

Mr. Little turned his head as Mack struggled to fasten the slide bolt to the storage room's sagging double doors to the storage room. The old storekeeper ate supper promptly at six every evening and it was now well past that. The inviting sound of an oven door opening and the comforting aroma of chicken frying drifted into the store from the living quarters Mack shared with his blind sister--a sure sign we should be going.

As we stood up, Mr. Little said, "Son, right now, you can't even think about gettin' old. I know. I was your age once, but if you live, *you will get old.* After Daddy died, I decided if we ever had a son, I was gonna name 'im Nelson Woods Little—for my uncle and my brother. Their names ain't on our old rock, see…*but they lived just the* same. I thought it would kindly keep their memory alive, but I finally had to give up on that notion. But, maybe you'll get lucky and have a son you can give it to."

Preparing to leave, Mr. Little picked up the denim jacket that was neatly draped over the back of his chair. Putting it on, he turned his green gaze upon me once more. "On the other hand, you could wind up just like me. You look around one day and ever'body's dead and gone. If that's the hand you're dealt, when the time comes, try to find the right man to give it to. Find a good man that knows a good knife when he sees one… and takes good care of it."

That was it-- the entirety of Mr. Daniel Jacob Little's presentation speech. He had done what he came to do, and with certainty in his voice, concluded the ceremony. "All right then, *young man*," he said, "here you are." Still warm from the touch of The Last Little, the treasured family heirloom passed from his hand to mine.

Mr. Little left the store shortly thereafter, and never spoke of the whet rock to me, ever again. To be truthful, I've never even used it—at least, not for its original purpose. Almost like it was a lost original copy of The Declaration of Independence--for fear of marring its surface, I left it just as it was. Far from being a venerated document in halls of polished marble, the lowly whet rock belongs among the common folk as the silent witness to one family's struggle for survival, and possibly even the lone artifact of its existence.

As Mack stood in front of the store with me, I suddenly remembered I needed to return his clipboard, still tucked under my arm.

Putting on his reading glasses, he reached for it. "Let me take a look at what you wrote down there."

My notes were a scribbled mess, but he turned both pages over, giving them a quick glance. As he handed them back, he said, "That was *one more story* you got to hear in there." I nodded in agreement, still amazed at the legacy I now held in my hand. Mack gave me his serious, over-the-glasses stare. "You know what all that was about, don't you?"

All I could say was, "Maybe?"

The old storekeeper gripped my shoulder, and spoke in brotherly, even affectionate terms of his old friend, "All in the world Dan Jacob wanted was for somebody to tell it to," he said. "…somebody young like you that *might listen.*"

During my three mile ride home with the whet rock in my pocket, I was struck by the sudden realization that this was the first time since The Declaration of Independence was written—in 1776--that a Little had not carried it. I know this may sound silly, for it is, after all, a rock-- but I felt unworthy to be its new owner. Both the blessing and the burden of its long, circuitous history were now mine to protect.

Now, nearly fifty years later, it is time for me to consider who should be the next keeper of The Little Whet Rock— to find a worthy candidate that would meet with the old carpenter's approval. It is a responsibility I accepted long

301

ago, *along with* the privilege of being its keeper –but only for a season.

Aunt Roxie's piano

Rose Petal Wine

I was helping Granny paint the living room that day—a chore I dreaded because it involved navigating around furniture. In particular I dreaded the piano, which required at least two strong backs just to move across the room. Two of its rollers were broken off and the undertaking usually resulted in additional casualties to the piano, the floor beneath, or adjacent territory. Three missing ivory keys knocked off by a falling vase evidenced the collateral damage from a previous move. The last time I managed the task, I said, "Granny, you don't even play the piano. Why don't you get rid of this thing? It's a man eater."

She said, "I love that old piano. My Cousin Arthur *gave it* to me."

"Would he consider taking it back?"

303

Slightly agitated, she said, "He's DEAD. He LEFT IT to me."

Even Granny's old helper Sister Simpson, the meekest, mildest soul that ever lived, said, "He's right. You need a piano about like a hog needs side pockets."

Granny felt the need to defend herself from our jibes. "I'll have you to know that my Aunt Roxie paid a whole lot of money for it."

"So she could learn to play?"

"Aunt Roxie? No, she bought it for Arthur when he was just a kid. Music was his whole life, bless his heart, but he just couldn't do much with it…not here, anyway."

"How come?"

Granny hesitated. "Well…Arthur was--different."

I searched her expression for some hidden meaning. "Because of a piano?"

She leaned forward in her rocker, studying her fingernails with paint underneath where she had opened the new can.

"Times was hard then. And a whole lot harder for him, especially. I always felt right sorry for the little feller on account of his daddy, my uncle Hetch, bein' so hard on 'im. Ever'body called him "Big Hetch" and he was--*great* big— a big ol' blacksmith—big *and* loud. At one time, they said he was prob'ly the strongest man in Fordville…weighed ever' bit of three hundred. When he was younger, he had the name of bein' the strongest man in Fordville, just like his daddy, my grandfather. One time I saw Hetch stand flat-footed and hold each arm out to the side at the same time with' a splittin' axe in each hand—holdin' it by the handle, this-away," she said, extending each of her own arms to her sides to demonstrate. "I've heard 'im joke and say that back in *his* younger days, his daddy could whip any man in Fordville—and that *he* could whip his daddy.

Hetch and Roxie didn't have children 'til late in life—'til Arthur come along. She'd lost two or three before they were born and she must've been up around forty when she had him. The first summer after he was born he took sick and started gettin' puny with what we used to call the "summer complaint." That's what the old timers called it. I don't know what it'd be now. They got real worried about him and sent for ol' Dr. Washburn from across the river. He'd known 'em both for years. They said he came through the door of their house down there in Fordville to see about little Arthur and he took one look at Roxie and said, "Why, Roxie, you're expectin' again." Roxie just thought she was gettin' sick with whatever Arthur had. Well, Arthur got better and Aunt Roxie got—bigger. So when Effie was born, there wasn't but about fourteen months' difference in 'em."

Granny shook her head, "Arthur and Effie were close in age, but they was miles apart every other way.

When they were growin' up, people around here said it looked like Mother Nature got her wires crossed up on them two. Arthur took after Aunt Roxie. She was tall for a woman—but as poor and thin as a whippoorwill. She had tiny little bones in her face and hands…she was just built small I reckon you'd say—and Arthur was the spit of her…almost like he'd been dug out of her with a grubbin' hoe. Then, when Effie came along, she was Big Hetch made over…built big just like he was—not nearly as heavy and strong of course. And to this day I've never seen a woman that could out-eat her. When she was up around fifteen or sixteen years old and we'd have big family dinners, I've seen her take one of her mama's big chicken

305

platters with three or four pieces left on it, and make a dinner plate with it—and pile it sky high. By that time, she was about as strong as any boy her age and she'd go out and work in the blacksmith shop with her daddy--and get just as black and dirty as he did.

People used to say that Effie belonged to Hetch and Arthur was Aunt Roxie's. The blacksmith shop set right next to their house and I'd get good and tickled when I was a kid. You'd be in Fordville and hear Hetch in his shop beatin' and bangin' away on a horseshoe or piece of iron and when he'd stop, you'd hear Arthur beatin' and bangin' away on this ol' piano here, if the windows was open. Even the sounds the two of them made was different as daylight and dark. Hetch tried his best to make a blacksmith out of Arthur, but it never took. If we were out of school, he'd take Arthur in his work clothes to get the forge fired up and there was always work for 'em to do. Hetch was one of the best blacksmiths in the county. But just as sure as he'd make Arthur work in the shop, Aunt Roxie'd come over and get him before dinner and take him back to the house to help her. He liked bein' in the kitchen--and to tell you the truth, by the time she died, he was about as good a cook as she was. He could bake the best angel food cakes I've ever put in my mouth.

Then, when Effie got up old enough to follow her daddy to the blacksmith shop, Aunt Roxie let her go. He'd show her how to do a few little piddlin' things that she was big enough to handle without gettin' hurt—and she took to it like a sunburnt pig to mud. As she got older, she got to where she'd help Hetch out there just like you'd a-thought Arthur would've, him bein' a boy and all. That was the *oddest* thing you ever saw. You'd go by there with a horse to be shod and Effie'd be there helpin' her daddy, all sweaty and black-faced--and if it was warm weather, you'd hear Arthur in the house playin' on that piano."

306

I said, "If you don't even play, why did he leave it to you?"

Granny chuckled, "Well, we thought a lot of one another growin' up. There wasn't but three months' difference between us and I just loved the little feller…hardly ever saw him after we got older, but Arthur was just…special. I reckon he wanted me to have it to remember him by. Your granddaddy said it was because nobody else wanted to move the thing.

When all of us cousins would gather here at Mama's or at one of the other aunts' houses, or at Big Granny's, most gen'lly he'd play with us girls. A lot of the time, we'd gather around this piano and listen to him play. He could sing like a canary, too…had a good tenor voice. The boys all teased him over it, especially Aunt Pearl's son John L…he was downright mean to Arthur.

One time, we had a big family dinner down at Hetch and Roxie's. The boys was gettin' Hetch to show 'em how to make things out in the blacksmith shop. He heated up the forge and all the boys was there but Arthur. He hated ever' square inch of that blacksmith shop, so he stayed on the front porch with us. Before long, here come John L. and two of the younger cousins and they commenced pickin' on Arthur. He never took up for hisself, so we just told 'em both to hush. They kept it up and I reckon he'd had enough. Finally, he stood up big and straight and told John L. and them to shut his mouth and ever'thing went downhill after that. He hauled off and gave Arthur a big shove over into his mother's rose bushes—they was all in full bloom and he squshed 'em flat as a flitter. By the time we got him pulled out of there, he had bleedin' scratches all over him—looked like he'd been tied up in a bag of cats."

Granny chuckled, "That's when I stepped in. I wasn't no older than any of the boys, but I was about a head taller; I got up in John L.'s face and told him to leave Arthur alone or I'd turn him inside out. I was so mad I could bust anyway, and well, you prob'ly never saw John L. but he was red headed like his daddy Uncle Ira, and just as freckle-faced. He'd been makin' fun of Arthur on account of how small he was and—delicate I reckon you'd call it, and I said, "John L. you're a fine one to talk about anybody's looks, after the old mare farted in *your* face."

I cackled out loud, "What?"

Granny looked at me blankly. "Oh, that was just an ol' sayin' about anybody that was freckled real bad—that "the old mare'd farted in their face."

Well, that did it for John L. He made a big step towards me like he was gonna push me or somethin', but I dodged him and then I got *me* a real good swing in-- and left my handprint in the side of that freckled face. Then the other two boys started to jump on me and Arthur ran right into 'em…poor little ol' feller--flailin' his arms at 'em like a windmill. We were all into it…and then here comes the other boys along with Effie and Big Hetch out of the blacksmith shop. I reckon that made it even worse for Arthur. And you know John L. never did have any use for me after I slapped him. I got me a good lick in for poor little ol' Arthur--and John L. had it comin'. I smacked the taste out of that red head and he took off runnin' to his mama, Aunt Pearl. She was in the house with Aunt Roxie and the other aunts. It wasn't five minutes before all of them started fussin'." Granny chuckled, "The family gatherin' got cut short that day. My uncles all thought it was funny, but that's the way some of them aunts of mine were. They'd rather've had somethin' to fume over than to eat sugar—and some of 'em were barely speakin' to one another all the way to Christmas that year."

Shaking her head, Granny said, "It's funny what makes you think of things from your childhood. I hate that memory in a way, 'cause it seems like things was never the same in our family after that. It wasn't long before Uncle Harve died from blood poisonin'—cut a bump off his jaw shavin' in a hurry to get to a horse and mule sale in Harriston. Then Aunt Roxie took sick, and when we did get together after that with my other aunts bringin' in food and settin' with her, why, Arthur would take off for the woods and none of us ever would see him. I think Hetch gave him a real hard time on the day we had that big ruckus. I can still remember the way he stood there lookin' at Arthur and you could see it in the old feller's eyes: he was ashamed of his own child."

Granny and Sister sat in silence for a moment on the sofa-- now all crammed into the middle of the living room with all the other furniture.

Although they'd performed this ritual many times over the years, it was getting more difficult for the two older women. They'd been cleaning all morning and taking pictures down in the living room and hallway, to get it ready for me to paint—under her supervision of course. Sister Simpson had helped Granny for so many years, she knew exactly what to do and in the order Granny preferred; in fact, this *was* the last time she would have a hand in the tedious process, although at the time she appeared to be in excellent health for her age. I still remember how Granny caressed the side of the piano as she told Arthur's story that afternoon.

"Poor ol' Aunt Roxie...she wanted better for *her* children than she'd had growin' up. She was raised *hard*--couldn't read or write her own name. But I've seen her count to ten and when she'd get past that number, she'd count out whatever she was doin' in *sets* of ten if they was a whole

309

lot of 'em, somethin' like ears of corn or 'taters. She'd say, "the second ten, or the third ten," instead of sayin' twenty or thirty, or what have you. But Aunt Roxie was a good woman, and a good mother. Arthur worshipped the very ground she walked on, and after she died, nothin' was the same for him--here."

Granny sighed through her nose. She reached over to run her fingers gently along the edge of the bass keys, releasing their deep and out of tune rumble.

"I don't know how to say it…but Arthur was just…unusual. He was too tender-hearted to live—here, anyway. His daddy, Hetch, made him go huntin' with him one Thanksgivin', along with him and some of the other men around Fordville—and then he cried when they'd shoot a rabbit or a squirrel. Those foolish cousins of mine made fun of him about that—for a long time. Hetch was a good man…a hard worker…and honest as the day is long, but he was just…real hard on Arthur. It was like they was worlds apart, them two.

But--there came a day later, after Aunt Roxie died…I'll never forget it. It was after dinner one Sunday. All my uncles and the boy cousins were out back at Big Granny's, target-shootin', that is, except for Arthur. Seems like he'd take off for the woods and just hide for a day at a time after Aunt Roxie died. I just don't think he could face livin' with his daddy if his mother wasn't there. He came around by the side of the house and my cousin John L. taunted him about bein' too sissified to fire a gun. Well, that did it. I reckon he made a beeline straight for him and reached for John L.'s gun and where they'd set the bottles up as targets, Arthur went right down the line and shot ever' one of em, dead center---and never said a word. He left all our boy cousins and their daddys standin' there with their mouths hangin' wide open—and his daddy, too, Big Hetch.

Nobody ever knew where he learned to shoot that-away, but he showed 'em."

Granny focused her eyes on the piano. "And I remember the very day when Aunt Roxie got this."

She chuckled and shook her head. "I forget just how much it cost her, but, back then it was a whole lot. Roxie and Hetch fussed about it, and then the other boys would say mean things to Arthur on account of him bein' more interested in his music than fishin' and huntin', such as that.

By and by though, Arthur and Effie both grew up. Arthur left here and went up north for his education. Effie married little ol' dried up Jimbo Jenkins and he was ever' bit of twenty years older than her. When auto-mobiles came out and the county built the Fordville turnpike, Hetch gave the blacksmith shop over to Effie and Jimbo and they turned it into a garage and fillin' station. That was the first 'n Fordville ever had. You might hear of it nowadays some, but back then you never saw—or even heard of a woman workin' on a car or motor or anything like that—not around here. I've known people that'd drive by there just to see Effie—with her all greasy lookin' and that ci-garette a-danglin from her lip. And cuss…my Lord, the words she used could kill corn knee-high. It looked mighty strange, but we all got used to 'em like that, Effie and Jimbo. Them two were as happy workin' together in that garage as if they had good sense and didn't know no better. That lasted a while, but then durin' the Thirties Jimbo got some wastin' disease and lost the use of his legs. Effie took care of 'im 'til he died, and her daddy, too—at the same time. I've seen her pick Jimbo up and carry him to the outhouse like he wasn't no more than a chunk of stove wood. If there was other people around, he'd give 'er some kind of signal so she'd know he needed to go. She'd clamp down on that

311

ci-garette in her mouth and say, "All right Jimbo, let's go potty." They didn't sell much gas or do much mechanicin' neither one down there durin' The Depression…but all that time Arthur kept sendin' 'em money to get by. He took care of Big Hetch and Effie both as long as he lived."

I wondered how I would have handled the kind of rejection that Granny's Cousin Arthur had experienced while living in the Fordville I had grown to love. I had never known anything from those around me but love and acceptance. What if I had been, as Granny said, *"different."*

I said, "Whatever happened to Arthur?

"He left here for good. After they buried Aunt Roxie, he boarded a train and I never laid eyes on 'im again for prob'ly ten or fifteen years. He worked his way through school up in Ohio somewhere. I'll think of it, direc'ly. He got to be a big concert piano player…traveled all over the country with an orchestra or somethin' of the sort. Then he taught music at a big name college way up in Illinois. I can't think of it either right now, but Arthur did right well for hisself. I know he made a right smart of money, 'cause that's the reason Effie doesn't have a care in the world now. He left her the biggest part of ever'thing he had.

After his mother died, I never knew of him to come back to Fordville—not one time. I think he sent letters to Effie, askin' about his daddy. But then you'd go to ask Hetch about Arthur and he wouldn't hardly answer you. It was like he didn't exist--and it hadn't been for him, they'd a-gone without. Right as rain, Arthur sent that check to Effie ever month for her and Hetch to live on. I've heard Effie say it herself, that Arthur always asked about "Big Hetch," that's what Arthur called him."

I said, "How did his piano wind up here?"

"Well…Hetch got up in years and died. They had the funeral down here at Coley Pepper's in Fordville. Knowin' how his daddy had always treated him, nobody much expected him to make it here for the funeral. Well don't you know, he *did* come. I hadn't seen him since Aunt Roxie's funeral, but I'd a-known him in a cornfield.

He stayed with some of the family while he was here and he came to see us a day or two before he went back to Illinois.

Hetch didn't have a whole lot but he'd made out a little will when he got sick. Come to find out he'd left what little money he had in the bank and that property down in Fordville to Effie—*just her*, and all Arthur got was this piano here and ONE DOLLAR."

Granny held up her bony little index finger.

"I know it had to hurt Arthur's feelin's, bein' kindly left out. Arthur didn't really need it, so far as that goes and Effie did. But to give credit where it's due, Effie told him that she'd tear up that will and divide what little there was between the two of 'em. Arthur said to her, "Ef,"—that's what he called her. He said, "Ef, if that's the way Big Hetch wanted it, that's the way it'll be." I always got tickled over that. Even after the way he'd done him, Arthur still looked up to his daddy.

I reckon you'd say Big Hetch disowned him in a way. If you ask me, leavin' somebody a dollar's worse than leavin' 'em out altogether--more like a slap in the face. But Arthur did love that piano. He paid a man a right smart amount to haul it all the way up to where he lived, almost to Chicago. Arthur'd lived in a house up there with some other man that was a big archi-tect, and he's the one that paid to ship the piano back down here to me when Arthur died."

313

Sister Simpson had been sitting in silence most of the time. She smiled and said, "Now wasn't that a nice thing to do? They had to be real good friends to live together that-away, didn't they? They *sure* must've thought a *whole lot* of one another.

Granny didn't make eye contact with Sister—or me. She was leaning her head back into the rocking chair. She just shook her head gently from side to side with her eyes closed and said in a sympathetic tone, "That's right, Sister. They were *real* good friends."

Sister said, "Lor-rain if I *ever* had me a friend like that I could've lived with, it'd a-been you, sure enough."

With her eyes still closed as she gently rocked back and forth, Granny said, "Sister…you had *Brother* to live with."

Sister's smile began to fade and she seemed confused. "But…Brother was *my* husband."

Seeing no future in the direction that conversation was headed, I said, "Granny, when did you get it?"

"The piano? Oh, I reckon it was about the time you were born, maybe a little before. Arthur didn't live to be too old. He took after Aunt Roxie in about ever' way a man could. They both died in their fifties.

But when Arthur died he had ever'thing spelled out to the letter. Effie'd done told him she didn't want the piano so he gave it to me. It's prob'ly traveled more miles than most people here have. Then he left a note to Effie, for her to scatter his ashes on their mother and daddy's graves down yonder in the Fordville Cemetery.

And your Granddaddy's hated that piano from the minute we brought it in here," she said.

"He's took the hide and hair off his knuckles I don't know how many times, movin' it through that doorway there so I could paint or hang wallpaper. It went through the floor over there in the corner about the time you came here to stay with us. Termites had chewed up a joist and that piano weighs an ever-lovin' ton…one corner of it squatted right down on top of it."

We returned to the task at hand, of moving and removing furniture and furnishings—of cleaning, and re-cleaning after painting one wall and part of a ceiling at a time.

Before I moved the piano, I knew enough this time to remove everything from its top. One of the items that had been there for as long as I could remember was an inexpensive oval metal frame on a lacy white doily, with a dried rose inside, the tiny barbs still clearly visible on its stem.

I said, "Granny's what's up with this?"

She said, "Oh, I've had that settin' up there almost as long as I've had the piano.

Arthur stayed around here about a week after Hetch's funeral. He'd go around and visit with some of the family he hadn't seen since he left here, when Aunt Roxie died.

He came up to see me that very day he left here, to go back to Illinois, and I'll never forget it. I reckon Effie insisted on givin' a dollar bill to Arthur out of Uncle Hetch's big old pocketbook that he carried around in his overalls. Holding up her index finger again, Granny said, "Arthur borrowed your Granddaddy's truck and took that *one dollar* to Harriston and bought a yellow rose bush for his daddy's grave. It was up in June when Big Hetch died--and hot as blazes. Arthur asked me if I'd go down to the cemetery with him to set it out. He'd asked Effie to help him, and

315

she said if he wanted it to live, then he'd better get me. We drove down there, and I took a grubbing hoe and little bit of sand...and some dried manure from the barn lot. Arthur wanted to dig the hole and set the rose in the ground. I covered it up and he watered it real good. Then, as we were leavin' he asked me if I'd look after it—and I told him I'd try to. Ever' spring and summer after that, I'd go over there about once a month and sprinkle me a little handful of Epsom salts around the roots and water it real good, and then I'd cut it back in the fall.

That little rosebush lived for several years—'til after Arthur died, but when I cut it back that last time, I could see it was startin' to look bad. When we buried Aunt Gracie, I looked over in that direction and saw that one little yellow rose bloomin'. It was fixin' to freeze again that evenin', so I took Russell's pocketknife to cut it and take it home with me. A day or two later, I decided to let it dry and put it in our big family Bible as a keepsake.

I never laid my eyes on Arthur again after the day we planted the rosebush. It wasn't but about three or four years after that Effie called and told me he'd died and they'd cre-mated 'im up there where he lived, Chicago or somewhere—never had no funeral nor nothin'. I don't believe in that...bein' all burnt up like a piece of light bread in a cookstove...and then crumbled up in a jar. I've heard of some people in these big cities have them jars of ashes settin' on their mantles and such as that. Some of 'em are real pretty--fancy lookin' things that cost a whole lot of money. I wouldn't mind havin' one on my mantle there in the dinin' room—but I wouldn't want nobody's ashes in it."

Granny shook her head. "No, that's nothin' I want to be a party to, but it's what Arthur wanted. Before he died, he asked Effie to scatter his ashes on their mother and daddy's graves. After he was cremated, why then, she called wantin' to know if I'd come to the cemetery when they had service for 'im. She found a preacher of some kind to read a few Bible verses and give a little talk, but he didn't know Arthur from a load of coal. Some of the cousins he'd kept in touch with over the years met down there, just a handful of us. Effie took the lid of that jar or…urn, whatever you call the thing, and scattered the little feller's ashes…and at the time I thought it was real nice the way she done it."

I said, "How *did* she do it?"

Granny searched for her words as if they were etched on the ceiling, "Oh, I don't know," she said, "…it just looked to me like she made the sign of The Cross with 'em, goin' this way and then that-away over Big Hetch and Roxie's graves." Granny made the motions and sifted her fingers together as if she was sprinkling her dead cousin's remains on the linoleum.

She said, "Then I saw Effie about a week later at the grocery in Harriston and I told her how sweet I thought it was, the way she did that, and she looked at me like I fell out of a tree. Effie was just like her daddy for the world—if she thought it, she said it. She stood there with that cigarette danglin' from her lip and she said, 'Lorene, honey, that didn't have nothin' to do with the service. The grass on Mama and Daddy's graves was lookin' kindly puny, and I thought Arthur might green it up a little. That's all that amounted to." Shaking her head, Granny said, "Effie sure had me fooled. I just thought she'd spread 'em out in the shape of a cross that-away, Cath'lic-like."

I couldn't help but ask, "Granny, have you *ever* been to a Catholic funeral?"

"Well, no," she said, adjusting her glasses, "I don't reckon I have, but it just seems to me that's like somethin' they'd do.

The last time we painted this room, I got to thinkin' about Arthur and I took that little dried up rose from Mama's big Bible and bought this frame for it at Woolworth's. It makes me think of him, and how he forgave Big Hetch and kept on lovin' 'im—'til his dyin' day."

With her arms folded, shaking her head ever so slightly, Granny said, "I don't care who you are, forgiveness like that takes a lot of grace."

She picked up the frame again and looked at it in the light. She said, "Along about the time you were born, we had a revival preacher at church that came here and stayed with us a few nights. In his last sermon to us he said, *"Forgiveness is like the fragrance a rose petal gives when it's been stepped on."* I don't know if he knew about it or if it was just a co-incidence, but there'd been a little squabble in The Ladies' Circle and two or three of our members weren't even speakin' to one another. Maybe he was pointin' that sermon toward them, but it did us all good to hear it, just the same. Arthur hadn't been dead just a few weeks then, and I couldn't help but think of the last time I saw him, on the day we planted that rosebush."

The small oval frame that went unnoticed for so long belongs with the piano, but I've decided to hold onto it for the time being. When I'm gone, my hope is that it will be reunited with the old piano--and their story retold. Until then, the forgiving rose that bloomed over Big Hetch remains on my desk.

Listening for Whippoorwills

She'd handed me three containers to open. Christmas Day
was approaching and it was time for Granny to make
fruitcakes and jam cakes. The spice rack in the kitchen was
hard to miss, for what was supposed to be Granny's name
was inlaid on the back-- "LOREN-- instead of "LORENE."
Our firstborn daughter was named Loren for Granny, which
is why she always thought the spice rack was hers. The
truth is Granny's name was misspelled by its maker long
before daughter Loren was even a gleam in our eyes.

An excellent old school cook, Granny didn't use many
spices except at Christmas when she would reach for the
walnut spice rack displaying her name—or most of it—
inlaid into the wood above the shelves. Also made of
walnut, each of the round spice containers had the name of
the spice inlaid into its wood surface just as Granny's name
had been. She had to pull really hard on the wooden
stoppers that sealed them, and even after years of use, they
were *still* that tight.

The freshly opened spice containers and the old
handwritten recipes in her mother's cookbook reminded her
of Christmases past. In particular, a 1944 Christmas shared
with strangers under her roof who had every reason not to
be, or feel, welcomed. Perhaps with them in mind, she sent
me to her bedroom to retrieve her large tin candy box of
pictures, kept in the bottom drawer of her dresser. This
was something she did only on rare occasions, each of
which is still vivid in my memory.

319

As she sat there looking through them, it was obvious she was searching for one in particular, although she would stop and gaze at those of my dead uncle, Johnny. Shortly, one photo in a small oval frame was set aside. While Granny carefully returned the others to the candy tin, I could see that across the bottom of the picture was written: "From Hans, Christmas 1946". I picked it up and studied the youthful face it contained. I vaguely knew that my grandparents had kept "enemy soldiers" during World War Two, but it was something they rarely discussed and until that moment I had never heard their names mentioned.

"I've wondered about those boys over the years," she said. "I wonder what they're doin'—if they've married and had families. They lived with us for a year or two." She gently reached for the photo in my hand and studied it.

They were German prisoners that stayed with us and worked here durin' the War…smart boys…right good workers once you showed 'em what to do, but they didn't know "b from bullfoot" about farmin'. We got a letter or two after they got back to Germany…. after the War--and when that Berlin Wall went up a couple of years ago, I wondered if they were in that part of Germany. Both of 'em were from small towns, and I don't remember their names. Couldn't say 'em if I did know."

At that time I knew essentially nothing about the German prisoner of war release program. I really didn't know much more about it until I was in college, but it had allowed thousands of German soldiers to live with and help American farm families during those critical labor shortage days of World War II—which Granny referred to simply as "The War."

Now here was a thought. Granny had lost her only son in the War-- in the Pacific fighting the Japanese. He had been a naval aviator aboard the ill-fated USS Benjamin Franklin, bombed by the Japanese very late in the War. She had not only allowed, but had volunteered to keep, feed and house German soldiers fighting on the same side as the Japanese that killed my uncle. For a twelve year old, that was a lot to take in. Most of my friends thought their grandmothers were saints, but Granny's decision to host our sworn enemies put her in a league of her own as far as I was concerned. As I came to learn, some of her neighbors *didn't* think so and bore some resentment toward her for doing it. She was to an exceptional degree a free spirit with regard to public opinion--at least, for her day and time. She always held her head high and did what she thought was right. Certainly, there was a practical side to it—extra hands to perform the never-ending farm labor. Still, I think much of it was doing for another young soldier what she couldn't do for Johnny. Although she never addressed it as such, I think for her there was a higher principle involved.

Raised on World War II movies and surrounded by that generation of men and their fathers, in my young mind there had been "them" and "us." That period in their lives was also a subject Granddaddy didn't care to discuss, for he and Granny had disagreed on their participation in the German POW program from the beginning, and which he resented even more after my Uncle Johnny was killed late in the War.

"Well, it's like this," Granny said to me years later, "some of the German people--them boys at least—hated Hitler about as bad as we did, here. Not only that, we and lot more families needed help gettin' the farm work done. There were people at church that held it against us takin' 'em in. Bad as it hurts me to say it, after Johnny got killed I think there was some around here that thought it was our come-uppins for takin' 'em. Your Granddaddy and me didn't much more than speak for a while after I brought it up. Then I got to thinkin' --What if it was Johnny that was overseas as a prisoner of war. How would I want *him* treated?

Your granddaddy didn't want us to do it and I let go of the idea. That was up in the spring, in '44, and it wasn't but a few days later we'd been out in the garden 'til might near dark, plantin' corn. We heard a whippoorwill hollerin' that evenin'—right up here at the edge of the woods. Sister had been here all afternoon helpin' me do the spring cleanin' and she stayed the night with us on account of Brother preachin' at a revival somewhere. So after supper we were out there in the garden and all of a sudden she stopped and listened to that whippoorwill call—you know it's kindly a lonesome sound in a way. Sister stopped to listen, and never moved a muscle. I didn't pay no mind to it. Well, we stayed up fairly late that night, me and Sister. Your granddaddy had already gone to bed and we were sittin' out here on the porch…it was a warm night for spring and just as we were fixin' to turn in, we heard another whippoorwill--up around midnight. It cried three times—I remember that as clear as day. Sister raised her head and got this real serious look on her face. She said, "*That means*

322

a death." Then she hopped up right quick and pointed in that direction—and just held her arm out like this here," Granny said, comically pointing at the cook stove with her flour-coated hand. "She never spoke a word. I said, "Sister, what on earth are you doin'?" and you know how superstitious she is.   She said, "That whippoorwill hollerin' means a death unless you point at it…and that charms it so nobody'll die." Well, I never slept much anyway in those days, with Johnny overseas and me worryin' over him. I tossed and turned all night long after Sister said that. Your granddaddy heard me and he asked me why I couldn't sleep. I told him what Sister'd done and he said, "Lorene, you've heard whippoorwills all your life. You can't pay any mind to that foolishness." He was right, and I knew it…but like Sister always said, "It plagued me."

I still don't know what came over your granddaddy. Maybe he felt bad about not takin' it serious, but the next mornin' at breakfast, out of the clear blue, he agreed for us go ahead and see about gettin' 'those German prisoners. I never knew why he changed his mind, but he asked me one more time why I wanted to do it, and I told him I just felt like it was somethin' The Lord was callin' me to do. I still believe there was some reason why He wanted us to have 'em. Maybe when I get to heaven, I'll know what it was.

But now, let me tell you, not ever'body around here felt like The Lord had a hand in it. Some people said we'd rue the day we signed up for 'em to come here, some of our best friends. Then somethin' else happened that I always thought was kindly strange.

About the time the Hitler part of the War started up
overseas, we had a bad storm to come through here. It was
in the summer and we had a big ol' walnut tree out yonder
where the fence is, between here and the hayfield, a big'n,
that got struck by lightnin'…killed it dead as a hammer.
Your granddaddy saw them dark clouds comin', so he
made a beeline to the house. Johnny and I had been
standin' there talkin' and waitin' for it to pass over, and we
saw a bolt of lightnin' hit that walnut tree and we jumped
two feet in the air. The ground shook under our feet for five
minutes, seems like. And that lightnin' must've followed a
big root on that ol' tree for thirty feet out into the field—
dirt flew up all around. It liked to have scared us all to
death. After the storm passed through, we ran out there and
it looked like somebody had plowed a furrow where that
lightnin' hit.

That fall your granddaddy had to haul dirt in from the
tobacco patch to fill it in. That walnut tree was dead but it
stood for several more years, 'til the limbs started fallin'
out of it. On account of it bein' so close to the house, your
granddaddy decided to cut it down for stovewood. Brother
Simpson started helpin' us some here about the time
Johnny went overseas and he was fixin' to start sawin' and
splittin' it up. They hadn't much more than started before
your granddaddy told Brother that lightnin' had killed it.
Brother asked him what he was gonna do with the wood.
Your granddaddy said, 'Well, I reckon we'll stack in the
woodshed and burn it in the kitchen stove.' Brother didn't
have but three fingers on that one hand but he pointed his
thumb at him and said, "Russell Hall, if you bring lightnin'-
killed firewood in your house, it'll cause trouble sure as

you're born." He believed wood that had been struck by lightnin' was bad luck if you brought it in the house. A lot of the old people used to believe that. Your granddaddy just laughed it off, said there wasn't anything to it, but Brother would not carry one piece of it into the house—not to save his life…said he didn't want to blame hisself if anything bad happened to us. He helped Russell might near all that day, sawin' and choppin.' They'd just about got it all stacked up, except for that one section of the trunk. Russell said the saw was dulled and needed sharpenin' and they left that one piece over next to the fence. That's when this big car pulls up our lane and two men in uniform were drivin' it—and it was them two German soldiers.

When they finally came, they couldn't hardly speak a word of English…and they were plumb scared to death. They were just boys—both of 'em younger'n Johnny. We knew they were comin' and we'd already straightened up the wash house out back—nothin' fancy, just fixed it up for 'em to sleep in. There was already a stove in there and the very first job your granddaddy gave 'em to do was to carry their stovewood into the wash house. He pointed to that pile of walnut in the woodshed that the lightnin' had killed and told 'em that's what we'd be usin'. He kindly laughed and said to Brother, "They're just as well to have bad luck as the rest of us." Course, he didn't believe any more in what Brother had said than I did. But, we shared ever'thing we had with them German boys…our stovewood, our food—every'thing we ate, they ate. Brother just shook his head. He couldn't understand why we'd allow Germans in our house. He said, "I'd just about as soon have that lightnin'-kilt firewood in my house as to have them

325

Germans. They're liable to kill all of you in your own beds." Poor ol' Brother…but, later on I think him and Sister both kindly understood why I wanted to do it."

I said, "Did anybody else around here understand?"

"Well…some of 'em did I think", she said, "but somebody—and I never knew who it was—turned us in once for feedin' 'em too much. We weren't supposed to feed 'em over so many calories a day, since so many of our soldiers were starvin' and dyin' in prison camps overseas. But never in my life have I allowed anybody to go hungry, and I don't care if they was Germans, or WOPS or little green men from Mars-- I wasn't about to let it happen in *my* house. We didn't pamper 'em none, but I think they appreciated us bein' good to 'em. I know they did. Hans made that spice rack in there for me, to say thank-you. He spent close to a year foolin' with it, off and on, and I didn't know a thing in the world about it.

One day your granddaddy had them boys splittin' more stovewood and he thought about the piece of that ol' walnut tree that was still layin' there where he and Brother'd left it. He said Hans kept lookin' at it, admirin' it. The best your Granddaddy could make out, he kept sayin' "Good , good." I reckon your Granddaddy finally got what he was sayin' to him and they sawed it into smaller pieces… said he wanted to make me somethin' out of it. Your granddaddy showed Hans where his tools were. Nothin' fancy, just hand tools. I don't think Russell was too keen on him knowin' where all the tools was, but Hans was a good worker, and he seemed to know that he had it better than a lot of our own boys in uniform. He got your granddaddy to understand that he needed to use a turnin' lathe to make somethin' for me, and sure enough, he took Hans down to Dan Jacob Little's workshop one evenin' and watched him turn ever' one of them spice containers out a of square piece of that walnut that he'd cut out.

To this day, I don't know how he made those pieces—ten of 'em, to hold the spices in that rack. He got lighter wood somewhere to make the inlay for the spice names—and then my name. Untellin' how long that took him." Granny smiled. "It's a funny thing—he spelled all the spices right and got my name wrong. It was the thought that counts, I reckon. Spring time rolled around again…the spring of 1945—the worst year of our lives. I think your granddaddy plowed the garden out the same day we got word that Johnny was killed on that carrier….The Benjamin Franklin--your Granddaddy and I both just went to pieces. It like to have killed us—your mama and Irene, too. They absolutely worshipped the ground he walked on. He was our firstborn--our only boy, not countin' the baby we lost. I remember Sister and Brother were here all that day…stayed 'til way up in the night. It was up around midnight when they got ready to leave and we were standin' out on the front porch, we heard a whippoorwill cry up yonder at the edge of the woods. Sister looked at me, and I knew just what she was thinkin'. She started to say somethin' about that whippoorwill hollerin' but then she turned her head like she'd thought better of it. I've always wondered if she was fixin' to tell me that that poor little ol' whippoorwill was announcin' Johnny's death. I never went in for all that stuff, but Sister and Brother lived accordin' to those kind of things—the signs. Well, in one way, it's a good thing we

327

had those German boys with us. By then they pretty much knew what had to be done here on the farm, and they went ahead and done what they could, Hans especially. I know they felt bad about us losin' Johnny. We were just gettin' to where we could communicate back and forth better and I think they appreciated bein' here. We never learned us a word of German, but they picked up enough English to get by. They tried to lay low for a long time after that, but it wasn't long after that when Germany surrendered anyway. It was the Japs that sunk the Franklin but they were on the same side. Your granddaddy couldn't hardly stand the sight of them boys after that. He treated 'em all right, but he said he just couldn't keep from seein' Japs when he looked at 'em. That was a hard, hard time for all of us. They just seemed like they belonged here in a way and we were just startin' to get used to one another. Even after all these years, I like to think there's a reason God wanted 'em to be here.

They stayed on with us for several months after Germany surrendered. Seems like it might've been fall before they left here, after them big bombs was dropped on Japan and then they surrendered. When that army man came here to pick those boys up, that's when Hans gave me that spice rack. I cried the worst you ever saw. Couldn't help it. Some of it was them leavin'….some of it was knowin' the house'd be quiet again and knowin' Johnny wouldn't be comin' through the door ever again. Hans'd worked on that thing with just a few hand tools your Granddaddy let 'im use and he found a can of linseed oil in the tool shed or somewhere and he just had rubbed some of that on 'em a few days before they left us. Come to find out his father

328

was a carpenter back in Germany and he grew up around tools…makin' things. He'd made a couple of pieces of furniture for his mother before the War.

Hans worried about his people a lot, especially his mother. I don't know where they lived in Germany, but he was afraid the Russians would get to 'em before the Americans did. We never heard from Wilhelm again but Hans sent us a Christmas card or two. One of 'em had that picture in it. I reckon they got on with their lives. I sit here and think about 'em ever' so often."

As she put the lid back on the box of old photos, the last thing I remember Granny ever saying about the German soldiers she once kept was, *"I hope they're doin' all right."*

The last comment Granny made was after she closed the lid and held the tin of pictures in her lap with both hands. She said, "It's funny now to think of those things…Brother afraid of that lightnin'-killed stove wood, and Sister thinkin' that whippoorwill's cry meant somebody was fixin' to die. We *did* have bad luck…but I don't think that old walnut tree had a thing in the world to do with it— *lightnin'-killed or not.* But, I will say I never cared much to hear the whippoorwills after that spring, neither. Always before, I kindly was glad to hear 'em, knowin' that winter was over and things were bloomin'. But, between the time Sister heard that whippoorwill cry at midnight, and then that last time, Johnny was killed…your Aunt Irene was married and gone…and them German boys was back overseas. It was mighty lonesome time around here for us. I'd be here in the house by myself while your granddaddy was out in the fields and your mama was still in school…and I wondered if Brother and Sister weren't both kindly right in a way…trouble…death…they was headed right toward us, but it was just like the ol' walnut tree that got struck by lightnin', there wasn't a thing we could do but just stand there and take it."

Oddly enough, during the Vietnam War, I met another soldier in Denang who had been stationed in Germany. He had dated a German girl who spoke fluent English, and her father had been one of the prisoners of War sent to the U.S. to work on a farm. He only saw the father a couple of times, but the girl's name was Lorena--not a common German name. He didn't know her father's name, or even remember what he looked like. It brought a smile to Granny's face when I later told her of the incident. "Maybe I've got me a namesake somewhere overseas, you reckon?" Although it took a few more years, she does in fact have a namesake in her great-granddaughter Loren, who now has possession of her walnut spice rack, the by-product of lightning, war—and grace.

As the mothers of all soldiers going into conflict are united in hope, it is especially true that the mothers of those who do not return home are united in the universal experience of grief. It took a leap of faith beyond my understanding for Granny to open her doors to those who fought under a different flag. At least one soldier far from home recognized that grace--to which the spice rack continues to pay tribute, for at least as long as its story is remembered.

Wounded Doves

At some point our daughters will both have to flip a coin to see which one of them gets either the Thanksgiving set or the Christmas set of Granny's china. Given the way they feel about cooking, maybe the coin toss will determine who has to box them up for the big yard sale that will surely take place when I have given up this coil of flesh.

That being said, I am glad we still use the old dishes on special occasions. More especially, I'm glad Granny told us about them before she died, for while there are two sets of dishes, their story is one. In household language, the Thanksgiving Dinner dishes were known as "The Pig Set" and those she brought out for Christmas were called "The Walker Set." Every November she would pay good old "Sister" Simpson to help her wash both sets in preparation for the big holiday dinners--every single dish.

After the "Pig Set" was returned to the china cabinet awaiting Thanksgiving Dinner, the two women attacked the "Walker Set," stored in the matching oak sideboard. Granny was convinced that the dishes *just had to be dirty* from being closed up all year long. Nothing would do but to wash them all again. You couldn't be too clean. Maybe there was something more to it…perhaps it was her way of remembering.

So far as Granny's history with them goes, both sets of dishes have their origin in the bitter year of 1930. They had lost the Aunt Mollie Moore Place and were forced to move in with Granny's parents just before their last child—my mother—was born in 1931. They came here to this farm in the same year—*temporarily,* they thought, with the hope of having a place of their own again soon. The hardships of 1930 made an indelible impression upon my uncle Johnny and caused him to be especially considerate of his mother. In the six months or so of that year that my grandfather had gone out west in a futile attempt to find work, at the age of thirteen Uncle Johnny became the man of the house. He and Granny had been especially close, and none of the things she left behind symbolizes that bond more than her holiday china.

During one of the last holiday seasons we shared with her before she died, I asked her how she came to own two complete sets of china, and even if she did, why it was necessary to use both.

We had just finished the jam cake that always concluded Christmas Dinner. In references to the dishes, I had heard the "Pig Set" and "Walker Set" for so long the oddity of those words had never sunk in until my wife Sandy apparently picked up on it for the first time.

Granny said, "Well, the Pig Set *does sound funny for somethin' people eat off of. Johnny started that.*" I hadn't made the connection between those dishes and my dead Uncle Johnny, though I was very familiar with his locally well-known pig story.

She said, "It was the spring we moved back here from the Moore Place….I was kindly blue over losin' it—and most ever'thing we'd ever worked for. I'd never had a nice set of china, and what dishes we had were boxed up when we moved back in here with Mama and Daddy. Then, one Saturday morning, your Granddaddy drove us into Harriston to run a couple of errands for Mama and Daddy. I was in the family way with your mother, so Johnny would've been fourteen years old, and Irene was about twelve. Your Granddaddy was loafin' at the feed mill and I made Johnny go with me. We were walkin' down passed Dowden's Department Store on Main Street and I saw their window display with this—"Walker Set" all spread out on a pretty white tablecloth. I just thought they were the prettiest set of dishes I'd ever laid my eyes on. The name of the pattern I think is called *Goldonia* on account of the color. But there we were in the middle of the Depression, and nobody had any money. I reckon they were in that store window all summer and ever' time we'd go into Harriston, nothin' would do but for me to stop and admire 'em.

Johnny was with me that first time, and he never gave it a thought, but Irene said to him later she thought I'd like to have 'em. I can't even remember how much they cost, but they were bad expensive. He was just a kid, but I reckon he got it in his head to get 'em for me for Christmas."

The smile gradually left her face as she said, "And—*I did get 'em*...but not that year.

Johnny mentioned it to your Granddaddy and you can imagine what *he* thought about buyin' a a costly new set of new dishes, after we'd just lost our farm.

Then one day, Johnny said somethin' to Mack Perkins
about gettin' his hands on some money to buy 'em for me,
and Mack was just jokin' and told him he should fatten a
pig up to sell. We had our own pigs but Johnny wanted to
keep the dishes a secret. J.B. found him a shoat to fatten up
at Doc Wilcox's place on the river where there was a pig
lot fenced on three sides—the river was on the back side of
it. Without me knowin' a thing in the world about it,
Johnny slipped off down there *every day* with corn to feed
to it. He did that for months—to fatten it up. He was
gonna sell it close to Christmas to help pay for the dishes if
Mrs. Dowden would let him.

Sometime when we were in Harriston, Johnny slipped off
to Dowden's with my mother and asked Mrs. Dowden if he
could buy 'em and pay on it 'til Christmas. He had a little
money he'd earned here and there from the time he was ten
years old. I didn't know it then, but he had a Liberty bond
from the World War that Mama and Daddy had bought him
when he was born. He didn't know any better, so he took it
down there and tried to use it to pay the difference for the
dishes. Mrs. Dowden said she hated to tell him that he
wasn't even old enough to cash it in his own name, but she
could see he had his head set on it. Mama was there with
him but she was over in the other part of the store and
didn't know anything about what he was plannin', and
really, I think Mrs. Dowden knew she'd help him find a
way to get the money if he needed it. So, she told him that
she'd let Mama hold on to that Liberty Bond until he could
sell his pig—and shook hands on it just like they'd made a
million dollar deal. The Dowdens were good people, but
they got hit hard like most ever'body around here and that

set of china had been there for months with nobody offerin' to buy 'em. Still, *they tried their best to help Johnny get 'em for me*. And when times got better I never forgot how good they'd been to us. I traded there with 'em 'til ol' Mrs. Dowden died and her children sold the store.

Johnny thought he had a good thing goin' with that pig because, accordin' to what J.B. said, it was gettin' fatter by the day. He went down there to the river to feed it without me knowin' a thing in the world about it, and the Dowdens took this set out of their display window and boxed it up for Johnny. The first time I walked by and didn't see 'em, it nearly broke my heart. I had no idea who got 'em, but I sure missed seein' 'em.

I think it was up around Thanksgivin' Day when Johnny headed down to the river at J.B.'s to feed his pig, and it was gone, disappeared into the thin air. He didn't know if somebody had stolen it or what, but I reckon he was one sad little feller. He didn't have no choice but to go into Dowden's the next time we were in town and tell 'em that his pig was gone and he had no way on earth of payin' for these dishes.

That's when *Mrs. Walker* spoke up.....*God love her heart.*

I asked, "Who?"

"Mrs. Walker—Olive Ann Walker, that lived in that big red brick house above Fordville. At one time, the Walkers practically owned Fordville--the Distillery and the sawmill both, 'til they closed down.

335

It just so happened that Mrs. Walker was in Dowden's Store that day and she overheard Johnny tellin' Mrs. Dowden that he couldn't pay for the dishes and he was bad disappointed. She told him he'd have to take his Liberty Bond home and she'd try to think of somethin' else she had there in the store he could get me for Christmas. I think she prob'ly would've called Mama to help Johnny get the money somehow, but they worked it out so she didn't have to.

The Walkers had plenty at one time but Mrs. Walker was the saddest little ol' thing. She lost Clevie in the World War *and he was their only child.* Her husband died about the time Irene was born, and she didn't have nobody—a few nieces and nephews, but they all lived away from here. She'd been standin' a couple of aisles away when she overhead Johnny, so she came over and spoke to him. She'd been his Sunday School teacher, and when she found out that he was tryin' to buy the dishes as a Christmas present for me, she offered to pay for 'em herself and let him pay her back *somehow.* Now, we're talkin' about a whole lot of money for them days—for anybody, let alone a fourteen year old kid.

Granny chuckled.

"Well, I reckon Johnny got it from his Daddy….he said he wasn't gonna have nothin' handed to him. He thanked Mrs. Walker but told her he just couldn't see any way in this world to pay for 'em. So that's when she told Mrs. Dowden that she'd buy the set herself and take 'em home with her. Then, while Mrs. Dowden was boxin' 'em up for Mrs. Walker, she says to Johnny, *'You know, I've been*

336

wantin' to get me a new set of dishes anyway. But now, that means I've got to get rid of that old set I've had so long and your mama's always liked it. Why don't you come by and see me sometime after school and let's take a look at 'em?'

It's a wonder he did it, but he and Irene both slipped off after school one day not long after and ran up the Walker Hill there and she showed 'em the dishes. Bein' a boy, I don't think Johnny thought too much about 'em either way, but bein' a girl, Irene knew more about what I'd like and she thought they were pretty. The trouble was that it was already around the first of December and Christmas was comin' soon.

So Mrs. Walker came up with a list of chores that Johnny could do after school and on Saturdays to help her around the house, to pay for 'em. To give credit where it belongs, your Granddaddy went along with it—even though he thought it was foolishness to be buyin' dishes and we didn't hardly have a pot to pee in. I thought Johnny was helpin' *him* a lot of that time, and there he was at the Walker place, workin' for these dishes. He had to work for her a pretty good while even after Christmas, but by that time I knew all about it.

Mrs. Walker even helped Johnny and Irene wrap up every single piece of it in newspapers and put 'em in some heavy wood crates that Mack Perkins let her have. As far as presents go, back in them days none of us ever had big doin's at Christmas. None of us hardly had a penny to our name, *but we always had us a big dinner.* Mama had her own dishes, but these were gonna be mine. Before

Christmas Day got here, they told her what they'd done, and she made up some big tale about why I needed to get Johnny to drive me over to Maud Ella Smith's and borrow somethin' she needed right before we ate our big Christmas dinner. I think it was bakin' powder or bakin' soda. I tried to tell her we could get by without it and she made out like the world was comin' to an end if she didn't have it. While I was gone, your granddaddy and Johnny set up the big drop leaf table in the dinin' room and Mama and Irene put all these dishes out. I came through the back door here, and when I saw it, my eyes very nearly fell out of my head. Mama had bought me a brand new linen tablecloth to go with it, just like the one Mrs. Dowden had in her store display. Mama said later, 'I can't believe Olive Ann Walker is partin' with her weddin' dishes.' It's a mighty fine set—the *Tea Leaf pattern*'s what Mama called it. The Walkers always had nice things, and she said this set was a gift from *her* mother-in-law when she married Big Jim Walker."

Granny chuckled, "I've always thought this was one of the prettiest sets of dishes I've ever laid my eyes on, and then one day Mama said Olive Ann Walker hated the ground her mother-in-law'd walked on, and she had to wait 'til the old woman died before she could get rid of 'em."

Never particularly interested in dishes, I was more concerned about what happened to Johnny's pig.

Granny laughed aloud.

"*My lord that was the funniest thing.* Ned Bishop was down at the store one day—you know he never came down

338

there much, but he was there one mornin' tellin' J.B. about a Poland China pig he saw swimmin' down the river. He was down there huntin' a cow for Doc that was tryin' to calve when he saw that swimmin' pig--said he had no idea where it came from, and for a long time nobody claimed it. Ned coaxed it to the river bank with a couple of ears of corn and he and his boy tied a rope to its leg and led it up to their place.

Ned said they kept 'im in their pen for a couple of days 'til they could find out who it belonged to. If you remember, Ned's wife Mary Lou ran that little restaurant in Harriston across from the courthouse. Every day she'd bring the scraps and soured milk and slop home in buckets. Ned had this barrel that set behind the barn, kind of down under it, where the barn was built on a hill. So every afternoon, he'd just back his truck up into the barn and empty the slop buckets into that barrel down below--just a little piece— about like this," she said holding her hands a foot and half apart.

Granny's face reddened.

"That was the strangest thing—even if it was sad for poor little ol' Johnny…but some way or another that evenin', Ned didn't close the gate, and that swimmin' pig got to smellin' the slop and came up through the barn. He trotted all the way to the little drop in the back where Ned poured his buckets out--and it fell head-first and drowned in the slop barrel.

I reckon J.B. got to askin' Ned to describe it, and about when the pig came down the river and it was the same time

Johnny's pig went missin'. Russell thought maybe a bobcat'd gotten hold of it or somethin' like that—even though he couldn't find a trace of blood, or bones—nothin'. Nobody ever gave a thought to a pig swimmin' off. J.B. told Ned that it was Johnny's, and those ol' men down at the store got the biggest kick out of that--*a pig that swam the river and then drowned in slop."*

"And don't you know," Granny continued, "that next spring, Perry Guinn Taylor had a sow to pig, and he brought one up here special for Johnny after it was weaned. Perry Guinn had such a good time tellin' that story, he felt honor-bound to give Johnny another chance in the pig business. Johnny named it Moses, on account of the other one bein' drawn from the water. And that didn't end too well, neither. Those loafers at The Children's Hour made a project out of Moses and helped Johnny enter 'im in The State Fair. They got 'im up to weighin' close to half a ton I think it was, and it died in the truck between here and Lousiville on the way to the Fair."

I said, "So Mrs. Walker let Johnny have her set of wedding china—the Pig Set?"

Granny replied, "That's where they came from. She was always close to our family but she dearly loved Johnny. I know you've heard me tell it, but her only boy—Clevie-- died in the World War, and that's when she and Mama got to be so close. He and my brother Harry Winston were big buddies, and after we got word he'd been killed in France, Mrs. Walker came over here to see Mama ever' few days and they'd both sit on the porch and cry together. Clevie died in trainin' camp not long before Harry Winston got his

340

draft notice and Mama would go by and visit Mr. and Mrs. Walker, and take 'em food of course. And then, when Johnny got killed in '45, Mrs. Walker came to see us ever' Sunday afternoon for the longest time. She was way up in years by then, but, bless her old heart, she would drive herself up here and we'd set here in the kitchen and cry over Clevie and Harry Winston, and now…now it was time to cry new tears for Johnny."

Tapping the big meat platter with the ends of her fingers, Granny said, "Mrs. Walker was a good ol' soul. Really and truly, both sets of china were hers. This set here was the one Johnny had *wanted* to buy, but they were a while longer in comin' here…prob'ly fifteen years or better. I doubt Mrs. Walker ever used 'em over a handful of times.

A while after the War ended—after that big bomb was dropped in Japan, Mrs. Walker came up to me in church one Sunday and said she was comin' to see us that afternoon. There was somethin' she wanted me to have. She drove up here with my Aunt Maude Venable…Cousin Andy's mother that cooked and cleaned for the Walkers. The two of 'em came up here with that set of dishes all boxed up. Mrs. Walker was up past eighty, and said she was gettin' rid of some things and wanted me to have that set of china on account of Johnny and him just a kid tryin' to buy 'em for me. She said she'd thought about that a lot after she heard he'd been killed."

"When did you start using *both* sets?"

"Well," she drawled out, "we didn't…*not for a while*."

Granny's face grew serious. "I'll just tell you. Mrs. Walker told me somethin' that Sunday afternoon that I…just didn't want to hear. She was talkin' about what a nice set of dishes they were—the ones I picked out in Dowden's Store Window—and then she pronounced the company name that was on the bottom of it-- "Nori-tocky" and told me it was *Jap-a-nese*. I couldn't believe what I was hearin'. I thought it was pronounced "Nora-take." All I could think of was that the Japanese'd killed Johnny. I appreciated Mrs. Walker givin' 'em to me, but when I found out the Japs made it...well, that…fixed it. I didn't want to have nothin' more to do with 'em."

This came as a big surprise. However, *what came next was even more interesting.*

"Mrs. Walker said to me, 'Well, Lorene, you know the Japanese *are known* for their craftsmanship. I have several Japanese things in my house and they're all *very* well-made.'"

I just tried my best to smile and tell her… I wished it wasn't Japanese. Of course, those dishes were made before the War, but it was just the idea that the same people that killed Johnny came from the same place as them dishes. That took a whole lot of the "pretty" out of 'em for me. *But, Mrs. Walker helped me to swallow a bitter pill* that day. I'm glad she did, but it was a big one to get down.

Mrs. Walker looked me in the eyes, and said, 'Yes, Lorene, I know how you feel. I felt the same way about the German people after Clevie died in the First War. And to be honest with you, when our boys were fighting The

Nazis, I felt that way about those German soldiers you all kept with you—*right here under your own roof*—those prisoners of war. It was the Germans that killed your own brother, and for all you knew one of their fathers could've been the one that killed Harry Winston. I couldn't have stood to have 'em on my property, let alone cook for 'em. But the way you handled that has helped me a lot—to forgive. I can't *ever* forget, but every day I can *choose* to forgive. I know more than anybody in Fordville just how hard that is, but maybe over time, it'll help you a little to use those dishes."

With a sigh Granny then paused and said, "I knew she was right. But I'll just tell you, *they stayed boxed up for another year or two*— 'til about the time you were born. I'd put 'em away in that sideboard there in the dinin' room and to be honest with you, as much as I thought of Olive Ann Walker, I never planned to use 'em. I figured your Aunt Irene might like to have 'em sometime, but she grieved over Johnny, and then your Uncle Matt was a Marine, and he'd fought the Japs, too…only, he got to come home. So, the bottom line was that she didn't want nothin' to do with 'em, neither."

Looking at me misty-eyed, Granny said, "You were born on the 10th of November in '50, and your mother brought you here when you was about a month old to spend the day with us. We got to talkin' about what all we were gonna cook for Christmas dinner and while I sat there holdin' you, all of a sudden, it all reminded me so much of Johnny…and… I… just broke down. I—hate—war, and what it did to me and Mama both…all mothers. Then a thought came to me—the hope that maybe *you* wouldn't have to go to war—to fight the Japanese like he did—*or Germans or anybody else.* That's one reason I took it so hard when you went off to Vietnam, but just like we had to let Johnny, I had to make myself let you go."

She said, "I reckon your mama and Russell both thought I was goin' to pieces, and I just cried my heart out...good tears...healin' tears. They tried to get you out of my arms so I could pull myself together, but I just told 'em to set still—holdin' you was the very thing I needed. I sat there for the longest time and then I told your mama to start unboxin' this--Walker Set of dishes for us to wash up for Christmas Dinner--and then we'd use Johnny's Pig Set for Thanksgivin' the next year...and that would've been in '51. You went to sleep while I was holdin' you, and just as soon as I laid you down, your mama and me went to work washin' these dishes."

Granny placed her gnarled hand on my arm and squeezed it.

"So, mainly on account of you bein' born, *we just started usin' both sets*...the Pig Set at Thanksgivin' and the Walker Set at Christmas. Ever' now and then I get to thinkin' about what Mrs. Walker said to me that day. It took me a while to understand it, but I'm glad she said what she did.

Ever' once in a while when I lay down to sleep at night, I try to say a prayer for all the mothers ever'where, that they won't ever have to feel the hurt I did over losin' a son-- *even the mothers in Japan.*"

344

As far as I could see, I think Granny was able to forgive the Japanese for what happened to Johnny—as much as humanly possible. I like to think that her special set of Noritake dishes played some role in that slow healing process.

They haven't missed a holiday season since The Christmas of 1950. It is my hope that tradition will continue.

My red fiddle

Fiddling to the Wolves

It was said she was stone blind by age thirty.

By the time I was born, "Blind Jenny" was already in her late fifties. It may seem cruel that she was thus known by her sightlessness throughout the community, and perhaps it was. Aside from red-faced "Red" Perkins, no other person I knew was identified by a physical feature, let alone a handicap.

I don't remember ever *seeing* Blind Jenny until I was about eight years old, but hearing her was another thing. Like most everyone else my age and older, I couldn't remember a time when I hadn't heard her fiddle tunes coming from the rooms in the back of the country store where she lived with her bachelor brother, store owner "Mack" Perkins. If her windows were raised on warm days, the faint echoes of Blind Jenny's fiddle would lie across Fordville, as light and airy as the sheets on a clothes line in May. On winter days, when the sky was iron gray, and the air cold and damp you

346

could hear the muffled drones of some sad and forgotten ballad of a tragic young death—or of a love as lost as the smoke drifting from the chimney above.

My first encounter with Blind Jenny took place when Granny sent me to deliver some freshly picked garden peas to the friend she had known all her life. Pointing toward the door in the dark corner of the store, she told me to take the brown paper bag and its contents to the reclusive old lady, who I knew only by her name and music.

Passing through the windowless storage space that separated the store from the living quarters, I could hear a fiddle tune as winsome and playful as that spring morning. When I tiptoed through the open doorway into her kitchen, the music stopped abruptly. "Come on in!" she yelled in a strong, almost masculine voice, not that of a frail, blind old lady that I understood to be an object of pity. To me, Miss Jenny was a mystery…and until that day, one known only by the distilled echoes of her fiddle tunes that trickled into our midst like fine Kentucky bourbon.

"Set the peas on the table and come over here and let me realize you". I still grin when I recall her words. Beholding a large white-sweatered figure at the far side of the room, I baby-stepped my way toward the big white chair where Blind Jenny sat on two floral cushions, holding her fiddle in one hand and bow in the other. Her unseeing eyes twitched involuntarily as I stood there, beneath a mop of reddish gray hair, gathered loosely into a bun on top of her head.

She carefully propped her bow up in the corner behind her.

I said, "Miss Jenny, it's me—Clay Hall."

She smiled and said, "Bless your heart, child, you ain't been to see me since your mama brought you --when you wasn't much more than a set-alone baby. Come over here and stand close to me, so I can realize you."

I was caught off guard as she lifted her hand and literally felt my face from the top of my head to down below my chin. "Well…I didn't know your daddy, but you've got the face of your Granny's people." This was my first conversation with a blind person, let alone one that could feel my face and tell me who I looked like and it made me wonder who she had in mind for my face—who from my family she'd known.

"Want a cookie?" she asked, leaning forward in the creaking wooden arm chair. Beneath its woven hickory-bark bottom wires ran crisscrossed from loosened rungs, holding it together along with several hit and miss coats of paint. Although handmade, these old chairs were commonplace and found in practically every home I knew. However, this particular model was Blind Jenny's dais, where she played her beloved fiddle. From this rustic throne many an old tune drifted through the store and onto the narrow stretch of road containing what was left of Fordville, Kentucky.

"Yes, Ma'am," I said. Blind Jenny rose and walked into the kitchen as if she could see as well as anybody. Standing alone in the small living room and staring at the fiddle, I couldn't help myself. Having heard the instrument being played for as long as I could remember coming into the store, I had never actually seen a fiddle up close and nothing would do but for me to pick it up.

My thinking was that I would just take a quick look, touch the strings and quickly put it back down before she returned from the kitchen. Of course, I nervously dropped it on the linoleum floor and the fiddle made a loud, but not unpleasant musical clang as it landed on its rounded bottom end. She darted back into the little living room like she was fired out of a cannon.

"Don't' bother that fiddle," she said, firmly.

I stammered out an apology, as Blind Jenny picked the fiddle up from the floor, caressing its front and back.

Although there was concern in her knitted eyebrows, Blind Jenny's expression seemed to lighten as she apparently felt no damage done to her beloved instrument.

"It's all right. It's not hurt none but the next time before you touch it, just ask me first. I'll show you how to hold a fiddle sometime. Would you like that?"

I wasn't sure about a next time, but I said "Yes, Ma'am, I would. " After a brief pause, I asked "How about right now?"

Slowly a broad grin made its way across her wide wrinkled face, making the whiskers on the ends of her upper lip recede into the folds.

"By Ned, " she said, half to herself, "you're plumb right. Right now's as good a time as any."

She patiently demonstrated how to hold the fiddle, with my left arm straight and palm positioned in such a way that I could "hold a walnut" in it. She reached over in the corner for her bow which had a loose string dancing daintily in the air. Blind, but sensing the fugitive's presence, she deftly snapped it off, raised herself from the chair and took my hand in hers. Smoothly drawing the bow over the strings, and then back again, in see saw fashion, I felt her surprisingly strong grip on both my hand and the well-worn bow. The sounds—screeches that issued forth that were hardly bearable to me, let alone the old instrument's master whose hand skillfully guided my own.

A satisfied smile came over Blind Jenny's face, making her appear for all the world like a plump, well-fed cat waking up from a nap in the morning sun. I gladly released my awkward grip and guided the fiddle and bow into their owner's hands.

"I've heard worse" she chuckled. "Maybe sometime I'll show you how to play a little tune if you want to learn one."

She sat down in her chair and held it upright with both hands.

"Here, take a good look at it…see where the music comes from."

I touched it carefully this time, running my pointer finger from the tuning pegs to the bridge and down to the chin rest. Its owner smiled again at my curiosity, and patiently waited for me to satisfy it. I drew my thumb firmly, slowly, across the lowers strings—beeeenn---bingg—bang—bung.

Ever curious about old things, I said, "It sure looks old."

"It *is* old," she said…"older than white thread, I reckon. Somebody *real special* gave it to me a long time ago…and it was old then."

"*Somebody real special…*" The way she said it piqued my curiosity.

 "Was it your husband?"

Every woman I knew had one somewhere, or once had. To this day, I don't know what made a ten year old ask such a question, but I still remember the expression on Blind Jenny's face. As a matter of fact, I had seen the same look on Granny's face not long before--on the day she discovered a Mother's Day card my dead Uncle Johnny had made for her at school thirty years earlier, lost before he could give it to her.

She didn't respond to my question and during what I recall as an awkward moment of silence, she changed the subject. However, I was much closer to the answer than I could have known at the time.

"Oh, Clay, here's your cookie." She reached for it, lying on the lamp table beside her chair, and then handed me a printed napkin with two more wrapped up inside wax paper. "And there's a couple extra, for later."

Nobody else, before or since made those pineapple and oatmeal cookies which she kept in a round tin with a few apple slices to keep them moist. Thanking her for the cookies, I rambled back through the storage room that separated the living quarters from the store, cheerless and dark even on that spring day. Flanked on both sides by shelves heavy with the weight of years and forgotten miscellany, the little room smelled of country ham, feed sacks, and kerosene.

Although it was nothing like a regular event, I did go back to see Blind Jenny every so often and at her beckoning would attempt a fiddle tune. Afterwards, she would happily entertain me by mimicking the sounds of bawling calves and mewing kittens. With her tongue stuck in the left cheek of her open mouth, she delighted in the host of sounds her winkled hands produced for an audience of one.

Over the next couple of years, on occasion I visited with this lady who underwent a transformation in my thinking, from being a semi -reclusive curiosity known as Blind Jenny, to simply Miss Jenny—even when she wasn't around. Of course, I never referred to her in person as Blind Jenny. Granny would've slapped my two eyes into one if I had done so in her presence. Over time, however, I found it increasingly difficult to refer to her as "Blind" although everyone else did, with no apparent disrespect. It's just that their paths and hers rarely crossed, and I never fully understood why she took an interest in me except for my lukewarm interest in fiddling, and maybe, one other factor that I became aware of when I was about thirteen.

This knowledge came in the form of a faded photograph brought to light onekk particularly gloomy fall day. I came home from school on that occasion to find Granny sorting through old photos in a big red box. It was one of those heavy days that never seems to be fully light and when inside lights are never turned off. I sat down with her at the kitchen table to find her unusually melancholy. Among those laid before her was a large sepia image of a group of people standing in front of our church in Fordville. I pointed to one particular young man who might as well have been me, minus the knickers, and at least some difference in age.

"Who's that?" I asked

"Honey, that's my brother, your great uncle, Harry Winston..Clark. We called him by his first and middle names run right together, "Harrywinston". That's Mack Perkins, and right here's my mother and daddy standin' next to him."

I had heard my great uncle's name mentioned numerous times, but had never laid eyes on him. Even by that time, the ranks of those that had known him as a young man were fading from view.

I asked "He got killed overseas, didn't he?"

Without raising her head, Granny nodded slowly, continuing to gaze at the photo.

She sighed, "In the World War."

As I always did, I asked, "Which one?"

We had the same conversation anytime the World Wars came up. Until Granny was middle aged, there had only been one "World War", which was not known as "One" until after "Two" was over in 1945. So, in her vocabulary, "The World War" was World War One, and "THE WAR" was World War II. She never got a good handle on the Korean Conflict and clearly Vietnam was beyond her reach of geography and interest at that point. At least, until I got there in 1969.

I digress.

In another group photo, I saw the same young man, with other young people roughly the same age, and a face that seemed oddly familiar.

"Who are these people?" I asked.

Granny told of this and that one that had moved away, or had died. "And there's Jenny Perkins --this was taken right about the time Harry Winston asked 'er to marry him."

I had never heard that story but instantly recalled the expression on Miss Jenny's face several years before, when I had asked if a boyfriend had given her the fiddle. Although I couldn't understand it at the time, in her blank and searching eyes, even an eight year old could see the look of remembered pain.

"They were gonna marry but decided to wait until after Harry Winston got back from overseas. Her daddy talked 'em into puttin' it off, just in case somethin' happened. "

Granny half mumbled, "And somethin' DID happen." She paused to look out the kitchen window. I remember the cool fall breeze whistling gently around the kitchen window, unevenly covered with a sheet of plastic, its gaps wheezing and puffing like the tired, dreary old day nearing its end.

"That fiddle Jenny plays was a gift from Harry Winston…got it for her the Christmas after he proposed. There was an old colored man that lived down toward Babylon ever'body called Uncle Alfred and he had the name of bein' the best fiddler in the county. He and Jenny's Uncle Henry used to play at dances together. He said it was the best'n he knew of anywhere, and if it hadn't been for Jenny wantin' one, nothin' on earth could've kept him from buyin' it for hisself. Uncle Alfred's son was a drunk and he let Uncle Henry have it for a jug of whiskey. Then, Mama and I wrapped it up in a big box with an old tablecloth, the spring before his unit shipped out to France. He asked us to see that Jenny got it for Christmas, and so far as I know it was the last thing he ever gave her."

I had always imagined that Miss Jenny had not learned to play until after she lost her sight as a grown woman.

"Um-Um" Granny said shaking her head, "No, she loved to dance better than she liked to fiddle, and that's where she and Harry Winston started courtin'—at a big square dance." Granny nodded toward the window as if I should know whereof she spoke, "down at Ned Talbott's tobacco barn. It was the biggest buildin' around here and they used to have dances there in the spring, before it got too hot. Jenny was her Uncle Henry's shadow when she was a little

355

girl. Many's the time I saw her followin' alongside of him, both of 'em singin' up a storm. When he would go to a dance, a lot of times she would carry his fiddle for him and when she took the notion to learn, he taught her to play. And it's a good thing. He taught her ever' tune he knew and she soaked it up just like a sponge.

After Harry Winston got killed, she quit goin' to dances and that's really when she took up fiddlin' if you want to know the truth. She just fiddled for herself, though. She went through a bad time…her daddy drowned a couple of years later, and it wasn't long after that when her eyes got bad and she kindly shut herself off from ever'body.

She went along like that for several years and we all just accepted it, but then, durin' that drought we had in 19 and 30, there was supposed to be another big square dance and ever'body was lookin' forward to it. It was up in the middle of summer and our crops were dryin' up right before our eyes and we couldn't do a thing in the world about it. Well, that very day, Jenny's Uncle Henry fell down a steep bank and broke his arm. He was the only fiddler they had around here then, and it looked like they were gonna have to cancel the dance, but after they doctored 'im, he had somebody to drive 'im down to Fordville to ask Jenny to go in his place. She told me about it years later. He said, 'Jenny, don't you think it's mighty strange that Harry Winston's last gift to you was somethin' he wanted you to share with other people? You're a good fiddler, and right now the only one. *Play for him.*' Well, that must've convinced her because she got ready and went with 'im. That was the first time Jenny ever played in public, and so far as I know she never missed another dance anywhere around Fordville. I've been there when she'd fiddle and it didn't matter if she was standin' or sittin', I wish you could have seen her feet move. She never danced with nobody else after Harry Winston. She said her heart wasn't in it no more, but that sure didn't stop her feet."

I have often thought of my conversation with Granny that dreary November afternoon. Over the years as I grew more interested in other things (namely Susie Anderson), my impromptu fiddling lessons ended, although I would on occasion stop by and visit Miss Jenny. Thinking that I might stay with it, Granny even bought me a smaller second hand child's fiddle for my eleventh birthday. It sounded worse than anything I've ever heard with strings on it.

Miss Jenny's only public performance that I ever witnessed took place at Red Perkins' graveside, after I returned home from Vietnam. Years before she died, Red's wife, Etta, had asked Miss Jenny to play an old hymn "The Lone Wild Bird," at her funeral. Even Red was reportedly moved by the performance, so much so that on the following day he asked her to play "Amazing Grace" at his funeral, if she outlived him. She did outlive Red, and play, she did. I was there that day as she was led in to the funeral home by two family members, one of which carried her familiar wooden arm chair and the other with her fiddle and bow. Already bickering among themselves, Red's children were soon comforted, and even brought to tears by Miss Jenny's arthritic fingers as they skillfully raised one last tune to honor Red's request.

What turned out to be my most memorable visit with Miss Jenny came just before going into the army-- right after my high school graduation.   I drove by the store near closing time one Saturday afternoon in early June to pick up a carton of buttermilk for Granny. My decision to enlist in the army had not been an easy road for my grandparents, but in the end, they accepted it with equanimity. My father had been in the European Theatre during World War IIj and was later a POW in Korea. He died a young man. Granny had lost her only son in "The War" at the age of 28 and had lost her only brother in France in "The World War" (One) before that. Although it was a novelty to me, war was a sadly familiar experience for my elders.

The storeowner, Mack Perkins looked at me sympathetically, and said "Clay, before I forget it, Jenny told me to give you a message. She wants to see you before you ship out."

I suppose I had hoped I could slip away without making much fuss about it--but I nodded politely to the old merchant who had weighed and measured the family's purchases since Teddy Roosevelt was in the White House.

Miss Jenny had already heard from Mack that I was enlisting in the army and on my way to Vietnam. I was not the only one in our community to go, and the three of us received firm handshakes and knowing pats on the back from our tribal elders as we prepared to go to basic training.

I tiptoed back to the back of the store, through the familiar dark hallway into the kitchen and called out for Miss Jenny.

She was seated at the kitchen table, almost like she was waiting for me.

Tersely, she said "Get you a seat!"

There on the table sat the familiar tin of pineapple oatmeal cookies. Instinctively, I reached in to take one. Miss Jenny said, "Take that whole tin home with you when you…leave."

She sighed through her nose, "Well, Clay, I reckon you know what you're doin', but we're sure gonna miss havin' you around here."

"I know what war is" she said with rueful certainty in her voice. "Anything can happen. I knew a couple of men from this county that didn't have the sense God gave a head of cabbage and they wound up bein' decorated overseas. Others I thought would come out of it just fine ain't been right since, if they came back at all. Ah Lord, war's a funny thing." Jenny looked toward the light of the kitchen window as if she could see, maybe sensing some of its warmth. After a momentary pause, she sighed, "Life's a funny thing."

Coming back to herself with some sense of urgency, Miss Jenny raised her voice above its usual low tone.

"Now Clay, I want you to listen to me. I want you to take somethin' home with you while I can give it to you. Pointing to one of the two kitchen chairs, she said, "Sit still here for a minute, while I go get it."

Miss Jenny tottered back into her tiny little bedroom and returned with a sagging shopping bag in her hand, its contents listing awkwardly to one side.

She came back into the kitchen, placing her hand on every piece of furniture she passed. I immediately recognized the scroll of her red fiddle poking out of the shopping bag and leaning against the recycled cardboard tube.

Standing before me at her kitchen table, she said "Clay, I want you to have this…while my hands are still warm… and one o' these days I want you to take up playin' again. These stiff ol' fingers don't work like they used to. Besides that, I've got another fiddle. No, now I take that back, there's two back there under my bed—one that my niece Gail bought for my 50th birthday, and another one that a man brought here for me to work on and he never came back for it.

But I've always come back to this one." She laid the bag on the kitchen table and spilling the well-worn horsehair bow out of the cardboard tube and onto the linoleum floor. Miss Jenny felt around and gathered her old "weapon" back in its holster. With one hand, she presented me the shopping bag and with the other came the cardboard cylinder. "That old bow needs re-hairin', but it's got a little playin' left in it yet. And somethin' else," she added, "I've ordered you a brand new case and I'll get it to your Granny when it comes in. That'n it came with has had the lick. Both hinges are missin' and I've got it tied together with some of my old hair ribbons…and they're prob'ly dry-rotted."

I was in a hurry that day—filled, I suppose, with nervous energy in anticipation of what lay ahead. In spite of myself, something inside of me said, "*Ask while you can.*"

"Miss Jenny, can you tell me what you know about it?"

She sat down across from me at the little kitchen table, and raised the fiddle from the shopping bag.

"Well, yes," she said, "That is, what little I do know.

Your great-uncle, Harry Winston gave it to me the Christmas after we got engaged. He was already in France by then but he'd paid Uncle Henry for the whiskey it took to buy it and his mother held onto it 'til then. Back before that, it belonged to an old colored man we called "Uncle Alfred," He taught Uncle Henry how to play—and Uncle Henry taught me. The summer he left for France, Harry Winston told Uncle Henry he wanted to get me a fiddle for Christmas. Uncle Henry knew about this'n and they drove down to Babylon and bought it from Uncle Alfred's son.

Even when he couldn't play no more, I've heard Uncle Alfred say out of his own mouth he wouldn't sell it for love nor money…but, in the end, his son let go of it for little or nothin'.

When Uncle Alfred got bedfast, he told that son of his he wanted to hear some good fiddlin' before he died. The son sent for Uncle Henry and I went along with 'im… and the whole time he was playin', Uncle Alfred's hands were just plain *hungry* for a fiddle. I could still see then and his hands would be workin' away like this--like he was playin'. It was kindly pitiful to watch. He'd fiddled might near his whole life—he said ever since he was a slave boy 'up around courtin' age' is the way he told it.

He said the man that owned 'im agreed to let 'im earn a little money fiddlin' for dances and such, and after he got his freedom, he left here for Texas with that man and his family. I don't know if he took this here fiddle with 'im or if he got it out there somewhere, but he came back to Fordville with it

Years and years later, when he got old, rheumatism set in on 'im and he had to give it up. When word got around that Uncle Alfred wasn't able to play no more, ever' fiddler in the county wanted to buy it, but he told 'em it it wasn't to be sold on account of it savin' his life one time.

Lord, I can hear 'im now, tellin' that tale and he nearly scared me into the sawdust with it.

Wherever it was they'd moved in Texas, he said there wasn't another fiddler for miles and somebody was always wantin 'im to play for dances. So, just before dark one winter evenin', he lit out on foot to play at a weddin' about three miles away. He said he knew right where he was goin' and there was a full moon, so he didn't carry no light a-tall, no lantern, torch-- nothin'. All he had was this fiddle here—and a bow, and when he got about halfway to where he was goin', he turned and saw a pack of wolves followin' along behind 'im. He looked around and there wasn't no place to go but this ol' fallin' down cabin up ahead of 'im. He was afraid to break and run because those wolves were kindly hangin' back a little and he didn't want to make any sudden movement. He didn't have no weapon—not even a rock to throw. All he had with this here fiddle and his bow in a homemade case. He said 'The onliest thing I could do was pray.' 'And right then,' he said, ' Right then somethin' told 'im to start fiddlin' …so he turned around to face them wolves comin' toward 'im and he set his case down and opened it up real slow-like and brought out this fiddle and bow. He left the case right where it was and started walkin' backwards toward that cabin and fiddlin' at the same time --and the wolves stayed still. He didn't know if it made 'em afraid or if they liked hearin' it. Well, when his arms got tired he had to stop and the wolves commenced comin' toward 'im again. He finally backed his way to that cabin and when he got to it, the door was gone but there was a loft and he climbed up in it and waited to see what was gonna happen. Direc'ly, he said, here the wolves came to the doorway, so he rared back and started playin' again.

AND he had to keep playin' or the wolves would get 'im.

He said that went on for an hour and it got dark on 'im. Finally, the people that he was to fiddle for that evenin' started wonderin' if somethin' had happened to 'im, and they lit torches and headed toward his house. They spread theirselves out a ways and before long, one of the men came close enough to that cabin to hear fiddle music. He'd hear it play a little bit, and then it would stop. He knew somethin' was wrong, so when he got closer, he saw the wolves in the moonlight where they'd gathered in a pack at the door o' that cabin and he fired shots at 'em. I think he said killed one, but the rest of 'em scattered. The other men came runnin' when they heard gunfire and by the time they got to Uncle Alfred, he was freezin' cold and weak as a kitten. I reckon they had to send for a horse to take 'im home.

Miss Jenny chuckled, "It wasn't funny, but I have to laugh when I think about how he told it. Uncle Alfred said, 'Never was in such a fix, not in all my born days. There I was, *fiddlin' to wolves in the dark.'*

It was funny, how he said it back then, but…I know now what that's like."

After a pause, Miss Jenny held the fiddle upright. Then, she carefully plucked each of its four strings, from the high pitched "E" down to the low "G" string. Making those last, simple sounds brought an instant smile to her face.

She said, "You know, that was the first thing Uncle Henry taught me—the order of these four strings here, goin' this-away--like this," her old voice cracking as she sang, "Pick—Up—Cow--Dung."

Miss Jenny recalled that memory with a smile-- and as tears formed in the corners of her sightless eyes, she stood up, holding the fiddle with both hands. Leaning over me, she laid it in my lap—into my hands. In that moment, I was instantly reminded of the morning I had driven Granny to visit a young tenant farmer's wife who had just given birth. In the same manner that young mother placed her newborn baby in Granny's outstretched arms, Miss Jenny said goodbye to her beloved instrument.

As I placed the fiddle in the shopping bag, she sighed, "Well, Clay, I know you're needin' to go. You've got things to do and I've kept you from 'em."

"I'm not in a hurry to leave, Miss Jenny, but you're right. I've got a lot to do."

She remained silent on the subject of the war in Vietnam— and of war anywhere, for long had its effects taken their toll.

At hand for her now was yet another parting, in a lifetime full of them. As foreign as this experience was for me, there was nothing new about it to her. At that moment, I thought of the final farewell and the last embrace she shared with my dead great-uncle, before his unit left for France.

Only once did I ever hear Miss Jenny mention her marriage that was never to be, to the young face I knew only through the faded photos in Granny's dresser. This was the occasion, and although we had never spoken of it, she rightly assumed I had been told.

She said, "If you can *keep* that girlfriend of yours, come back to her." Miss Jenny knew about Susie. News traveled fast in Fordville, if nothing else did. I didn't have the heart to tell her that we had more or less parted ways.

Rising up from her seat, she said, "Harry Winston didn't get the chance to. The German Kaiser got HIM."

Looking back, maybe I should have taken the time to learn more about her relationship with my great uncle. I was just too preoccupied with my pending departure to Vietnam to appreciate the moment. Miss Jenny stood at the little kitchen table where she and Mack shared their meals, alternately holding and releasing the knobs on the back of the chair.

She gently let go of her grip and stepped over to give me a one armed hug. She reached to touch my face, feeling from forehead to chin in the same gentle sweeping motion. At that moment her hand was the camera, and my face the focused image. Without saying a word, she gently patted me on the shoulder. Not knowing exactly how to respond, I said "Miss Jenny, Granny will get word to you when I'm in Vietnam. You take care of yourself, and Mack."

Her only response came along in a trickle "You…get yourself back here--safe. You hear?"

I gave no answer, nor do I think she expected one. I made my way out the kitchen door with the bulging shopping bag, and back through the familiar dark hallway as I paused to take in and savor its lingering earthy smells.

Miss Jenny's gift and farewell touch forced me to think of the great uncle that had also said his goodbyes before sailing to France fifty years earlier, "to make the world safe for democracy." Was he excited, scared, sad, or like me, all the above? Although he had been drafted, and I had volunteered, I could not help but think the feelings were the same. I wondered about when my great uncle, whose name I barely even knew, was standing deep in French mud waiting for the dreaded blow of an officer's whistle, announcing a deadly charge toward enemy lines. I wondered if in those moments, he thought about what his family and friends were doing at that very instant, half a world away, and if they were thinking the same thoughts about him.

As I departed, making my way across the store's uneven floorboards, I avoided eye contact with the village elders of my youth who seemed to understand the nature of our parting, though none spoke of it. I thought about how my life would change from this scene now before me. Six months from this very second, what would *I* be doing in Vietnam? Searching for an unknown enemy in the tall elephant grass, or eating my cold rations in the rain? Where I was standing right now, would Mack be leaning back in the same worn out kitchen chair? Would I be holding my rifle over my head slogging through snake infested water like the poor guys I saw on the evening news? Or, the biggest thought:

Would I "**be**" at all?

Luckily, I did return home safely from Vietnam, and two years before she died I visited Miss Jenny one last time.

I was still on active duty, but back in the U.S. when I read her obituary in *The Louisville Courier-Journal.* Virginia Elmore Perkins, known simply, if not tactlessly, as "Blind Jenny" to most of Fordville, had died in a Lexington hospital. In all that time, I never knew her actual given name.

For the record, I did eventually take fiddle lessons, and have played Miss Jenny's fiddle for over twenty years. Honestly, I still don't know if it's because I was truly interested in returning to it for the sake of music alone, or the fact that I am now the fiddle's caretaker, and the unworthy heir to Miss Jenny's legacy. Either way, I am grateful that I did experience a renewed interest in playing, as she hoped that I would. And like her, I have a couple of other fiddles--but I still keep coming back to the one she gave me.

A few years after Miss Jenny's death, I met the niece who cared for her in the last weeks of her life. The chance meeting took place at a church homecoming dinner, and there we shared memories of Miss Jenny. As we stood in the serving line in the fellowship hall swapping stories, the niece whispered loudly, "Tighten up your strings, Boys." Seeing my puzzled look, she explained.

"I was with Aunt Jenny when she died. When she was lying there in the hospital bed, fading in and out, those were the last words she spoke."

The niece paused, and smiled as she recalled the poignant memory.

"Aunt Jenny used to get the biggest kick out of telling that story…so much I think everybody in Fordville's heard it."

With my bulging paper plate in hand, I sat down with her at the long table to hear the rest.

"When Aunt Jenny was just a little girl, she would tag along with Uncle Henry to square dances and carry his fiddle. His eyesight was always bad and by the time he died, he was totally blind, just like she came to be later. Maybe it's because of that, but those two were as close as they could be. There would be two or three fiddlers and other musicians at those dances—maybe one on the guitar and another playing the banjo. Just before they would begin playing, they would tune their instruments. Aunt Jenny said that Uncle Henry would pick her up and set her on a chair so everybody could hear her yell big and loud, 'Tighten up your strings, Boys!'

The niece said, "Aunt Jenny *always* said those were her happiest days…always."

I often think about Miss Jenny's story--how she kept on fiddling in the dark, and to the wolves of her darkest days. Before I play a tune, I sometimes pause in gratitude for having known her and for the fiddle, given to me in remembrance of the great-uncle I never knew, and the husband she was never to have.

Miss Jenny was at peace when she left us, and it brings me comfort to know that at that moment, she was in the company of fiddlers, and looking forward to something good.

Sarah's Oak

Gliding her hand along the edge of Granny's dining room table, Sarah Herndon declared, "You know, it's hard to beat good oak."

 "Lorene," she said, "I don't know that I ever told you, but this table and set of chairs were the first things I bought with my own money after I went to live in town. I bought 'em second hand from a friend that hardly ever cooked…about like me," she mused, before taking a sip of the coffee from one of the china cups Granny brought out for company.

Until then, I never knew the oak dining room furniture, the solid, square table with six heavy round legs and matching chairs, hadn't always been in that room. Seven sturdy oak "leaves" extending the table were stacked neatly in a closet under the stairwell, although I never saw all of them used at one time. From the time I came to live with my grandparents when I was eight years old, the "big table" dominated the dining room, which was closed up during cold weather and opened up only for special occasions such as Sarah Herndon's visit.

As the five of us sat at the dining room table, Sarah continued caressing the smooth tight grain, occasionally glancing down. She caught herself, and inconspicuously folded her hands in her lap as she and her nephew visited with my grandparents and me that Sunday in late December. By mid-afternoon, dessert plates and empty coffee cups still sat in front of us as the three elders reminisced.

Sarah asked "How long's it been since I sold you all this set?" I could tell by her expression that she suddenly wished she hadn't brought it up. It was the look of remembered pain.

Granny said, "You remember. It was durin' the War, prob'ly in '42 or '43, right after Johnny…enlisted." Miss Sarah nodded gently with a knowing smile, "That's right, I remember now. The Murphys just had opened their new furniture store and I bought that dinin' room suit I have now. To tell you the truth, that was just about the first *new* furniture I bought after I gave up the farm." I can still hear that curious phrase "gave up the farm," and thought it sounded odd, even as a teenager.

"I was bound and determined to have somethin' *new*," she said. "I'd been surrounded by old things my whole life. Especially after what I went through to get out on my own, I started buyin' new furniture a little at a time, like my dinin' room suit. Mahogany they said it was. But, I'm sure I'd been better off to have kept this oak set."

Although I probably never saw Sarah Herndon over three or four times in my life, in that first encounter she made an indelible impression on me. Early that Sunday morning, Granny had said "company's comin'—an old family friend," as she opened up the cold dining room to circulate heat from the coal stoves in the kitchen and living room. As I was soon to learn, Miss Herndon had also been "the

371

insurance lady" my grandparents had done business with for decades.

She and her nephew had arrived early in the afternoon and coming through the front door, she hugged Granny and said, "Lorene' it's my last business call. I wanted to bring the new calendars around myself this time to my oldest customers". Sarah Herndon had an aura—a presence about her which demanded attention, and above all, order. She was past eighty and couldn't have been much over five feet tall. Granddaddy said she got around like a gray squirrel, standing erect as her little frame would allow. She wore a matching navy blue "Mamie Eisenhower" pillbox hat and dress, in contrast to her snow-white hair permed hair. Wearing white gloves against the black cane in front of her battered and beaten Buick, she appeared misplaced. As she entered the house, Granddaddy said quietly, nodding in her direction "That little lady right there's livin' proof that size doesn't tell the whole story. If it did, a cow could outrun a rabbit." Totally at odds with her manner of dress and speech, Sarah had arrived in a faded black car, adorned with beaten fenders and dented chrome wheel covers. Granddaddy looked out the front door as we heard her pull up. Pointing toward it, he said, "That car right there's a '48 Buick Roadmaster. She went to the Oldsmobile Garage to look around. She liked it, and somebody said she counted out the cash right there on the hood and drove it home."

I could not imagine this regal old lady scratching, sneezing or using the bathroom. She seemed incapable of such earthy functions. "I'm turning the insurance business over to Woodrow," she said, nodding in her nephew's direction.

"I'll probably come by the office once in a while, but it's all his now." Still, you got the impression she wouldn't be far away.

After a brief lull in their dining room table conversation, Miss Herndon turned toward me with her whole body, leaning on her cane, looked me dead in the eye and somberly asked, "Now young man, what do YOU wish to make of yourself?"

There was an unspoken demand in her voice that haunted me. As she studied my eyes in those few seconds, it was as if she looked down into my thoughts—and into the very soles of my Sunday shoes. It was one of those chance encounters that has an impact on your thinking, totally out of proportion to its duration. That visit probably lasted two hours, but I have spent much more time since, pondering the question put to me so directly by Sarah Herndon and at a time when I needed to hear it.

For the first time in my young life it dawned on me that someone outside my immediate family was taking notice of what I did with my life. Maybe I had best devote some thought to it. There was more to her prodding than vocation—more than trade or course of study. Her pensive stare and pointed questions marked her interest in purpose and direction—*"how,"* maybe as much as *"what"* I chose to do.

As I was later to learn, this grand old lady had gone quite literally from a farm off Fordville Road to the White House. As I was to learn that December afternoon, the surplused oak table in Granny's dining room was one artifact of that long journey.

Caught off guard by Sarah Herndon's question and her fixed gaze into my soul, I mumbled "Farming…I think I want to be farmer, ma'am."

Never taking her dark little eyes off mine, she nodded thoughtfully. "It's a noble thing to cultivate the soil…to work with nature. Then with knitted eyebrows she said, "and sometimes *against* it. My parents farmed the land, and my grandparents. I did plenty of farm work, back in my younger days. We all had to work. But I did well in school and my parents sent me to Richmond to the teacher's college there--The Normal School's what they called it then. I went two years and then taught two years."

"Did you like teaching" I asked

She thought for a moment, glancing at both my grandparents.

With pursed lips she replied, "I did….*very much so.*" She paused, looking at the crumbs on the table which she gently swept into her palm and sprinkled them into her dessert plate. "Family circumstances forced me out of teaching— farming too, for that matter. I had *my part* of the family farm on Foaling Ridge but one of our neighbors has rented it from me for years."

Granddaddy studied the old lady who he'd described earlier that day as "independent as a hog on ice." He said, "You still charge one dollar a year rent for that place, Sarah?" Clearly, he already knew the answer to the question. There

374

had to be a story. I was no businessman but one dollar a year rent for any farm was unheard of—unless it was a mere formality.

"Oh yes," she said, decidedly. "When I left the farm, I leased it to John David Evans for one dollar a year *and I've never raised my price.* He paid me five years in advance with a five dollar gold piece--*and I've still got it,"* she said, beaming.

My elders grew conspicuously quiet and the conversation shifted to other topics before Sarah haltingly made her way toward the door with her nephew in tow. She still had stops to make before dark she said, leaving a new 1965 calendar with Granny. The three of us waved goodbye from the porch as she started the engine. The Buick shuddered, firing a smoky salute as its white haired captain awkwardly attempted a three-point turn and backed over two of Granny's wintering peony bushes. Finally negotiating the turns and cuts, Sarah Herndon rattled down the farm lane in the hulking old car, fenders quivering with each bump.

The next Sunday afternoon, my buddy Mike, his father and I drove up to Foaling Ridge to go rabbit hunting on Sarah Herndon's land that Granddaddy pointed out to me earlier in the week. The presence of three massive stone and brick chimneys where once stood a family dwelling caught my attention. Perhaps a hundred feet to the left of the house site was a row of rotting logs, most of which had long before settled into the ground. "Too big for fence posts," I thought. *These* were cut for a purpose.

That night at supper, Granddaddy asked how the rabbit hunting had gone.

I said, "We got three, but I know how you all feel about eating rabbit, so Mike kept them. That's what they're having for supper tonight." As we ate, I recalled the naked chimneys in the open field on Sarah Herndon's farm and the nearby pile of logs.

Granddaddy had his thumbs behind the suspenders on his overalls as he chuckled and said, "That's more or less what got her to move to town in the first place."

"What did?"

"Them logs."

Granny said, "What it amounted to was that Sarah's brothers thought they were gonna tell her what to do and when to do it, but it didn't work out that way for 'em."

Nodding in affirmation, Granddaddy said, "She was the smartest one of the bunch."

Granny said, "Sarah was the oldest child in that family and her parents were good people--but they thought the sun rose and set in *those boys*. They sent Sarah off to get her an education, but she didn't teach very long after she got back. Her mother got to needin' her on the farm when her daddy got sick —but the boys all married and started families."

"She never married?"

"Nope," Granny continued, and tapping her finger on the kitchen table, she said, "Sarah stayed right there on that farm and took care of ever'body. And just as right as rain, every Sunday those brothers expected to have a big dinner at their mother's and of course Sarah had to do the biggest part of it—more as time went by. She worked like a dog, and helped look after her mother and daddy's business. She's sharp, let me tell you. After her daddy and mother died, a man at the bank in Harriston knew Sarah was good in school and he knew of an insurance company lookin' for an agent, somebody smart, good with the people, and honest. She started off sellin' fire and life insurance on horseback, and took to it like a duck to water. She bought a second hand Model T Ford with her own money so she wouldn't have to be out in all kinds of weather. I reckon her brothers thought she ought to stay on the farm and take care of the home place. They were against the idea of her gettin' out on her own—havin' a life of her own.

Never mind that each one of them had. I know Sarah's mother and daddy didn't mean to hold her back the way they did, but when her mother made a will, she divided that great big farm—seven or eight hundred acres, between Sarah and the three boys, but she tied Sarah's part up so she couldn't sell it."

Granddaddy said, "The heart of that farm-the middle of it went to Sarah, but only for her lifetime. She got the part with the house and outbuildin's, and all the best barns. She was past havin' children by then and her mother didn't want the land to leave the family if she married. But what made it so bad was that she had to consult her brothers—*all three of 'em--* about the least little thing she did on it—and all three of 'em had to agree. If there was any timber cut, or anything like that to be done, she had to have their permission. Sarah was allowed to keep *half* of whatever income came off her part of the farm during her lifetime and the rest went to the brothers. The will *did say* that the brothers had to keep up the barns and out buildin's and pay for that out of their own money, since the land would be goin' to them or their children when Sarah died. She outfoxed 'em all, though---her mother *and* the brothers when she left the farm and struck out on her own. All these years they haven't been able to use her part of the farm or the barns, but they've had to see they're halfway kept in repair.

Long about then, Sarah bought that secondhand Model T Ford, to call on customers and she hired Willie Ross to teach her how to drive it. He's joked for years that she took five years off his life and then tried to sell him life insurance. Then, fall came and she got the idea she wanted to have a garage built near the house to keep her car out of the weather. That's when it got real interestin'.

Sarah walked out on the land herself with an axe and marked the oak trees she wanted cut into lumber for her new garage and she had me cut 'em down--in that stand above the hollow…got my team of mules to snake 'em down to the field where Sarah told us to put 'em."

I could tell that my grandfather admired the old lady's spunk as he spoke about dragging the logs into the field where they remained. I said, "I'm guessing the garage never got built?"

Granny said, "Nope. Her *very own brothers* went against her. They told Sarah she hadn't talked it over with them first. You might say that log cuttin' business was the last straw. There she was, forty-odd years old, and had given her whole life to the family. That was in late winter or early spring, and things went along like they had the rest of that summer and fall, and the logs laid right there in the pasture. But... on the first day of January, she marched across the road and had a good long visit with John David Evans. He was her closest neighbor back then. On that first Sunday in January, Sarah's brothers and their families went to the home place after church like they'd always done, expectin' one of them big Sunday dinners. They got there and Sarah had made up some cold sandwiches and that was it. She had her trunks packed up and told 'em she'd leased her part of the land to John David for five years. Her brothers just about had a fit—all three of 'em. They stormed out of that house and I reckon they threatened to take her to court and the whole nine yards. But—ol' Sarah knew what she was doin'. She was tryin' to teach 'em a lesson and saw a chance to help somebody else at the same time...somebody that deserved it.

John David Evans and his wife had lost their farm over on Dodd Lane and a little store there, before he moved across the road from the Herndon Place. He was too good hearted and he let too many people have credit. They took advantage of him. Then his own brother-in-law that held the note on his farm foreclosed on him. John David lost everything he'd paid on it and all he had left was his farm tools...and a good team of mules. He'd rented that little Sam Norris place, across from Sarah, just a house and ten or twelve acres—just enough to have a garden and a few cows you might say. The Evanses were good neighbors to Sarah and they helped her a lot when her daddy and mother were sick. She got to be real close to that whole family."

Granddaddy said, "Yessir, they had a hard time," dragging out the word "hard" sympathetically. "John David and his wife had lost a little girl to diphtheria the summer after they lost the farm--and still had six more to feed and clothe."

Reflecting on the story, Granddaddy added, "I've heard John David himself say that gettin' to rent that place from Sarah put him back on his feet…gave him a second chance to get ahead. When his boys got grown, it helped them all get a start and they've all done well. Sarah thinks as much of them as she does her own blood kin. In a way, she kindly adopted that whole family."

Picking at a piece of cold fried chicken, Granny said, *"It wasn't about the money.* I don't think those brothers of hers ever understood that. The Sunday they all had that big ruckus at the home place, they knew she'd already found a little house in town to rent. She finally bought it," and with a chuckle added, "and ever'thing else on that street."

Granddaddy said, "I would like to have seen the look on her brothers' faces when she told 'em she had rented her part of the farm out to John David. Those boys never dreamed but what they wouldn't have the run of that whole place--and it was a lot harder without Sarah's part. The best barns were on her part …and the best ponds. That one decision they made to keep her from buildin' her a garage cost 'em dear."

Granny said, "Sarah sold her milk cows, pigs and the chickens, and loaded up two big trunks. So far as I know, that's all she took with her. She left that house just like it was—didn't take not one stick of furniture. It wasn't a week later before the brothers went to see her in town and tried to smooth things over. When they came to see her, Sarah gave 'em all the keys to the old Herndon house and all the outbuildin's and said, "'You're my brothers, and I love you, *but it's all yours now*-- and everything in it.'" She told 'em she was doin' good with the insurance business and thought she could make a go of it—but even if she didn't, she'd never come back to live on the farm. Here's a funny thing too...she sold insurance, but Sarah told those brothers that since she wasn't livin' there and the house wasn't really hers anyway, that they would have to pay the insurance on it. The way it was fixed, if anything happened to Sarah, her part of the farm was to be divided between the three brothers *but* if Sarah outlived her brothers then it was to go to *their* children, her nieces and nephews when she died.

Abruptly, Granddaddy asked, "Lorene, what year did that Herndon house burn down?"

"Oh," she said, "I don't remember the year, but it was probably five or six years after Sarah left it, maybe '31 or '32, along in there somewhere. They thought lightnin' struck it. Nobody was livin' there...burnt clean to the ground one night and all that fine furniture, antiques and such. The funny part of it is… those brothers couldn't agree on hardly anything, and not a one of 'em had

381

bothered to take insurance out on that house. Nobody got a dime."

With a slight grin on his face, Granddaddy said, "And to beat it all, the way her mother wrote the will, Sarah was to get half the profits from her part of the farm, *but she didn't say that her brothers got the right to farm it.* It's probably what ol' Mrs. Herndon meant, but it wasn't in writin'. When they met Sarah at that little house she'd rented in town and tried callin' her hand on it, she showed 'em the will—and she was right. Sharp as a rat's turd, that one is.

And she told me she reached in her purse and counted out the change for 'em—two dollars and fifty cents--and laid it on her kitchen table. Sarah had leased her whole part of that place for five dollars—one dollar a year--and she told her brothers that it was their half of the profit from rentin' the farm for the next five years and *they* could figure out how to divide it three ways. She had it all drawn up into a legal contract between her and John David—quoted her mother's will and all such as that. She showed it to me. Sarah would've made a smart lawyer if she'd had the chance. The funny thing is they thought it would all blow over…but it didn't." Clearly, the little old lady still had a strong personality and sense of purpose about her.

At school the next day, I told my friend Mike about the meeting with Sarah. Billy Stewart was eating lunch with us in the high school cafeteria. "Boy Howdy," he said. "I know that crazy old woman." Billy worked after school at a full service gas station in Harriston. "She comes to the station all the time, wantin' somethin' done to her ol' car."

He said "I couldn't believe it, but she pulled up one day in that old wreck and asked me to change the air in her tires!"

"The air?"

"I kid you not," he said, holding his hand up in affirmation. "Kenny (the owner) came up and spoke to her and called her by name, so that's how I know who you're talkin' about. I asked him what to do, and he leaned over to me and whispered, "Billy, do what the lady says. She owns ever'thing between here and the courthouse.""

I later told my grandparents what Billy had said. "Oh, Lord, yes," Granny said," Sarah Herndon's a wealthy woman but you wouldn't hardly know it. She's never put on airs… and just as common as an old boot."

Granddaddy said, "I'll tell you this—people in this county trust that little lady and she's earned it. In the Depression there were a lot of people that had a hard time payin' their insurance—life insurance and property mostly. In the early thirties…well, really up to the War, it was tough goin' around here. I went to her once somewhere in there and told her I didn't have it to pay. I wasn't the only one, either. There were plenty of people in that shape. Sarah said it was all right, and that she understood. I never heard one word from the company about my little burial policy bein' cancelled and I forgot about 'it. Come to find out, Sarah paid the premiums for a lot of us *out of her own pocket*. She knew times wouldn't always be as bad as they were then and she carried us, you might say. I never forgot it neither, when times did get better…and I paid her back when I was able, *every dime of it.*

A long time after that I asked Sarah how she knew to trust people she did business with, and she told me the funniest thing I've ever heard. She was speakin' of farmers mostly but Sarah said she studied a man's knees and the seat of his pants—that she'd take a chance on him as long as his knees had more wear than his be-hind. In other words, if it looked like he *worked* more than he *sat*, she'd take a chance—and said she got it right mostly, except for one time, when Pee Wee Purvis stole his brother in law's britches off the clothes line and wore 'em into town."

Granny said, "She's kindly quiet about it, but Sarah does a whole lot for the community—Harriston mostly. She was real active in the Red Cross durin' the War—even rode a train to Washington for a fancy luncheon with Eleanor Roosevelt at the White House in a group of Red Cross big wheels from all over the country. She told me about it not long after she got back home. President Roosevelt wasn't even supposed to be there, but he came by for this meeting and somehow he found out Sarah was a stamp collector— evidently, he was, too and they hit it off. He showed her some of his collection and autographed a picture for her. She's got it hangin' there in that insurance office."

Christmas break ended and when I came home from school just a few days later, Granny informed me she had gotten a phone call from Sarah Herndon who wanted me to stop by her office sometime—she said she had something she wanted me to see. Neither my grandparents nor I had any idea why.

I wasn't driving yet, but the next Saturday morning we rode into town as usual and while my grandparents ran their errands, I was sent down Main Street to the Herndon Insurance Company office to find Sarah Herndon. She had told Granny that she still came into the office on Saturday mornings because her oldest customers still followed the practice of country folks of coming to town on Saturdays to do business.

I found her in the office chatting with a customer. She seemed not to recognize me.

"Hi Miss Herndon, I'm Clay Hall—Lorene's grandson. You sent word you wanted to see me".

Looking into my eyes again with her pensive stare, she suddenly came to herself and said, "Honey, I'm sorry--I had to place you. You look so much like your grandmother's people I should've known you in a cornfield." Taking me by the hand where she was seated, she said, "I knew your daddy, too…and I know his parents, your other grandparents. Your daddy was a fine young man. This community lost something when it lost him. I want you to come back here to my office," she said, grabbing her black cane and walking unsteadily on the uneven hardwood floor, "I've got something I want to you to see."

We turned the corner into her office and she pointed to her left--to a huge, glaring portrait of General Robert E. Lee in a magnificent brass frame. Hanging directly above her massive oak roll top desk, it dominated the room. Like Sarah Herndon, the Old General had the command of all who entered.

Gesturing toward it with a sweep of her little hand, Sarah said, "*I just wanted you to see The General.* I can't help but believe that any young man can only be a better person if he just looks at this picture. My daddy was named for Robert E. Lee and my grandfather was a chaplain in the Confederate Army. One of the officers kept in touch with him after the War…they attended some of the Confederate veterans' gatherings together. He sent this portrait to my daddy after Grandfather died. It hung in the parlor at the home place and I've always loved it. That's the only thing I've got that came from the old home place and IT wouldn't be here if I hadn't taken it into town to have the frame repaired. It would've burned up along with the rest of the house."

"So," she said, prodding me into a reaction, "What do you think of the General?"

I said, "From what I've read about him Miss Herndon, he was a true gentleman."

Sarah nodded approvingly and continued to gaze at the portrait as if she could never get enough of it. "Clay, I believe I showed this picture to your father when he was a young man—probably about your age…maybe a little older. I had his father, your grandfather bring him in here when we were tending to some business years ago. I've shown it to a good many young men over the years. It seems to me that just looking at General Lee ought to make any young man want to do better—*be better*."

I wondered to myself if in fact it had helped my father be a better man. He was a good man who died way too young. I stood there looking at the huge portrait of General Lee and wondered what he had thought when he once fixed his own youthful gaze upon it. Over the years I've heard the same story from a dozen or more men who remembered Sarah Herndon and the Herndon Insurance Company. For a number of young men in the county, it had become something of a rite of passage.

Sarah questioned me about farming again, which she obviously remembered as something like my plan for the future. "O, how I loved being on the farm…always something going on…and I still love every foot of it. One of my favorite days in the whole year was when we butchered hogs."

Caught off guard, I could not imagine this impeccably dressed little old lady anywhere near blood and guts. She was full of surprises. "My grandmother would pick the day and set the whole process into motion," she said. "And my MOST favorite thing was when my daddy would give my brothers and me the pig's bladder."

I was surprised she would even say the word "bladder."

"Miss Herndon, if you don't mind my asking…. what on earth did you did you do with a pig's bladder?"

Puzzled, she looked at me for a moment and said, almost with disgust, "I guess kids these days don't have to make their own fun, but that was a big time to us. We would blow up that pig's bladder and make a balloon or ball out of it and play with it all morning." She giggled like a child recalling the event.

Now this was something. This lady in front of me whose lips had blown up a freshly slaughtered pig's bladder had sipped tea and ate finger sandwiches on White House china. The same little hands that gathered eggs fresh with chicken poop had shaken the hand of the most powerful man in the world, and petted his little dog Falla.

We sat down in her office for half an hour or so as Sarah Herndon shared other fond recollections of her life on the farm. Never once did she make reference to leaving it, or the disagreement with her brothers that had prompted her departure. Her favorite memories seemed to be of her family working and living together on the land, apart from complexities of the rapidly changing adult world she and her brothers would soon face.

I never visited with Sarah Herndon again. As my life took shape—graduating from high school, going to Vietnam, and finally college, I lost touch with many of the people I knew in the county, especially in Harriston. However, I did come back home on weekends as often as I could. While we were visiting with Granny one Sunday after church, she was catching me up on news of people in the community. At some point I glanced down and saw her new Herndon Insurance Company calendar lying on the dining room table—coincidentally, Sarah Herndon's old table.

I told Granny it brought back memories of the afternoon the old lady came for a last call on her customers and the brief encounter I had with her in the insurance office.

"Oh, I meant to tell you about her. She just died here a month or two ago," Granny smiled as she spoke the words,

"I believe she was either ninety-six or ninety-seven, and still walked down to that insurance office nearly every day 'til she fell and broke her hip."

As my wife Sandy and I left Fordville that day, we drove to the old Herndon Place on Foaling Ridge before heading back to Louisville. The gate was locked, so we climbed over and walked up the long dirt lane toward the three lone brick chimneys. To my amazement, the oak logs I had seen a decade earlier were still intact in the adjacent field. Sarah was clearly justified in her admiration of oak. Later that evening I phoned Granny to tell her we had driven to Sarah Herndon's land on Foaling Ridge as we drove back to Louisville and that I'd told Sandy the story of the domineering Herndon brothers--and the oak logs left to rot.

Granny said thoughtfully, "You know, I've been sittin' here thinkin' about Sarah since you all were here this afternoon. Seems like I do that a lot more, now that it's just me here most of the time starin' at these walls. She kindly puts me in mind of a fire in the grate that's been smothered down. The hot coals just lay there hidden in the ashes for a long time seems like, and you don't think it's doin' a thing 'til you throw somethin' on it that'll burn. Then directly, here come the flames."

Before she hung up the phone that evening, she said, "Oh, Clay, I meant to tell you this earlier today--Charlie Herndon died back in the spring. He was the last one of Sarah's brothers left. None of 'em got a foot of *her* land— or her money, for that matter." With a chuckle, Granny said, "She outsmarted 'em all--*and then* she outlived 'em." It may have seemed spiteful of her on the surface, but I had to admire the old lady's spunk. Clearly, she was ahead of her time in many ways—something her unfortunate brothers learned the hard way.

Granny was later informed that Sarah Herndon had not cut her family off from her bounty entirely—she had simply skipped a generation. One by one, as she came to know each of her brothers' sons and daughters—and even their children, as individuals with minds and plans of their own, she generously helped most of them along life's way in the time and manner of her own choosing.

The solid oak dining room furniture has never left Granny's farmhouse since she bought it from Sarah Herndon in 1942. We still use it for all major holidays and family dinners—sometimes with all seven leaves extending it nearly the full length of the dining room. The oak table's sturdy construction and enduring presence continues to bear testimony to its former owner--and kindred spirit.

The claw footed tub in the downstairs bathroom

The Cleansing

Granny met me at the door with worry in her eyes. "Russell wants you to go with him to Doc Wilcox's place. It's J.B."

"It's J.B." Those two words would generally let the hearer know that you could expect almost anything to follow.

Using her pet phrase for one of his extended drinking spells, I asked, "Is he on a 'high lonesome?'"

She shook her head gravely.

"He's been layin' out at Doc's place for a week. Says it's just the flu, but Doc thinks there's somethin' else goin' on with him. He says he can't get 'im to go to the doctor and all he's used to treatin' is cows and baby pigs."

She continued drying her hands on the dishtowel. "Russell's fixin' to go right now, so go ahead and start the truck. I was in the middle of cookin' supper when Doc called, so you all go on up there and find out about J.B. We'll see what your granddaddy thinks we ought to do."

Granddaddy dreaded whatever was ahead—as he usually did in his assumed role as J.B.'s reluctant keeper. As always, he faced it, silently, and we soon arrived at the Wilcox place. A lifelong bachelor, the old veterinarian lived alone on the farm where he was born, a place well known as a laying-in house for local drunks. As such, J.B. was eminently qualified for temporary residency.

Doc met us at the door and we were ushered into the living room where J.B. was resting, something at which he excelled. One of the more memorable quotes attributed to him was "When have you ever heard of a man restin' hisself to death?"

Doc said, "Russell, see if you can talk your baby brother here into goin' over to Veterans' Hospital and get looked at. Somethin's not right."

J.B. was lying on the couch with his feet propped up on the end.

With an audible sigh, Granddaddy stepped in front of the couch to take in the full length view of his brother in the closed up room that smelled like a brewery.

Never had many words passed between my grandfather and his only sibling, his younger brother by five years. Yet, they seemed to understand one another intimately, and could in fact communicate when forced to do so.

The older brother addressed J.B. as he might have a six year old. "Doc here says you need to go to the hospital and you ARE goin', so you might as well get your shoes on and get to movin'." The command proved effective in stirring the seventy-two year old child into a sitting position. Despite J.B.'s longstanding resentment of his older brother's ministrations, he obediently rose up from the couch without making a sound, and began putting on his muddy pair of shoes.

Stepping again into his elder brother role, Granddaddy said, "You'll go home with us tonight. Tomorrow's Saturday, so Clay here can drive us to the Veterans' Hospital early in the mornin.'" J.B. offered no resistance but neither did he respond. Like an errant child sent to bed without supper, he skulked around the room to gather his few clothes into a brown paper bag. As J.B. moved slowly toward the truck, Doc gave us a quick summary of his old friend's declining health as we prepared to leave.

A long short ride is the best way to describe what followed and reminds me of the journey home from school with Granddaddy after I got into a fight with Buddy Evans--the dreaded, simmering silence and that "Just wait 'til I get you home" feeling. I don't think my grandfather or J.B. felt it, but I felt it enough for all three of us.

J.B. had always been knowingly or unknowingly "looked after." First, and longest by his widowed mother, who, even from her grave in the Fordville Cemetery continued to do so. Years before, he had talked her into selling her little farm near Babylon to buy a house in Fordville. Granddaddy claimed it was so that J.B. could be closer to the bootleggers. Whatever the case, J.B. lived there with her until he was middle aged, and at her death he was to have lifetime use of the house. She didn't will the property to him outright for fear he would get drunk, sell it, and then run through the money. At J.B.'s death, the house was to pass to Granddaddy's children. Secondly, and from a cool distance, he had been provided for—begrudgingly, by his older brother. Debts of one variety or another that J.B. accumulated--which he had every good intention of paying--were often paid by an embarassed Granddaddy for the sake of family pride.

The comical result of the provision made for J.B. by his distressed mother was that he preferred not to live in the house; instead, he rented it out, a shrewd, somewhat lucrative move that provided him with the only reliable cash income he ever had. Not only did old maid school teacher Miss Tib Johnson pay her rent promptly at the beginning of every month for the next twenty something years, she often prepared meals for J.B. and even delivered them to his encampment on the river. He was truly an independent gentleman. Even as a reluctant landlord, J.B. had it made. Knowing fully well that his younger brother would never maintain the property which would eventually pass to his own children, Granddaddy became its unofficial caretaker. This burden he gladly shared with me in the form of my conscripted labor. Many a hot summer day did I spend scraping and painting on that old house, puttying windows or smearing tar on its old roof, while J.B., the Lord of the Manor, was off somewhere fishing in the shade.

We pulled into the driveway with J.B. sitting between us and filling the truck cab with his…aroma. I helped get him into the house, and Granny took it from there, persuading him to take a bath and clean up. "You'll feel better," she said, sympathetically.

Granddaddy grumbled "I don't know if he'll FEEL any different, but maybe he'll smell *some* better."

While Granddaddy sat down at the supper table and fussed over cold mashed potatoes, Granny fussed over J.B., getting him this and that to clean himself. She mothered him like she did everything else that came within her reach, and I think Granddaddy resented the preferential treatment J.B. received at her hands.

While J.B. was soaking in the claw footed bath tub, Granny asked Granddaddy what they ought to do with him. "Veterans," he said tersely, referring to Veterans' Hospital in Lexington, forty- odd miles away.

Yes, surprisingly, J.B. had once served in the U.S. Navy. Granddaddy said, "Naturally, it was durin' peacetime." He had actually been honorably discharged.

J.B. rested well that night in my bed and early the next morning we were up and on the road to Lexington, with me behind the wheel since Granddaddy didn't like driving out of the county. It was a long, long day for all three of us, at the end of which we had J.B. admitted as a patient.

I came home from school in the middle of the next week and my grandparents were seated at the kitchen table drinking coffee, something they often did at that time of day. Granny looked up at me. "I've been on the phone this morning with J.B.'s doctor. They think he's got a cancer."

"No small wonder," Granddaddy said. "He's smoked enough of them Little Camels to sink a battleship. Started when he wasn't twelve or thirteen years old. When he came home from the Navy, I heard Daddy say he knew for a fact that J.B. had smoked a million cigarettes while he was in uniform. Daddy read somewhere that there were half a million men in uniform and he knew J.B. had bummed two smokes off every one of 'em." His numbers were way off for the naval forces of that day, but the economic principle was the same: J.B.'s resourcefulness knew no bounds when it came to living off his environment, wherever it happened to be.

Another week passed and once again I was met with a solemn huddle of my grandparents as I came home from school.

Granny said "Clay, we need you to stay home from school tomorrow." That was the only one of two times I ever recall such a request. "We've got to go to Veterans' and get J.B. I reckon he's gonna stay here with us for a few days." She was unusually quiet that afternoon, and I think they had been discussing the matter for some time, and likely disagreeing on that particular course of action. The few days turned out to be the entire fall and winter of my junior year in high school, and for all its frustrations, one of my more special memories.

We brought home the sanitized version of my great-uncle that afternoon. Granny insisted we stop at J.C. Penney's and buy him new clothes and pajamas . Even Granddaddy agreed to the expenditure as the three of us went inside, leaving J.B. to bask in the warmth of the car's back seat, like a groundhog in the afternoon sun.

"I'm not havin' you wash his nasty clothes," Granddaddy said. "Like as not, you'd catch some disease from 'em."

Granny commented on how good J.B. looked after being well fed and kept clean at the Veterans' Hospital.

"Well, he's a goner now, " Granddaddy quipped. "The microbes wouldn't bother him much until he's cleaned up."

With what amounted to an entirely new wardrobe, the three of us came out of Penney's loaded down like pack mules to an unimpressed, if not unappreciative J.B., who cared nothing for clean clothes, let alone new.

On our return trip home, J.B. asked me to drive by his shack on the river where he'd lived for probably fifteen years, that is as much as he lived anywhere. He said he wanted to bring a few things with him to stay at our place. It was a warm day, and we soon were forced to climb out of the car to wait for him to reemerge. Granddaddy had just started to enter when J.B. finally stepped down from the graying structure with a beaten suitcase in his hand, tethered with several pieces of baling twine.

I was unaware that he even owned one, but it had probably been hidden under his bed with Lord knows what else. It became clear to me on that day that J.B. was a sick man. Frailty was written upon him from crown to heel in the way he shuffled his feet when he walked, and especially in his breathing. Just before getting into the car, he turned to look at his humble riparian abode and he glanced upstream in the same direction I had seen him stare for hours at a time.

Looking back, I think he understood then he would never return. I also remember how strangely he acted when I offered to carry his battered suitcase to the trunk.

"Nope, I got it." That's all he said. And, when we returned home, the first thing he did was to carry it upstairs and put it away, out of plain sight, as if he wished for whatever was contained in it to be kept hidden. Of course, I wondered then what could be in it. I had stayed many nights with the man "camping out" in that river shack and never saw evidence of anything that had merited his concern so far as material objects go, apart from the pocket watch which he kept with him at all times.

The next six months were probably among the longest of Granddaddy's life, but he generally bore it with a measure of grace. Suppertime could get interesting, however. The only thing J.B. would eat for that one meal was cornbread—like his mother had baked for him every night until she died. So, every evening, Granny indulged him by preparing his own personal skillet of cornbread, most of which he crumbled up in milk. Conversation was extremely limited between him and Granddaddy, especially when J.B. would tell of his adventures.

Fact or fiction, they were great stories. He had hoboed his way across the central and southern plains. He had worked as a foreman's assistant in a CCC camp in Idaho at one point before getting fired for showing up drunk. He had harvested wheat under the hot Kansas sun, and had slept under the giant redwoods in California. Death had missed him by inches wherever he'd traveled. Professional baseball players, actors, wanted fugitives, musicians, and one ex- President had been among those he had seen or met personally, to hear him tell it.

Once a tale was underway, Granddaddy would generally conclude his supper quietly and push his chair back under the table. You could hear the screen door to the front porch close gently. To his credit, it was a mild protest of the wearisome younger brother's celebrity status in his own household. Even Granny would sit with me for an hourk at a time listening to J.B., knowing good and well that what she was hearing was along the same factual level as her treasured "Days of Our Lives."

Granny prepared the spare bedroom upstairs for J.B. She even had me set up another old single bed that had been in the attic and bought a new mattress and box spring for it.

Granddaddy groaned, "He'll lay there smokin' one night and burn this whole house down." Surprisingly, J.B. never again lit another cigarette. But, it didn't matter at that point. The untold thousands of his smokes had done their damage and as Granddaddy said, "the hay's in the barn."

Occasionally when he felt like it, J.B. would attempt to assist Granny with small household chores. She wouldn't let him near the kitchen, nor was he wont to do so. He wasn't much of a worker, but he was great entertainment for any worker present. He liked to stay up late and watch television with me after my grandparents had gone to bed. The man absolutely loved westerns, and once again, to hear him tell, had witnessed "some pretty rough stuff" out west.

The days turned into weeks, and the weeks into months. We noticed that J.B. gradually ate even less than he usually did, and was losing what little weight he had when he came. Even his special pan of cornbread was left mostly uneaten at supper. Doc Wilcox began driving him to his doctor appointments at the Veterans' Hospital, and he likewise observed that J.B.'s days were numbered.

He coughed and gurgled a lot during that time and he couldn't sleep well. Still, J.B. seemed to enjoy sitting up late at night with me watching what little television was then available. My grandparents usually went to bed by 9:00 PM, so it was relatively late by 10:00 for them. It was during those times that I learned the most about the restless spirit that resided within him.

In early April, J.B. got up exceptionally early one morning and declared at breakfast that he wanted to go fishing one more time. He called up his old friend Doc Wilcox who soon appeared in his truck and away they went, for one last hurrah.

Granddaddy was shocked. "I've been givin' him up for dead, and now, he's gone fishin'"

400

It was a short-lived fishing trip. Doc brought J.B. home before lunch that day.

That night my grandparents sat up later than usual talking to him, even after I went upstairs to bed. They sat much in silence, the three of them. I was at the kitchen table doing homework when I heard J.B. tell Granny that he wanted to be baptized.

You could hear a pin drop. Although he had been to church in my lifetime, you could easily count those Sundays on one hand.

With resignation in his voice, J.B. said, "I reckon it's about time."

Blunt as always, Granddaddy said, "I think you're right. From the look of things, Brother, I don't think you're long with us." J.B. searched his older brother's eyes for comfort he could not give. He dropped his head and nodded without saying a word.

We were between regular preachers at our little church in Fordville, and were being served by supply pastors. Finally Granny was able to hunt down one of the preachers that had established some kind of rapport with J.B. years before and he agreed to baptize him at church in three weeks on a given Sunday.

However, by the time the appointed date came around, Granny and Granddaddy decided that J.B. was too weak to travel to church, and the preacher and two deacons came to baptize him in the only place we could gather reasonably clean warm water: the old claw footed bathtub in our bathroom.

I remember well the day of J.B.'s baptism. Granny was always meticulously clean, but that day she attacked the old bathtub with conviction in her heart and a can of Comet in her hand. She practically stood on her head scrubbing the old tub as if it had dark sins of its own to wash down the drain. About dusk that evening the preacher and deacons arrived. Clothed in his new J.C. Penney pajamas, Fordville's most popular alcoholic was baptized and accepted into the membership of its one and only remaining church.

The preacher and deacons helped a now frail and gasping little J.B. out of the bathtub in which he'd been baptized, and he looked like a half-starved rat caught in a storm drain as he stood dripping water on the bathroom floor. Granddaddy and I dried off his gaunt, wet little body and restored him to another pair of pajamas and a bathrobe after which we helped him get back to the couch where he lay down on a blanket. The preacher and elders had a long, pleasant—if not somber visit with J.B., who, though weak as a kitten, seemed to enjoy the whole experience.

That particular night, I told my grandparents that I would sit up with him. Since it would be Saturday, I could try to sleep during the day and give them a well-deserved break. After they went upstairs to bed, I turned on the television to watch it with J.B. as I had done so many nights since he came to stay with us. He'd been sitting in silence the whole time as we watched late night television. That night, J.B. was looking into something beyond the big knobs and snowy images of the black and white floor model RCA. At the time it seemed like J.B. wasn't himself in a way. As I look back now, maybe he was **all** of himself that night— baring it all emotionally as he had spiritually, rising from the bathtub only hours earlier.

He really hadn't been paying attention to the television program, and appeared to be miles away in thought. He said abruptly "Clay, go upstairs to my room and bring me my old suitcase. It's up under the bed."

I hadn't seen it since he returned to our house with it when we brought him home from the hospital. It was still tied up when I found it.

Setting it down in front of him, I stepped away as he fumbled with my pocketknife to pick at the carefully tied knots to open them and reveal its contents. Inside was a fistful of old newspaper clippings that included a photo of J.B. with his famous pair of coon dogs that appeared in the Harriston paper when I was too young to remember. His discharge papers from the Navy, a lapsed burial policy his mother had started for him, and her worn Bible were all that remained. He reached for his pair of dime store glasses and tilted the lamp shade toward him for better lighting.

Opening his mother's Bible, he sifted through some of the folded articles and non-discernable fragments of paper that I wanted to look through, but didn't. J.B. was clearly on a single-minded mission.

I tried to turn my attention to the television, to afford him some degree of privacy as he opened and examined some of his mother's carefully kept newspaper clippings and letters. Within a few minutes, he declared, *"Here they are!"* with as much enthusiasm as I had heard him say anything since he came to stay…to die with us. Gasping for every shallow breath he took, J.B. sat there studying the photo.

He turned toward me and eagerly angled the lamp shade toward his knees where he held out the photo for me to examine. "That's *my family*," he said, pointing proudly to the smiling couple. "That's us, right there in front of where we lived."

I attempted to take the picture from his hand so that I could see it better, and strangely he didn't act like he wanted to let go of it. The small, dog-eared photo of a young J.B., an attractive young woman and an infant in her arms was taken in front of a plain one story house that needed a paint job. An unsmiling haggard old lady stood just behind the younger woman.

Tapping her image lightly with his shaking thumb, J.B. said softly, "Bessie was her name." His words spoke came out of the clear blue, as if we'd already been talking about her, "Bessie Mae Hargrove.

She was a Methodist and she let her ol' granny name our boy—right here, you see 'im?" I nodded. J.B. very much wanted me to see his one and only son. Finally, he said, "That there's John Wesley…Hall." He chuckled and wheezed together at the same time, "I reckon there was a man named John Wesley years and years ago that was a big Methodist preacher somewhere. Bessie and her granny

404

thought our baby boy might grow up to be a better man if he had a powerful name to live up to." Chuckling, he said "I reckon she knew then the little feller would have a hard row to hoe… if all he got from me was *my* last name."

I sat in something like stunned silence as I had never even heard these names spoken.

"I ain't seen 'em since 1935, or '36…I'd done been gone for about three years when I came back through there and I knocked on her granny's door way up in the night. Ol' Mrs. Hargrove came to the door with a coal oil lamp. She wasn't one bit happy to see me, but she did let me in and went to get Bessie and my little boy. It took her a few minutes, but here she came in her nightgown carryin' Little John Wesley. He wasn't but three or four years old, and he looked like he was halfway afraid of me." J.B. gasped again, and gurgled as he laughed. "And the little feller—he didn't know me from buckshot. He tugged at his mother's nightgown and asked her, "Bess, is that my daddy?" That tickled me—him callin' his mother by her first name. Lord, she looked rough as I did, but it was a different kind of rough, I reckon. She spoke to me a little…fixed me a plate of somethin' to eat left over from their supper. She offered to let me sleep on the floor in the livin' room that night but, shoot, I couldn't stay there. I laid down for a little while and took a nap…but I left before daylight without even sayin' goodbye to 'em and I ain't seen neither one of 'em since. I reckon Kansas is where they live…or did live when this picture was took."

Two or three minutes passed and J.B. continued looking blankly into the television screen, still holding their picture in his hand. "Harper, Kansas," he said, as if to affirm its existence, and that of the life there he once had.

I got up the nerve to break into J.B.'s trance to ask him why he left.

He never took his eyes from the picture as he spoke. "Ahh Lord...it's hard to say why a man does what he does at the time. We were livin' there with Bessie's granny and she was a bossy, naggin' ol' thing. You couldn't pour a glass of water to suit her. Me and Bessie was plantin' the garden the day I left there. Dry as it was, I studied that little garden patch and decided we'd be better off to put the beans out in the back where the ground looked like it would hold moisture better when it ever did rain again. Bessie said, 'I'll have to ask Granny first.'"

"Well, that just ran all over me. I was doin' the work, and I wasn't about to ask some foolish old woman where to plant beans." Like Granddaddy might have, I wanted to point out that the foolish old woman was the one paying the rent.

"Then Bessie yells up on the porch 'Granny, J.B. wants to move the bean patch!' –just like she was tellin' on me for stealin' candy or some such foolishness as that.

Well...that did it for me. I wasn't about to ask that ol' hell-hag where to plant the beans... that I'd be raisin'.'"

I knew J.B., and the likelihood of him tending a garden was at best optimistic.

He continued his account of the parting event. "So I just threw my hoe down right where I stood...*right there* in that bean patch--and left…and I stayed gone for about three years."

"Where did you go?" I asked.

"Different places," he said. "I rode the rails for a while. Them was Dust Bowl days, boy, and I was in good company. There was a whole bunch of us doin' that. I left Kansas…made it all the way up into Washington State. Picked apples up there one summer. I done different things to get by, a little o' this, and a little o' that."

He did not seem to express regrets but it was clear to me that the family he abandoned was on his mind as he contemplated what his life had been, and presumably what he would soon leave behind. That tiny little window into his soul was painted shut before morning and the subject never mentioned again. Labored breathing and shortened words and phrases characterized the days that followed.

A week later, Doc Wilcox asked if he could come and sit up with J.B. at night, to help us out. Rightly so, he was with his old friend when he went to sleep for good – peacefully, on the couch in the living room. Doc woke Granny and Granddaddy to tell them he was gone, and Granny woke me. Doc turned J.B. on his side, facing the couch so that our last memory of him would not be his death gaze that would otherwise be toward us. The four of us sat there in the pre-dawn dark, sipping strong black coffee and waiting for daylight while J.B. appeared to be laid in for a long night's sleep.

Within a week of his funeral, the slow rhythms of daily life eventually returned to normal for my grandparents and our household. Granny did buy a new couch because she kept thinking about J.B. dying on the old one; it was of course still green, but a new couch. Granddaddy clearly had mixed and unspoken emotions about the complicated relationship he shared with his younger brother, but he was also glad to have his household back. And, although it was again functioning as it had, something special was missing both there and in my mind. While J.B. was living, there in my imagination, I could always think of what adventures he might be taking part in, if he wasn't drunk on the floor of his shack. Even while sitting in a geometry class, it would bring a smile to my face knowing that at least one person I knew was probably having a good time. It might be fishing, hunting or trying to engineer a salvage operation to drag something out of the river that he could sell for a few bucks. It made me sad to think of the abandoned shack on the river bank—and no more stories of J.B.'s misadventures.

Granny sorted through J.B.'s few papers and mailed several letters to officials in the area of Harper, Kansas, inquiring into the whereabouts of his long-deserted family. Eventually, a former resident living a hundred miles away learned of Granny's quest. It was probably a year after J.B.'s death before a letter arrived in the mail from the elderly widow, stating that Bessie and little John Wesley had left after Bessie's grandmother died in the late Thirties. She thought the family had moved to Idaho—or Iowa. She knew it started with an "I," and sounded like one of the two. She had gotten a letter or two from Bessie and remembered that she had changed her name when she remarried, not long after leaving Kansas, and most importantly, that the new husband had formally adopted little John Wesley and gave him *his own last name*.

J.B.'s little family had vanished into thin air, carried away by the Dust Bowl wind like the tons of parched earth it claimed. And when the winds ceased their howling, J.B.'s abandoned Bessie and their little John Wesley not only lived under another man's roof, but under his name. So, in the end, we didn't even have a name to hunt for. It was as gone as the bean patch the young couple had once argued over in the Kansas dust. Back here in Kentucky, the muddy old river that J. B. loved so well continued in its course, flowing past his empty shack. Tales of his exploits continued to entertain and amuse those who remembered him, but for me, Fordville would never the same.

For months, I couldn't even enter the bathroom without seeing J.B. in the clawfooted bathtub on the night of his baptism. The first time I took a bath in it following J.B.'s death, it seemed like the desecration of a sacred object. Of course, it was the same old tub that had been there for years, but it seemed different somehow--*holy*, even.

As a teenager, I would rather have listened to J.B.'s stories than eat ice cream. But, as much as I enjoyed his company and as much as I loved him, it would be easy—and a mistake-- to romanticize the life he'd led. He was his own man and did what he wanted, when or if he wanted: his was a life, by many to be envied.

Over the years, however, I had many opportunities to take a good hard look at the lives of these two men, this unlikely pair of brothers. Although I loved and learned from each in his own way, I will always feel fortunate that my grandfather was not the fun brother, and that I lived under his roof and under the blessings of his name.

At Granny's death we bought her old home place and when we remodeled the house, the claw footed tub was restored to its original condition. It might have been easier to replace it, but no one I know can say their bathtub has witnessed an event to equal the cleansing, healing baptism of J.B. Hall.

About the Author

The author, Todd D. Moberly, is a retired high school teacher and lives with his family near Berea, Kentucky.

12891942R00230

Made in the USA
Middletown, DE
24 November 2018